the Sanibel-Cayman disc

the Sanibel-Cayman disc

Thomas D. Cochrun

Guild Press of Indiana, Inc.

GUILD PRESS OF INDIANA, INC.
435 Gradle Drive
Carmel, Indiana 46032
www.guildpress.com

ISBN 1-57860-041-3

Library of Congress
Catalog Card Number 99-67763

Cover design by James Wille Faust
Text design by Sheila Samson

Printed and bound in the United States of America

Also by Thomas D. Cochrun:

The Sanibel Arcanum

(Guild Press of Indiana, 1994)

To KWC-father and friend.
  "Make the most of each day."
LAC-friend and mentor.
  "sail, with the wind or against,
      but you must always sail . . ."

*Train a child in the way he should go, and
when he is old he will not depart from it.*

Proverbs 22:6

*We were made to be neither cerebral men nor
visceral men, but men. Not beasts nor angels,
but men . . .*

C. S. Lewis

Writing on the Sky

THE RED RAY KITE soared and dived against the terra cotta evening sky, followed by a ninety-foot tail of silk-like mylar. It wrote letters, curlicues and zigzags in front of a sun about to set into the horizon. The surf lapped gently at Tim Calvin's feet. A cabin cruiser, strung with twinkling lights and Christmas garlands, carried a band of holiday merrymakers over the blue gulf. Only a handful of people were on the beach to catch the "sweet light" in which the manta-ray-shaped kite played high on the breeze. A white heron drifted lazily onto the beach between Calvin and the man working the guidelines. The sun's warmth and the kite's acrobatics lulled him into a mind-resting peace, heaven on earth. For a moment, the puzzle in his life was put on hold.

The electrical tape was cutting a ridge in the side of Judge Malcome Browne's mouth. His shoulders burned in pain as his arms were stretched behind his back so his wrists could be taped together. The last six hours had been an absolute terror. He had returned to his friend's Sanibel beach home to continue the chore of closing it out, making it ready for the nature conservancy to take over the property.

It had been six weeks since C. G.'s funeral, and while his work was on schedule, the law firm that represented C. G.'s estate had asked Browne to provide personal letters and effects "which might have a bearing on the disposition of the estate." That sentence had been running through his mind as a curiosity, since it was well known that C. G. had deeded all of her properties to environmental and nature conservancy groups.

Following some of C. G.'s last personal instructions to him, Browne had been boxing and labeling personal papers, preparing them for the Gulf Coast Environmental Fund, when he was grabbed and struck from behind. Now he was taped to a chair and gagged, listening to the person or persons behind him rifle through the packed boxes and half-full book shelves. The only relief he had from his fright and pain was watching the scene through the study window: a man with a long-tailed red kite which was creating an aerial ballet against the evening sky.

It was just about closing time, and Dave Hockett was thinking about the chicken he was going to grill that evening. His wife, Barb, had picked up jumbo shrimp which would also be part of the grill feast. A clock was running in his mind. Should the bird go on an hour before, or should it go on forty-five minutes before the shrimp? He was savoring the sweet taste and feeling the emptiness in his stomach. Soon he would tell Barb she could close up the pottery shop so he could get to the house to get the grill started. Looking through his workshop window, he saw a large yellow Mercedes crunch onto the gravel drive and park. Hockett never minded customers coming to his pottery and ceramics shop, except when it was right before closing time on a night when he was hungry. Resignedly, he went into the showroom.

"I've seen some stuff on Koppel and *Sixty Minutes*. I've read a few pieces in the *Times*, but I had no idea it had gone so far," said Larry Conroy as he mixed another whiskey and branch water for his old friend and political colleague, Lee Hamblin.

"What you're saying, Lee, scares the hell out of me. Biologically and chemically engineered Armageddon. I keep thinkin' of my grandkids and kids everywhere. What kind of world are we handing them?"

Hamblin stared into his drink. "You know, Larry, C. S. Lewis seemed to capture our plight in *That Hideous Strength*."

"Lee, retirement is giving you the opportunity to get philosophical," Conroy said wryly.

"Well, yes. Anyway, Lewis said, 'There is even less room for indecision, and choices are even more momentous. Good is always getting better and bad is always getting worse.' He said the possibility of neutrality always diminishes. I suppose that's why I'm so consumed with the report for the President and Congress." Hamblin accepted a refill, then raised his glass. "To good men who act on their good intentions."

The men sat on Conroy's screened porch, in what he called his Captiva den. The wall was lined with photographs of Conroy with presidents, senators, athletes, and stars. He had been an influential Senate committee counsel, a state office holder and a candidate for governor. He now worked for an international commercial real-estate firm. His political connections made him an important asset. In turn, he used his influence with the firm's ownership to direct large amounts of money and resources to community projects and social-service needs in nations where the company did business.

"Larry, it's very good of you to allow me to stay here," Lee said. "I need the insulation from all the distractions back home. I know I can spend the day working on the horrible business I must assess. The real blessing is the antidote, just out the window here. If I must consider these weapons of mass destruction, I prefer to see the sun and beach."

◆ ◆ ◆

Tim Calvin loved the sublime contemplation of waves and horizon. He and the girls had walked and waded from Captiva to the north end of Sanibel. Now his mind drifted in a kind of free float, as the darting kite was being reeled in by its pilot. Until that evening he had been concerned, perplexed, trying to figure out his next move. He had masked his concern, wanting Laney and the girls to enjoy this chance to stay at the beach home, a Christmas gift celebrating the publishing of his book on the news industry. He should be absolutely blissful, he thought. His communications consulting business was growing; he was in the midst of book signings and interviews; and he had purchased what he hoped would be his retirement home on Sanibel. It was currently being leased by a nice couple, so the monthly mortgage was covered.

Everyone was well. He and Hockett were still celebrated as island heroes by people who remembered all the business about the old metal plate, the ancient manuscript, the family kidnapping, and the animal-assisted escape, which the Fort Myers press had memorialized in an article called "The Sanibel Arcanum." It had made other Florida papers and was even covered on the cable news network. But instead of peace, he was full of a longing, a kind of unresolved quest. Who was he? What was his destiny in life? What kind of mark should he, indeed could he, leave?

It was natural, he figured, for a Boomer at his point in life to begin thinking about the second half, about the significance of a life. This was the place to let it flow, he reasoned.

"Hey, buddy, are you getting hungry?" Laney broke into his thoughts as she walked up beside him. She was carrying *Sanybel Light* by Charles Lebuff, which she had been reading while enjoying the afternoon in the beach lounger.

"Mr. Hockett will be ready for you to help him with the grill. You know how persnickety he is about getting things going on time. We'd better get ready to go. We should walk back up to Captiva while the tide is out." She put her head on his shoulder.

"That's beautiful, isn't it?" He slipped his arm around her tan shoulders as they watched the kite man.

"And that would make a great picture, too," Laney responded, nodding to their left, where their eldest, Elizabeth, stood fishing in the surf. Her golden brown skin was set off by her black bikini, sun-lightened blonde hair, golden necklace, and red sunglasses. She appeared to be washing seaweed off the bobber.

"I hope she'll get some diving in while we're down here. It'd be a great break from student teaching. And I expect she'll do some good painting," Calvin said with fatherly pride.

"You'd better enjoy that sight," the voice interrupted Browne's thoughts, " 'cause you're about to take a ride."

Malcome Browne had been watching the family and the kite flyer, thinking how odd it was for such an idyllic vacation scene to be playing out just yards from where he was being held captive. Now, at least, he knew what one of them sounded like. These were the first words he'd heard as he regained consciousness.

"Oooh! That is one hot dollbaby," the voice said, more to himself than to Browne, but Browne thought he detected a slight accent, maybe Russian.

Strange Customers

Dave Hockett could see that the tall, muscular man was in a hurry when he came into the shop. By the look in his eyes, Dave could tell that the man had no desire to be browsing through a pottery shop. It was clearly the well-dressed and seemingly well-heeled woman at his side who was driving the decisions.

"You figure that's a trophy wife?" Barb smiled and whispered to her husband, referring to the obvious age difference between the fifty-something man and the younger woman who was spending a lot of time examining the items on display. Barb was at the register tabulating the day's receipts. Tall, bearded Hockett smiled back at her.

"Maybe just a girlfriend," he said, shuffling past her behind the counter. He then made a long-strided but slow amble into the showroom.

"If there's anything I can do, let me know," Hockett said, watching the man. He tried not to stare at the woman, whose expensive but sheer beach outfit revealed a generous amount of shapely physique.

"Well, if dinner's going to be late, this is okay," he said to himself with a smirk.

"Nah! We not be long," the man snorted, not looking at Hockett but at the pottery his lady had pulled off the shelf. They conversed with each other in low, intense tones.

Hockett recognized a Russian accent from his numerous church mission aid trips to Chegdomyn. He considered a Russian greeting but hesitated. There was something about this graying and flamboyantly dressed man and his beautiful young companion that didn't invite welcome. His instincts were sounding a message.

Ever since he and Calvin had gotten involved in the Arcanum mystery, he read people differently. The old army master sergeant personality lurked just behind his easygoing, old boy, laid-back island potter demeanor. Now his senses told him to be wary of this man. To others he might appear to be a rich tourist on a Sanibel holiday, but Hockett sensed there was something else. He could also tell this man was reading him with some presentiment. The man's steel-gray eyes had a fierce, cold look, out of place in the vacation atmosphere of Sanibel Island. The piercing eyes were looking deeply into Hockett's. He knew that both he and the man were, at the moment, caught in some primal engagement, two predators circling a territory, each sizing up the other and trying not to become prey.

By now, Southwest Regional Airport had quieted for the day. The blazing glow of rose and pink in the clouds and sky filled the large windows of the gate area. Airport personnel were uttering sighs of relief as dusk settled in, ending another frantic day of arrivals and departures. The place now slipped into a relaxed mood, more reminiscent of the old Florida nights captured on the 1950s vintage postcards: coconut palm trees against the sunset, gardenia bushes sweetening the air.

The man who had attacked Malcome Browne was forcing him, drugged and in despair, onto an airplane. They approached the only active gate. Most of the seats were full, as a somewhat exotic mix of people had begun their wait for a 9:45 flight to Caracas, Venezuela. Browne's heart began to rip at his chest in fear. He now knew his most immediate fate, but there was nothing he could do to prevent it. The why of it he could not even consider.

To all those who stared at him now—some with pity, others with a kind of disgust—he looked like a victim of a stroke or perhaps someone with advanced Parkinson's symptoms. His left arm and wrist twisted in the distortion of paralysis. His neck and face were frozen, his mouth half open, twitching, and his legs dragging and groping more than walking on feet now so neurologically crooked that only his toes stabbed at the carpeted floor. Maybe he would see someone he knew. But what chance would there be in an almost deserted airport? Even if he recognized someone, he could not talk. He knew his captor would have a story.

The place on Browne's neck where the syringe had jabbed into him burned and itched, but he was unable to navigate his tight and seemingly useless muscles to reach it. His ability to reason compounded the horror. He wanted desperately to scream out that he had been drugged, that he was about to be put on a plane for heaven-only-knows-what reason, yet he was powerless to do anything but move at the direction of the man who held his right elbow with a crushing grip.

"My uncle is not well, as you can see," Browne heard the man say to the ticket agent. "He can toilet for himself, but he must not eat until the plane arrives in Caracas. He will need only a little water."

Browne was not sure he could care for himself. Since he had been injected, he had been almost powerless to control his muscles. All he could manage was a spasmodic fit of moves. Was this a permanent condition, or would the drug wear off and allow him to regain his mobility? What fate awaited him in Caracas? Would he now be a helpless old man, a ready and quick victim of a vicious street crime? And what in God's name caused this Russian to do this? Could it have anything to do with C. G.'s estate?

"I'll need to see his identification and ticket please," the agent said, looking at Browne with what he sensed was a tinge of contempt.

"I'm sorry. This ticket is for a Mr. Josef Morello to Santo

Domingo," the agent said with some puzzlement on his face. "The name on your uncle's passport is Browne."

"Oh, it is my apology. I simply pulled the wrong ticket from my pocket. Here is my uncle's ticket."

By the time the man and his girlfriend left the pottery shop, the Hocketts were six hundred dollars richer. One of Hockett's large coffee table urns had been packed in wads of newspaper and bubblepack. Still, his stomach was growling and his mood was a bit nasty.

"You're so good with people, darlin'," Dave said to Barb, locking the door while watching the happy shopper slide into the car. Her boyfriend held the door while staring back through the window pane at Hockett.

"I just got a weird vibe from that guy," he continued, pulling down the shade on the door.

"Well, I guess you did," Barb shot back with emphasis. "All you two did was stare each other down. Thank heavens Miss Vogue was interested in your urn. I haven't seen you act like that with anyone before."

Fourteen-year-old Celia Hockett came through the side door into the office, a bundle of energy and a storm of questions.

"Hi, Mom. Hi, Dad. That was, like, a cool car! Did they buy anything? I'm hungry. When are the Calvins coming over? Can Katie spend the night? Dad, are you grilling tonight? Can we go home now? I'm really hungry."

"So am I, babe, and I think we can finally go now."

Sanibel at Evening
and Cayman by Night

"After dinner we'll walk along the beach. I want you to see the old C. G. King place. It's just across the pass on the end of Sanibel. The beach code on this island is very protective, so there's a lot more green." Larry Conroy stood poolside, pointing to the south.

Lee Hamblin was a tall, angular and elegant man. He looked at Conroy and beyond with a distant gaze. His host was to provide him a beach home so he could complete work on a government research project on bio-weapons. They stood on the front deck overlooking the small copse of Australian pine and Brazilian pepper.

"Lee," Conroy said, "I've known you for thirty years, ever since you were elected to Congress. As much as I hated to see you retire, I've admired what you've done. You were a great college president. And since then, presidents from both parties have relied on your advice. Practically every one of 'em has wanted you for their cabinet. But I've never seen you so morose and somber."

"I'll be all right. I'm looking for spiritual solace. It's a difficult thing, that's all. I've spent a great amount of my life trying to build up and reach for ideals, and now it comes to this task."

"I shouldn't have to tell you that what you're doing is part of the first step. We can't control these poisons and killer germs until we know where they are and who's doing what with them. Lee, your report is part of the cure."

"I'm sorry to bore you with my own dilemma. I'm really more disappointed than anything else," Hamblin sighed, gazing out at tree limbs moving gracefully in the first breeze of evening. "Almost five decades in public service and education and I find what could be my last significant contribution is a listing of how nations want to unleash lethal intentions in the most horrific of ways. I'll be fine, Larry. It's depressing. It is horrible work, that's all. I keep going back to C. S. Lewis for the *raison d'être*. He said, 'It was necessary and the necessary was always possible.'"

"We can eat at the condo every other night," Barb said to Laney, slicing tomatoes for the salad. Calvin sat on the bar stool and swirled a glass of merlot in his right hand. He pointed to a computer printout of a review of the Lantana restaurant with his left. The Hocketts and Calvins were working on plans for their summer trip to Grand Cayman. Up until thirty minutes ago Tim Calvin had been online, getting information about the island. He was finally bumped from the Hockett PC by his younger daughter.

"Dad, I've got that site you found back up on the web. I also found one about Cayman. I think you can see the condo where we'll stay. Do you want to get back online?" Katie walked around the corner from Dave Hockett's study, where she had been busy at the computer desk. At twelve, she was excited about the snorkeling she would be able to enjoy on this trip, having missed out on previous Cayman visits. A quiet and graceful child tottering on the edge of her teen years, she found on the Internet a community congenial to her interests. And there was e-mail, even on vacation.

"Have you been chatting with Julie and Colleen and Mandy?" Calvin asked, smiling at his daughter.

"Not Julie. She's at the lake," Katie answered, spreading smoked fish dip on a cracker. "Mandy hasn't answered her mail and Colleen is sending weird jokes. You want to see this Grand Cayman site?"

Putting his hand on her shoulder, Calvin said, "Sure, lets take a look. We'll be there in a few months."

Katie Calvin was thin and long-legged like her mother. She had not yet hit her growth spurt. She would mature soon enough, and Calvin enjoyed these last days of having his little girl. He still hadn't forgiven himself for the anguish she suffered when she was abducted with her mother, sister and his goddaughter, Celia, when he had gone off chasing the mystery of the old metal plate. She was young enough to forget most of the ordeal, though he hadn't.

The Sanibel Arcanum mystery was celebrated all over Florida. When Tim and Katie dug up the old engraved metal plate, he had no idea it would put him into the midst of an international intrigue and a centuries-old mystery. It had nearly cost the entire Calvin family their lives. Even though it ended happily, with a wild rescue when the family was held prisoner on the beach at Captiva and Calvin himself being a hero of sorts, he had never forgiven himself for exposing his family to danger.

Calvin never traveled anywhere in the world without worrying about his family's well-being. Both Katie and her older sister, who had grown into a beautiful young woman, were the delight of his life. These family vacations was the kind of brass ring he longed for, especially now that he was caught in his own search for meaning. The upcoming summer trip to Grand Cayman inspired him; it was something to plan for.

Increasingly, Calvin sensed what he needed in his life was a quest, a mission, something that put him outside his comfort zone. He had always been that way, full of zest for an adventure. He blamed it on two books: *Treasure Island*, which he read as a nine-year-old, and *Journey Without Maps*, which he read in high school. As a kid, he'd created his own treasure isle in a field behind his house and played for hours in that fantasy world. Later, after reading Graham Greene's account of his trek across uncharted Africa, he was struck by wanderlust.

Adventure-questing always thrilled him, especially if it involved danger or travel. Now it was clearly part of his middle-aged rumination. He was Jim Hawkins in Scotland, longing to run away to the sea, or Graham Greene, creating his own trail through jungle bush, pushing into the unknown. But tonight was an oasis, one of those pauses when he could enjoy how good it was to be at rest among family and dear friends.

The yellow Mercedes cruised over the causeway. The couple sat in the backseat as the woman admired the corner of the urn she could see in the box. The driver was on a cell phone, talking with a flight hangar on the international grounds of the airport. The muscular man with the fierce eyes and the Russian accent stared out at the darkening sky. He was thinking about the couple at the pottery shop, especially the woman. Sweet face, kind eyes. She reminded him of someone.

Katie stood by the printer, waiting for the job to be completed. She lifted the corner of the paper to see the full-color print.

"Hey, Dad. You can see Seven Mile Beach and the condo where we're going to stay."

"Cool." Calvin had linked from the Cayman site to Net19 which offered the Expedition Channel and pages on Cayman and other locales in the world.

"What are you looking at, Dad?"

"You know how much I like to travel and to read about other people's trips. I've got a great site up, written by some other road warriors."

"What a road warrior you are yourself, Dad." She smiled down at him.

Retrieving the print, Katie headed to the kitchen. Calvin

immediately absorbed himself in an article about an archeological expedition into the jungles of the Dominican Republic. It was the work side of his life.

"Dave wants you to help him with the grill," Katie said from the doorway, breaking his concentration. "Mom says you can wait to go online until after everyone goes to bed."

"She's right, sweetie. You know how I get lost out there." He smiled at her as he shut down the computer. "You want to help your pop and Dave with the grill?"

"Celia and I are going to play our flutes." She ducked breezily out of the room and out of smoky grill duty.

"That's probably just as well," Calvin mused. He and Hockett gabbed as they grilled and engaged in old-fashioned horseplay and joking around, not always appropriate for daughters. Sergeant Hockett was a demanding grill master, adjusting coals and applying marinades as carefully as he watched his pottery kiln.

◆ ◆ ◆

"All right folks, consider this: U.S. forces are leading a UN relief mission. Their job is largely peacekeeping. A couple of African nations are suffering famine, along with the death and dislocation of civil war. Islamic fundamentalists and a few warlords in the region have threatened violence. They call the mission an invasion." Lee Hamblin paused as he re-lit his pipe.

Larry Conroy had lost the affable grin that seemed painted on his face. His eyes were grim as he waited for Hamblin to continue.

"We've got eleven thousand troops on the ground. French, British, and a few others round it out to just under twenty thousand. During the second day, some of the forces begin getting the flu. This thing continues to spread. By the end of the week, eighty percent of all the troops are disabled, down, totally out of service."

"Good Lord! How real is that?" The question was fired by Claudia Prouse, Conroy's executive assistant. She scowled as she looked at the former congressman.

"Let me continue. Those who can stand are busy taking care of the sick. Now the mission is totally off-line, powerless and cut off. The warlords have carte blanche to step up their offensive. The fundamentalists are crowing about divine retribution, and the whole mess swings out of control. We've got thousands of sick troops and are totally incapable of dealing with them."

Silently, Conroy turned to his wife, Mary Lou, and Claudia and shook his head. "What is this, Lee?"

"It's a National Command Authority training scenario," Hamblin explained. "It's the type of drill that they run to evaluate several layers of command and control issues. Of course, the political issues are on top of that. This is the type of thing I've been working on, complete with horrifying details. The report I'm assembling will be fed into their war-gaming computer scenarios."

The GulfAir jet lightly touched the runway outside Georgetown and moved gracefully toward the private hanger. Except for the runway flashers and the stars overhead, the tower lights and those near the hanger were the only illumination. Midnight was a very quiet time at the Grand Cayman airport. Only a handful of necessary personnel were on duty, who told themselves they were fortunate; these assignments put fish, chicken, and beans on the table. They'd started when a Mr. Bokanyev had begun his late-night arrivals and departures from places like Fort Myers, the Dominican Republic, and Havana.

Craig Merryman was not on duty, but he had assigned himself off-duty surveillance when these suspicious flights began. He had taken up a vantage point in his services-and-operations office and had trained his field glasses on the thirty yards between the hanger side door and the waiting limo and escort SUV. Craig didn't approve of what he saw. Once again, this mysterious man Bokanyev had arrived, surrounded by men with guns on their sides or holstered to their backs. Craig dropped the glasses to his chest and readied a camera with a telephoto lens.

"Why do these men need guns on this gentle island, mon? I keep asking myself the question," Craig said as he watched the entourage get into dark vehicles and roll away into the night. Only the motor drive on his shutter penetrated the thick, dark silence inside his office, located on the drive approaching the Owen Roberts Airport terminal building. When the cars had disappeared, Craig switched on a light at his desk and entered in his pocket notebook the specifics of this most recent arrival of Bokanyev.

The limo and its escort turned right off Owen Roberts Drive onto Northsound Road. Bokanyev relaxed; they were going to the right instead of left, which would have led to Eastern Avenue into Georgetown. In addition to avoiding people, one of the advantages of the late flights was being able to skip the shopping that Monica seemed obsessed with. He looked at her cradling the urn in the large box, her eyes closed and her head leaning against the deep leather seat.

As the driver turned right onto the new Harquail bypass, he accelerated. The new road was built over drainage canals and was cut out of scrub woodland through the heart of the island; it was desolate. It amused Bokanyev to think the Caymanians had built the road to relieve what they considered traffic problems and to cut down on the backups along West Bay Road and North Church Street, or Eastern Avenue going into Georgetown. In his years on Cayman, he had seen an increase in cars and traffic, certainly that was true; still he considered a ten to fifteen minute drive to town as nothing compared to the traffic problems he had seen in Mexico City and Santo Domingo.

"So this is good," he mused as he looked at the virgin roadside, thinking of the private canal and road he planned to build up to the deserted coast on North Sound. He contented himself that very few people ever thought of that part of Grand Cayman. Most of the population lived in an area running from West Bay on the Northwest Point, along Seven Mile Beach into Georgetown and then along the south through Savannah and Bodden Town, past the breakers to the East end, then around the Queen's Highway up to Old Man's Bay and Rum Point, which was far out on the northside.

A little thumb of a peninsula stuck out southwest from Rum Point. An almost direct shot west across the sound from there would put you behind West Bay on equally unpopulated Morgan's Harbor, with the northernmost Conch Point just above it. For the most part, the large, U-shaped sound to the south of those two points was ignored. The commercial development, local villages, tourist hotels, condos, and dive and snorkel sights were located on the remaining perimeter of the island. The isolation of the North Sound was perfect for the business plans Bokanyev had been developing. The highway that he had pressured the government to build and that he had helped pay for in "gratuities" would make life a little easier once he began to store his product here. The Cayman site would give him three locales, now that he was taking care of the obstacles in the Sanibel situation.

Tim Calvin was pleased with the arrangement he had made with his laptop on the porch of the Captiva beach house. The extension cord and phone lines were long enough to allow him to clack away while he also enjoyed the fresh night air. Laney and the girls were preparing for bed. He sat at the table listening to the surf on the beach, while he did a different kind of surfing on the Internet. He was visiting bookmarked sites on Grand Cayman and the Dominican Republic, planning for their annual trip. He liked the idea of sitting on this island in the Gulf of Mexico, preparing for trips that would take him down into the Caribbean. And all this on the eve of his first book signing. "This is one way to deal with middle age," he mumbled to himself.

The limo and escort vehicle pulled off West Bay through the automatic gates onto the long drive. This had been the Royal

Caymanian Resort, one of the original compounds of British elegance and style in this part of the Caribbean. Now the long, sweeping drive past tennis courts and cricket green to the large pink hotel behind the line of palms and the extensive beach front was the private domain of Yuri Bokanyev, former agent of the KGB, and now a very rich man.

When he was on active duty, Bokanyev had been posted to Cuba, the Dominican Republic, and Mexico. While his old employer, the former Soviet Union, was collapsing, Bokanyev was building networks that would supersede the pedestrian games of intelligence and information in the new life that would evolve for him when the Iron Curtain crumbled into a rust heap. He had been involved in reading the economic and political winds and was at work on building a serious fortune with trophies like this former resort, now a residence and a place where he planned to broker his product.

Monica had gone off to bed, exhausted by the flight. Still, she had taken a moment to create a place for the new large piece of pottery on a marble-topped credenza that stood between the sets of French doors opening onto the Caribbean. She had been slightly puzzled by the rattling sound the urn had made as she had moved it around to get it situated. Bokanyev told her he had dropped a computer disc into its depths for safe keeping. Used to his somewhat curious ways, she thought nothing more of it. She admired the new piece, which sat next to a Minguet she had collected on St. Martin, and then, satisfied with her new acquisition, retired.

Bokanyev sipped a gin. He was pleased she had not turned on the jazz and opened the hall doors leading to their bedroom, signaling him to join her for an amorous romp. In the five years they had shared, Monica had become closer to him than anyone. She brought him pleasure and company, so he took the emotional risk of growing close to her, but he toughly reasoned she never got more from him than what he parceled out, never got closer than he permitted.

Tonight he was glad that she had not made demands, even for the physical encounter. He was not in the mood. He recognized that it was the physical companionship that allowed him to keep such a long lasting, intimate relationship. Still, he was truly fond of her. It went against all his training.

More importantly, it violated something more rigid, the protective containment wall which separated his day-to-day living from his inner world, his soul, if you wanted to call it that. To look at that divide deeply was to look into horror. When he took the time for such inner inventories, he was pleased with himself, pleased that he had been able to segregate so deeply the terrible thing which once seared his heart and scarred him. He had come to discount this idea of soul and reasoned that what he confused for such a thing was only the romantic notion of a young boy.

At any rate, he thought, he had learned how to dispatch such sentiment, cordon off the thing that once meant pain, and convert it into a controlled rage, which he channeled into extremely capable job performance, first as an intelligence officer and now as an international broker of weapons. A government psychologist once told him what he had mastered was a constructive use of hatred. Bokanyev was not much for the kind of psychobabble and "navel contemplation" on which such conversations hinged. He had simply learned to segregate a part of his life.

But there was something about that lady he had seen this afternoon in the pottery shop, that woman with the angelic smile, which seemed to stir up the demons he had buried so deeply inside. Bokanyev wondered why now, after all the years of successful suppression, he should be spending an increasing amount of time thinking about things in his personal life. He fixed the reason to be his age, fifty plus, and the fact he was now wed to a life-style where psycho-pop and culture often met. Television and other media were full of the personal. But enough for tonight, he concluded, as he initiated a call to his associates in the Dominican Republic and at the hotel in Puerto Plata. They had artifacts and caves to discuss as part of his grand master plan.

Helpless in the Terminal

MALCOME BROWNE REASONED it had been more than an hour since the frustrated flight attendant left him sitting in a wheelchair in the terminal of the Caracas airport. He heard her telling airline, airport and customs officials that he was a stroke victim, but no one had come to meet him. The security man he was left with had nervously smoked two cigarettes, looking at Browne with a sneer before departing into the crowd. Thank God he had been able to sleep during most of the unscheduled stop in Santo Domingo. He wasn't sure how his captor had convinced the flight attendants to continue to give him "medicine," but every six hours they had nursed another pill into him. Maybe he was lucky that during the delays he had been kept doped up, so he could sleep through most it. Now Browne thought he was once again beginning to regain some muscle control and strength, but any effort to move or speak ended in what seemed like a case of the shakes. He noticed he was being watched by two and then three young men in leather jackets and expensive sports shoes. They didn't look like the tourist or business travelers, nor even the South American locals in their colorful traditional dress.

Two men—one dressed in khaki adventure clothes, another an older, bearded, bald man carrying a small camera—had stopped to ask if they could be of assistance. Desperately, Browne had tried to speak, but was unable to do anything but twitch. The younger man looked deeply into his eyes and seemed to sense something. He straightened Browne's sport coat and helped him sit up in the wheelchair, looked to see if there was someone with him, and then reluctantly left. Most people, though, looked away from him, avoiding eye contact, except those who stared, including the men in leather jackets.

They looked at each other and began to approach him. Browne felt his heart begin to race. He struggled to speak. His jaws seemed more pliable, but still he could manage no sound. Why had this happened to him? Surely it was something to do with the environmental work C. G. King had started. Maybe there was some sort of real estate grab going on. C. G.'s property was worth millions. A developer would love to have it. The SOB who had drugged and gagged him seemed foreign. He sounded as though he had been going through files. Now here he was, helpless and being approached by three men. Were they connected to the man who kidnapped him?

"*Buenos noches*, Grandpa," said a man with a weathered face that looked older at closer range. The other two looked more Indian, with narrow-set eyes. Maybe they were brothers. One of them had a scarred face.

"How are your kidneys, old man?" the brother with the scar asked with only a hint of an accent.

The third, who appeared younger than his companions, grabbed the handles of the wheelchair and spun it a half turn while tilting it back, raising the front wheels off the floor.

"Welcome to Caracas," the leader said darkly, looking at Browne's watch and then patting his sport coat, feeling for the billfold.

Helplessly, Browne saw himself being wheeled through the bustling terminal, its exotic and pungent aromas filling the air. The older brother stopped at an open food stand and purchased something that resembled a sandwich while the younger tilted the wheelchair back in a rapid series of jerks.

"Easy with Grandpa," the leader commanded. "He needs to be well for the surgery." He bent down and leered in Browne's face.

"He is an old croaker. His kidneys will be no good," the scar-faced man said.

"On ice they will look good," came the response. "Black market buyers are not too careful." His weathered face and head nodded toward the door as his eyes scanned the terminal.

Browne felt clammy, as though blood was draining from him. He knew now what lay in store for him. He had read of people on foreign travel, even in the U.S., who were kidnapped, drugged, and then used for organ harvest, with their livers or kidneys sold on the black market. The people who had kidnapped him wanted him dead.

They exited the terminal and were bumping along a sidewalk, choked with bus and taxi exhaust and the stalls of street vendors, when Browne made eye contact with someone he knew. His heart leapt.

Donna Iemer was grabbing a shoulder bag from the taxi curb when she turned to see the trio with Browne in the wheelchair. She did a classic double take and then eyed the men.

Browne at once recognized her. She was a longtime political operative from his party and had been on the staff of his old friend Lee Hamblin when Hamblin was in Congress.

Iemer, a short, lean, and sinewy blonde, normally wore a slightly bemused smile. The smile disappeared and her eyes widened at what she saw.

"My God, Judge Browne! Are you all right?" she exclaimed, striding toward them.

Browne managed to utter a sound, a twisted garble, his tongue and jaw still under the influence of whatever he had been doped with.

"All right, guys, what's going on here?" Donna demanded, dropping the bags in front of the wheelchair and placing her hand on Browne's forehead as though checking for a fever.

"You are mistaken if you think this is your friend," the leader of the three men said, malevolence in his voice and eyes.

"I'm not mistaken about anything. This is Judge Malcome Browne and I am his friend," she said in a quietly defiant manner.

She caught what she thought was a look of surprise or perhaps fright in the eyes of the youngest of the three, the one who had been pushing the wheelchair.

"I said you are mistaken. We are taking this man to a clinic and you are going with him," the leader said, pointing his hand in a rapid fashion to the eldest of the brothers.

The man had close to a one-hundred-pound advantage and was almost a foot taller. He started toward her in an effort to grab her arm. But Donna, who had crewed on sailing yachts in the Caribbean, was toned and tougher than her pixie-like appearance implied. Her knee connected strongly with the man's groin and her left elbow, driven by her open right hand slamming into her left fist, caught the doubled-over assailant in the temple and sent him reeling back onto the sidewalk, where he fell into a group of tourists and sprawled over their baggage.

Stunned as he watched his accomplice tumble, the leader took a hard whack to the side of his head with something metal. As he recoiled, he heard, and then felt, the sting of mace or pepper gas spray. Iemer eyed the youngest of the three, who was still standing behind the wheelchair. His eyes darted from his brother to the leader on the ground, who clutched his face, screaming. He turned and ran.

Donna bent down to the side of the wheelchair and was soon joined by other travelers and two men in uniform. Malcome Browne had been rescued.

Book-Signing Flashbacks

THE LINE IN THE MACINTOSH Bookstore was about seven deep. Tim Calvin sat at a card table covered with a floral cloth and lined with stacks of his book *The NewsCenter*. Outside, the 1:00 P.M. sun dappled through the Australian pines and Brazilian pepper which lined Periwinkle, blazing hot on the beaches and golf courses. Refugees from the sun, along with the lunch crowd and afternoon shoppers, mingled with the serious book people.

A young woman from Rochester, New York, had enthusiastically informed Calvin of how much she loved the book and especially the characters. She was the first person to have read his first novel before getting his signature. A man had quizzed him about the title.

A woman he later learned to be an English teacher from Springfield, Massachusetts, had caught his eye as she stood about three people back. Calvin felt her continuing stare as he signed for others and chatted with them.

"May I tell you something about your book, Mr. Calvin?" she asked when she reached the front of the line.

"Certainly," he offered, wondering where it was headed.

"I teach high-school English."

Calvin's heart sank. "Oh boy," he offered in a sheepish bravado. "I'm in trouble."

"No, not at all. There are a few small printing errors, but those I'll overlook," she replied. "It's the splendid research you've done. I've been in some of those locales and your descriptions were wonderful. What I am especially pleased by is how accurate you are. I intend to offer it to my classes as an example of fiction that trades scrupulously on reality."

"Are there some scenes in particular you're thinking about?"

"I don't know Indianapolis, but I've traveled to Europe three times and I do know Chicago quite well. I grew up there." He nodded, pleased with her comments.

◆ ◆ ◆

After the first hour, people dribbled in in small groups or one at a time, leaving him sitting at his table amidst the shelves of books. Solitude gave Calvin a chance to reflect on the book and its creation. He randomly opened to a page, trying to put himself in the mind of a book browser who was trying to decide whether to make a purchase. Instead, he rambled back in his memory through the research and process of writing from which a particular scene or passage derived.

He had good friends in the television news business and it was easy for him to get access to news crews for his research. His intention had been to write a semi-scholarly evaluation of broadcast journalism, how it functioned in the last half of the twentieth century and how it had changed both the society it reported to as well as itself. He enjoyed the time in the newsrooms. He was fascinated by the parade of egos, politics, critical decision-making, and the ever present crisis mood and mentality. The personalities were large and strong, and the day-to-day dramas were complex and often amusing. What he found was the stuff of fiction, so instead of a nonfiction analysis, he turned out a potboiler mystery, though it still took some broad strokes at the serious issues. It was the story of an idealistic reporter who refused to buckle from the pressure to ignore an important story even though a cocaine-addicted news director tried to ruin her life.

He was pleased that critics had praised both his insights about the process and his view of the implications of television news. While in graduate school pursuing a Ph.D. in history, he had worked as a newspaper reporter. A family illness had intruded and he had never completed his dissertation, but his few years as a reporter had been an important influence in his life. It had served him well when he worked in advertising, marketing and corporate communications before venturing out and setting up his own consulting business. It was that background and his love for history that was, in part, behind his wild idea to write a book. For his own edification, the most instructive part of the research was done about two years ago, when he spent time with the investigative unit.

During the research period he had become friendly with Steve Stearns, a skilled veteran photographer. His colleagues raved about Stearns' shooting ability, but Calvin was impressed by the man's matter-of-fact coolness, even though he had seen and done it all. Stearns didn't say much, but when he did, it was worth listening to. Twenty-five years in the news business had honed Stearns' instincts and offered him plenty of opportunity to study people and their behavior.

He had the outward appearance of a hard-ass: lean, angular, weathered, and strong. His eyes gave little hint of what he was thinking, but they observed only as someone who made a living with camera lenses could do. Stearns didn't so much look at people and things as he studied them, finding a unique angle or essence. Calvin thought if he had been a television journalist, Stearns is the fellow he would have wanted to work with.

After spending several days shadowing Stearns, Calvin found himself enjoying beers one evening at the Elbow Room with the ace photographer and a couple of other shooters and producers.

"I hear you've got a place on Sanibel Island," Stearns said as he lit another cigarette.

"I'd like to retire there, or figure some way to get there on a more permanent basis. You know the place?" Calvin said, nibbling on popcorn.

"Was there on an assignment. Got to do some tarpon fishing. I'd like to try that again sometime." Stearns was known as a guy who preferred to have a fishing rig in his hands as anything else.

"You know the name C. G. King?"

"Know the name, and a little about her reputation," Calvin responded.

"We were there to interview her. I don't remember all the details, but she was a former ambassador somewhere. She'd been a business big shot. Had property all over the world, and she said she was going to will it to nature and environmental groups."

"Didn't she live here? Isn't there a Hoosier connection?"

"Used to be, after she married William King of the King Steel family. But C. G. had lived on Sanibel for years. There was some research project she was giving to an environmental defense fund. We were there for an interview and got to shoot her making her statement, signing the papers." Stearns signaled the bartender and Calvin did the same. "They were going to put her on some new kind of disc. You might want to get to know her. It was one of Riley's stories. You ought to check with her."

"Before you sign my book, I have to ask you a question." The voice stirred Calvin from his reminiscence. Before him stood a dimpled and blushing young woman whom he estimated to be about the age of his eldest daughter, Elizabeth.

"I'll try," he smiled.

"I'm from Indianapolis, and I think your character of the TV anchorwoman is based on Annie Riley of *Action News*."

"What makes you think so?"

"Because I shadowed her when I was in high school during professional interest week. I've kept in touch with her, and hope I can intern at her station. She is my role model and there are just too many similarities."

"Hmm, you could be right," he conceded, nodding pleasantly.

"Maybe some other people in Indianapolis will figure it out, but how do you think she'll appear to people from elsewhere?"

"Oh, I think it's great. I mean you changed her enough that some people may not recognize her. She's a great character."

As the would-be TV anchor walked away, Calvin surmised he had adequately answered her question. He had built a type of template response when people asked from where he drew his characters. He usually lapsed into telling the story of English novelist Graham Greene, who wrote *The Power and the Glory, A Burnt-Out Case, The Third Man, Our Man in Havana*, and many other books as well as screenplays. Greene borrowed from life so accurately, he sometimes risked anger and even legal battles. One work even drew the wrath of Shirley Temple advisors. Calvin wondered if the young woman who had just left even knew who Shirley Temple was. Left alone again, he turned to a page where the anchorwoman confronted a producer; it launched him back to a memory of the real-life prototype.

Calvin had met Annie Riley and had admired her work. She was a local girl who had become a favored anchor. Short, and a real head-turner, she had a sophisticated air and a spirit and spunk that made her accessible to viewers. With an academic pedigree from one of the nation's leading journalism schools, she was a strict custodian of principle, which in modern television news meant she sometimes battled with that side of the business which sprang from entertainment values. He knew he would cast her as a prototype for a character after he learned of the battles she had waged to get her regular feature, "Faith Journeys," on the air.

Ironically, he later learned it was a "Faith Journey" story that had taken her to Sanibel for the interview with C. G. King. Following Stearns' advice, Calvin had called Riley to schedule a time he could talk with her about her visit with C. G. King. She had suggested they meet at the television station at the beginning of her shift. Calvin appeared and they sat in the glass-walled conference room overlooking the hustle of the cubicle-filled newsroom. Calvin listened as Riley told the remarkable details of C. G.'s plans to deed her considerable property holdings to a special nature conservancy group and international network.

"Her will contained some interesting codicils. Her property on Sanibel is deeded to local government and is to be maintained by a trust fund as an environmental study center and retreat, provided zoning and building regulations within a particular distance of the property are never changed."

"That's generous."

"It's her way of assuring that some restrictions would provide for a continuity of 'class and a perpetual concern for environmental impact, fulfilling our role as stewards.' That's a direct quote. She fears that someday developers bent only on greed will get her large parcel of land and turn it into palatial homes or condominiums. She particularly detests the 'Miami school of garish and ostentatious.' " Riley smiled and then sipped her black coffee.

They watched the glass wall as a couple of reporters and photographers yelled at a woman, the assignment manager, who was sitting below the large assignment board. Riley shook her head in a bemused manner. She then told Calvin something else that roused his curiosity.

"C. G. had funded a study on the impact of shoreline and port development at many locations around the world. It took years and required the hiring of academics from a variety of international schools, which in turn led to linkages with a handful of government agencies both in the U.S. and abroad. When she was up for confirmation to be an ambassador, there was some thought that her privately funded study might create the perception of being too meddling in the affairs of other nations."

"Yes, I remember that story, vaguely."

"Well, to stave off the controversy, she got an old friend to quietly move the management of the research and its funding mechanism to a little-known independent research agency. The potential confirmation crisis was thus avoided. But while she served as an ambassador, the agency that had taken possession of her project was, in essence, purchased by the U.S. federal government. What had actually occurred was that the director of the group was hired by the mapping and reconnaissance division of the national security council and he simply took his data with him, including the C. G. King-funded research."

"He was treating it like it was his private property?"

"Not really. C. G. told me he had done it to protect the entire concept. At any rate, it took the extraordinary efforts of C. G. King's friend, an old CIA executive, to get the research back in her hands after she retired."

"Do you know who the old CIA guy is?"

"Not right off. I can check my notebook. Why?"

"I know a former deputy director who used to live on Sanibel. He became a friend. In fact he really pushed me to chase my dream to write a book."

"Oh yeah. I remember a couple years ago, when you got involved with some old inscribed metal plate. Something about a UN commission. You were getting help and direction from that retired CIA man, right? I remember the Florida press ran some big stories. I read about it on the wire. Could be the same guy. Can't imagine there are too many guys like him on Sanibel."

"Go ahead with your story. Sorry to stop you. I'll check it out myself. I'm sure I'm going to want to meet with C. G. sometime."

"I think you should. You'd like her."

A bearded man, his tie loose at the neck and a stack of video tapes in his hands, shoved the door open with his shoulder. "Annie, I need you to tape the tease and the sneak. And when you get through, I want to talk to you about the page-one voice over. Sorry to butt in."

"All right, Kevin. I'll be done here in a couple of minutes."

"Cool." He retreated to the newsroom.

"Sorry about that. It's almost getting to be crazy time around here. Tape and script deadlines. People get a little nutsy. Anyway, once

C. G. got the research back, she proceeded with the construction of her will, written so that funding made it possible to continue the research and to continue to monitor its findings. It was for that reason she has deeded property to conservancy groups and environmental funds. After her years as ambassador, she began to spend some of her great fortune to buy strategic parcels of land around the world with the intention of someday giving them to groups which would maintain them naturally and present a continuing foil or obstacle to shoreline degradation or the building of ports in places where there would be negative environmental impact."

Calvin was amazed by Riley. She had briefed him from a set of notes in a reporter's notebook and did so in a rapid-fire manner, even through interruptions and phone calls. Annie Riley was the definition of professionalism.

As Calvin left the television station, he was struck by two thoughts. The elder CIA executive had to be the same man as his old friend and mentor, Valmer. Riley was right. How many men with that kind of background could live on Sanibel? Calvin left that meeting with Riley, determined to meet this C. G. King.

◆ ◆ ◆

Letting his attention return to his book signing, Calvin enjoyed a quiet second hour. With only an occasional interruption by purchasers wanting him to sign their books, he could relax and observe the passing scene and reminisce as well—opportunities that had been in short supply as he worked to meet publishing deadlines. As he sat there signing pre-ordered copies of his book for the store, his mind continued to travel over the past, the untold story he had learned while researching *The NewsCenter*.

◆ ◆ ◆

Death had intruded before Calvin was able to learn a great deal more. His old friend and associate Valmer's health had deteriorated and he had moved to mountaintop property in North Carolina.

Calvin had spoken with him by phone a few times. In each subsequent call he sensed it wouldn't be long before the Cold War warrior, worn out by the active and dangerous life he had lived and his increasing illness, succumbed to his own wishes and at last joined the ages.

In the longest, though not his last, conversation with the former deputy director of the CIA, Valmer told Calvin how he had helped C. G. King get her research moved to a think tank, and then regain control of it. It was in that period, when others had access to the data, King gained some allies in her clandestine and honorable plan. Valmer said he had helped her approach many private interests, individuals and organizations who were thought to be kindred spirits, to help her facilitate her goals.

As a few people milled around the bookstore, Calvin closed his eyes and thought back on that conversation. He had called from Indianapolis, while Valmer convalesced on his mountain.

Valmer told Calvin that he himself made the pitch. "After all, I had the credibility. Remember, I was deputy director until a dispute with LBJ forced my retirement. I chose Sanibel above many other locations in the world because of its strict environmental policy and resulting quality of life."

"I know you served as mayor. You helped codify environmental policy, didn't you?"

"Yes. I knew it would be my last operation. But it was damned important. I helped C. G. King make her multiple international land purchases in strategically chosen spots. Her purchases were designed to stymie proposed commercial or industrial development in key places like Sanibel."

"I wondered how that got scoped out."

"With the help of friends and old associates we gained information from files, records and open sources on proposed or speculated development." Valmer's voice was hoarse and sometimes hesitant, but his mind was obviously as strong as ever. "C. G. told me she was surprised to learn how many people in the intelligence communities of the world were deep down 'greens.' Her land was purchased and deeded so that the purchase would become environmental study centers or buffer zones. With inside help and knowledge, they were set up, organized to be staffed by nationals, and funded by her. Upon her death, her own estate on Sanibel would become the international headquarters, and funding would flow from the disposition of her vast holdings, much of it going to a newly established foundation."

"Who was going to carry on the work? She had heart trouble, didn't she?"

"Well, the first director was to be C. G.'s longtime associate Malcome Browne, a former law-school professor, federal judge, accomplished scuba diver and outdoor enthusiast, who had been a friend of both C. G. and her late husband. You know, Tim, I think it's a great thing we did. It's up to your generation to protect it from here on in."

Malcome Browne! The thought of the old judge as he recalled his conversation with Valmer snapped Calvin back to the present. Hockett had called him at noon, just before he left for the book-signing. Malcome Browne had just been brought home from Caracas, where he had been found, apparently the victim of a kidnapping. He was unable to speak clearly and was debilitated, as he if he had suffered a stroke. They thought he might also have some type of amnesia.

A couple of Venezuelan men had been taken into custody by police, but they had subsequently disappeared. It wasn't clear how Browne had gotten to Caracas or why. Hockett had phoned Calvin with the bulletin after his late morning coffee with Sanibel police chief Stiner. According to the report, Donna Iemer, who was returning from a vacation on some neighboring islands, just happened to luck into finding the judge at the airport. He was in pretty bad shape. Donna arranged for medical care on the flight home.

He opened his eyes, clutching the book, and noticed he was still alone at the table, alone with his memories. He knew he wouldn't be sitting at his own book signing if that persistent call of adventure had not put him in touch with Valmer. He felt a deep regret he had never gotten to the North Carolina mountaintop to see his old friend. It was Valmer who had changed his life by thrusting him into the intrigue of the old metal plate, operating as his control as Calvin dashed around France to solve the puzzle. After the episode concluded, he and Valmer had become good friends, as though bonded by the experience, until Valmer's worsening heart problems began to take a toll. Calvin had heard in the old spymaster's voice that edge of control as Valmer outlined the work he had done for C. G.

Now Calvin sat and leafed through his book. Valmer had cajoled and, for all intents, ordered him to write it. Valmer was intense, compelling that way. Having recalled their conversation, Calvin now understood for the first time that it was probably the self-induced strain and sense of orderly control that Valmer always mandated for himself that had sapped him of his last energy. The last phone chat was just a couple of weeks before Valmer died, and he was confined to his lounger chair, looking out over the valley. His voice was weak and his mind had become somewhat confused, but he spoke with some pride about the King land deals, which he called "Operation Buffer." To the very last, the old patriot gave himself to a greater cause.

As Annie Riley had suggested and Valmer had urged, Calvin finally secured a meeting with C. G. King, almost a year ago. He had gone to her home with the intention of learning more of her Operation Buffer plan so he could write a magazine article. Confined to a motorized transport because of a bad leg, she suffered what she called "a bad ticker and a variety of other maladies," but she still described herself as a "feisty old bird."

"So you think this crazy environmental plan of mine is a good idea do you?" Her voice was stronger in intent than her aged vocal cords would permit. The result was delivery in a kind of quavery vibrato.

He assured her he thought it wonderful that someone was trying to leave a legacy.

"Well, we'll just see about it. I'm doing it for the future generations. I'm leaving the business end of it to Judge Browne. I'm too lazy and too much of a short timer to do any more." Her eyes, narrowed and tucked in a face now deeply wrinkled, were strong and mirthful.

Calvin had immediately liked the old gal, and she seemed to appreciate that he was a younger man who let her ramble and wasn't impatient to get to a point. For three and a half hours they talked and laughed. They were joined occasionally by Judge Browne. Calvin learned of her career in the WACs, her marriage to a steel-maker, her insistence in working with him, his early death, her taking over the business and succeeding. Her success in business provided the beginning of her philanthropy which was followed by her time as ambassador and as a friend of presidents.

Her commitment to the environment, though, was the result of her years on Sanibel. She and her husband first came to the island before the causeway was built. They were introduced to Sanibel by Adlai Stevenson, the governor of Illinois and presidential candidate. C. G. said she "had been a city girl and knew only the beaches of the Great Lakes or New Jersey's Atlantic shore. The first look at the turquoise Gulf of Mexico and the shell-strewn sand opened in me a curiosity about the ecosystem of warm-water lands." Since that first visit in the late 1940s, C. G. had made it her business to know the who, what, when, where and why of island development.

"I made my first trip here when the only route was a ferry," Calvin said. "All my daughters know, though, is the causeway."

"In so many ways it's sad to see all the building that has occurred on this wilderness island. But I am a pragmatist, a realist; I know we can't deny the future, which is, of course, an increasing commercialism of just about everything. However, we have established a strong environmental stewardship here. Thanks to the wonderful efforts of Ding Darling when he worked for the federal government."

"It is remarkable what his vision means to us now."

"Half of this island will always be natural, a wildlife sanctuary. Where we build, we have strong codes and, because of that, we are an example. That is why, Mr. Calvin, I am endeavoring to sow little seeds of the Sanibel experience in other places. We must have little islands of this spirit to stop our descent to our own worst inclinations. I just pray this will work." As she finished her thought, she looked through the floor-to-ceiling window to the gulf, waiting beyond a patch of sea grapes, saw grass and the stand of banyan trees ablaze with orchids. She was looking beyond the horizon to where turquoise sea met royal blue sky.

Calvin was sorry that had been the only meeting with this exceptional lady. His intention had been to get together with her again, but the business and routines of his life prevented it. He also felt a pang of anxiety over the well-being of Judge Browne and what his incapacity might mean to C. G.'s noble plans.

Twice on this afternoon of his book signing Calvin had regretted his inaction. It's odd that those who purchased his book would read and remember the story in their own way, while his own reflective reading took him to entirely private places. Still, he felt there might be some unfinished business. He felt a new link to Valmer and C. G. and their Operation Buffer dreams. "Maybe this next part of my life is about legacy," he thought.

"Hey Dad, you're on Amazon.com!" Katie had dashed out of the office of the MacIntosh Bookstore and was beaming as she broke into his reverie. "Philip let me use his PC and we found your book."

"Cool." Calvin looked at his watch. "About another ten minutes here and we can get back to the beach, kiddo." Katie had wanted to stay at the beach rather than come to her father's book signing, but had decided it was important to be there. Now he was ready to give her a break. They could leave soon. He too was ready for the beach.

Terror and Dinner

THE MOVIE-LIKE SCENE added luster to what had been a remarkable day for Calvin, his first book signing and the active recall of some strong memories. He and Laney sat at the glass-topped table on the porch, sipping glasses of cabernet and watching the sun set on the gulf in a blaze of colors that matched the art of his book jacket. Piano music from the stereo floated in from another room, giving an elegant musical background for the choreography of the palm trees, whose fronds waved near the shining gulf and white beach. It was a wonderful moment, one to savor for a lifetime. The Calvins embraced, happy with their choice of home for when the time for retirement came.

The holiday vacation mood was scheduled to continue with cocktails with new friends and then dinner with the Hocketts. All of the activities of the week were in support of the publication of *The NewsCenter*. Dave Hockett had made the acquaintance of George Romano, a film director who split time between Sanibel and Pittsburgh. Romano was an independent thinker who refused to surrender to the industry pressure to live in California. He and Hockett connected, in large part because they were both men who chose to live their lives as they wished, rather than as convention or professional norms might dictate.

The Romanos, like the Hocketts, lived in Gumbo Limbo, a quiet neighborhood built around three lakes and hidden in the middle of the island off Dixie Beach Road.

"I enjoyed your book," Romano said to Calvin as the couples took chairs at a table, poolside under a screen cage. The pool lights glistened, giving the lanai deck an electric blue mood. A Christmas tree, still clad in lights even though it was the week after Christmas, stood behind the window in the family room.

"It'd make a great film. I don't think I'd do you any good because it's not my genre. People know me for something else, but I could give you some names, make a couple of calls if you'd like."

"What kind of budget would it take, do you estimate?" Calvin asked.

"Well, when one of your lead characters, the news anchor, goes on assignment in Europe, you drive it up a bit. European locations . . . decent talent . . . you don't need a huge star . . . I'd say seven to ten million. Now if you get a big name attached, someone who likes the property, all the numbers change."

Laney and Elizabeth Calvin, Barb and Dave Hockett, and Chris Romano listened as Tim and George talked about filmmaking, the delivery technology, and the coming changes in the industry while the girls Katie, Celia, and Tina Romano played upstairs.

"What are you working on now?" Calvin asked.

"Do you mean what is he obsessed with now?" Chris Romano responded. She poured wine in the emptying glasses.

"I'm looking at a property now that's a little out there, but there is something so chilling about it I can't get the right handle on it. It's about bio-weapons and bio-terrorism. Actually it's really about something else and goes off in a different direction, but I'm hung up on this bio-terrorism stuff. I just didn't know how serious all that was."

"Man, it's real serious," Hockett offered. "In all my trips to Russia, I've picked up on that. The Russian Mafia is into that big time. A lot of former military and some of their old KGB agents are getting rich peddling the stuff, so they say over there."

"The trouble is, they'll sell to anyone," Calvin added. "It's fueled the rise in what they call 'non-state terrorism.' Anyone with an issue or grudge and the money to pay can play. When I was researching *The NewsCenter*, I spent time with an investigative unit that was trying to get some stuff on the air. What they had developed really opened my eyes. It is a frightening thing," Calvin said shaking his head.

Romano nodded agreement. "I don't want to jump in and do a slasher with this though. I'm trying to figure a take that will please the money people, put fannies in the seats and still tell the story."

"Right now the guess is ten to twenty countries have the capacity to use or make biological weapons. As many as one hundred countries are working on getting to the point they can," Calvin said.

"It's called the poor man's nuke 'cause they're relatively cheap to make," Hockett added.

Laney, Barb and Chris stood and walked around the pool deck to look at orchids, which were growing in Hockett pottery. They remained in earshot of the conversation.

Romano reached for a stack of papers on a nearby butler's table. "The lethality of this stuff is unbelievable. Ten grams of anthrax can kill as many people as a ton of the nerve agent sarin. Botulin toxin is probably the most dangerous poison on earth. This stuff is so bad, if you inhale even a nanogram you're gone, and in a terrible way."

"The skin burns and blisters; flesh can be eaten away; organs shut down; people choke on their own blood and suffocate, or they get incredibly sick, very quickly, and die, in just hours. I learned so much from the news team. It's horrible," Calvin said in a somber voice.

Romano flipped through his stack of papers. "The crazy damn thing is we've been doing this for centuries. In 1200 B.C. they used something called "Greek fire" at sea. Pitch, sulfur and quicklime was set on fire and thrown onto enemy ships. The Spartans made clouds of poisonous sulfur dioxide during the Peloponnesian Wars and used it if wind conditions were right when they besieged a city. Hellebore root was used by the Athenian Solon in 600 B.C. to poison rivers of a besieged city. Hannibal won a sea battle in 184 B.C. by throwing pots full of snakes onto a Roman ship."

"Well, you know," Hockett added, "I remember hearing, when I was in the army, about what they did during the bubonic plague in the Middle Ages. When ships bearing the plague arrived in port, they'd be turned away and sent toward commercial rivals' or political enemies' ports."

Calvin looked thoughtful. "And didn't the Brits send blankets loaded with smallpox to the Indian tribes fighting against them?"

Laney returned and stood behind Calvin. Barb and Chris were at the bar, freshening the cocktails and appetizers. "I just can't believe it. I didn't think any of it started until World War I," Laney added sadly.

"That's when it got real hellish," Romano shot back. "Good old Fritz Haber, director of the German Kaiser Wilhelm Institute, used chlorine gas as a weapon. He kept tinkering with it. Added phosgene and then mustard gas." He sipped his wine and consulted his notes. "Says here, on the twenty-second of April in 1915, Haber used mustard gas against French troops at Langemarke near Ypres in Flanders. A retired U.S. Navy Captain named Stuart Landersman did some research. Said a green cloud five feet high hugged the ground and moved in on the French troops. It hit them. Screams of pain and panic. Three-hundred-fifty dead. Total casualties, seven thousand."

"That is awful, just barbaric," Chris said, handing Hockett a refill.

George nodded agreement. "Then Italy used mustard against the Abyssinians in 1936. Japan used it against China in 1937. Egypt used gas in Yemen in the 1960s. The Russians had stuff in Afghanistan. Saddam used bio-weapons against Iran, then he used it against his own people, the Kurds. Then what scares the hell out of me is that incident in 1995. The Aum Shinrikyo cult used sarin gas in the subway in Tokyo. These things cause horrible deaths, massive."

Barb advanced on the group, hors d'oeuvres on a plate and a frown on her face. She'd heard enough. "Why don't we change the subject? I want to enjoy this evening and the girls will be coming downstairs. I don't want them to hear this."

"Now you say that. It's too late—we've already been listening to your gross conversation," Celia said as she, Katie, and Tina stood up. They'd been sitting on the edge of the pool, kicking their feet in the water and listening with fatal fascination. The men, whose voices had grown agitated, had not been aware of them.

"Really gross! Not a very nice dinner conversation, Dad," Tina added.

Katie stood on the threshold and looked at her father. "Sick! Why do people do such things?" she said with emotion.

"The Captiva Inn dining room is considered one of the great quiet rooms in southwest Florida," Romano told the group as they walked from the parking lot toward the building.

They entered a space with the look and feel of a room in a fine home. It offered rich and personal intimacy, creating a mellow mood. The relaxed conversation ceased only when the entrees were presented and then sampled. Seared sesame yellowfin tuna and vegetable fried rice with chili sauce, Caribbean snapper with avocado and lime cream sauce, New York Strip, portobello mushroom sauce and re-mashed potatoes with goat cheese and Gouda were choices in the party of nine. A bottle of St. Emillion Grand Cru and a Conundrum from Caymus Vineyards balanced the table and offered both red and white wine, which helped celebrate the accomplishments of the chef. The evening fairly raced by with humor and friendship.

Celia sounded advice to the group. "You've got to try some of the desserts. They are really killer!"

"What do you recommend, Cee?" Calvin asked his goddaughter.

"The apple crisp with ice cream and the bourbon pecan chocolate pie in butter crust and topped with vanilla." As she spoke, she eyed a giant chocolate silk mousse being served at the next table.

◆ ◆ ◆

Hugs and embraces sent the Romanos and Hocketts back on their way along San-Cap Road to Sanibel. The Calvins had only a short drive to the beach house where they were special guests during this book-launch week. Even though he was partial to Sanibel, Calvin liked Captiva and was enamored of the elegance of the Simmington home, which had been offered to him for this post-Christmas week by Dyane Simmington, an environmental, social and political activist whom he had known for years. Married to an international business mogul, she had decorated the house with great charm and would often offer it to friends for special occasions. She had deemed the publishing of his book such an occasion. Since his own more modest place on Sanibel was currently being leased, Calvin was pleased by the kindness of the offer.

Slightly stuffed from dinner, Calvin looked forward to a walk on the beach. On this point, he conceded, the South Seas Plantation complex was arranged so that the private beach homes were indeed private. On his anticipated stroll he would probably have the beach to himself. He needed to think some things over. The day of book signings and socializing had provoked powerful memories and had opened his mind to looming issues, principally his interior battle over what he was going to do with the rest of his life.

Thinking it Over

THE BREEZE WAS ON his face as he sank his bare feet into the cool, damp sand and stretched his arms at his side. The lights of the beach house made strange shadows of the palm trees. There was no moon, but the star field was full. It was one of those nights when the froth of the lapping waves seemed to glow as though illuminated by a sea light. The beach at night was his own; even the shore birds had taken shelter. Calvin was glad for the space. The sea evoked in him creative ruminations, but it also loosed an expansive stirring of restlessness. He was convinced there was a genetic predisposition to this. His father used to love to just stare at the surf and let his thoughts wander.

Step after step, sinking into night sand, Calvin experienced a refreshing contentment. He needed to think. He had been lucky and had enjoyed a decent run at his consulting business, but he was unsatisfied. He spent too much time worrying about financials, courting new business, piddling with "personnel" issues, which, when reduced to their essence, were nothing more than personality issues, often petty and even childish. He had written his book on a whim, later motivated by the continuing support of Valmer and Laney. He had done it by borrowing time early in the morning, late at night and on weekends. Writing his book was the single most satisfying experience of his professional life, but there was no indication it could be family supporting. The new business, tough and unpredictable as it was, had proven its ability to provide an income.

"Middle-aged and still enamored of his boyish dreams, that was his situation," Calvin mused, doing an impersonation of an overwrought newscaster as he walked. He was looking for a new angle to his plight. He was still Jim Hawkins with the breeze ever beckoning and the sail set to some place of adventure.

Calvin knew from experience he was about to undertake some energizing enterprise. Always when he found himself confronting his own balance sheet of being and measuring the success of his own life, he found a new path to travel or life would simply intervene and place before him some new project, curiosity or other endeavor which would, for a short time, consume him. He didn't have to think in order to confront ultimate self-examination that way.

He suddenly realized his stride had become brisk and his heels were pounding down, digging into the sand and launching him in a rapid forward motion. He had walked a great distance. He slowed and then stopped. As he allowed his mind to quiet, he became aware of other life on the beach.

The odd noise sounded like a blend of a hiss and an airy snort. Then there were quick retorts in what sounded like voices in quick blurted bites. Calvin had traveled to an area of beach where the houses were spread and separated by stands of Australian Pine and patches of thick sea grapes and saw grass. Surprised by how far he had walked, he realized he was only a short distance from the C. G. King property. A few dozen yards ahead, he could see a flashlight held by someone who was obviously struggling. His heart rate, already elevated from his brisk walk, seemed to pace ahead. He had left his glasses behind and strained to stare through the darkness for a better sense of what was happening. He crept up to the tree line and edged south toward the scuffle, listening intently.

"Grab that end and help me drag him into the water," a voice said. Immediately Calvin sensed something unusual.

"Have you done this before?" came the second voice, measured, cultured, and familiar.

"Once, several years ago, when the kids were young. That was during egg-laying time," was the response.

Two shadowy figures struggled with something large on the beach.

"Well, we'll certainly work off a few calories," said the second voice.

"Speak for yourself; it's not like *you* need to."

Realization flashed into Calvin's mind even before he could clearly see the two men and their unlikely situation. Two Hoosier power-brokers were wrestling with a loggerhead turtle which had somehow wandered onto the beach. It was an old boy, and heavy. Larry Conroy, wearing a flowered shirt and long, baggy swim trunks, was trying to grab the shell behind the head and avoid the turtle's snapping mouth. Former Congressman Lee Hamblin wore a seersucker shirt and long slacks which he had rolled to his knees.

"Mr. Conroy, Mr. Congressman, I presume this is a high level political discussion," Calvin said as he approached, startling the two men whom he knew from back north.

"There you go, Calvin, true to form. You're a consultant, so that means you talk while everybody else does the work. Get your hands dirty here, boy." Larry Conroy was an old political pro and longtime friend of the Calvins who had often entertained Laney and Tim Calvin at his Captiva Beach home. Always a jokester, he hadn't missed a beat, and his big grin beamed in his gray beard. Conroy had a cherub-like round face, and his eyes generally twinkled with a sense of humor. He made Calvin think of a story-telling and mischievous Santa Claus.

"Well, Mr. Calvin, you'll remember how Larry never overlooked a possible vote anywhere. I think he's doing a kindness for this loggerhead in hopes he'll remember him when he goes into the turtle voting booth. But you know, no one has called me 'Mr. Congressman' recently. These days I am simply 'Professor Hamblin.' " Lee Hamblin had had a distinguished career in the House before retiring to academia. His opinions were sought by politicians of both parties and he had on three occasions turned down cabinet appointments.

Calvin lent a hand and, after a couple of shoves, the turtle began to lumber off into the gulf on its own power.

"Well, gentlemen, we've earned a drink," Conroy said with his flat, nasal twang. "Calvin, can you join us? Or is it past your bedtime? Lee's going to stay in our place for a while," he added as they walked toward the house. "We're just down here getting him set up. I thought you were strictly a Sanibel snob."

"Strictly speaking, you are both on Sanibel. We crossed over the pass: the tide must be out." Calvin paused. "You guys gave me a bit of start, dragging reptiles around."

"Taking a walk to recover from your book signing? Sorry I missed it. I saw the piece in the paper," Hamblin said.

"The beach is a great place to think," Calvin answered.

"Well, I intend to do a lot of that," the former congressman said. "I've taken a leave so I can write and compile a rather somber piece of business."

"I don't know whether we should discuss anything in front of him or not," grinned Conroy. "After all, he's a writer now and has been known to associate with card-carrying journalists."

"If a few more journalists paid more attention to some of this dreadful business I'm studying, a few more governments in the world might take the problem of biochemical terrorism and warfare more seriously," Hamblin opined.

"We were discussing that tonight with a film director. Our consensus is that not enough people are aware of how serious the problem is," Calvin explained.

"Well, of course, I'm inclined to agree with you. The academic and scientific research is sobering enough. I'll also be working with a task force from several nations, government people with intelligence analysis," Hamblin continued.

They had reached the path that led back toward the beach and the Conroy house.

Calvin shook his head. "What a burden it must be to have to immerse oneself in such a horrible problem."

"Oh, it is a strain, but I think the beauty of these islands will help. They are a kind of balm to the spirit."

Hockett was having trouble sleeping. He didn't think it was the second cup of espresso as much as the troubling conversation he and Romano had on the drive back to Sanibel. He had hoped that he and Barb were providing a safe world for Celia to grow into, yet he knew that forces beyond the gentle barrier reef island could also intrude into the world his daughter would inherit. The fact that a renegade Saudi billionaire, an Irish zealot, an American political extremist or just a plain wacko could wield so much power in the balance of terrorism made him angry. Anyone with the money and the reason, even if it was a delusional one, could poison a water supply, release a nerve agent in a mall, or spray an area from a plane. The more he thought, the angrier he became. Unable to sleep, he got up and went to the computer to e-mail friends in Russia from his church mission trips. Somehow he wanted to share his deep concern to internationalize it. Spreading the burden around a bit seemed to diffuse it.

Bokanyev sat in his hideaway study in the turret tower of his Cayman beach front estate. When the place had been a resort, the tower was an open lookout, a place for resort guests to look over the expanse of Seven Mile Beach and the rolling Caribbean. Bokanyev had installed small satellite dishes, satellite phones, tinted glass, computer ports and hidden files. His desk was a virtual circle, broken only by the entry. He commanded a 360-degree view.

Tonight he felt powerful. He had spoken with his employee in Indianapolis, a lawyer, and was assured the legal matter was being handled. Bin Laden's organization had e-mailed their counterproposal for a product he had in shipment, bound eventually for his new property on Sanibel. He would send it once the legal arrangements were done.

Even though Monica had prevailed and they had gone out to dine at the Wharf rather than eat in and enjoy the cuisine of his Cayman chef, it had worked to his advantage. She was gratefully affectionate and their passion began to bloom as they drove home. Monica enjoyed going out, flaunting her sculpted body, displaying her dazzling wardrobe. She seemed to need public adoration, at a distance anyway. It was a cycle he knew well. Show her off, let her be seen and draw stares, and then enjoy her payback. She had tapped the button to put up the divider between the limo driver and the backseat, then began her ritual of arousal: gentle kisses behind his ear and down his neck with a delicate anatomical brush of his body. The slow, erotic disrobing was timed to arrival through the gates and into the estate. From there it was into their bedroom lair, into an incense-and-perfume scented atmosphere filled with soft jazz and the breeze of trade winds to cool their perspiring bodies.

Now, as Monica slept below in the boudoir, he sat typing a message to Santo Domingo. Indeed, he did feel quite powerful.

Calvin knew this would be a day he'd spend walking the beach and thinking. He stopped to watch the pelicans cruise near the shoreline in packs, skimming the top of the gulf and soaring in wide arcs and circles, eventually cutting the green surface in their predatory dives. He was amused by the couple of terns and gulls which followed behind, barely able to keep with the pack. One of the terns would consistently follow a pelican into the water, landing on the large bird's head or back or splashing alongside as though he too could grab a harvest from the gulf. On takeoff, the pelicans looked as though they used their web flippers to run across the surface of the water. This was exactly the type of diversion Calvin was looking for. Watching the pelicans in their early morning work helped him focus on the tasks that lay ahead. Priority one was to get out of his middle-aged, "now-what-do-I-do" funk. Number two was to organize a trip to the Dominican Republic for a magazine article he had been hired to do free-lance. Number three was to decide what to do about his business. Should he plan for expansion and go for more financing, or should he try to sell it or phase it down? Itemizing this way gave him a sense of mission. Perhaps Lee Hamblin was someone who might be able to offer a little sage wisdom as he entered this next stage of his life. Would it be presumptuous to ask for his advice? There was something about that man that had always given Calvin a sense of confidence. Perhaps it was his integrity and intelligence. In the conversation after last night's turtle-wrestling incident on the beach, he saw Hamblin in a new light, as a kind of pragmatic philosopher.

Last night, as they sat there on the Conroy screened porch and philosophized, enjoying the jokes and conversation, Conroy observed "this was one of life's golden moments. Three Midwestern guys enjoying drinks at midnight while listening to the gulf, saving turtles and solving problems. Pleasure."

Hamblin offered with a smile, "like the man said, *a pleasure is full grown only when it is remembered.*"

Indeed, it had been a pleasurable evening and Calvin knew it was one of those occasions he would recall with fondness. Over time and through the service of remembrance he could understand how the pleasure would grow. It sparked a realization that there were other moments in his life which he could and indeed should count as mature pleasures. There was a lot of meaning in moments of quiet, satisfying pleasure, and he needed to remember that.

The day drifted by in beach strolls, solitary and with the girls, lazy poolside reading, and naps induced by the sound of waves. It had been a day to "unplug" and drop into deep relaxation. At 6:00 P.M. he was strolling back to the beach house to ready for a party on Sanibel. The pelicans were back, in formations of three, five and seven, soaring over the foliage line of the beach. A yellow parasail with two riders drifted in from the south about midpoint between the shore and the blue edge of the gulf. Beyond that, a two-masted sailing ship cut the upper third of the water, its naked masts silhouetted in the river of diamond light left by the sun beginning its evening descent. A few osprey and a rare solo pelican skimmed the top of the turquoise water just behind little foam waves which tumbled the shells. Now, small shore birds picked among them.

Calvin felt a type of completeness. The pelicans had been busy on the water in the morning, but now they soared above the trees. They too were preparing for the evening ahead. He hadn't decided much, but he had relaxed, and that in itself was a good first step. He felt a sense of openness, a willingness to listen to life. He had reaffirmed for himself that simply enjoying his family and friends was a worthwhile priority, and that everything else could follow.

Party on West Gulf

THE CALVIN AND HOCKETT families walked under the arbor along the path to the entrance of the rambling house. The front door opened into a courtyard which led to an Olympic-sized pool and a bridge to the main house, all decked out in Christmas trimmings and lights.

Hockett was telling about the host. "Don McKenzie is from a coal mining family in Pennsylvania. They winter on Sanibel. He and his wife, Sara, came into the shop about eight years ago. He's made it a point to know just about everything about the island. I think he may run for mayor when they move down here full time."

From a corner of the pool deck, a reggae band washed the scene with funky rhythms. Three or four dozen people milled around the balconies, decks, bridges and sitting areas in the home.

"Everywhere you look, you see Hockett pottery," Laney said quietly to her husband as he waited for a glass of champagne.

"Tim, Laney, I want you to meet Don McKenzie, our host," Hockett said behind them.

Calvin turned and offered his hand and complimented the host on the elegant beauty of his home.

"My wife, Sara, takes the credit. She designed it, wanted it built around the pool so you can see water from every window, either the gulf or the pool. We love it. Say, Tim, I've got to tell you how much I enjoyed your book. I don't usually read novels, I stick to business books and biographies, but I got hooked and thoroughly enjoyed it. Dave tells me you may do some more writing, some magazine work in the Dominican Republic?"

"One of the great things about working as a consultant is being able to take on free-lance writing assignments. There's an archeological mystery down there in the eastern part of the island. They've found a couple of caves. I've been hired by *Outdoor* magazine to do a story on the archeology and dive teams."

Don McKenzie nodded his head with interest, then he said, "Dave, you might be interested in this as well: there's a little mystery right here on Sanibel. Remember the old King estate?

"Well, I went to pay a visit to Judge Browne today; I knew he was taking care of things since C. G. died. I wanted to see if there was anything I could do with our foundation and all that to help run the place."

"You hadn't heard the news then?" Hockett said.

"No. Sara and the kids and I have been off on the boat. We get out there and we're out of touch. It's a kind of holiday tradition for us. So, no, I hadn't heard a thing, and there I was on my way to see the old boy. But of course no one was there and the place looks like it's been halfway packed up. Now, I went back later when I passed the drive and saw a car. There was some fellow who was very unfriendly. Said he was preparing the place for a new owner. New owner! I said, what the hell did he mean new owner? I said the place was supposed to go into a trust and be an environmental center. He said, 'Not anymore, the place has been sold.' And that's all he would say."

"Whew," Hockett said.

"That can't be," Calvin added.

"I know C. G. had made a formal presentation. I told this guy there was proof of her intent—it was clear. A TV crew had been there and even recorded her making a record of it. The tape had been dubbed onto a CD or a disc of some sort and it was probably on a shelf in the house. Well, what's he do? He slammed the door in my face. Now there are some people here tonight I want to ask about that. Sure is weird." McKenzie shook his head in a kind of wonderment as he finished. He was then interrupted by other guests and the conversation broke up. Calvin had a rare moment alone, then Laney came up and slipped her hand in his.

Shrimp, pineapple tidbits, and skewered mushrooms were being passed around. Hockett cruised by, popping small barbecued sausages into his mouth.

"You know, Dave, I'd like to drop by the King estate tomorrow. Something is very odd." Hockett looked at him long and hard. Calvin was off again, contemplating another adventure, another unmarked path.

Laney withdrew her hand and set her drink forcefully on the table. "Tim, I want you to stay out of this. You know what happened the last time you started sticking your nose in somebody else's business. You almost got yourself killed at Chartres Cathedral! Remember?"

Calvin stood looking at the river of moonlight on the gulf. A large quarter moon and a star were in the upper left sky and were shimmering on the rolling surf. The floor-to-ceiling window in the study of the McKenzie home made a perfect contemplation point. The moon was occasionally obscured by a bank of dark clouds, looking like an eye peaking out of a shroud. A couple of champagnes had left him seriously considering walking over to the King estate that evening and checking for himself, despite Laney's admonition.

"Hey! You being antisocial?" Hockett asked as he approached the window.

"Would you like to join me for a quick trip over to the King house to see what we can see?" Calvin asked.

"And leave this party? Leave Barb? How do you think you can get by Laney? No sir, mister. Whatchya gonna see?"

"Ah, there you are." Don McKenzie entered the room with a glass of bourbon. "This is one of my favorite rooms. Like to read the

Sunday paper here. But listen, I've picked up the weirdest tidbit tonight on that subject we were discussing." McKenzie drew the small group together. "Charlene Thomas, the broker with the office in Periwinkle Center?"

"Sure. We know her, she helped us buy our place. I'm sure she hears a lot," Calvin said.

"She fills me in with the latest real estate information. She tells me tonight she heard that a European named Bokanyev—sounds Russian to me—has paid the tax on the King property and is apparently going to take up housekeeping.

"What about C. G.'s environmental plan?"

"Apparently the idea of the study center is shot and there doesn't seem to be anything anyone can do."

"I know she intended otherwise. She was very dedicated to making this the headquarters of a network of environmental study centers. What about her will?" Calvin asked.

"No one knows. Apparently it's now in the hands of a firm back north. Charlene says a Fort Myers lawyer named Clifton handled C. G.'s personal matters. He died before C. G. got it all put together. All of the King Steel Company work was done by an Indianapolis firm that did it for decades. Well, when Clifton died, C. G. had it all shipped to that firm. Judge Browne was apparently trying to tie up loose ends when he was kidnapped. Charlene says this Bokanyev guy is apparently changing the title. Something's missing, isn't it?"

"Seems that way. It's very odd."

◆ ◆ ◆

Calvin looked longingly down the shoreline. If he could just go see what was happening at the King estate. The urge to go was compelling, almost electric.

"You couldn't get through that hedge. There are a lot of old peppers in there and they'll catch at you until you can't move." Hockett's warning was clear and it was about more than peppers. "Fence on the other two sides. I've heard there's even an inside perimeter of wire. It was set up when she was ambassador and would take vacations here. She just kept it with that intense security. You couldn't get in there tonight and even if you could, your wife would kill you, and maybe me for helping you." His voice was insistent and reasonable. Calvin wasn't buying it.

"The way in is through the gate and up the drive?" Calvin asked. "Didn't you say there was another drop arm on the way?"

"It's as much a barrier as the link fence outside her lawn. Plus, I'll bet she had motion detectors put inside that cabana tiki."

"Hey, Pop. What you are talking about?" Elizabeth, carrying a sparkling glass of champagne and glowing with the joy of the evening, joined Hockett and Calvin.

"Talking about the King place," Calvin said to his daughter, smiling with pride in his eyes. Her hair was pulled back and she carried herself with grace. She was at a searching time in her life, examining relationships and considering what she was going to do. Student teaching was the last academic act. Tim and Laney had urged her to add a teaching certificate to her undergraduate degrees in art history and studio. She was an advanced scuba diver, a wilderness canoeist, hiker and survival camper. Still, he wasn't sure what he thought of seeing her enjoying the champagne. Well, she was certainly old enough to decide what she wanted to drink. He wanted to say, "Be careful, don't drink too much," but he stifled it.

"This is a great house and very nice party," Elizabeth said. "When Ben gets down here, we're going to canoe to Buck Key." Ben was her steady boyfriend.

"Could you guys swing by the northeast and take a look at something?" Calvin asked.

Hockett shook his head at Calvin and shot him a "don't even think about it" look. Then he muttered a dramatic, bullet-fast, "Leave it alone."

"Sure, Pop. What is it?"

Moonlight on the Woods

IT WAS LATE JANUARY and the warmth in the room felt good. The light from the fireplace flickered across the room and reflected in the side window which looked onto the front porch and portico of Tim Calvin's Indianapolis home. The reflection provided a slight distraction as Calvin sat in the overstuffed chair reading Martin Gilbert's *Churchill: A Life*.

But that wasn't what broke his concentration. It was the beauty of the moonlit evening. He walked to the front window, a ceiling-to-floor expanse which was recessed and almost as wide as the room. Calvin was soothed by the scene. A bright moon glistened on snow that was piled on the rail fence running along the lane which wound back in off the road through the woods. It had been a great Florida Christmas vacation and the family had returned to a snowy homecoming. The picture-perfect woodland beauty diverted his mind from a bewildering situation that had continued to develop since the end of the holiday trip to Florida. Something quite sinister was beginning to stir on Sanibel.

Elizabeth's photos were proof of something. She and Ben had canoed past the King estate and collected a roll of shots. There, unmistakably in living color, was the top floor and roof of the King estate now fitted with what looked like gun mounts. In addition, there were views of three satellite dishes which Calvin assumed were also new. Ridiculous. Three was overkill for television viewing. Calvin strolled from the window to the desk in his study where the pictures were spread. It was clear that Elizabeth had alighted from the canoe and sneaked onto the ground to get some of the shots. While he felt a sense of pride in her pluck and courage, he winced at the thought he had clearly put his daughter in harm's way. Anyone with gun mounts on the house would disapprove of a clandestine approach to the property.

Calvin sat at his desk and turned on the computer so he could read again the e-mail from Edward Earl. Earl was the former associate of Valmer who had taken direct control of efforts to get Calvin's family and goddaughter released when they had been taken hostage three years earlier. Calvin learned about Earl's role later, and he and Earl had formed a friendship. A former intelligence officer and prosecutor now in private law practice in a small town, Earl still had great sources. Again, Calvin read the gripping reality:

Re: the King estate.

This will bear scrutiny. Maybe it should go to some of the pros at FBI or CIA. The name Bokanyev is bad news. Yuri Bokanyev was a colonel in the KGB. Now part of one wing of the Russian Mafia—really more of an independent. A loner. The speculation is he brokers old weapons, maybe bio-weapons. In the attachment are some URLs and passwords to give you more. For God's sake, be careful. Don't do anything with this until we have spoken.

Calvin opened a file in which he had stored a video clip of Bokanyev. It was apparently shot by an agent in Santo Domingo. There were also photos, giving Calvin a chance to see the face of the man who represented the evil prowling behind the palm trees on Sanibel. Calvin made a note to ship the file to Hockett, then moved on to another subject and another electronic file: the details of his upcoming business trip to the Dominican Republic, as compiled from the Internet.

His company was in a bleak quarter. Cash flow was low, and things were not expected to pick up for a couple of months when projects would be finished and checks cut. The magazine assignment in the Dominican Republic was a way to get a cash infusion as well as being interesting to him. After all, *Outdoor* was a national magazine. The writing job would give him a chance to keep his authoring skills honed. He opened the slats of the wooden shutters on the window at his left shoulder and looked out at the snow-covered garden and woods. His mind was stuck on the Bokanyev connection on Sanibel. He shivered, not so much from the cold draft and view of the winter night as from the thought of what was happening at the King estate and to C. G.'s dreams.

Billable Hours

HIGH ABOVE THE GRAY slush and creeping traffic, Richie Peabody of McAtee Cheskin Ford and Hendricks strolled past the vacant conference room with its commanding forty-second-floor, glass-walled view of Indianapolis. Peabody carried a hard copy of his most recent message from Bokanyev. He detested Bokanyev; still, he was his puppet, pulled and jerked around. In this instance he would respond as he always had to. As Peabody walked into the file room, he caught a lingering sweet scent: the perfume of one of the office women. It started his mind on a journey back to the time of another such scent and the beginning of his vassalage to Bokanyev.

◆ ◆ ◆

It had been about two years ago. Peabody was in Mexico City at a continuing legal education seminar with the express objective of learning about converting aging files to electronic storage and access. At the last minute, his wife had canceled her plans to travel with him, so he found himself alone. Most of the other attendees were accompanied by companions. He remembered leaving the crowd at the cocktail party to go sit solitarily at the bar to wait for dinner.

Peabody loved to eat, which explained his pear-shaped body and round face with double chin. Because he was soft and fleshy and disgusted with his corpulence, he took notice of men who were the opposite. He had made eye contact with a hard and chiseled fellow as he pulled away from the lawyers. The man had been standing with three lovely women just behind the gaggle of squawking lawyers.

As he sat looking at the wine list, his nostrils were filled with a rich and delightful fragrance. He became aware that people were taking seats on the stools next to him.

A Euro-something—perhaps Russian—accent interrupted his contemplation. "My friend, you are alone in Mexico City and this is no good."

Peabody turned to see the chiseled-face man smiling at him. He was accompanied by two of the women.

"I am Yuri Bokanyev, also a lawyer. My friends here do not want to see you so lonely."

"I know just want you need," a seductively sweet voice said from behind him. "A margarita."

Peabody turned on his bar stool to look into the dark eyes of an absolutely stunning woman. She pursed her bright red lips into an air kiss.

Peabody shuddered as he recalled what happened next. There were a couple rounds of the powerful drink, the dissolving of any will power, an aroused libido and then a hazy encounter in his hotel room of which he could recall very little. What he would never be permitted to forget was the horrible moment of waking up to the lights of the video camera. In a groggy act of desperation, he pulled the blankets over his head, only to have them tossed away as his companion slithered her naked body around his, kissing his ears and rubbing her hands on his saggy chest as Bokanyev smiled and videotaped.

"Oh, what wonderful memories we make here my friend," he said, moving in close as Peabody's bedmate was joined suddenly by one of the other women he had seen in the bar. Both of the women straddled their legs around Peabody. His protruding stomach was now entwined from both sides by the legs of the naked women.

"Smile, Mr. Richie, so you may never forget this moment!"

As he sat in the file room, Peabody smoldered. As hard as he tried, he could never recall what actually happened. To this day he would swear that he had just fallen asleep. The video tape, though, could not be argued with. He felt so pathetic, his large white belly and rolls of flab jiggling as his "playmates" engaged in their staged amorous gymnastics. No, there could be no explaining the tape, he thought. He looked both guilty and repulsive, and it had been easy for Bokanyev to shame him into compliance. Mostly what he had done for the man was non-billed legal work and research at McAtee Cheskin Ford and Hendricks. It wasn't until a couple of months ago that he really crossed the line, violating not only legal canons, but quite clearly the law. All because of his own corpulent, disgusting lust.

"At it early again are we, Peabody? Your billable hours must be way up." The voice of Don Southland penetrated his self-loathing.

"Uh, this transfer of the records to electronic files is more intricate than our estimates," Peabody bleated back.

"Yes," Southland trailed off, looking at him with what Peabody read as disgust.

Southland was a senior partner preparing for retirement. A tall and trim man, he had a quiet, aristocratic air, though he was a tenacious tennis player and had been a combative litigator. Peabody sensed that Southland never liked him. Southland was a Midwesterner; probably he held Peabody's South Carolina heritage against him. That he had attended law school in Virginia was an asset and in his favor with everyone but Southland. Peabody knew what Southland held against him most was his nonathletic personality, his "chubby sissyhood," a phrase he had overheard in the steam room at the Athletic Club.

The conversation then had been between Southland and John Ford, the patriarchal founder of the firm. At issue was the assignment of managing the transfer of the firm's old hard-copy files to electronic storage—a massive and important job.

"You know he's the perfect type. We used to call 'em bookworms. Today it's nerds. He's done a fine job with the real estate work," Ford had said through the steam.

"You may be right, Johnny. I just can't get around his wimpy, chubby sissyhood."

On hearing that, Peabody retreated from the partially opened steam room door and retired to the lockers. From that day, he gained a personal incentive in his forced cooperation with Bokanyev. He'd show them who was a chubby sissy.

"Good evening, Mr. Calvin. It is good to see you again." Maître d' Simon smiled and offered his hand as Tim Calvin and Frank Phillips, *Outdoor* magazine's feature editor and an old colleague of Calvin's, entered Something Different.

"Simon, it looks great this evening." Calvin moved past the coat room and large windows into the dining room. "How is your family?"

"They are wonderful. My youngest is teething, but it hasn't been too bad. Thank you. Robert will be your server tonight. Enjoy yourselves, and bring Mrs. Calvin in soon." His British accent and polished body language added a touch of elegance to the already classy atmosphere.

"This is a beautiful room. I guess it's modern, metro style. Has a hint of a Frank Lloyd Wright in it," Phillips said, looking around.

Calvin smiled and watched Robert pour water onto paper-thin lime slices in the goblets before them. "This is a new location. Larger than the old place. Laney and I have been fans since Susan and Drew ran the place. They've got a great place in Chicago now. This one has always had great chefs. Steven is a superb young guy; he sort of grew up here and in other kitchens."

"Well, I don't think you'll be eating like this in the Dominican Republic," Frank Phillips said, sipping the lime water. "Looking at your pitch proposal, it appears you'll be spending most of your time in the jungle, or the 'tropical forest' as some would prefer." Phillips opened the packet of papers. En route from the West Coast, Phillips had stopped to consult with Calvin on the assignment he had taken.

Calvin opened the large menu. "We'll be there two weeks. I think we should spend a little less than half of that in Santo Domingo, at the conservation lab and talking with the academics. The rest of the time will be split between Isabela and the caves. There are also a couple of private collectors I'd like to get to see."

"I think your budget is fine, but I'd like to spread some of this to your pre-trip research. I'm sure you already have some hours in and we'll take care of those now."

Calvin smiled at the idea of an early payment.

Peabody was surprised to find people on the partners' and senior associates' floor. He thought the only individuals working this late would be the worker bees who were building their careers and jockeying for favor from their smaller offices on the floor below.

"She's been a whiz with puzzles since she was a little one. The judges said her 3-D jigsaw puzzle idea was the best explanation they had seen on bio-engineering." Southland was speaking to his assistant and a couple of others as they walked toward the elevators. Standing next to him was his ten-year-old niece, whom he doted on during her visits, and of whom he often spoke.

Southland had spotted him. "Peabody, when do you figure to begin transfer of the section-five files?"

"Mid-February is what is projected. Why do you ask?"

"We've had some items sent to us from Florida. C. G. King's personal estate. I did most of her husband's corporate work. She had an attorney friend handle her personal work after she retired down there. She was setting up a foundation. Her attorney died and she asked Judge Browne, whom you may not remember, to start gathering her papers and to send them to us. Then C. G. passed away. I haven't been through it all yet, but I'm sure most of it is history and should get into the transfer schedule. I hope to be working on it next week."

Peabody stood up and nodded eagerly. It was the C. G. King estate that Bokanyev had ordered him to snoop on. He couldn't believe his good fortune. He'd thought he had been given a task of finding a needle in a haystack. Bokanyev had no idea which Indianapolis firm would be handling the King estate; he only knew that it was being sent north. Peabody had been ordered to learn where and then intercede.

Even with this bonanza, he could not forgive Southland for his condescending attitude. That line about not remembering Judge Browne. Did Southland really think he was an idiot? No, of course not. No one in the legal community could *not* know of Browne and his record. Even though he had started with the firm after the judge's retirement, Peabody certainly knew who he was. Then there was the recent news accounts of Browne's kidnapping and rescue in Caracas and his subsequent disabilities and memory loss. Southland's sneering "whom you may not remember"—so typical of him—was just one more shot at demeaning him.

"Of course I know of Judge Browne, and I'll be pleased to integrate the King files into the section-five transfer. I'm sure you'll have all the time you need to finish the work before we transfer and then batch and dispose of the old files."

"Thank you, Peabody. Come on, Teresa, everyone will be waiting for us at Shapiro's."

Peabody nodded and returned to his office, thinking of the e-mail message he was about to send to Bokanyev on Grand Cayman.

Long Lines and Old Memories

IT HAD BEEN ONE of those days of forced memories which brought a sense of sadness and a rush to adjust the business of life to the pause of a passing. Calvin stood looking at the ornate woodwork and sculpture that adorned the Scottish Rite Cathedral. From his spot in the viewing line, he could see those leaving the inner room as well as those who were coming into the building to pay their respects to Baldridge Blake, community leader, philanthropist, and business and political power broker. Politicians, sports and financial stars, educators, and others by the hundreds were on queue for as long as an hour and forty-five minutes to speak with his widow and family.

Follow-up details to his dinner meeting with Phillips had given Calvin more to add to his to-do list. It had been a hectic day. Calvin had rearranged an afternoon meeting to give him time for the drive downtown. He was glad he had given himself extra time before his evening meeting. Thinking about the busy schedule while waiting to pay tribute to someone who was now beyond the frantic pace of life gave him cause to think again about what he was doing with his own life. Others in this line were surely doing the same thing. No one needed to exchange words on the subject. It was just one of those moments when an event, in this case Blake's sudden death, created a shared moment of reflection. Many of these people waiting in the long line were the powerful and prominent, and all of them self-absorbed.

It gave Calvin time to measure his own mid-life angst against the finality of life itself. He thought it just might be the gist of his own troubled searching. Was there really that much time left? What had he really accomplished? His abandoned Ph.D., the years in promotion and advertising, the starting of his own business, volunteer work at the church and on community boards, and now the book. Thinking about it sometimes spun him off into a kind of desperation. So much to do.

Oh yes, he had come to grips with the idea there were some things he would never do, some achievements that were now beyond him. Even though it angered him to admit it, he knew he could not accomplish the unending list of possibilities he had contrived for himself as a younger man. He ought to be happy and content, certainly. He truly felt as though he was blessed. Health, family, home, opportunity, good friends, a mature spiritual understanding. . . . Still there were things he wanted to do, places to see, mysteries to delve into. He wondered if he wasn't running out of time for personal dreams, while he spent time dealing with business. He was chasing money instead of contemplating great thinkers and moments of history. Lee Hamblin back there on Sanibel at Christmas had it figured out: He was taking time to philosophize, to deeply savor friends, to help mankind.

Was much of what he was doing a waste of time? He thought God had given him talents and skills that could be used in better ways than business. Write another book. Maybe even bring closure to his unfilled desire for a Ph.D. Why couldn't he just be content with a comfortable life? Why hadn't he outgrown his wanderlust or his nose for a mystery? As Calvin moved through the line, passing through mahogany portals of the cathedral, he was absorbed in thought. The Masonic order had been around a long time, some said since the construction of the Great

Pyramid. All of the members of the fraternal orders, through countless generations, had found their meaning in sharing brotherhood, ritual and service. There were many ways to add value to life. And here were the pictures of Baldridge Blake in his active life: official at the Speedway, officer in respected corporations, family man on fishing and boating expeditions.

The entrance of Judge Browne created a stir and it brought Calvin out of his reverie. Everyone had read of the kidnapping and rescue in Caracas. A more recent newspaper article detailed his long hours of physical therapy to improve his speech and movement. He had made progress in speaking, but still suffered a short-term memory loss, which had stymied both the investigation and legal efforts on the King estate. He looked reasonably well but showed signs of the ordeal. He walked with a cane and moved slowly. Behind him, coming through the large ornate doors into the waiting hall, were more familiar faces: Larry Conroy, Lee Hamblin, Claudia Prouse, and Donna Iemer.

"Well, it looks like the Sanibel contingent is all here," Conroy said, extending his hand to Calvin. He was solemn in mood though his eyes still twinkled. In a dash, he was off to speak with others in line.

"I've been holding your place; we'll all do that now," Calvin called after him. He figured the little fib might explain the line cut to those behind him. Nobody seemed to care anyway. After all, this was a distinguished party and they were all friends. Hamblin, Browne, Donna, and Claudia greeted Calvin and took a place in line, nodding to those who were behind them.

"It is a sad passing," Hamblin said, shaking his head, "but what a marvelous life Baldridge led."

Browne and Donna had walked arm-in-arm. The judge then spoke to Hamblin in a quiet tone.

Donna and Claudia turned to Calvin. "Mary Lou had business in Naples so she couldn't get back," Claudia said. "Larry, Lee, and I just flew in from Fort Myers. We are all going back tomorrow. Larry is in the middle of a deal. Lee is still working on his report."

"You all made quite an entrance, I must say," Calvin said.

"We just bumped into each other in the parking lot. A driver let the judge out, and we were right behind him. Lucky timing," Donna explained.

Claudia lowered her voice to just above a whisper. "The judge is still having trouble. It's as if he has amnesia. He can remember very little about the past year, just bits and pieces. It's got him very frustrated, but he says the doctors tell him it's probably a combination of the drugs and the trauma of his ordeal."

"They think it's the body's natural defense mechanism to the effect of the drug. They're not even sure what it was. But he says he's getting stronger," Donna said.

"He told Lee out in the parking lot that he hopes it will eventually clear, but he's not even sure of that. He is also very embarrassed about his affected speech," Claudia added.

Calvin nodded with concern and looked toward Hamblin and Browne, who were standing in front of them, speaking with others who had come by.

"I know the congressman is staying at the Conroys," Calvin said. "Aren't you getting involved in his research?" He turned to Donna.

"Yes and no," Donna said with a grin. "I'd like to be heading back down there, but we've got too much going on with the park." Calvin knew Iemer was referring to the state park project she was helping to manage. "I'm probably going to help the congressman when he gets toward the end of his bio-warfare project. If I'm lucky, that means going back to Sanibel-Captiva."

"It is a bit confusing, but a writer like you should be able to figure it out," Claudia said, smiling through her sarcasm. "Congressman Hamblin is staying at the Conroy house; they're letting him stay there while he's doing the report. Because of that, Larry and Mary Lou are staying at the Simmingtons', a place you are familiar with, Mr. Calvin."

Calvin nodded, again grateful the Simmingtons had lent his family their Captiva beach house at Christmas.

Claudia continued, "In fact, before we left this morning your friend Dave Hockett was there delivering a huge new urn that the Simmingtons had ordered. Dyane Simmington loves his work. He said he had sold a similar piece to a Russian and his girlfriend when you guys were down over the holidays. Beautiful, blue, very unusual glaze."

"There's the Bokanyev issue again. Shall we get together afterwards for dinner. Can you get Larry and Lee together and make the arrangements?"

"Listen, I've been planning meetings, dinners, events and fund raisers for twenty-five years," Claudia responded. "It'll be a piece of cake."

◆ ◆ ◆

Calvin noticed the heads turn as the maître d' led the group through the crowded front chambers of the St. Elmo Steakhouse to the quiet room with windows, more recently called the New York Room. Lee Hamblin quietly nodded to those who waved or spoke, while Conroy shook hands or fired one-liners at some of those who recognized him and the former congressman. Donna and Claudia, veterans of many political campaigns, simply smiled, having seen this type of scene hundreds of times. The din and buzz of the venerable old steakhouse was a good antidote to the contained seriousness of the mourning visit they'd all just paid. A couple of drinks and the sinus-blasting sauce of shrimp cocktails allowed the group to transition the mood and topic. It also provided an opportunity for Conroy to get them laughing with his story-telling.

By the time the sizzling filets and prime rib were delivered by the tuxedoed waiter, Calvin had led the conversation back to Sanibel.

"Tim," Hamblin said, "I find it an enormous irony: here I am editing a presidential report on the threat of bio-terrorism, and, if your information is correct, an active marketer of the stuff has designs on property near where I am working." Hamblin's look was serious.

"Lee, I wonder if there is a connection. How coincidental can this be?" Claudia said, fiddling with her cigarette pack.

"How can the King will and real estate be overturned like this? That's what we ought to look at. Something stinks." Conroy looked at Donna and then at Hamblin.

"The judge has already started on that. Trouble is, he can't provide any details," Donna said. "The authorities in Venezuela could never come up with much on the men who had him. They looked strictly local to me. The embassy down there says he was just a victim of opportunity, wrong place at the wrong time. Man in a wheelchair, left alone. They're probably right. The guys at the airport were probably just after his kidneys."

"Who in the hell would have kidnapped him up here?" Claudia asked.

Hamblin pushed back his plate. "Whoever they are, I presume they simply wanted him out of the way. If there is some legal game or some real estate fraud about to be perpetrated, it would be much easier with someone as formidable as the judge to be gone."

Donna leaned forward and spoke to the group. "Well, the judge told me something tonight as we were going through the line. This is interesting: McAtee Cheskin Ford and Hendricks is handling the estate. Don Southland used to handle all of the King corporate business. When C. G.'s Fort Myers lawyer died, the judge started to work with her in an effort to get it all sent back to Indianapolis. After C. G. died, Judge Browne was working on the details of her will and had just sent all of her files up here when he was kidnapped and sent off for that hellacious trip to Caracas."

"So who's behind it? The guy who apparently is getting the house is a bad character named Bokanyev," Calvin said.

"Bad character is an apt description, Tim," Hamblin offered.

"No one knows for sure, but it's a strong guess it was the Russian's man who did it," Donna said. "I guess they figured somebody would probably kill a crippled old man, maybe just for his clothes. Thank God I happened to be flying out of there. It's like it was Divine Providence. Anyway, Southland told the judge they had received the material, but he had not really gotten into it. It had arrived, but it was going to be transferred to electronic data before someone could dig through it. He said that would make it easier to work with. But there's been a glitch in the transfer process and everything's been delayed."

Claudia tapped an unlit cigarette on the table. "Typical of computers."

"You know, Lee," Conroy said, gesturing for the check, "I know you are busy with the biochemical weapon report, but I think we need to put some kind of group together to deal with whatever this intrigue is on Sanibel. I've got to think there's something more than just a real estate grab here." Conroy looked dead serious.

Hockett and his daughter were driving over the causeway, watching the last of the color of the sky begin to fade under a darkening cloud blanket.

Celia had been to band practice. Though it meant a commute, Hockett didn't mind. Cee had shown a real talent for music, and even though he'd lived on the island for twenty years, he still enjoyed the view from the causeway.

"Mom said we had a letter from Grand Cayman. Is it about our summer vacation with the Calvins?"

"No. It was from a woman who bought one of the two large cobalt blue urns."

"Oh, I remember her. She had the cool car. What did she want?"

"The companion urn. But I already took it up to the Simmingtons as a gift."

"Way to go, Dad. Lost a big sale. Six hundred big ones. I'm hungry. What's for dinner? What is Mom making?"

"She's had a parents circle meeting, so we're going to Jerry's," Hockett said, only half interested in the dinner plans. He was thinking back over the letter from the Cayman shopper. She had written that she would be moving to Sanibel and that she and "Yuri" wanted the other urn for their new Sanibel home. Could it be the same Yuri that

Calvin told him about. The former KGB man? The guy who might be doing something with bio-weapons? And just yesterday Calvin had called to tell him about the Indianapolis group's concern—a plot to overthrow C. G.'s will—and do what? Calvin said he would send a photo file. Hockett was sure he could match the face if, as he believed, it was the same man he had the staring match with back during the Christmas holiday.

Assignment in the Dominican Republic — Bad Dreams at Home

CALVIN WAS GLAD HE was sitting in the front of the plane. The buffeting from the wind always seemed more rocky in the back half, as the tail seemed to slide around. He couldn't remember ever landing in such a heavy rain storm. The water raged outside the window like an angry river. Suddenly, the plane jerked; passengers gasped or cried out as the nose went into a steep climb. Calvin was pushed to his left by the force of the rapid bank to the right. He could see nothing from the window but more water. An eerie silence filled the cabin and Calvin wondered whether he should pray for safety or as though he was about to meet his Maker. He opted for the former.

"Dear Lord be with us—whatever it is," he mumbled as the pilot came on the speaker.

"Well folks, I'm very sorry. I didn't like that either. The truth is, I just couldn't see the runway. We got socked by a heavy squall that just seemed to come out of nowhere. I made a last-moment decision to bring her back up here and see if that storm cell doesn't clear out of here. We have plenty of fuel and we'll give it a few minutes. If it doesn't clear then we'll go south to Santo Domingo and we'll have buses bring you up here. I'm sorry for the roller coaster ride there, but flying in over these mountains can be tricky."

Tricky wasn't the half of it, Calvin thought.

Hockett heard the sobbing, first thinking he might be dreaming as he roused from his sleep. He knew it was late. Barb had switched off her reading light and was in a deep sleep. He turned over and cocked his head. No, it wasn't a dream. The sobbing was coming from Celia's room, through the bathroom.

The glow from the nightlight slivered out the door as he leaned forward to observe. Cee's face was buried in a pillow and her body heaved as she tried to muffle her anguished crying. He entered her bedroom.

"Cee, darling what in the world is wrong?"

His inquiry was met only with an outburst of tears.

"Celia, tell me what it is. Are you sick?" he asked, rubbing her shoulder.

"What's the matter here?" Barb, suddenly wide awake, had come to the door.

"It's horrible," Celia blurted. "It's awful!" Her face was red and her eyes were swollen. She was gasping for air.

Both parents embraced her.

"What is it, honey?" Barb asked, keeping her voice calm. "Was it a dream?"

Celia nodded. "It was the chemical weapons. Everybody on the beach was dying. They had growths on their skin. All the fish and turtles were dead. The birds were falling out of the sky. Mom, it was coming inland! It was coming toward Periwinkle! Dad was out in the front of the shop and . . . and . . ." She shuddered and buried her head on her father's shoulder, sobbing furiously. She threw her arms around his neck and squeezing as though to keep him alive.

Barb and Dave exchanged wondering looks over their distraught daughter's back.

◆ ◆ ◆

It was late and only one customs line was open at the Puerto Plata airport. The walk across the tarmac from the rolling stairs was a sweet and fragrant stroll. A damp haze, thick with floral bouquet, rose from the blacktop and seemed to hang in the air. The island vegetation seemed to be celebrating the safe landing. Calvin certainly was.

"Thank you, Lord, terra firma sure feels good," Calvin said. He peered, frowning, through the darkness at the masses in the distance—the mountains they had flown over before they dipped down into the valley and located the airport.

Calvin didn't mind the intense humidity inside the terminal. A German charter plane had also prevailed against the wind and rain, and the last of their contingent was finishing processing through the passport and customs line. Calvin didn't need to understand what they were saying to each other; gestures and facial expressions spoke of their anguish in the air and relief to be on the ground.

◆ ◆ ◆

Calvin was pleased he would have the next day to settle in and get organized before he began his round of interviews and site visits. The magazine piece could run as long as seven thousand words, so he would be able to use a lot of local color as well as the background history of the dig sites he would be visiting. He hoped that he'd also get a few good stories to tell when making pitches or entertaining clients in his consulting business. Even by the street lamps he could see that the resort village of condominiums had a comfortable charm. Each of the units, built in Caribbean cabana style, appeared to stand alone. Wrapped around cul-de-sacs and community greens, the condos were vaguely reminiscent of an English village.

Checked in, bags deposited, clothes hung up, and the overhead fan set on the speed of preference, Calvin pulled the sheet up to his chest, stared at the whirling blade, and let the tension of the flight and the lateness of the long day drift away.

◆ ◆ ◆

They're right about the azure sea and alabaster sands, Calvin thought as he pulled into the parking lot next to the wind surf shop in Caberete the next day. The mid-morning sun sparkled off the Atlantic. Several wind surfers were catching the trade winds and working the sea. These were the pros who made it look effortless; nearer to shore there were several knots of instruction groups. Racks of gear and rigs were lined up, indicating that this beach was one of the world's busiest and possibly one of the best for wind surfing competition.

Calvin checked his watch. It was too early for lunch, though his stomach had been growling since he caught the aromas coming from the La Puntilla de Piergiorgio restaurant back in Sosua. He had stopped to make sure he could find the place that evening for his meeting with his in-country contact, Pedro Perez. He unfolded the map on the hood of his rental car and calculated the drive time to Samana, the mitten-like peninsula which looped eastward into the Atlantic above the massive Higuey province and jungle, his eventual destination. Samana was being built up like Puerto Plata, with condos and hotels. The airport had been expanded, and it would eventually prove to be competition for the older resort.

Calvin shuddered as he drove east, thinking of the scar on the mountain he had seen that morning. A large chunk of the green edge of one of the slopes outside Puerto Plata had been dug out. Gray and chalky, it was the looming reminder that a few months before, a German charter plane, unable to find the altitude it needed when attempting a takeoff in a storm similar to the one in which he arrived last night, had exploded when it slammed into the peak. The new Samana airport outside Las Terrenas was free of the green mountains, thank God.

◆ ◆ ◆

Laney left school after teaching her third-period class at the middle school and dashed home to check on Katie. For a couple of days, Katie had no appetite and seemed listless. Usually, her after-school routine consisted of a stop at the refrigerator for a snack of cheese or lunch meat, then up to her computer room for a check of e-mail before a combination of homework, radio, computer chat, and telephone calls. This customary practice included bounding up and down the steps two at a time, another stop at the refrigerator, and inquiries as to what was for dinner. But the last two days had been different. She lay on the couch, not really watching television, though it was on. She had only picked at the spaghetti and salad she usually loved, and had made no runs at the refrigerator. Now, today, as the school day began for both mother and child, Katie had come down pale and mopey to tell Laney she didn't feel like going to school and wanted to go back to bed. Katie was a thin child to begin with, and Laney was concerned by her failure to eat. None of her friends had been sick and there didn't seem to be any other symptoms except this general malaise.

Laney heard the television as she opened the door from the garage, but Katie was not on the day couch in the kitchen.

"Katie, I'm home. Where are you?"

"In here," came the puny reply from the living room, where the girl was stretched on the couch, covered with a burgundy throw. There were dark circles under her eyes and she looked terribly sad.

"Katie, what is wrong with you?" Laney asked, instinctively putting her hand on her child's forehead to feel for signs of a fever that did not exist.

"Mom, look at this," Katie said, sitting up and reaching for a sheaf of papers that had been put on top of a magazine at the couch's end.

Laney looked at computer printouts from some online data source. She leafed through the pages, quickly scanning the headers: *Anthrax . . . Sarin Gas . . . VX Nerve Agents . . .*

"Mom, it's like the black plague. Why do they make this? Who are they going to use it on? What are they going to do with it?"

"Oh Katie! Is this what it is?" she said, looking at her daughter with a heavy heart and eyes full of compassion. "This all goes back to the day at the Romanos and all that horrible talk. And now you're obsessing about it and researching it on the Internet, aren't you?"

"Mom, I'm very worried," she finished, and limply opened her arms for a reassuring embrace.

Dinner at Puntilla

THE DRIVE TO SAMANA and back had given Calvin a chance to relax and begin to think through the assignment. He had arrived back at the resort in time to catch an hour of beach time before getting ready for his dinner meeting. This might be a great place to bring Laney, Elizabeth and Katie. The northern coast on the Atlantic featured beautiful beaches and large expanses of palm and green, rambling mountains which rolled toward the heart of the island. Tomorrow he would head west toward Luperon, then south and west in the direction of Haiti, until he arrived at the desolate fishing village of La Isabela. It was there, in a tiny town that, for centuries, some have said is cursed, that Christopher Columbus built a home, established his first community. Fate had been unkind after that. This would provide a point of departure for that part of his story which dealt with "Columbus: Hero Worship or Hatred."

◆ ◆ ◆

The tall torches in the walkways and the low, rounded globe lights on the cliffside balconies gave the La Puntilla de Piergiorgio restaurant a magic and festive glow. The seating was open air, amidst a rich atmosphere of tropical lushness. The place had been the home of diplomat and writer John Bartlow Martin, former U.S. ambassador to the Dominican Republic. As he walked to his table, Calvin understood how Martin could have written his books here. Built on a cliff overlooking the Atlantic and the blue profile of the famous mountain Isabel de Torres, which Columbus had called the Silver Mountain, the place was magnificent. In 1989 it caught the fancy of Italian fashion designer Piergiorgio. Now the Victorian-style architecture set in a Caribbean paradise provided the perfect setting for one of the world's great restaurants. Calvin's table was at a rocky ledge of a sheer cliff wall, bounded by a white stone railing. Stars swept from the horizon into the sky and disappeared behind luscious royal poinciana, frangipani, and bougainvillea.

Pedro's voice interrupted Calvin's reverie. "Ah, it is my good friend Tim Calvin."

"Pedro! It's great to see you again. How are things in your new position?"

"I love my old home country, now with a new leader."

"Yes, I followed the election."

"It truly is a new day for the Dominican Republic. After twenty years it was time for a new leader. Leon truly wants to lead us to a better place."

"You have no regrets leaving the States and moving back? Adele is happy about it too?" Calvin had known them since he and Pedro worked at the same small newspaper. Calvin had been in graduate school and Pedro had only recently emigrated to the United States. They had been friends since.

"We were able to buy a very lovely home outside Santo Domingo and get a place in the mountains with what we sold our place for in Evanston. I will miss my marketing work with the Cubs and Bulls, but we have good baseball here too, you know. My years in advertising and public relations are very valuable to the new government, so I am able to come home with a great joy in my heart. Adele always longed to return, to be on the soil of her ancestors. The President and the legislature both agree that those who left and became citizens of other countries may now return. It is a sign of health, don't you think?"

Calvin's regret that he could not share the lovely scenery with Laney was lightened by seeing his old friend. The crashing of the surf and the wafting strains of music from under the central cabana meant relaxation, though the knowledge that he was about to undertake arduous work lingered at the fringe of his thoughts. Still, this was the sort of thing he loved. He wrote in his notebook that the tagliatelle and baby lobster were to be added to his best-ever list.

Calvin noticed that Pedro's mood changed visibly as they watched Buffalo Bill, the restaurant's mustached, flaming-crepe and dessert-cart showman. Bill performed his comedic juggling dessert routine at the seaside table to the immediate left of them, but Pedro's eyes were elsewhere, scanning the patron's tables.

"Pedro, are you okay? You seem distracted by something."

"It's just that I see a man who is a symbol of our past, one of the obstructions to making a new way here. The cigar smoker with the gold chains, do you see him? He is Abelardo Rota, real estate and finance. He made millions in the old government. He was inside on deals and developments. The word is he was being paid by the Russians and the Libyans and everyone else who wanted to curry favors or develop an agenda." Pedro busied himself with the silverware. His voice was low. "Stinking new money. He has homes all over the island, including a virtual palace at Casa de Campo. He is a collector of artifacts. In fact, Tim, we think he is behind a raid on one of the archeological sites you will visit."

Calvin scribbled. "Abelardo Rota of Casa de Campo. I've got it in my notebook."

"Be careful where you speak his name. He is a serious player, my friend."

In what Calvin interpreted as a strange move, Pedro abruptly stood and walked away from the table, toward the central cabana. He then observed that Rota and his dining companions had gotten up and were walking in the opposite direction, toward where he sat. They were en route to the exit. Calvin caught a glimpse of Pedro standing behind a line of dancers.

Calvin occupied himself with his wine glass, but sneaked a look at the trio and strained to overhear the conversation.

"My client is quite particular and does not want there to be any kind of development near his land," Rota was saying. "I don't know what he wants to do with the caves. Maybe put gold there. Maybe put women there. I know only he wants privacy and he can afford it."

It was a tantalizing trail of conversation he heard from the cigar-puffing, barrel-chested Rota.

"Excuse my odd behavior," Pedro said, coming back to the table. "I did not want to make eye contact, or I would have had to speak and introduce you and explain that you are here to write an article. I think it best that you and Rota not meet."

"It's too bad Dad isn't here. I think the jaeger schnitzel tonight is as good as it's ever been," Elizabeth said to Laney, Katie and Calvin's mother, Mary, as they sat beneath the laced curtains of the Café Europa.

"Look at how Katie has cleaned her plate. Poor thing must have been starving," Mary said, purring in grandmotherly concern.

"Barb said they've had a couple of sessions with a counselor for Celia. They figure this whole thing started when the girls heard us talking with the Romanos, during Christmas, about biological warfare. Some kids respond that way. Anyway, Barb says Cee's stopped having her long, complicated nightmares every night."

"But she says she still has short ones," Katie added. "We were chatting today, until Dave told her he needed to go online."

"The situation is, honey, you just can't worry about some things," her grandmother said. "When your daddy was a boy, he used to have nightmares about mushroom clouds and the atomic bomb. Your grandfather and I had to get him to think about other things. You just have to do that yourself or you'll make yourself sick. Will you do that for Grandma?"

"Yeah, uh huh," Katie said, trailing the fork around in her applesauce.

A Spider and the Web

"IF WE CAN GET away by midday, we can get to Jarabacoa by sunset," Pedro said. "Adele will have a dinner set on the patio. It will be lovely watching the sky in the mountains. You and Dr. Morales will be able to conduct your interview there. Tomorrow morning you can relax and get some shots around our end of the Ciboa Valley and then spend the rest of the day driving to Santo Domingo. I have arranged for a driver. If you don't mind, I'll bring your rental car down the day after, when I join you for the trip to the east." Pedro spoke as the gold of the sunrise shone in the rear view mirror.

"Sounds good. Pedro, let me run some of this by you to make sure I've got the history right." Calvin watched the rising sun light up the green of the palms and verdant mountainsides as they drove past patches of coast on the way to Isabela.

"Shoot."

"Let's see, Columbus got to Isabela almost by mistake. Tracking back into a storm, he put into the north shore and decided to set up an agricultural community. He built his house, his first permanent residence, and tried to establish a community. He lost most of a fleet of ships in a hurricane in 1496 or '97. Eventually he abandoned Isabela."

"Okay so far. Go on."

"They've recovered some of his original home and other plazas, and a team is working to find what they believe are remains of the fleet in the bay."

"That is the summary, yes. What you do not mention is the immense tragedy of it all. It is here where Colón became inflamed with gold fever. He began making slaves of the local tribe, the Tainos. Columbus had encountered the terrible and savage Caribs elsewhere in the Caribbean. The Caribs would ritually eat the dead. Maybe he believed all Indians were bloodthirsty. The Tainos were the "good people" though. That is the meaning of the translation of "Tainos." They built communities, they farmed, they were organized and I suppose too passive for the Spanish who decimated them."

"I thought the wars and bloodshed came later."

"Yes, there were conquistadors who came and brought the bloody history to completion. But it was started by Columbus. When Columbus arrived, there were between a half-million and maybe three million Tainos. Seventy years later, they were almost extinct. The caves you will visit in Higuey province may hold clues to this elusive and tragic race of people."

Distant mountains, wide valleys and green hillsides continued to roll by, increasingly bright through the windows as the sun's presence flooded the landscape.

"Where did the story of the curse of Isabela begin?"

"From the many deaths of Columbus' men from disease and mysterious origin. From the loss of the ships in the storm. From the failure of the agriculture. From the mistreatment and death of the Tainos. Of all the places to build a community, this windy desolate point in the Atlantic is one of the worst. Villagers throughout the last five centuries have struggled, fishing boats have been lost, homes have been destroyed. Today it is a very poor village, and only a few people live there. Only those who are not superstitious dare try it. Still they do not prosper. I too have to wonder if there is not some curse. Why would the place of the first permanent home of the great admiral be a poor and cursed village today?"

◆ ◆ ◆

Calvin watched as a young mother in an orange T-shirt fashioned into a dress chased a naked baby toward the door of a palm wood shack. An older woman with a lined face, wearing a dirty shirt, sat on the steps of the wooden slat house. The door, apparently the only opening in the long structure, was in the middle of the end of the building. The roof was tin. The house was surrounded by a line of branch posts, leaning and drooping to the ground, heavy with wash hanging on connecting lines. A dirt path wound between other makeshift homes situated on a hillside and the bottom of a valley. It was washday, and the squalor of dry, unpainted wood and corrugated buildings was brightened by points of color—bougainvillea and an occasional blue or orange shirt or pair of pants. Calvin waited for Pedro to return to the car after seeking directions to the dig sight at Isabela.

◆ ◆ ◆

The broken and pot-holed blacktop and dirt roads gave way to a well-graveled road. They passed signs indicating an historical location was ahead. The nine o'clock sun was surprisingly intense, and the heat and humidity grew as they approached the work site.

Pedro pointed, as Calvin began his work of photographing the site. "This stone wall is where the admiral's house stood. Take your time. A guide will be here later. I am going to sit in the shade."

Calvin was moved by the sense of history of the place. He stood on the high bluff looking out to the vastness of the Atlantic waves and watching the sea crash on the rocky coast. It was here where two worlds met, where the native Tainos first sighted the masts of the caravels that brought to their land the men they thought were gods. Gods indeed! He enjoyed the respite of the bluff view with its constant breeze; it cooled the profuse sweat which soaked him.

Back amidst the ruins, he was pestered by swarms of tiny mosquitoes which seemed to move like a cheesecloth blanket over his arms and face. Calvin understood this was why he was taking anti-malarial medicine. Despite the admonition of the doctor that it gave some users hallucinations and vivid dreams, the medicine was necessary to prevent the malady that had plagued tropical adventurers and explorers through the ages.

After he completed his conversation with the site curator, which gave him necessary background, Calvin toed at some of the abundant pottery shards and stone pieces that littered the ground. There, at his feet and in his hands, was what remained of the first European civilization on this site five hundred years ago. These were fragments of what had been part of the age of exploration. Today, all of it was surrounded by jungle and would be completely overgrown and forgotten were it not for the work of these dedicated archeologists, anthropologists and historians. For a moment, he thought of C. G. King's plans for his beloved Sanibel and wondered how someone five hundred years hence might find or regard that island.

"You can buy all the clay stuff you wish, but I tell you I will not eat on anything but china. Do you know why, Monica? It's because I can." Yuri Bokanyev spoke without waiting for an answer as they flew from Cayman back to Fort Myers. He didn't intend for his comments to sound so gruff.

"I just mean you can buy all you want at that little place on Periwinkle." He smiled at her. He was in a good mood because today the world was moving in his direction. His lawyer, Peabody, in Indianapolis with that prestigious law firm, assured him he would soon have clear title to the Sanibel house. Bokanyev was told he would be able to sell the West Gulf condo he had purchased, and make a tidy profit. His man in the Dominican Republic had given him good news about his cave, too. Rota was going to use his connections to close access to the neighboring caves where archeologists had been working.

That prevented Bokanyev from having to use the more messy technique of explosive closure. They would be closed—so what? The old cave paintings were part of the past. They belonged to the ages, not to the future, not to those like him who could wield power. Academics tromping around the network of caves could only interfere with his intended use of the deep, dark hiding places, perfect places for his product. His only annoyance was his Dominican partner's obsession with his own collection of stuff. Why did Rota go on so about what he had and how it made him feel? To each his own. He'd let Monica collect whatever things she wanted. His own desire was the money and the power he was building. It would lead to even greater wealth. Today was a good day.

◆ ◆ ◆

Calvin clicked the film canister shut and slid it into the flapped pocket in his cargo pants. He was on his sixth roll and was pleased with the exposures he had so far. The mountain views of palm trees and rich vegetation and the tobacco plantations on rolling hills backed by mountains and dotted by thatched-roof drying sheds helped to capture the lushness of the Ciboa valley. He had studied the maps but had not comprehended how large the island was. He wasn't sure yet how some of the village scenes, homes made from royal palm slats and thatch, spread along winding mountain roads, would work into the magazine story he'd been commissioned to write, but they'd make great memories. Naked babies, chickens in side yards, burrows on the road, people sitting on curbs, mountain villages of only a few houses, lean-to fruit stands, slabs of pork and goat meat hanging in open air stalls, piles of fried pork on wooden stands, brown and yellow shreds of dried pork looking like tobacco threads hanging on stands: he had shot it all and was sure some of the exposures would be good enough for the story.

Now that they were headed south and had driven over a mountain, the sun was blocked by the towering peak beside them. Even though sunset was still a couple of hours away, the tropical foliage and looming peak made this a cool and dark descent into a valley. They would be in twilight before they would again gain altitude and the sunlight. As they wound under a rock outcropping, Calvin spotted a likely scene and asked Pedro to stop the car. There, below, on a hillside, was a palm-built lean-to with an open door. Light flickered out as it did when old-time movies played. In the midst of this shadowed, cool darkness, the blue light of a television set was shining in the blackness of the cabin.

"Man, is this ever a metaphor for the global village!" he said back in the direction of the car as he clicked several shots.

Just a bit further in the next mountain village, Calvin took a shot that evoked both a smile and tears. A tiny palm slat house, really no larger than a walk-in closet, stood proudly at the roadside. Its doorless opening revealed a bright yellow flower bouquet on a simple wooden table in the miniature room. As he clicked, an old woman, bent at the waist, appeared from the darkness of the room and hobbled outside. She met Calvin with a weathered but saintly smile. The love of beauty is universal, he thought, particularly so for women. Laney loved gardening and flowers. He recalled his wife's proud smile as she displayed a homemade bouquet on the kitchen window or placed a lovely floral centerpiece on the dining-room table. She could toil for hours, bent or kneeling in the dirt, struggling with the ground and weeds, exhausting herself to create beauty. She would love to see some of these scenes. He looked forward to sharing them with her.

◆ ◆ ◆

Pedro explained to Calvin that many professionals from Santo Domingo and the other larger cities of the Dominican Republic kept mountain homes as retreats. Dr. Morales of the University kept a place near Pedro and Adele's new home so it was a convenient place to do the interview.

The full day; the long drive; the magnificent purple, gold and rose of the sunset over the mountains; the dinner of fried corn, boiled plantain, yellow rice, shrimp, grilled beef, beans, and fresh salad; and the two hours of talk with Dr. Morales, the expert on the Tainos, left Calvin ready for deep sleep. The cool breeze rifting through the windows carried the night sounds of the mountains, and Calvin was soon in deep delta-stage sleep.

♦ ♦ ♦

The smell of rich, dark Dominican coffee lured Calvin to the kitchen. He could see Adele was out picking hibiscus and delphinium. He retreated to his room for a review of his notes from the interview with Dr. Morales.

At the wet cave, where Morales had helped direct recovery efforts, they had found a number of carvings of zemis, the spirits the Tainos worshipped. The Tainos believed the zemis controlled the world. In a spirit world of opposing forces, the zemis created balance and represented good and evil, life and death. There was Guyuba, lord of the land of the dead. Attabey was the mother of waters, the sustainer of life, and Yucahu, lord of the yucca, was the source of bread and life and the supreme being. Morales showed him slides and color plates of the spirits resembling bats, turtles, and frog-like creatures. The Tainos believed that all life emerged from caves, which is why the sites Calvin was visiting were so important.

♦ ♦ ♦

The intense sun and the weak air-conditioning in the van made Calvin glad he had chosen to wear hiking shorts for the shoot. The driver Pedro had hired was a colorful fellow named Alexander Eve. Full of good cheer, he introduced himself as "a very black man." He and Calvin shared an enjoyment of cigars—Alex had a fresh supply from a factory in Santiago. After a couple of hours of travel, Alexander learned to anticipate the type of lookout or scene Calvin was searching out. He had driven the roads enough to know side jaunts that would provide extraordinary vistas of pineapple, orange, flowers, tobacco plantations, and fields.

They stopped to pick up a couple of soft drinks and then drove up a lookout outside of Maimon on the south edge of the large lake Hatillo. Calvin climbed up a short bluff and walked around some scrub grass. He stood on a large boulder and enjoyed a commanding view of the blue sky reflecting in the lake surrounded by green. When he got back in the car, Alexander noticed blood on Calvin's leg, inside his thigh just above his left knee.

"Tim, what is that on your leg? You look as though you bleed."

"Must have scratched myself," Calvin said, wiping the droplets of blood with his left hand. "Huh," he said on closer examination. "This is strange, it looks like a couple of little holes, almost like fangs. Looks like one of the mosquitoes nailed me a couple of times."

"Oh my God, mon!" Alex said. "I hope it is only mosquitoes. Let me know how you feel. There are plenty bad spiders in this country."

About fifteen minutes down the road, Calvin began to feel odd. His stomach was queasy and his head had begun to ache. Alex scrutinized him as he drove.

"I think it not be too bad, or you be much sicker. I think it only a little spider that bite you, Tim."

Calvin nodded. Alex was trying to be upbeat. In another few minutes the headache had intensified, flashing malaise down his spine and into his shoulders. His face felt hot, and his eyes hurt. The queasiness edged closer to nausea. His joints began to ache. The sound of the engine and the jostle of the rough road seemed to conspire to make him feel even worse. The car's inept air conditioner, emitting its pitiful stream of unchilled air, did nothing to help his increasing dizziness.

He leaned his head against the window and door jamb, which offered a slight coolness, and swallowed down the horrible taste of his rising nausea. Alex's occasional inquiry and sporadic comments about "getting to the hotel, getting into air conditioning, getting to bed" punctuated Calvin's intoxicated, ache-filled mental haze. He felt only a slight retreat from the ringing in his ears and fevered dizziness when he drifted into a kind of drugged sleep. In and out of this semi-alert stage, he was vaguely aware of Alex helping him into the lobby of the hotel. All of Santo Domingo had gone by in a blur of horns and lights, turns and climbs up hills. Old buildings whizzed by, hundreds of motor scooters buzzed through loud traffic, snatches of festive music could be heard, and an odd array of aromas borne through the humid air were, at times, almost suffocating.

The chill of the air conditioning in the expansive lobby seemed to give Calvin a renewed vigor, but as he was signing in he began to chill.

"Are you all right, sir?" the young woman behind the desk asked.

"I just need to get to my room, please," Calvin said weakly, suddenly feeling nauseated.

"Tim, Mr. Pedro said that some of the expedition team are coming here to meet you at the hotel tonight. You be sure to tell them you have a spider bite. I must get the van to the garage for a night appointment or I be forced to pay a fine. I can have my wife bring me here later to check on you if you wish."

Afraid that he was about to be ill, Calvin quickly dismissed that idea.

"I think I'm feeling better. I just need to lie down for a while. Thanks, I'll see you tomorrow, Alex." Calvin walked toward the elevators, carrying his suitcase and laptop shoulder bag; the camera hung around his neck like dead weight.

In his room, Calvin turned the air conditioning fan unit to high and the temperature back to sixty-five degrees, as low as it would go. There was a knock on the door. He stumbled toward it and looked out the view hole to see a young bellman.

Opening the door, the bellman handed him a plastic bag with three bottles of Evian water.

"Your driver said you needed these."

"Thank you very much."

Calvin twisted the top and began to down one of the bottles. The cool liquid felt very good on his hot and dry throat. He was operating in a fog, with everything experienced distantly. Each movement caused his head to throb. He swallowed two Advils and found his bag containing Sudafed. He took one, then collapsed on the bed.

◆ ◆ ◆

Calvin didn't know how long he had been unconscious when he was awakened by the phone, but the room was beginning to chill.

He heard the hiss and echo of a cell or satellite phone. "Tim, this is Charles Williams. One of our divers got sick and had to be air-vacked out of the site. We're not going to make it to dinner tonight. I'm sorry about that. We'll just have to see you over here in a couple of days." The signal echoed and hissed again. "We got some rain on this communications gear and I'm not sure our signal is too clear. Pedro Perez has been working with the national guard pilots so he'll get you here. Wait to hear from him. We'll see you in the bush. Clear."

"Okay, Charles. I got your message. That's fine. I'm a little under the weather myself. I'll see you over there. Clear." The hotel phone clicked off.

Calvin felt as though his head was a three-alarm blaze. He walked to the bathroom and was startled to see his face was crimson and his eyes looked as though they were bleeding. He put his face next to the mirror to look more closely at his eyes. They were so bloodshot they looked like open wounds.

He soaked a face towel in cold water and took two more Advils, then peeled off his shorts and shirt and flipped them onto the second bed. He opened an alcohol swab and wiped the bite, which now seemed barely noticeable. After drinking the first bottle of water, he made a serious start on the second. Then he crawled under the covers, clicked off the light, and dropped back into fever-drugged sleep.

The light through the open drapes hit Calvin's face, making sleep impossible as it brightened. His head and body ached as though he had the flu, but he felt less feverish than he had the night before. He went to the bathroom and saw that his crimson hue of his skin had faded, though his face was still swollen and puffy. His eyes, though still bloodshot, looked much better than they had.

"Guess the worst is over," he mumbled, turning on the shower. Maybe there was something to the curse of Isabela. He put his head against the tile of the shower and let the hot water run over his head and down his neck and shoulders. Steam filled the room. Dreamlike thoughts flitted through his mind. Laney had told him that the conversation about bio and chemical weapons had given the girls nightmares. Well, his sleep last night was filled with hellish scenes too: victims of mustard gas in World War I movies he had seen, staggering in no man's land, choking to death; the victims of sarin gas in Tokyo, being taken out of the subway; Lee Hamblin's face contorted with disgust; people suffering chemical burns; news footage of men in biohazard suits; headlines about anthrax scares; Hollywood visions of bio horror, the bloated red bodies and people retching themselves to death. Who is Yuri Bokanyev and why is he interested in Sanibel? Calvin asked himself emphatically.

Why had Bokanyev suddenly entered his mind? He felt weak and light-headed. He turned the handle to douse himself with cold water.

By late morning Calvin had e-mailed Edward Earl the name of the shady Dominican lord, Abelardo Rota; had talked with Laney, neglecting to tell her about the spider bite; had spoken with Elizabeth and Katie about some of the sights he had seen; and had been treated to a tour of Santo Domingo. He was feeling terrible, but marveled at what he was looking at. He was in the plaza across from the Santa Maria Laminor Cathedral, the oldest church in the Americas. Alexander told him construction on it had started in 1523. Calvin sat on a stone bench beneath a spreading giant of an acacia ginkgo tree, whose trunk looked like a bundle of individual trunks. A group of young shoe-shine boys were busy near the shade and a group of old men sat across the plaza under the shade of red and white San Miguel umbrellas at a sidewalk coffee bar. They slowly sipped beers. Close to noon, the energy of the plaza intensified. Families and couples strolled by, and school kids in blue shirts and khaki slacks and skirts moved through.

A sudden sprinkle sent people scattering. A fruit vendor, whom Calvin was planning to photograph, covered the pineapple, papaya and oranges in his bicycle cart with a blue tarp. Calvin ached and hoped the people from the conservancy lab he was scheduled to meet at 12:30 would be late. He leaned against the tree and felt a mist on his face. He put his head against the trunk and watched as little lizards climbed the gnarls just inches from his face. His stomach hurt, his body ached, and he felt as if he was wrapped in a toxic waste cocoon. People stared at him; and he thought he must resemble a bloodshot rummy, leaning against the tree, or some Graham Greene character, far from home and in bad shape. He simply wanted to be at home in his own bed and to feel better.

◆ ◆ ◆

Calvin's interview with the conservancy lab staff finished mid-afternoon, after he shot photos in the lab and at the cathedral where the Dominican government claimed Columbus' bones were found. He looked forward to down time in the room before the evening plans, which included dinner and a visit to the famed *Faro Colón*—the Columbus Lighthouse. How revered the memory of Columbus was here! The team from the conservation lab had given him ample information about the zemis, the figures representing the Taino gods, which had been recovered from the well cave. Other artifacts from the well had been stolen, these scientists believed, and the well had been raided since the team of Indiana University researchers made their first dive.

The buzz of the phone jarred him.

"Mr. Tim Calvin, there is a fax at the business center. Would you care to have it sent to your room?"

◆ ◆ ◆

"I'm telling you, this process had to be done first," Peabody told Bokanyev, who was in Sanibel, on his car phone. "I need to establish some history to her files."

"The place is vacant," Bokanyev snorted. "We sent the rest of the boxes to your address and burned the papers on the environmental study institute. You've got to make sure none of that stuff gets put in the official file."

"I don't officially have control of all the material yet. I should get it tomorrow. I told them I need to start transferring it to electronic storage. I have read much of it; that's how I know we have this problem."

"Why the hell can't you fix it now? Just amend the will. I don't want any of the locals to raise a stink. Who'd have thought the old judge would have made it back alive? I had to send Josef off to the Dominican Republic. It's an extended holiday that is costing me plenty. He's spoiled goods here; people could recognize him. If that judge were ever to show up down here, he might identify Josef."

"I doubt that, and—"

"People at the airport or the neighbors might. He's out of here, so get the damned thing done so I will have no more snooping callers!"

"You are supposed to be a smart man, Yuri, so stop your ranting and listen to what I say. The copy of her will is now a hard copy, signed by her. She made a tape of the signing, so it could be part of the institute's archives. A TV crew did it when they were interviewing her for a story. What I am going to do is post the will and organizational papers to her file site. I can do that with a program I have."

"What in the hell good is that?" Bokanyev steamed.

"Listen to me. I can put a new date time on her will; it can be a fix. I will batch all the material in a download. What we scan here will go into a file that can be selectively deleted when it's mixed with the material that will come from her electronic records."

"So you are saying, in your techno-babble, that we change the will, obviously. What about the institute she was setting up?"

"Once I have control of the records, we can change names and dates and transfer of property. I will do that on the inner pages and architecture of her file; no one will know the difference."

"But you said there was a TV story and a record about the institute. Won't someone remember that?"

"Most of that can be taken care of by the rewrite, which becomes the official record when it all gets merged. I can protect the date of the amendment to her will by inserting it into her files and then merging it with the data we will scan here. The original gets overwritten, but the program I use will leave no trace. Since the will is going to be, in essence, transferred from her electronic files, we lose the hard copy and establish the file copy as the real will. You become the entitled owner of her house."

"No, I still don't get it. You have not solved the problem of the institute that is supposed to be here! These damn greens know about her wishes. They'll squawk and raise hell. They may be starting already. I heard that some young couple was on the grounds taking pictures."

"The new will can permit the sale of the property, with the proceeds going to the other centers. In the case of the Sanibel estate, your purchase will fund the establishment of a research site at Woodrings Point."

"So you do have some strategic intellect after all. I see. You control the information, so you can make it appear there has been a sale and transfer of money to the Woodrings site, which is, of course, already under our control."

"Yes, and to make it even cleaner, I can designate either Josef or someone else of your choosing to be the 'quote' director of the institute. It will all be a part of the files that I merge from her file site. Such marvelous tools, the Internet and electronic storage. The disc that you took from Sanibel to Cayman will be the only record of the woman's original intentions."

"Should I destroy it?"

"I never counsel clients to destroy originals. It could have a later use. Soon, you will have the Sanibel estate and the Woodrings Point property, and you will be in control of the environmental institute, which may even have some funds."

"Let me think about who to set up as director."

"I need to know quickly, because I will have to author that data into the web coding."

"Use the name Abelardo Rota, from the Dominican Republic. Set him up as the director. And get this done quickly. My woman has already started decorating the Sanibel place. You know how women can be, don't you? They can make you do things beyond yourself, no?" Bokanyev hung up with a malicious chuckle.

Peabody grinned with delight, despite Bokanyev's dig. He knew he was going to have the last laugh.

"You Russian bastard! International properties are part of the King estate. Guess you're not smart enough to know that, or to figure it out. A lot of oceanfront land will soon be mine." Peabody chortled at the thought of how many delinquent tax violations Bokanyev's new real estate would bring to the Russian, major trouble. "And I'll not be here when you cry for help. Yes, it is a morality tale after all."

◆ ◆ ◆

Calvin thought about burning the fax. He didn't want the information to haunt him from some unknown quarter. Still, Earl's fax was vague enough to pass notice, though short and chilling.

"The name you supplied is linked in several data sources to the new man on the shell beach. Remember the Dominicans hit well in the big leagues. Stay in center field and be ready to run."

So Rota is tied to Bokanyev, Calvin thought. Earl's message about the big-league hitting and center field was clearly a warning to stay clear of him. Calvin could still feel the poison in his system, and perhaps because of that he was quick to anger. Bokanyev, the former Russian agent and now mobster, was getting a foothold on Sanibel. For what reason? He was linked to Abelardo Rota, a shady operator suspected of raiding archeological sites. What was Rota saying the other night about wanting to get land for his associate? Something about keeping women or gold, a metaphor for keeping something of value? Perhaps gold indeed, or stolen art. Maybe another place for bio-weapons, God forbid.

Earl had said Rota was a broker of stuff from the old Soviet arsenal. Calvin made a note to send word to Conroy and Hamblin to be wary of going around the old King estate. Maybe Donna was able to turn up something about the King real estate. It now seemed obvious to Calvin that Malcome Browne's kidnapping was linked directly to Bokanyev. He had, after all, been working on the details of settling the estate.

Here he was in the Caribbean, sick from a spider bite, angry about a sinister man and his devious real estate grab near his intended retirement home. And that wasn't all. His business tottered, he was vaguely restless in his life, he had a magazine assignment to complete, he felt horrible and he had days in the jungle ahead of him. What a load! His mind was cloudy, but he still felt some deep thrill. He was again in the midst of deep intrigue.

Spirits in the Jungle

Latin and merengue music came from a ballroom located down a long hall. Calvin's head was tilted back on the overstuffed chair in the Santo Domingo Sheraton's large and busy lobby. He was staring up at baby royal palms which reached to a high ceiling, watching blue cigar smoke curl up and disappear in the glass-drop chandelier lights just above the top of the potted palm heads. He was smoking a Partagas Churchill, fresh and rich. He sipped a beer, his feet resting on a low stone table which fronted his small sitting area in the lobby. Next to the chair was a long leather couch, which was, for the moment, unoccupied. Nearby were arrangements of wicker chairs around an elegant stone-top table and other arrangements with formal wingbacks.

It was evening and the lobby furniture groupings buzzed as people rendezvoused, came and went, preparing for an evening at the neighboring casino or on the town. Calvin was beginning to feel less toxic, enough so that he could take note of how many women here preferred tight slacks and skirts while men favored open collars and neck jewelry. There were some who wore evening gowns and sport coats or suits and ties, but many of the local tourists, people in town from other cities, went for tight and flashy. He loved to people-watch, and at moments like this he missed having Laney at his side to share the sport. As he checked his watch, he spotted Pedro leading a group of others through the long glass front of the hotel.

"I've just been making arrangements with Alexander for the drive tomorrow," Pedro said. His tone was scolding. "He told me you were quite ill from a spider bite. Tim, I am angry and hurt you did not call me. You should have seen a physician."

"Those little buggers can be very nasty," Charles Williams, the head of the archeology team, said. "I've seen them practically kill a man."

Williams was a ruddy-skinned man with a weathered face, who reminded Calvin of a drill instructor. He was a skilled diver, more adventurer than academic. Calvin had read a newspaper story about his work on the island and called him to discuss doing a pitch for a magazine piece. He had seen pictures of Williams, but this was his first face-to-face encounter with the man.

"We've got just the cure for you tonight, if it doesn't kill your stomach," Williams said with a grin. "El Conuco, a fine eating place—all island cuisine. Watch out for the green stew!"

"This is very traditional. Does it not look like some of the places you saw up in the Ciboa Valley?" Pedro asked Calvin as they got out of the car and faced a large thatch-roofed building. "There is an old saying that the soul of this country lies in the Ciboa. Here we are! El Conuco, a Dominican soul-food restaurant."

Calvin's queasiness had faded and he realized he was hungry, but he wasn't sure how much he should or could eat. He was amazed at the length of the buffet table spread and the exotic nature of some of the dishes. Drums and spirited music blasted through the long building. In front of a thatched cabana bar, barefoot dancers worked to a feverish pitch. A woman did something that seemed to defy physics. She stood on top of a vodka bottle, strong toes gripping the bottle's lip. She spun in rapid revolutions while other dancers whirled in circles around her. Diners at long wooden tables covered with country-checked tablecloths laughed, conversed loudly, and drank beer. The place was full of a genuine joy, and it began to act as an antidote for Calvin's complaints.

Nursing the remains of a beer, Calvin declined to go back for one last trip to the buffet table. He had sampled the rice, plantain, guava, plantain and meat casserole, pork, catfish onion bake, chicken, red beans and rice, tripe stew, green stew, coconut and sweet potato pudding. There was simply no room for the candied and glazed fruit that looked like flowers, which Pedro said were made of sugar cane and trimmed with Cayena flowers. Full and relaxed, Calvin believed Williams had been right. This place was a cure for the spider hangover. Now he was ready for a plunge into the jungle.

"I have arranged for a very special treat tonight," Pedro said, coming back from paying the bill. "We have been given permission to watch the lights come on at the Faro Colón."

"You'll love this. It's outstanding, man!" Williams said for the benefit of Calvin and the remainder of the entourage.

"The Faro Colón is truly one of the most remarkable structures on this planet," Pedro said with a proud smile.

◆ ◆ ◆

"Faro Colón, which translates 'Columbus Lighthouse,' is a combination of the Washington Monument, the Vatican, and the Smithsonian. It's where Columbus' bones are, in a setting fit for a pope, and it's where many of the artifacts from the period of exploration are stored." Williams spoke as the van approached the private ellipse parking lot. The van had been cleared and passed by the military guard and stop points.

Calvin had seen the massive structure in daylight. Now washed in dramatic lights, the monument seemed more significant, more impressive. Three or four blocks long, it resembled an Aztec or Mayan temple in the way the stone was laid, rising to a center height. Faro Colón was laid out in the form of a cross, with the crossbar section one and half to two blocks in length. In the center, an ornate marble and stone sepulcher rose behind elaborate iron grill work. Marching armed guards protected the mortal remains of Christopher Columbus. There was a sense of reverence and respect about the place.

All of the men were bathed in sweat as they walked up and around tight concrete-encased steps working toward the top of the monument. It seemed to Calvin that about every three or four levels they would depart through a side door and go through darkened, clammy chambers into what would appear to be a hidden stairwell. It was decidedly unpleasant; the massive stone building seemed to collect the tropical humidity. On one of the levels, they passed by what Calvin assumed was officers' quarters. A radio or television sounded down a lighted hallway, and Calvin glimpsed uniformed men and felt the slight cool wind of an air conditioner or fan. That cool and the scent of cooked meat were odd intrusions in a bizarre, flashlight-led ascent through the shrine.

Passing through a level that contained buzzing electrical motors and generators with ample warning signs, they emerged onto the top of the center of the cross at the height of the towering monument.

"This view of Santo Domingo at night is phenomenal, just fantastic!" Calvin said as he began to set his camera for exposures. The breeze was a welcome blessing as well.

"It gets even better," Pedro smiled in response.

Shouts in Spanish directed everyone's attention to the long, declining slope of the length of the monument. Calvin heard loud clacking metallic sounds and a slight buzz, and was then overwhelmed with sensation as dozens of colossal search lights clicked on along the top of the expanse. Each blast of illumination seemed to Calvin to roar in a transfixing radiation. An even more powerful rotating lamp, like those used in lighthouses, swept across the night expanse of Santo Domingo and beyond. Warnings not to look into the light seemed unnecessary, Calvin thought. This *faro* light on the top of the Columbus monument was clearly one of the brightest lights in the world and he could almost feel the electrical currents that fueled it.

"This is better than anything in *Star Wars*," John Anderson, one of Williams' associates said to Calvin, as they both tried to capture the remarkable sight on camera.

"It's a wall of light," Calvin responded, fascinated by the sparkle and shifting contour of each brilliant beam as humidity and insects hovered in the modulating brilliance.

"And now you must look up," Pedro said to Calvin.

Calvin pulled the camera from his face and tilted his head back in the direction Pedro looked. In the night sky above the island was a gigantic cross.

"It works this way only on nights when there is a good, high cloud cover." Pedro spoke as he looked toward the heavens. "The higher the clouds, the larger the cross."

Calvin had never seen anything like it. The massive cross seemed sculpted by the roaming clouds on which it was illuminated.

"Pilots say they can see this from hundreds of miles away," Pedro told him.

"I've got to say this is one of the wonders of the modern world," Anderson murmured.

"Right here in my homeland and little appreciated by the world," Pedro affirmed.

"Well, it's good you boys are seeing this tonight because tomorrow night, you'll be in the sticks. It gets a little weird out there," Williams chuckled, pointing the way for them to descend.

"We talked with Dr. Bright after church last Sunday, and he said we can't ignore Celia's concerns, but we have to get her to focus on activities that keep her occupied and thinking about the future." Barb's voice, on the phone to Laney in Indianapolis, was full of concern.

"I don't want her to have to take the prescription. She's too young to take sleeping pills," Hockett said emphatically on the extension.

"Katie seemed to be over it, until the local TV stations covered one of these anthrax hoaxes. That just set her off again. She goes from normal to this sense of dread. I notice it more when she's tired, but now she's talking about doing a school research project on bio-terrorism—in the seventh grade, for heaven's sake!" Laney was outraged.

"It's a rough world for these kids, isn't it?" Hockett felt his anger building too, as he considered the implications of his words.

◆ ◆ ◆

The next morning, the eastern sky in Santo Domingo was incandescent. Williams and his team, Pedro Perez, and Calvin had loaded the helicopter and were waiting for the horizon to toss up the orange sun, giving the pilot the light he wanted to begin the flight into the jungle.

Pedro had filled the time telling Calvin about the chronicles of Bartolomé de las Casas, an early sixteenth-century priest who arrived during the period of conquest. Las Casas' version of that encounter between the Tainos and the Spanish records and details one of history's most barbaric dramas. Spanish brutality was so severe and Las Casas' portrayal so graphic, it moved Pedro to tears as he recounted the tale. Calvin was stirred by Pedro's emotion.

He thought of his daughters, Elizabeth and Katie, when Pedro spoke of how the women and young girls were forced to submit to the desires of the Conquistadors. The specific details of the enslavement of the men—the disembowelment, the cutting off of hands, the plucking of eyes—were revolting not only for their savageness but for the contemptuous and arrogant hatefulness it represented in the Spanish officers. The torture seemed to be as much for sport as for control of the compliant, kind and trusting Tainos.

"Because of the genocide, there are very few people of Taino bloodline left," Pedro said. The chopper engines were coming to life while the copilot checked the fit of the restraint belts on the passengers.

"That's what's so special about a couple of our porters and dive assistants," Williams said over the engine roar. "They're Tainos and still hold the old beliefs of their people. Pretty amazing guys—a little weird though."

♦ ♦ ♦

The morning sun glistening off the tops of palm heads made the chopper ride a beautiful pass over the verdant island. It was like gliding over a green sea. A landing zone had been cleared and burned into the thick jungle, with a red flag tied to the top of a stripped tree limb to mark the spot.

Williams led the group toward the well site. "Once we cut away the overgrowth," he said, "we could see these large limestone blocks which formed a plaza, a ceremonial plaza. This was obviously a big village and the well was important. In fact, we think it's the well in the woodcut illustration that was in Las Casas' chronicle."

"A well of this size would have drawn a lot of people. We think this could be the center of the Taino capital," Anderson added as they followed a narrow trail deeper into the heat of the tropical forest. They were heading toward the well.

"Measuring and mapping down there is a pain in the butt," Williams barked. "The divers can spend only ten minutes on the bottom before they have to come back up. I mean, they are working at about 190 feet and that's a deep dive. We are starting to use nitrox—a nitrogen-oxygen mixture to give us a little more time, but coming back up is slow to avoid the bends."

Calvin was fascinated by the well which suddenly opened before them. It looked like a giant yawning hole on the jungle floor. It dropped into a large dark expanse, now lit by work lights. A few rubber rafts had been laced by rope and were anchored to the cave wall. From that spot, sixty feet below the surface of the jungle, the divers began their descent to almost two hundred feet to find the remains of a once-vibrant culture.

"We are not sure how or why the artifacts got to the floor. Were they thrown in as a last desperate act by the Tainos, or by conquerors, or as ritual?" Pedro spoke to Calvin as Calvin began shooting the divers descending to the dive platform rafts by a series of ropes.

"How was this cave formed?" Calvin asked.

"A limestone cap rock broke away centuries ago," Williams answered. "It dropped into the aquifer, coming to rest in such a way that it formed an underground mountain probably three hundred feet steep. The mountain in there spires up. It's from the top and the slopes that we're getting the good artifacts." Williams' attention was diverted to the new divers who had just geared up.

"Nobody goes below one-forty unless authorized. Bottom time is fifteen minutes." He gestured toward a gnarly, tough-looking middle-aged man. "Enrique, you lead the archeology team and start working the provenance." Williams looked at Calvin and Pedro. "That's an archaeological measuring form." He looked back at the divers, "Okay from the bottom up, three minutes on O2 at each stop. I'm going to suit up and join you down there. Let's go!" Williams moved toward his tent to get rigged.

As Laney reached for colored construction paper, she brushed against a stack of papers on the corner of Katie's computer desk and they fell to the floor. Picking them up, she glanced at the type and felt a sinking in her heart. One article was a reprint of a *New York Times* piece: "Former Congressman, College President and Presidential Advisor to Draft Bio War Report." Katie had written across it, "Dad knows him." Below that was the UN report on chemical and biological weapons in the twenty-first century. A third, and what appeared to be a largely technical piece, was headlined "Finding the time/date footprint on pre-Y2K programs—more fun from Cyberfools." She thought of her husband down in the Dominican Republic and wished that he could be home to help Katie regain her emotional balance.

◆ ◆ ◆

Calvin sat on the folding stool outside the flap of his tent, looking at the long coil of wire that ran to the generator. His step-down transformer had been gaffer-taped to the plug-in, so he could use his laptop on power without problems caused by the generator current blowing circuits. He reviewed his notes of the day and entered them into the file, feeling a very comfortable buzz from a refreshing beer.

In mid-morning, after the first dive, Enrique, a native Taino descendent, had led some of the team and a burro through the jungle to the dry cave site about five miles away. They were going to see cave paintings five hundred years old. The ten-mile round trip in the sweltering heat had drained Calvin, and he worried about dehydration. He was surprised at how quickly the cold beers went down, and how they did in fact have a "carbo replacement" effect, as Williams said they would. He felt both replenished and relaxed, and while he missed Laney and the girls, he was torqued up by the reality of his jungle adventure.

He examined his notes from Enrique's explanation of the hundreds of hieroglyphs, or cave paintings. He felt again the thrill of standing in the darkened cave, of looking at what was probably the first native account of the contact period, when the old world met the new. They were crude in their form, though complex in detail. Some kind of brush or stick had been hand-fashioned, dipped in an early form of dye or paint and drawn on the uneven wall. One patch looked to Calvin like a crown or headdress, and another patch seemed to depict a boat next to a rectangle. He also made note of the Taino rituals of welcome, which Enrique explained to him as they walked along the cave wall casting bright lights on the paintings. There were symbols of the exchange of names between the Taino cacique, or chief, Cotubanama, and Juan de Esquivel, the conquistador. It was a declaration of eternal brotherhood, two men from two worlds becoming one. It was an encounter fated to end in tragedy.

Now by lantern and firelight amidst the buzz of mosquitoes and the night sounds of the jungle birds and frogs, it was easy for Calvin to get into the mind-set of that age, five hundred years ago. The three-quarter moon had risen above the jungle canopy, and the aroma of the cooking beans and spices urged his stomach to anticipate the deepening darkness. The smell of the cooking food also offset the strong odor of the high-powered mosquito repellent, deet, which now enveloped most of the men and their gear.

Calvin listened to Williams and his men talk through the technical and detail-laden evaluation of the day. They were sharing a meal around the campfire. A dirty and worn oversized cooler supplied cold beer. A spirit of companionship pervaded the scene, but the archeology teams' words were angry. The greed of the conquistadors, it appeared, was not confined to that time when they savaged the Tainos.

"We compared some of the photos from our original dive, three months ago, to what we've gotten since we came back last week, and it's clear someone has been here," Williams said. "Some of the ceremonial stuff we mapped on the left side of the slope has been invaded."

The Dominican archeologists shook their heads and, speaking rapidly in Spanish, lamented the plundering. John Anderson translated for the remainder of the group. The conversation then ranged over who could have been behind the raid, and who could have afforded to pay professional divers to undertake such a hazardous venture into the well.

"I know it is but one man who do these things. Five hundred years ago his people from Spain come to rape and kill and steal. And now he comes to steal our spirits, to defile and to disturb Guyuba," Enrique said from the edge of the fire. "It is Abelardo Rota. I have seen him before—the bloodsucker. In his house are many things from Taino, from Aztec, from Maya, even from Carib. He has many paintings that came from the Jews of Europe. He has things from American wars. I have even seen he has a piece of the space shuttle that blew up."

"Yeah, I figured it was that son of a bitch." Williams drained a beer as he spoke. "He's a leading underground collector. Stuff that he has no right to. Most of it should be in museums, but he gets his jollies by having it and one-upping the other sick bastards who collect."

"I hear, too, that he seeks to buy cave spaces. Some say it is so he can store other stuffs," Enrique added.

Pedro leaned over to Calvin. "That's what I meant the other night, when we saw him up at the restaurant. He's a rough customer, as we used to say in Chicago."

Calvin's mind moved between the outrage shared around the campfire to his own anger at the plunder of artifacts. Then, too, there was the growing puzzle of Rota and his connection to Bokanyev. What were these two men up to? What in God's name were they planning to store in these caves? And again—was it connected to Sanibel?

"I thought you were staying on Sanibel," Peabody said to the speakerphone. "I was ready to send you title papers for signing there."

"A local issue here requires some attention," Bokanyev said sitting in his Cayman command office, looking at the lights on the fishing boat. The moonlit Caribbean washed in along his private beach front.

"Is it a legal matter?" Peabody asked.

"It is about money, I think. A local hero, a bike star who talks a lot, is creating an issue over my men who carry weapons. It is something I can probably make go away with cash. This fellow Craig Merryman is not rich. If I find the right button, I will play him and he will be my ally. You know of these things, don't you? Or I can eliminate him, that is always possible."

"You have gone too far, Mr. Bokanyev. I will not condone your thinking nor do I like your tone. As your lawyer, I tell you your comments are wrong."

"What is this? Sudden outrage from you? You weasel! Either you will listen to me, or your wife will. Which is it?"

"Even though your comments could not be used in court because of our relationship, they could be used against you by investigators. *You* are an outrage! Keep in mind, you are not on a secure line. I am ending this conversation now."

Peabody clicked off the phone with a vengeance. He knew he had angered Bokanyev, but he didn't care. In fact, he had been looking for a chance to provoke such an exchange. Now the power had shifted his way. He had the real estate under his control, and he would have the final word when he tipped off the IRS to "irregularities in Bokanyev's holdings," irregularities which he of course had created. All the while he would himself take control of other properties, clear and clean.

"You fat wimp. You have done what I needed you to do. The Sanibel property is mine. But you are getting too bold." Bokanyev spoke into the dial tone, but it gave him still a modicum of satisfaction. "Maybe I will arrange for an accident to befall you, or, maybe better, your wife will see your party in Mexico."

"Okay, mon, we shall see what button you want to play. And maybe I'll play this tape," Craig Merryman said from the captain's cabin of his cousin's fishing charter as it bobbled on the surf. Merryman could see Bokanyev through his infrared field glasses now that he had put down the parabolic antenna, which was attached to the tape recorder he had borrowed from his cousin who worked on the Cayman/Commonwealth criminal investigative force staff. His fishing trip had been successful: the conversation had been caught.

Cigar smoke mingled with smoke from the campfire. Some of the team had gone into their tents. Calvin had packed his laptop and was slowly drinking a beer and enjoying a cigar under the moon while he ruminated about business, Bokanyev, and the classic betrayals which seemed to befall good people through history. Pedro was in his tent and Calvin had the quiet to himself. Williams, Anderson and a couple of the other divers stood under the thatched tiki near the edge of the cave, poring over maps and charts.

"Tim Calvin, I have seen you worry about Abelardo Rota, who is somehow tied to your life." Enrique startled Calvin as he came from behind his tent.

"You spooked me, Enrique. I'm sorry. Yes, I do worry about Rota,"

Calvin said. He noticed that Enrique looked different. The man's eyes were somewhat fixed, the pupils wide and the whites bloodshot. Calvin figured he was feeling the effect of too many beers. "But how do you know of my concern over Rota? I've said nothing about it."

"I can see it in your eyes when I say his name. I know these things. Tim Calvin, my ancestors tell me you are a good heart, that you have remorse for wrongs done by people who are not yours, that you feel pain for those who suffer."

Enrique was acting strange, his voice and actions somewhat distant and mechanical.

"Do not be frightened. There is no harm to come to you, but Guyuba, lord of the land of the dead, is restless. Yachu, lord of the yucca, the source of bread and life, the supreme being, cries for justice." He stood holding his hand as though to motion Calvin to stand and follow him into the jungle.

Calvin was nervous. Was Enrique high on something other than beer? All this seemed odd and bizarre. But he sensed, just knew in his heart, that Enrique meant him no ill. He would go with him and he would be all right. His heart beating rapidly, Calvin followed Enrique into the darkness. In a couple of minutes, they had reached a smaller fire in a clearing surrounded by large pieces of stone which had been assembled into a pattern of rows.

Enrique offered Calvin a ceramic bowl carved with a zemi image. "Attabey, the mother of waters, sustainer of life." He motioned for Calvin to drink; he did so.

"All of life comes from the waters, from the floods. From out of the caves, a turtle rose up to create our island land." He paused then said, "Yachu. Our holy bread." Enrique had picked up and offered to Calvin another, more intricately carved ceremonial bowl which contained a gummy, bread-like substance.

Calvin responded by chewing it and swallowing. Fascinated by this moment of comradeship, he no longer worried. He was thrilled by the experience.

"These pieces come from the ancestors. Up from the cave, I bring them. Across five hundred years, the ancestors travel," Enrique said, handling the ceramic ware.

Enrique knelt before the fire and placed a device that looked like a long tube between his knees. He lifted a pipe from a flat rock and lit it with a twig, then inhaled the smoke and passed it to Calvin. Reluctantly, Calvin accepted it and meekly drew from the rough-hewn stem. It seemed more mild than his cigar smoke and he watched as Enrique exhaled from his nose. Calvin did likewise and was surprised he did not cough or choke.

Enrique then bowed his head to the tube between his legs.

"*Cohoba*. It allows us to communicate with our spirits."

Enrique put his nose on the tube and inhaled deeply. Silhouetted by the leaping flames, he threw his head back with a gasp. Then he extended his arms and opened his hands, palms skyward. From the shadows, another man Calvin had seen at the dive site came forward, lifted the cohoba tube from between Enrique's knees, and handed it to Calvin.

Was he really doing this? Was it harmful? It didn't appear to be. It seemed only natural to respond in kind and to follow Enrique's lead. This must be an act of deep friendship, a sacred ritual. Calvin snorted a pungent and mildly aromatic, tobacco-like powder. His nostrils burned and he forced open his mouth; then he too, like Enrique, gasped, throwing his head back.

Calvin's ears buzzed, and his heart beat ever more rapidly. Everything he heard came to him from a distance, thinly, with whooshing background static. The stars seemed to sparkle with bejeweled brilliance and then he became very sleepy, though his eyes were not heavy. A Novocaine numbness was working from the back of his throat into his brain and behind his eyes. He stared at Enrique, who was mumbling and jerking his arms and legs. Within a couple of minutes, the surrounding trees, rocks and flames seemed to twist into contortions. Calvin consciously knew he was hallucinating; reality had been convoluted. He was merely a passenger on a psychotropic thrill ride.

Enrique stood, casting shadows against the jungle foliage. His own dance-like movement around the fire combined with the hallucinatory effect to create vivid images which captivated Calvin's attention. The second man finally took Calvin's arm to lead him to his tent. The walk back through the tropical forest felt as though he was walking through a moving passageway that seemed to expand and contract inexplicably.

The camp was silent, although a couple of the tents glowed with lights. Calvin thanked Enrique's assistant, zipped his mosquito flap shut, and was soon on his foam pad feeling as though his mind was rushing through the stars.

Upon waking, Calvin checked his possessions to determine that he had not at sometime during the night left the tent again to return to the jungle. He had the distinct feeling he had been away and had only recently returned to the tent, though nothing had moved since he made his intoxicated return from the cohoba experience. He felt as though his sleep had been deep. His dreams had been vivid, though not clear nor lucid. He remembered dreaming of Laney and the girls, Barb, Dave, Celia, Larry Conroy, and Lee Hamblin engaged in some hard work, such as digging, or pushing an object. He knew they were on Sanibel, but little else was clear. He recalled something that looked and felt like a museum and the feeling of running or being chased. Very odd night. There was clearly something to the material he smoked or snorted, though he felt no ill effect.

Calvin heard activity outside where he could smell coffee. He recognized Pedro's voice and looked out to see him speaking with Enrique near the hose which drew washing water from the depth of the cave. Calvin splashed his head and face; the cold water refreshed him. He had decided against a shave and was ready to move.

"Enrique has asked to accompany you and me on the trip to Alto de Chevron," Pedro said as he and Calvin enjoyed a cup of the powerful Dominican coffee and munched pineapple slices. "When the helicopter brings in the fresh water and food, it will fly us to Casa de Campo, where we will get a car for the drive to the art colony. You remember the picture I showed you of the palm-lined river? You will be able to shoot from that bluff and get some wonderful scenes."

"Great. I'll enjoy that."

Pedro's eyes grew serious. "Enrique wants to point out to you where Rota lives, and where he keeps his stolen possessions."

"Hmm, whatever they are. Okay."

Calvin had taken a couple of rolls of film at Alto de Chevron, a replication of a sixteenth-century Spanish village. A beautifully designed art colony, shopping and restaurant district, it was a favorite of those who kept homes at the exclusive Casa de Campo enclave. As Calvin descended the stairs of the small church balcony, he was startled by the sight of Abelardo Rota and a small party walking toward a cafe-bistro on the plaza below.

"Enrique, Pedro. Rota is here. He and a group are sitting down at a cafe," Calvin told his companions

Enrique excused himself to take a closer look. "This is very good," he said, coming back around the wall of trimmed conifers which separated the overlook from the plaza where the Rota party had taken seats.

"He is with his man Josef, the Russian, and a group of his guests. They will be some time at dining. Luncheon here takes two hours. I know where he keeps his stolen treasures; I think you should see them, maybe write a story for the world to know."

Calvin's attention fastened on what Enrique said: "The Russian." This had to be another connection to Bokanyev. "I shouldn't take the chance. It's a little risky." A pause. "But yes, let's go see what we can."

Passing the security point was no trouble, since Calvin and the party had been there earlier. The compound had become a favorite of

the wealthy dilettantes from several nations. Some homes were very private with mountain views, some stood next to the famed Teeth of the Dog golf course, others were beachside villas.

Pedro went to the hanger at the end of the private runway, which was bounded by fairways and the ocean. "Enrique, be careful with Mr. Calvin!" he shouted, then he got into a golf cart and headed west.

Calvin and Enrique took another cart through the course, toward the east. They stopped at the bottom of a long, sloping incline. To their backs was the sea, and in front of them a long, green expanse rose up like a small mountain. At the top perched a sprawling, red-tile-roofed, glass and adobe villa. It spread over the private hilltop.

"This is the palace of the thief," Enrique murmured as he and Calvin walked toward the pool and cabana, through a garden resplendent with fountains.

"What are we going to do? If someone is here, I'll tell them I'm here for a magazine article." Calvin was feeling temporarily confident about the foray.

"No one is here. Josef is with Rota. Rota has no family, he lives here only with the security man; Josef, when he is here; or another man, who I know."

"What is Rota's secret? How does he stay out of trouble?"

"Connections. He make many pay off. He have politicians who owe him many favors. But his time may be running out. The new president is different. The new party leaders have not received his favors. Perhaps his past will bring him a bad future."

Enrique led them into the cabana bathhouse and into the pump room. He lifted a small trapdoor below a pump housing.

"Now we go see what this man has. He steals from the cave, I just know it. My wife's brother helped to build these homes. It is good to know these things." Enrique smiled, then turned and dropped about three feet into a crawl space. Calvin followed. They wriggled beneath a couple of water lines until Enrique pushed open another trapdoor. They were in the equipment room of the house, ironically bypassing any security alarms.

Calvin's stomach was fluttering. This was dangerous territory. As a writer, he'd been willing enough to put himself on the line for a story, but this was different. Wasn't this breaking and entering? Still, he did not retreat. They climbed short flight of stairs into the main salon. The villa was immaculate and richly appointed, though extravagantly overdone. The tile and wooden floors shone. Fresh flower arrangements of gardenias, birds of paradise, orchids and frangipani were everywhere. The commanding views took in the sea, the mountains and the beautifully manicured golf courses. The place offered many shelves and display arrangements that featured pre-Columbian artifacts and other extraordinarily expensive items. Oil paintings were generously placed on walls.

"Do you see the glass catwalk to the other wing? That wing is where he keeps his most prized loot." Enrique pointed through the large glass-walled room with the western exposure, toward what looked like a cut-crystal door and, beyond that, an enclosed bridge over a waterfall.

"This place is unbelievable," Calvin said numbly.

"Oh, you don't know how much so. I am going to get us into that wing."

"I don't know about that, man. Do you think we should? Time is passing here."

Enrique ignored him. "I must be careful because he have many types locks on that crystal door. It came from a palace in France."

Calvin had no trouble believing that. The paintings he studied included Renoir, Monet, Modigliani, Picasso, Warhol, Dali. There were glass hutches and curios that displayed Fabergé eggs, gold sculptures, pieces of jewelry. Each item almost defied belief. He mused over how ostentatiously the treasures were displayed. It was obvious Rota was a compulsive show-off as well as a major thief. His fascination took the edge off his nervousness. But occasionally he would hear something, and it would give him an electrical jolt of panic. What was taking Enrique so long?

"Enrique, we should get out of here. If this Rota comes back—"

"No, no, Tim. I am almost in. You must see these things."

"I've seen enough. We could be accused of being thieves, or we could get shot. We should go."

"Tim, you must see this display room. The piece of the space shuttle, the gun that kill John Lennon, bloody gloves from Mrs. Kennedy—"

"I believe you. Listen—this guy is nuts. We've been in here too long. We should get out of here, get back to Pedro."

"This is for me, for my people and the ancestors. There is something I must do here. Just a few more minutes and then we go."

Calvin's mouth was like cotton. He was almost overwhelmed by fear, but every cell in his body felt vitally alive. He considered the grandeur of this home and compared it to the places he had seen coming down through the Ciboa Valley. Somehow this guy was tied to Bokanyev. Obviously they were heavy players and could probably be very tough. These people clearly had money and could sustain a long legal fight over the King real estate issues.

But how did they get into the King estate in the first place? What do they want with a Sanibel place? Was it just another playhouse? Were they planning something more? Earl's information about his brokering of bio-agents had worried Calvin from the moment he read the e-mail. Was this guy Rota part of that as well? As Calvin riddled thoughts through his mind, he recalled Earl's warning to "stay in center field," meaning stay away from Rota. He had completely disregarded the advice. It was part of the old urge inspired by *Journey Without Maps* or *Treasure Island*, which he had always either fought or indulged. It could get him into deep trouble now.

"Tim, we are in!" Enrique called.

The glass walkway over the garden waterfall led to a majestic room resembling a fine museum, complete with lights and exhibit cases. Enrique was drawn immediately to a group of items. Calvin took in the outside view and noticed a couple of golf carts rolling along the ridge of the course, silhouetted against the water. Almost simultaneously he saw Rota's desk and computer.

Calvin could tell by Enrique's excited speech that he had found something of interest. So had he, but it caused his heart to thud. On the desk lay a communiqué to Bokanyev:

The humidity of the cave causes the casing to sweat. Over time the casing will corrode and the cap stabilizers will be ineffective.

Calvin grabbed the paper. His hand shook. Casings? Cap stabilizers? This was about bio-weapons. Poison. Death agents. He realized the snippet of conversation he had heard at the restaurant about a client and caves related to this. "Bokanyev is using Rota to find places to store bio or chemical weapons," he said aloud. Instantly, his daughter's anguished face leapt into his mind.

He looked down at the desk and stared at the paper beneath the memo he had grabbed and folded into his pocket.

It was the printout of an e-mail.

A former comrade says some of the oldest Russian systems are flawed. Not all the weaknesses are known. In addition, the east caves are too far from shipment points. The archaeology work makes them too crowded. Salt water immersion or sand storage is probably better.

Sand storage? Salt water immersion? Caves not okay?

"Tim, Rota is coming. Quick! Quick!" Enrique slapped Calvin's shoulder and dashed toward the glass walkway. He was carrying something in his hands, but he was moving too quickly for Calvin to see what it was.

Calvin saw that the golf carts he spotted earlier were now parked at the edge of the waterfall pond. He ran through the glass catwalk. Looking out the window, he made eye contact with a man who had returned to the carts. Standing below the bridge, he was just twenty or so feet away, outside. Sudden surprise moved through both sets of eyes. The man began yelling.

Calvin and Enrique dashed to the equipment room. They could hear voices and commotion on the upper level. Calvin's heart pounded in his ears. He had forgotten he still clutched the second memo, until he folded it and shoved it into his cargo pants. He ran. He and Enrique traversed the crawl space in a hip-and-thigh crunching crabwalk. They listened for a moment at the trapdoor in the pump room of the poolhouse. There were no voices. Enrique turned to Calvin.

"Hold these. Protect them. They belong to history, not to the grave robber. I will look above." He handed Calvin a magnificent carved ceramic and a strange wooden piece, also carved.

Enrique pulled himself out of the crawl space and motioned for Calvin to hand up the two artifacts. They slipped out of the cabana and dashed across the pool terrace into the fountain garden, looking back at the house, then bounded down the hill to the golf cart. By going east they could go with the flow of the course and back around the house. But that wouldn't work; they needed to go west, to the hanger to meet Pedro. Enrique attempted to keep the golf cart at the base of the hill, out of sight, until a stream made it necessary to pull into the open. They had just barely reached the service path, which paralleled the runway, when they were spotted from the villa on the hilltop.

Calvin and Enrique had a considerable head start, but Calvin's confidence dissolved when he heard the explosion of gunfire and the spit of dirt to the side of the cart. He felt vulnerable, exposed and terrified.

Enrique turned to him. "Don't worry. You carry sacred objects. The ancestors protect you. But hang on. I'm going for the runway."

Getting across the ruts and hard scrabble almost threw them from the cart, but the drive along the runway proved to be a brilliant move. A couple of airport service workers looked at them as though they were crazy as they whizzed by and around the small office to the space near the hanger door where the chopper was waiting.

Calvin didn't understand the Spanish, but he got the drift of the shouted conversation. The pilot fired up in a manner that probably violated most international flight regulations, but they got off the ground rapidly. As they banked away from Casa de Campo and headed back to the cave site, Calvin felt absolutely drained, but relieved. They looked down on a golf cart carrying Rota and two other men bouncing along the service road.

"Do you think they know the guys they want are up here?" Calvin asked Pedro and Enrique.

"I hope they do not. I hope they did not see you. I think it is wise for you to return home. I hope you have enough information for your article." Pedro was clearly concerned, but not for himself, it seemed. Calvin looked at him questioningly.

"I have my own network of protection here," was all Pedro said.

"I've got enough. I was just looking for more color, but I think I've had all that I need, definitely."

"Tonight we'll fly you back to Santo Domingo," Pedro announced. "I'll work on getting your return flight moved up. Enrique, what have you taken?"

"No, no, you should say, 'What have I returned to my people.' It's a zemi stone of Yachu and a piece of a duhos, the ceremonial stool of a cacique ruler, probably Cotubanama. I saw this last night."

"Enrique, You could have gotten yourself and Tim killed!" Pedro said with some anger.

"No! No! You do not understand the zemis. The ancestors will protect."

Pedro shook his head, frowned deeply, then closed his eyes and leaned back against the seat. Calvin soon followed his example.

A Quick Good-bye

CALVIN WAS GLAD he had packed lightly. His shoulder bag could pass as a carry-on. He was pre-boarded, so he could go directly to the gate. It was good to be leaving. He faxed Earl, saying they needed to talk and that he'd send him information soon. Last night, after getting back to the hotel, he and Pedro had taken a walk to the headquarters of one of the political parties in the block behind the Sheraton and Intercontinental hotels.

Elections were coming up, and Pedro wanted Calvin to explain news about Rota to a couple of party officials. The competing party headquarters, painted in bright pinks, yellow and purple, were in the same neighborhood. On the return to the hotel, they stopped at Charlie's, a garage-like building under a bright neon sign on Colonel Mallecon. The extent of the place was a bar set up under a thatch roof, with bottles placed neatly on it. Six or seven white wooden tables, each with a bottle of wine in the center of the table. It was a quiet, out-of-the-way retreat that had been around for a while. Two hard-looking, older men sat chatting at a table on the sidewalk. A Mercedes was parked on the sidewalk near their table, and two other men, who looked like bodyguards, stood near the Mercedes. Pedro directed Calvin to a seat at a table inside while he went to speak with the two seated men. A couple of times they turned to look at Calvin. He learned later that that meeting probably saved his life.

Pedro explained the "old boys" were members of a *patronato*, or ruling council, a kind of unofficial board of the powerful. It was "a Caribbean kind of thing," where elements from government and all walks of business got together and "worked things out." The old boys had heard that someone had gotten Rota angry, and that he had determined it was the Yankee magazine writer. Rota's surveillance cameras had gotten a couple of frames of a North American standing by his swimming pool. It wouldn't take too long to figure out who and where he was. It could go much further in terms of police and politics, but Rota and the others didn't want that kind of scrutiny. So it was a good thing that Calvin wanted to leave.

These two men of the *patronato* didn't particularly care for Rota, he was a trouble maker, but he had his friends. And although the members of the *patronato* didn't know Mr. Calvin, they didn't want an international incident, so they agreed with Pedro's decision to get the North American out of town soon. He was ready to go.

Another hour at the hotel, and he would get a cab to the airport. They had decided that for Pedro's benefit he should not be seen with Calvin, in case Rota was at the airport. Calvin decided to snack at the La Canasta restaurant next to the casino. It was quick, dark and not as crowded as the other dining rooms, partially because of some of its menu items—tripe stew and frontier goat.

He was getting on the elevator in the lobby to return to his room when he caught a glimpse out of the corner of his eye of someone looking at him. He turned as he boarded the elevator and saw he was looking at the man he'd made eye contact with at Rota's house. The man dashed for the elevator, but the door closed. What a break.

Calvin was glad there were three other passengers on board, each of whom had tapped buttons for other floors. They gave him strange looks as he keyed in three more floors above his own. "Just a little game I'm playing with my wife," he said sheepishly.

He had planned for a hasty retreat. He ran to his room, grabbed his bag, and dashed to the end of the hallway to a door opening onto a balcony. He was glad he got the bad end of the floor this time. It had come in handy. One level below him was a gravel-topped roof with fans and air-conditioning units. It was an easy hop. From there, the roof ran toward the back of the hotel, the tennis courts and a fenced-in garden nursery.

He remembered last night, when Pedro and he walked to party headquarters, they noticed the open service gate. He thought at the time it would be easy to hide in the thick mini-jungle of the nursery. A shed in the nursery was covered with a corrugated metal roof. If he landed right, he could simply jump, squat, then slide down the roof into a row of potted palms. It worked. Oooh! Trouble sitting for a while, but it would pass.

He slipped out the gate and made for party headquarters, wanting to avoid the cab stand at the front of the hotel. His heart sank as he rounded the corner and saw hundreds of people in the front yard of the party building as well as at the opposing party building just to the north. A rally or major event was underway, one which would force him to the street to hail a cab. That was not a good idea because it would put him back on the Mallecon and dangerously close to the hotel and all the lights. As he examined his options, he looked along the block and noticed Charlie's neon sign. Once again, a large black Mercedes was pulled up onto the curb. Adrenaline was flowing. He made for the place, which looked like a classic Mafia bar, to ask one of the old dons for help. He had nothing to lose.

The old man recognized him from the night before and, with a simple flip of his head, summoned his body guard driver. "I need to stay, señor, but Alvarado, you get the man to the airport with no problems, si?"

The swarthy, pockmarked Alvarado nodded and pulled a nine-millimeter Glock from the holster on his belt in the center of his back. He checked the clip, looked down the sights, put it back in the holster and smiled at Calvin.

The half-hour drive out of Santo Domingo went rapidly along the coast and the American Avenue, past what once must have been a series of lovely medallioned crest posts of the nations of the world.

Now they stood broken, missing, in disrepair, symbols of the cor-
ruption and neglect the old regime had inflicted on the island nation.
It was men like Rota who had benefited. Now men like his friend
Pedro and the new government would try to restore dignity to the
oldest of the American cultures.

The trip passed in absolute silence.

"American TransAir, please," Calvin said as they approached the
terminal. The driver raised his steely eyes briefly. As he stopped the car,
he turned his head slightly, signaling Calvin to exit.

"Gracias," Calvin said. The driver returned only a blank stare and
then sped away from the curb.

Calvin passed the six glass-boxed customs booths along the
marble-flecked floor of the gymnasium-sized terminal. Lines of people
stood to clear security. Lit pictures of resorts and shopping centers
lined the walls. Aromas of tobacco, coffee, spicy meats, Chanel, and
cheap Passion Wave mixed with the smell of sweat in the humidity of
the night. Exhaust fumes of old taxies swept in when large glass doors
off the arrival drive opened. Calvin wore a cap and tried to keep his
face hidden behind those in line in front of him. He scanned the area,
looking for the man or men who might still be looking for him. He
was hopeful he had given them the slip.

He cleared security and saw the gate number ahead. He would
have about thirty minutes to wait, but he could bury his face in a
newspaper. Only ticketed passengers were supposed to get beyond this
point. He began to feel safe, as though home would soon be his. He
had much to do, a lot to figure out, but he actually looked forward to
the normal hassles of business.

He moved toward the lounge area and was stopped in his tracks by
the sight. There on the wall was a lighted, full-color ad for Rum. It
featured a picture of a Taino zemi. The caption, in Spanish, read
something to the effect of "Welcome to the house of our ancestors, we
have good spirits here."

Indianapolis Gray Skies
and Sanibel Clouds

"YES, IT'S BEEN a long winter," Calvin conceded to Edward Earl. "We're all ready for spring break. Of course, I wonder what's happening with Bokanyev getting the King home." Calvin was at his desk in his Northside Indianapolis office looking out at the week-old snow on the parking lot. "He's had two months to do whatever he's doing."

Earl's voice chuckled at the other end of the phone line. "Well, I don't know whether you put them on notice with your Dominican escapade or not. We'll try to figure that out. Thanks for inviting us down to Sanibel to be with you over spring vacation. Judy and I look forward to some of that famous R&R you talk about."

"I'm glad you'll be able to make it. Laney will love seeing Judy."

"Of course, the last time I was on your delightful island we had that business of the kidnapping and the old artifact you were chasing around. There wasn't any down time. But it sure was a memory maker. I'm really glad to have gotten to work with Valmer." Earl paused and his tone changed. "Have you been able to develop anything new on the King situation?"

"Since I was in the Dominican Republic, I've been trying to stay out of trouble, but I have been poking around a bit, by Internet mostly. Unfortunately Judge Browne can't help. He's got some serious memory loss, so the authorities have sort of put the case on hold. I'm sure that Rota's accomplice Josef is probably the same guy who grabbed the judge. He's got to be Bokanyev's stooge. But we've got no proof. Conroy's got his executive assistant, Claudia, digging around in real estate. Donna Iemer—she's the gal who rescued the judge—is taking a leave of absence to work with Browne to get the study institute mess figured out. She can do that because she's also working with Congressman Hamblin; she's editing his report."

"I've got to tell you I've enjoyed the phone chats with Lee Hamblin. I see why he is so highly regarded. And this Larry Conroy is a character, a thousand ideas flow from him all the time. Since we've been talking about this trouble, I must have gotten seventy clips from him—magazines, newspapers, Internet reprints. The guy must read everything. He's really quite a guy. I see why you are so fond of him."

"Ed, it's really great of you to get involved like this."

"Look, Tim, I'm semiretired. I've worked for the federal government; I've been a local prosecutor; I've filled in as a judge; and I've got to admit, this small-town legal work doesn't give me the adrenaline rush I was used to. Besides that, I know how much Valmer loved the island. If you've got a bad character down there who's up to no good, it gives me a chance to dust off the old skills. And Judy and I get to travel together."

Calvin walked over to shut the blinds on the gray snow. "We get in on Friday. You can reach us at the condo or through the Hocketts. Larry and his wife Mary Lou will be staying with Lee at their home on Captiva. I think he's planning lunch, or should I say Sunday dinner. When you're at the Conroys', you are just a short beach hike away from the King home."

"Tim, I've told Larry Conroy to stay away from there. Beach walks are expected, but no snooping, no photographs. What your daughter got was great, but very foolish. Anyway we'll meet on Sunday and plan our next move. You sound beat, so relax. I don't think this thing is so out of hand that we can't figure a way to work it out. I think you're going to like Doug Garret. I let him in on all the pertinent stuff. Told him you'd call. I've worked with him a couple of times since he retired from the bureau. He's a good guy. He's right there in Indiana, and he's got good connections too. Remember, you're supposed to be taking a vacation."

◆ ◆ ◆

As he drove up Allisonville Road, Calvin began itemizing points he wanted to make in his lunch meeting with Doug Garret. Retired from the FBI, Garret now took on special assignments in which his investigative and legal background were needed. Edward Earl had met Garret at a former agent's golf outing where Garret confessed to him that he was flirting with getting his PGA qualification.

Calvin remembered what Garret said when he had called to schedule a meeting. "It ought to work out. I can't get a tee time anyway when snow's on the ground. I'm available for a lunch meeting, so long as IU's not playing an NCAA prelim."

Calvin turned left on slushy Eighty-second Street, and eventually into the plowed parking lot of the Malibu Grill. He'd asked Garret what he looked like so he could recognize him. "Don't worry," Garret said. "I'll recognize you."

The aroma of the grill tempted Calvin as he approached the door. As he reached for the handle, it swung open and there stood an athletic-looking man only a few years his junior.

"Tim Calvin. I'm Doug Garret. I understand you're a basketball nut too!"

◆ ◆ ◆

Dave Hockett read the telltale signs on his desktop and in the configuration of his home screen. Celia had been online again, seeking information on chemical and biological weapons. He had tried to reason with her about obsessing over the topic. He asked her to consciously avoid reading or studying anything more about it.

"Barb, Cee's been surfing for more stuff," Hockett called around the corner to his wife, who sat on the screened porch reading.

She put down the book. "She's apparently told some of the kids in the band that her nightmares are back. She was okay for a couple of months, but now it seems worse." Barb stared off at the lake behind the house. "Laney says Celia and Katie are chatting regularly online and apparently little Katie is pointing Celia to some of the sites."

"This has got to stop. Celia's a nervous wreck; Katie's not eating. I think Tim and Laney and you and I should have a long chat with the girls," Hockett said with emphasis.

"Well, honey, take your own advice. You've got to stop all your worry about Bokanyev. There are some things you can't fix. All we have are suspicions."

"It's got to be more than suspicions, Barb. Tim thinks the memos he found in the Dominican Republic at that bozo Rota's house show for sure that some kind of containers are on the way to Sanibel."

"David, you listen to me. He's turned the information over to authorities. Nothing more can be done. Worrying over it is not good for anyone."

"Well . . ." Hockett trailed off and began thinking about his upcoming mission trip to Russia. His circle of friends was small, but they too had networks. Perhaps he could discreetly inquire as to Bokanyev's background and, more importantly, about what might be his intentions.

Calvin was impressed with Garret's quick mind and ready read of the situation. He was also pleased with Garret's reaction to *The NewsCenter*.

"You were right on, Tim, the way you got the media process, at least according to my own experience working with the media. I bet my wife Sylvia that your female anchor character was based on Annie Riley," Garret said over the top of the menu. "By the way, I've already spoken with the lovely Ms. Riley."

"About her knowledge of C. G. King, I presume, not about the book," Calvin said with some uncertainty.

"Oh, she's got her own take on where you got the anchorlady. No, this is about the Sanibel stuff. I started my investigation by talking with Riley. After Ed told me what you were dealing with, I wanted to get as much info on the line of title to the property as I could. Apparently, the old gal made a taped statement about her mission for the international study centers and even identified some of the property she owned. I guess she put it all on a disc of some format."

"That's what's so troublesome about this property change. Somebody's engineered a takeover. I can't figure out how the property ownership could get changed. It had to be in her will. Heaven only knows where the disc is," Calvin said, shaking his head.

"It's an interesting point. If you had the disc, you'd have the old bird using her own words. Of course, some of these scumbag solicitors can be clever in what they do with legal documents. We could have a lawyer on the take.

"What I've learned is that C. G.'s lawyer died shortly before she did and that she was having all the paperwork organized by Judge Browne, then sent up here to McAtee Cheskin Ford and Hendricks. Don Southland was the attorney of record for the old King Steel, so it probably goes to him, but he's about ready to retire. He's been on a long cruise, so he hasn't done much with the case. He read it quickly and turned it over to their MIS guy."

"So they are supervising it. I guess that's good news." Calvin dipped a piece of bread in the olive oil on his plate.

"Not really. From what I hear, the will's being used by somebody to purchase the property. Institute still functions though. It's on the up and up, so they say. They're in the process of turning all their paper into electronic files but there were some early bugs, so that got delayed. What it means is that not a whole lot has been done. What worries me is that they are depending on electronic files. I feel more comfortable with the old hard copy; you can see where it's from."

The dashing Garret nodded at a group of businesswomen who had been watching him during lunch. They smiled at him on the way past the table.

Calvin considered what Garret said, and then stared out the window at the steel-gray March sky.

"What about this character Bokanyev?" Calvin asked.

"Everybody knows about him. The Bureau, CIA, NSC, DIA. He was a major operative in Latin America and the Caribbean. Earl's right, the guy is Russian Mafia, at least connected. It looks like he's an independent and stays out of the mother country. Can't blame him, huh? But the truth of the matter is, he's only one guy doing his own thing; and he's not high on anyone's agenda. They figured he was dealing arms, but apparently they got some communication linking him to Bin Laden on some bio stuff. Right now he's an ancillary. The real focus for the government is on that son of a bitch Bin Laden."

"That's understandable. What a dangerous man!" Calvin said.

"I'm not suggesting no one cares about Bokanyev, but it's a matter of resources and jurisdiction. Who's got the time and money to go after him, and on what charge? It's only suspicion. Our last president let manpower and resources slip so much, everybody is strapped. But I guarantee you the south Florida field office will probably start keeping an eye on him. What this means is that whatever we do, we won't be screwing up somebody's investigation. In fact, what we get could help put this sleaze away."

"I'm not an investigator. I'm just a guy who—"

"Hey, bucko, I heard about what you and your buddy, the old army sergeant, pulled off a couple of years ago. You were being run by a legend, man. I mean even guys in the bureau knew about Valmer's career at CIA. If you satisfied him, you had to do something right. What did the Florida newspapers call it? The Sanibel Arcanum? I also heard about your caper in the Dominican Republic. Plus, you're hooked up with Ed Earl. You're no cherry!" Garret smiled.

"I don't know . . ." Calvin sighed.

"Hey, doesn't it steam you that his guy may be setting up shop on Sanibel? This is your chance."

◆ ◆ ◆

It was one of those pleasant surprises in life. Calvin had ducked into the bookstore to pick up some vacation reading and, to his surprise, he spotted Laney in an aisle, doing the same thing.

"This is like a date," Laney said, smiling as Calvin sat down the steaming drinks at one of the bookstore's cafe tables.

"Thankfully, Katie ate some turkey bacon this morning and part of a bagel. It's really odd. Some days it's as if there is no problem, others she's in deep," Calvin said, blowing on the top of his espresso.

"Dr. Cooksey said it's not a normal eating disorder. It doesn't follow a pattern. I hate to ground her for this."

"Oh, I know. Bless her heart. It's just too much for a little girl to worry about."

"Lots of middle-schoolers, seventh- and eighth-grade girls, get worried, depressed. You know that book *Reviving Ophelia*? We had a teachers' meeting just a few weeks ago where we discussed the problems preteen girls have."

"Yeah, I know. That's what's worrying me."

"How was your meeting with the guy Ed put you in touch with?"

"Excellent. His name is Doug Garret, former FBI. He's a great guy. Big IU fan. IU law school grad. Loves to cook. Says he owes a favor to Earl, so all he wants for his time is someone to pick up his greens fees at a couple of great courses in Florida. He said his wife Sylvia is an even better golfer than he is, but he'd never admit that to her. Anyway, he figures this is a chance to stop Bokanyev before he gets a foothold on Sanibel."

"How is he going to do it?" she asked.

"Well he's got some ideas for Dave and me, some ways to get some information. Plus Earl set up a meeting with Conroy and Hamblin for the Sunday after we get down there."

"Tim! This is a vacation. You've got no business sticking your nose in it anyway. This is not going to help Katie." Laney's face reflected not only worry, but wifely disgust. He was skirting the line, definitely.

Spring Break Shellers

"OH, SMELL THAT AIR!" Laney enthused as she rolled down the window of the rental car. The sun splashed across the turquoise waters of San Carlos Bay as they drove over the causeway to Sanibel.

"Dad, you seem to chill by the time the plane gets into Fort Myers," Elizabeth observed from the back seat.

"Really!" Katie added.

"Mellow is the goal, kiddo. This island just works on me. This is one of the great joys of life. I feel especially blessed when I'm standing on Sanibel and I'm with my family." Calvin smiled. He could feel the tightness in his neck and shoulders begin to relax.

Laney gave her husband a sideways glance. Her voice was strong with wisdom and firmness. "Let's all remember this is a vacation, and it could be the last time Elizabeth will be able to join us, since who knows where she's going to end up living and working."

Calvin looked into the rearview mirror to glimpse the reaction in the backseat. Was Elizabeth considering the admonition in light of her curiosity about the King/Bokanyev property she had slipped onto back in December? Katie looked down at her hands, maybe thinking of the computer chat she and Celia had conducted on the prospect that chemical weapons were someplace on Sanibel, the latest of Celia's nightmares.

Clear, bright sunlight spread across West Gulf Drive, illuminating palm trees and vegetation with a sharp green. The sky was clear and the blue was deep and royal.

"Ah, wonderland again. This is just beautiful. It's worth everything we do to get here." Calvin drove toward Rabbit Road past West Wind Inn, Sanyana Sanibel, The Atrium, Villa Sanibel, High Tide, By the Sea, Royal Tern, Waterside Inn, and the other condos on West Gulf. "Even the signs are tasteful and classy. They actually add to the serenity."

"There aren't many places that care so much," Laney said, looking at the sunny and green day pass by. "I mean, just look at how beautifully everything is landscaped. No neon, no big signs, no ugliness. Everything for the eye and nature."

Elizabeth leaned toward the front seat and spoke. "I think it's wonderful and everything, but if you guys really want to retire here, you're going to have to deal with the hassles. After all, it's not perfect."

"Give me a for-example," her father said.

"The traffic. In season, it takes forever to go anywhere on Periwinkle."

Calvin cleared his throat. "So, we stay off Periwinkle in mid-afternoon during season. That's only a month or so."

"Plus your father and I are going to ride bikes when we're down here," Laney said.

"Better wear helmets." Katie joined the chat.

"Yes, and what about the deep-injection well controversy?" Elizabeth peppered back. "You know, that may not be a good way to get rid of waste water."

"Kiddo, your dad is not afraid of a little controversy. Nor is your mom. I agree with you on the deep well. It may not be the best method, but this island is about as good, on the issues, as anyplace you'll find. Something I hope to be able to do when I retire is spend time on environmental issues. This will be a great place to do that, controversy or not. It'll give me something to get riled up about as an old man."

"Like you'll really need that," Laney whispered to Calvin.

"What did you say?" Katie asked.

"I was talking to your father."

Elizabeth leaned forward again. "Well, what if they build a new bridge, with more lanes? That'll just make it easier to put more people on the island. Right?"

"Good point. I think this island is right in the cross hairs of one of the great issues for the new century. The balance between tourism, ecotourism even, and the damage brought about by it. But again, this is one of the places that's made a lot of right decisions so far. I look forward to being part of the discussion, or debate."

"Cross hairs, my eye," Elizabeth snorted. "You know I love it here, but I just don't think it's perfect, and you should be careful about where you want to live. Mildew, humidity, there's stuff you've got to think about."

"It's perfect to me," Katie said, breathing in the salt air. "But you guys can't move before I graduate from high school."

Calvin stayed on Gulf Drive across Tarpon Bay Road, and wound around the turns through the vegetation and past more of the gulf-front condos. In-line skaters and bike riders were out in number enjoying the sparkling day.

The Calvin family passed the Casa Ybell resort, the Algiers beach road and the turn to Middle Gulf Drive, and then around to Periwinkle, just opposite the entrance to Jerry's. A Sanibel police officer was directing traffic flow as sun splashed through the Australian pines along the main road of Sanibel.

"Elizabeth is right about the traffic," Calvin mumbled.

"I've got a list, so let's grocery shop quickly. I want to get back to the beach. We don't need a lot of corn chips and cookies," Laney said with an edge of command in her voice.

Groups of people stood in front of the bird cages, calling and coaxing for the beautiful featured creatures to respond. Calvin spotted the macaw as he walked up the steps to the store's entrance. The old bird seemed more interested in napping in his feathers than talking back.

Inside Jerry's, Calvin was immediately drawn to the aroma of the fried chicken at the deli case in front of the small restaurant area. Jerry's restaurant was a regular stop of the Hocketts each Sunday after church. Calvin enjoyed the special Jerry's link sausage so much he convinced Laney to add it to the shopping list each trip they made to the island.

"Where are you going?" Laney asked.

"Seafood salad and kaiser rolls," Calvin said. "The girls will want lunch."

"Very good," Laney replied in a rare sheepish moment. "I forgot to put those on the list." She stopped the cart. "See those people? They're looking at your book, Tim. That is so exciting." Calvin was looking for lip balm.

He nodded, somewhat embarrassed by watching people pick up and thumb through *The NewsCenter*. It was the first time he had seen the book display in Jerry's and it gave him a sense of pride . . . and uneasiness. He watched the couple while fiddling with different lip balms.

"This looks like something you'd like," the woman said to her companion.

"Great cover," was the response.

"I feel like telling them the author is right behind them," Laney whispered.

Would she do it? Maybe.

"Let's go get the shrimp," Calvin said, putting his hands on the cart handles and steering it toward the meat and seafood department. "This is nerve-wracking. Let's get back to the beach."

♦ ♦ ♦

The glow of the lights against the plants and portico created a festive feeling. The smells of grilling fish and steak filled the evening air as the group walked across the parking lot into the chic charm of the cottage-like restaurant called the Mad Hatter.

"This is kind of sad," Elizabeth said with a melancholy smile.

"Yes, but all things change," Calvin mused. "Selling is what Brian and Jayne want. They've given a lot of their lives to this place." He put his arm around Elizabeth's shoulder as he and Laney held hands.

"It won't be the same without them, will it?" Barb asked.

"Why did they have to sell it? Couldn't they just rent it?" Celia asked with a sense of indignation.

"That's not how business works, Cee," Hockett responded as he reached for the door to hold it open for the party. He smiled broadly, "Boy, we're acquiring some beautiful women here, Mr. Calvin."

Calvin was fascinated by a cloud bank. As he looked out the window toward the gulf, the cloud configuration reminded him of a framed work of art. In the upper right quarter of the frame was a cumulus grouping that looked to him like a staircase—leading up to some ethereal point of departure into the unknown. Pelicans and frigate birds soared against the graying work of "nature's art."

He sipped at the last of the wine in his glass. "That sky out there is sort of symbolic. Can you see that looks like a staircase?"

"Yeah. Where you going with this?" Brian, the Mad Hatter's owner, asked, taking a break from the roast lamb entree he had quartered for himself. Only a few customers remained.

"I don't know for sure. But changes are happening. We are all on a path to something new in our lives, and there is some uncertainty. We have an idea of where we are headed, but we're not exactly sure. Not even sure if we have much influence."

"Profound." Brian smiled, lifting his wine glass as in a toast. "I know where I'm going—to Grand Cayman with you in June. This time we won't have to hurry back to run this place."

"One other thing is sure, Mr. Calvin, if you don't get to that crème brulée of yours, I will," Hockett said as he continued to attack the rich chocolate creation named "Jayne's Addiction," which sat obscenely large in front of him.

"I'm going to savor this moment—every bite," Calvin said. "This is a celebration of what has been a fantastic run of chow at this magical little establishment. A lot of great memories are here and I'm going to take it out slowly." He took a bite and proceeded to savor it for a long moment, whimpering and sighing with pleasure.

"Dad!" Katie exclaimed.

Calvin cast a quick glance at her and then a questioning one at Laney.

"I don't think she wants you to make those noises, what you call your 'moans of ecstasy,' which you sometimes make when you eat."

"Yeah, it's, like, real strange," Celia added.

"Who me?" Calvin asked, all innocence. Katie glared, mortified.

"I'll save them for later," he whispered into Laney's ear.

"It was a bittersweet night wasn't it?" Calvin said, looking at the growing ash on the end of his cigar. He and Hockett were up on the open deck of the West Gulf condo, while the gals stayed below.

"There's an awful lot going on now. A lot of confusion. I'm trying to get ready for the mission trip to Russia. Celia's having this trouble with the dreams and nervousness. There's Bokanyev and his tricks that nobody can seem to pinpoint or stop. Barb and Laney are in a hurry to finish the plans for the Cayman trip, which is only a couple of weeks after I get back. Yeah, I guess you're right. Bittersweet. It's sorta like Brian and Jayne's selling the Hatter is a symbol of all the changes and confusion."

"Like the old song, 'Oh them changes.' Guess it never stops."

"The island's going through some changes too. Things never stay the same."

"We're just at that age, bud. I don't know what I'm going to do with the business. I'd like to get down here full time. Elizabeth's trying to figure out her life, which is normal, she's just twenty-four. Well, I'm over fifty and I'm still trying to figure out my life."

"Growing pains. I guess they never stop tweaking at us."

"One thing is for sure, we've got to get Cee and Katie off this bio-weapons jag. Worry is making them sick. It could have permanent repercussions. That's got to be priority one."

"Well, how are we going to handle the Sunday lunch at the Conroys? I guess the girls can stay here at your condo. They can swim and beach."

"That'll work. Let them hang out here. I don't want them even near any of that talk." Calvin paused and drew on his cigar. "In the meantime, listen to that surf. It's probably not a sound you are familiar with, Sergeant Hockett. You live only a few blocks from here and you never get to the beach. You're too busy, man. Kick back and listen. It's good for your soul. For all the pleasure you get out of those palms and sandy shores, you might as well live in Brooklyn."

"I've got a living to make," Hockett responded a little defensively.

"Well you're on vacation tonight. And, by the way, this *is* living." Calvin paused a long time as they listened to the waves.

"You'll be in Russia soon enough. I hear the sirloins there are a little difficult to find."

"Those poor folks don't have sirloin, but they'll give you the best they've got. God love 'em. I hope they're generous with information."

Calvin looked at his friend and knew immediately the kind of information he would be looking for. The odds weren't good. It would be an off chance that any information would surface.

The spring vacation fun continued on Saturday. They spent the day fishing on the boat of Dr. George Roppe, a friend from back north. The doctor had a winter home on Sanibel and kept a forty-foot boat with a flying bridge, captain, and first mate on Captiva. During the season, he and his sons and their families and friends kept it busy.

Off season, the captain did commercial fishing. For the past few years, the Hockett and Calvin families had accepted George's invitation, taken their motion-sickness pills, and loaded up for a full day of fishing, lunch, and great sight-seeing. This Saturday was spectacular. The captain had found three holes, the first about thirty-five miles offshore.

It was all the first mate could do to take the fish off the line and bait the hook in time for another go. The girls were almost screaming with excitement. Even Hockett, who had done a lot of fishing, couldn't believe how good the bounty was. The only slow time was at the third stop. Even though the sonar showed there were fish down below, the heat of the day had apparently quelled their appetites. Just as well, Calvin thought. Even though Dr. Roppe's wife, Peggy, was used to fixing fish dinners on the boat's return, there was a limit to how much everyone could eat.

"I'd say it's been a pretty successful day, wouldn't you?" Roppe beamed as he sat on the bridge. He and Hockett conversed with the captain. Below deck, Katie and Celia were napping, tired from the excitement and a little drowsy from the motion-sickness pills. Laney, Barb and Elizabeth sat on the bench seat and nodded off.

Calvin sat outside with his feet up on the side of the boat, content and clear-minded. Being on the water was a real tonic for him. It gave him a chance to fantasize about someday having a boat of his own and taking it out, dropping anchor and writing. He never was on a fishing trip that he didn't recall reading that Ernest Hemingway, who loved to fish the gulf stream, was so good because he could see motion in the water, sense where the big game fish were running, and anticipate when they would hit. And he could turn this closely observed experience into vital fiction.

As they were approaching Blind Pass, Roppe called everyone's attention to the line of white pelicans that were hatched not far from there. It was a spectacular sight, hundreds of the white birds set against the afternoon sky. They flew in a single formation. From a distance, it looked like a chain, hovering just above the surface of the water and extending hundreds of yards, thin and link-like. About every quarter of a mile, the line would loop up as the individual birds reached a certain point over the water. It looked as though they were putting on a flying show—mounting up, as if flying up and over a hill, then settling back and continuing a water-hugging flight line. This went on against the horizon and held everybody's rapt attention.

"It's the thermal currents," Roppe said. "It's amazing how intricate all this ecology is out here."

Calvin smiled in quiet satisfaction. This day in fresh air and water had given him a stronger resolution to deal with the issues that would be presented at the Sunday lunch meeting. This would be a good confab, those concerned with the King estate and the issues that clustered around it.

◆ ◆ ◆

"This is quite a gathering." Conroy stood and held up his wine glass. "Here's to a healthy future for Sanibel-Captiva, free of any bio-weapons. May God smile on our efforts."

Seated around the table with Tim and Laney Calvin were Larry and Mary Lou Conroy, Larry's executive assistant, Claudia Prouse, Ed and Judy Earl, Barb and Dave Hockett, Lee Hamblin, Doug and Sylvia Garret, and Donna Iemer.

"Larry, thanks for your hospitality," Edward Earl spoke as he sat at the head of the table on the Conroy porch on Captiva. "We'll hear from Tim, discuss strategy, and update you on the latest from Craig Merryman on Grand Cayman. And we'll talk about the newest chapter in the saga—the odd man out, Richie Peabody."

"I've heard about the louse Peabody," Claudia said loudly. "He's a real snake. I knew him from the press club."

"What's he got to do with this?" Calvin wanted to know.

"I'll get to that later," Earl told him.

"I don't know Merryman," Claudia interjected.

"He's a young friend of ours," Calvin said. "A bit of a local celebrity and activist on Cayman. Has family all over the island and he's visited us in Indianapolis. Good fellow. He's very concerned about Yuri Bokanyev's influence on his island. I put him in touch with Ed and Doug."

Earl fiddled with his water glass. "He tells us he's turned over material about possible criminal activity to the Queen's Council and the Cayman police command. Trouble is, Bokanyev's a sly old fox. He's been careful to make a lot of friends, and very few mistakes. Merryman is looking forward to the visit of the Calvins and Hocketts. He'll probably have more to tell you."

"You guys need to stay cool when you're down there. Nothing— no activity—unless Ed or I say it's all right," Garret said gravely.

Earl cleared his throat. "Now, I think a good way to get everybody up to speed is to hear from Tim about some of his experiences while he was in the Dominican Republic. Tim, I don't think you've shared this yet."

Calvin speared a piece of avocado and shrimp, then he obliged the group by recounting most of the Dominican Republic adventure.

◆ ◆ ◆

"So clearly Bokanyev is operating out of the Dominican Republic." Calvin took a sip of lemonade. "What worries me is the business about the unsuitability of cave storage."

"Folks, there are important elements here," Earl said, looking at Hamblin. "Congressman, would you go first please?"

"Please, Lee is fine. What is particularly troublesome is the memo Tim retrieved, which talks about the weapons." He put on his glasses. "It reads:

An old comrade says some of the oldest Russian systems are flawed. Not all the weaknesses are known. The east caves are too far from shipment points. The archaeology work makes them too crowded. Salt water immersion or sand storage is probably better.

Lee Hamblin put the memo on the table and looked at those in the circle. "Now, what we know is there are Soviet weapons known as the Petrov-class. They were developed for Afghanistan and are particularly unstable. These things are under a pressure system which intelligence and, in fact, practical experience, have shown to be entirely unpredictable. It is typical of so much of Soviet defense technology." He paused to take a sip of his bourbon and water.

"The fact that Bokanyev has told Rota that all the weaknesses are not known worries me very deeply. What we, and by that I mean western intelligence, have learned is bad enough. If what he has been storing in caves is the Petrov-class nerve agent he may have compounded the trouble. A cave's natural moisture and humidity can only worsen matters. The pressure seals are given to sweating, which causes the Russian rubber to rib and warp. A hard jostle can actually begin to activate the depressurization."

"That's damn frightening," mumbled Claudia.

"We know they had that trouble in Afghanistan. They stored some of the metal canisters in coolers. Once they were removed into the heat of the day, the canisters sweated and, intelligence sources say, there were at least two incidents of premature release."

The group sat transfixed. A light rain fell and rattled the palm branches; nobody noticed it. Hamblin continued.

"The Muja captured some supplies and had the same trouble. They tried to blame the deaths on Iraqi weapons, but it was the Petrov supply. What makes this worse is Rota's comments about storing in salt water and sand. I'm afraid he may be talking about Sanibel. Who'd ever expect that sort of thing down here?" Hamblin finished and sat back and shook his head, looking at the rain splash on the screen.

Earl pointed to Garret. "Doug, I believe you've got something to add to this."

Garret's face was scarlet with sunburn. He touched his nose gingerly. "A little more sun block tomorrow," he muttered, then stood and wiped his brow with a handkerchief. "First, the point of storage. Some buddies in the south Florida field office have taken a, quote—

unofficial interest in the Bokanyev property. These guys love to fish and they've been taking the opportunity to watch what's going on at the old King estate around the boathouse. It looks like he is probably doing something to allow him storage and shipment. He doesn't need a lot of room for these systems, so it could be easily hidden in a structure like a boathouse or even a covered boat rack. It would be an ideal place for a shipment delivery. No customs, no clearance issues. A boat could off-load a smaller craft, simply cut the gulf to Bokanyev's canal, move up to the boathouse, and it's a done deal."

"We know Bin Laden was around these Petrov-class weapons in Afghanistan," Earl interjected. "Excuse me, Doug. He saw the Muja use it. It's our hunch that it's what Bokanyev is trying to broker to him now."

"That's my next point. I said our office has an unofficial interest, because right now we have no probable cause to suspect activity. We can't open an official case. It's not our people who have the Bin Laden communiqué; that came from someone on the spook side. But if we can make some connections here, I can go to some folks and, as a former fed, we can get them to go at it." Heads nodded. Conroy got up to close a couple of windows as the former FBI agent continued.

"And here is where I think we may get something going. There is a slimy little toad lawyer who somehow got on the staff at McAtee Cheskin Ford and Hendricks. Turns out he's the connection. Somehow he's tied to Bokanyev. His name is Richie Peabody. He's told the people at the firm that he intends to leave and move from Indiana. Says he's inherited some property. One of the partners, Don Southland, is on to him like a hawk. Everybody is giving him plenty of rope. This is a great story."

Everyone nodded encouragingly.

"In case you don't know him, or just to remind you," Garret said, "Don Southland is a senior partner and a good man. He used to handle all of the King Steel business. When C. G.'s lawyer down here died, C. G. asked Judge Browne to send all of her stuff up to Southland. Southland's about to retire, so he's looking to hand off a lot of his detail work. Well, Southland plays tennis like a demon." Garret paused to flip a note card and clear his throat.

"He's at National Institute of Fitness and Sport one evening and gets into a doubles match with Ms. Iemer here." He nodded toward Donna. Heads at the table turned.

"The guy is an awesome tennis player," Donna said, shifting in her chair.

"They start talking about Judge Browne and his kidnapping and her breaking him out, and one things leads to the next. Southland says he's been suspicious of this dumbsquat Peabody. He thought he'd been cheating on his billable hours time log. Said the guy had just been acting suspicious. Was there at strange hours, very secretive. Just something about him didn't add up."

"Southland says the guy is a real wimp. Sorta like a big crybaby. It blew me away when we made the connection," Donna said, smiling. "And it gets even better."

"This is almost too much." Garret set his vodka martini down. "Southland's niece is a puzzle genius. Jigsaws, those new stand-up-buildup jobbies, computer puzzles, anything. I mean she's even won awards, beating people three times her age. Anyway he gets the cleaning crew to bag up Peabody's shred bag and trash and his niece puts it together. She finds some stuff, including some communications to and from a Yuri Bokanyev. Boom!"

"That's incredible," Conroy exclaimed, prompting others at the table to exalt the discovery as well.

"Let's hear it for the kid and the cleaning crew," Claudia said, getting up to stand by the window to light a cigarette. Rain began to pelt the window. With a smoke in her mouth, she cranked in a couple of the louvers, finally giving up and snuffing the newly lit smoke, which had gotten damp from the blowing rain. "I'm trying to quit anyway."

"It's about time," several people muttered.

"Well, it's not so clean, folks," Garret countered. "I hate to deflate your hopes, but this is not so easy. Donna, tell them what you've learned."

The wiry blonde stood and, with an ironic smile on her face, spoke in a low key, matter-of-fact tone. "Peabody's in charge of the transfer of hard files to electronic storage. All of the King files have now been batched and transferred. What it gets down to is what's in the file. All of the old hard copy is under Peabody's control, so what he didn't want, he could destroy. All of the files are now computerized, so who knows what he's done? Malcome Browne is still sick, and he still can't remember details. So it is not provable, legally, that C. G. willed her estate to an environmental conservancy."

Doug Garret stood. "Bottom line? Bokanyev may be a legal landowner."

"Engaged in highly illegal pursuits," Calvin interrupted. "What about the tape and the disc C. G. made of her will and the plans for the institute?"

"Good question, Sherlock," Garret fired back. "What about it? Where is it? All we've got now is Judge Browne's hazy, partial recollections of the files versus Peabody's new electronic file. Even with what he can remember, Browne was never the attorney of record. Without the disc, we've got a 'he says' while Peabody has the records."

"Damned outrageous," Claudia fumed, getting up and reaching for her cigarettes.

Garret glanced at her and then back at the group. "My old employer will be watching Peabody to see if he slips up. If Bokanyev's got him on the string, something will come up someday to make him vulnerable. Southland's been helpful. I talked to him before we flew down. He says it looks like Peabody is doing some real estate work of his own. And now we have this statement that he is going to resign. This is my gut hunch, I think the toad is ripping off Bokanyev, probably taking the balance of the King properties for himself. If he is, he'll get nailed. That is, if Bokanyev doesn't kill him first."

◆ ◆ ◆

Calvin's mind was working at high velocity as he turned the key to the condo's front door. The deep blues of the sky and the gulf were what he needed to slow the pace, encouraging serenity to return. The sun flowed in shafts through the seagrapes and palms into the porch and formed squares on Elizabeth's smooth, golden-brown skin. She lay in a gentle, somewhat crumpled repose, swaying slightly in the hammock, a book on her knee, her hands at her side. The little upturn of her nose, her graceful jaw and cheeks as she took in a peaceful island nap, enchanted him. He looked to the pool where Katie and Cee were busy practicing their homegrown variety of a water ballet, splashing and laughing in the unaffected mirth of innocent childhood. For the time being, all three girls, his daughters and goddaughter, were free of the fear and paranoia they had developed about the future. The very peacefulness they enjoyed seemed unsettling.

"What in heaven's name have we done to this world? What insanity have we unleashed for these kids? How on earth can we in any way justify the creation of bio-weapons? You know I'm all for a strong defense, and we need to be a superpower to keep everyone honest, but not this," Calvin said to Laney as he walked into their room to change into his swimsuit.

"It's insane, isn't it?" She shook her head.

"What makes this even more sickening is how this Bokanyev can totally pervert the plans C. G. made to give stewardship of the earth a chance. I don't mean to be overly simplistic, but it's just plain evil. And he's getting away with it. Government agencies overlap; the laws are too easy to skirt; nobody can prove anything. But we know what he's up to. It's nuts!"

"Right now you need to pick up your book and go down to the beach and relax. I'll say it again—this is a vacation. You need a break." Laney rubbed his shoulders and gave him a hug.

◆ ◆ ◆

A wind began to stir up a bit of a chop on the gulf, and the pound of the surf provided a lullaby for Calvin's afternoon nap. Between episodes of drifting into slumber, he read or watched the surf with a parade of shellers passing by. He thought of his late father who used to watch the surf roll for hours. Like father, like son, he thought. He watched as a father and young son of a new generation worked the shell line with two long-handled, basket-like devices. The father wore a red T-shirt. The five-year-old was in yellow swim gear and top. They were colorful as they waded to the edge of the rolling surf. Father would place the basket devices into the surf and with a great flair and seeming effort, pull them out, walk up to the dry sand and dump the baskets. The lad jumped up and down and bounced around, waiting to sort through the shell pile.

Other shellers with their own collection of nets, bags, scoops, buckets or full hands would pass by, giving the father and son some attention. Calvin enjoyed watching the style of gait and manner of approach as the line of walkers passed up and down the beach. It entertained him. Such simple pleasures. This is what the world, the future is really all about, he told himself. It's living for moments like this, moments of contentment, which serve like beacons, guiding to happiness, as one deals with the pressures and stress of everyday life. These are the treasures that any adventurer on the journey of life should seek.

◆ ◆ ◆

Yuri Bokanyev watched the computer screen lower its glow as it went into a sleep mode. He liked the numbers he saw on the spread sheet. The Cayman offshore accounts were pleasing to his eyes. Maybe he should get out of the business and spend some of the money he'd already made. Not yet. These old weapons systems of the Soviet Army could mean lots of cash, and that could buy security. Yes, maybe someday he would just quit it all, but not yet. He was just beginning to build his strength. Someday he would be the most powerful broker in the trade. He had connections, supply, and the unlikely safe haven of Sanibel, with its open access to the gulf and Caribbean. Such an open border.

Bokanyev surveyed the horizon from his command turret. He clicked among the cameras mounted around his waterfront estate, checking them. On the monitor flashed a series of shots: beach, property lines, fence, front gate, driveway, supply shed, pool, cabana, living room, verandah. Monica was standing on the verandah, watching the sun set. He zoomed in. She held a book in her left hand. Perhaps she would like to go out this evening. He longed to enjoy the pleasures he derived when he allowed her to be seen and displayed, and if the truth be told, in spite of himself, he enjoyed her company.

The evening delivered another sensational Sanibel sunset. As the swipes of orange and pink washed across the horizon, the colors reflected in the languid gulf. Calvin had managed to relax through the day, and they had eaten lightly on chilled shrimp and salad. Elizabeth was returning from her beach stroll and Katie and Celia were anxious to get to the Hocketts to watch a video. The mood of the mellow day had settled itself in Calvin's mind and he was less tense about the Bokanyev affair. Cee and Katie had been snacking on chips and cookies, and, for once, he didn't mind the junk food binge. At least Katie was eating and Cee had been laughing.

The moment he entered the Hockett house, Calvin sensed that Hockett was in a sour mood.

"Yeah, how you doing?" Hockett barely looked up from the computer screen as the entourage entered. Barb shot a quick side look at her husband and then back at the group and shook her head.

"David, your daughter is home," she said with a bit of an edge.

"Hey Cee. How are you?" He turned in the chair as she bent down to give him a hug.

"What's your problem?" Celia shot back.

"Oh, I've just got some things on my mind," he said as the girls left the room, heading for the TV.

"You seem a little glum," Calvin observed.

"I'm trapped. I'm so ticked off after our porch conference at Conroys. I want to drive out to the King estate and take the place apart. I want to smash that evil jerk. I really want to bust him up. Beat him to an inch of his life. I've just been thinking all day about how to get him. But, I know that's wrong. And that makes me mad too. I know I'm supposed to forgive him. The church tells me I'm supposed to love him, but, for the life of me, I just can't do it."

Calvin eased in. "You're mad at yourself, too, sounds like it."

"Well, yes. Damn right I am. I'm mad. I mean, when are you supposed to stand your ground for something? Are you ever supposed to not turn the other cheek? This guy comes down here and brings the worst of the world with him. Why? For money? Isn't that getting us to the root of it? How am I supposed to let this guy create chaos and not do something. Cee's having nightmares and maybe working on a nervous breakdown. Katie's in the same condition. She can't eat half the time. This guy may be trying to sell bio-weapons from here! Just let me have a half hour with him. Maybe I can save his soul after I kick his ass!" He picked up a can of computer-cleaning air and blew it loudly into the silence.

Calvin sat down next to his friend. "Well I don't doubt that you could do it, but it's like Earl and Garret said, this guy's a heavy player. Remember what they tried to do to Judge Browne? Remember Elizabeth's pictures of the gun mounts on the upper porches? That's heavy stuff. This is not a guy you can sneak up on. What are you going to do, bust up all the inventory in your shop if he comes in again? Drive him off the road?"

"I know, I know. Barb's been all over me. What upsets me is that I am powerless. I mean, I know what I want to do, but I know I shouldn't even be thinking that way."

"Well you are human. Wasn't it Peter who cut off one of the

guard's ears when they arrested Jesus? Anger is natural."

"Who are you? Dr. Calm? Doesn't this drive you nuts?"

"Yeah it can drive me nuts. And it will if I let it. Hamblin got me interested in C. S. Lewis. So I chilled all afternoon reading him. Good for my head. Good for my heart."

"Too literary for me. That doesn't take the problem away."

"No, but I know Earl and Garret are right. We let this work out the right way. Let them put the thing together. Here we've got a chance. Obviously, this guy Peabody has doctored the will and the real estate papers. Let the authorities catch him. It's going to take a while for all these wheels to work."

"If they do!"

"They will. That'll shut him down on the island. Possibly— likely—they'll even get all of C. G.'s properties back so the study centers and institute will be back in business. At least it'll stop Bokanyev from doing business from Sanibel. And if the feds or some intelligence agency can, they'll crack him for trying to deal in bio-weapons. I think the solution is in front of us."

"I heard all that today. But I also heard the thing about the computer files. You're a Mac guy, so you have a different take on computers. I've been an IBM and PC person for a long time. Trust me on this. If that toad guy that Garret talked about, that lawyer . . ." Hockett looked at Calvin.

"Peabody—at McAtee Cheskin Ford and Hendricks," Calvin replied.

"Yeah, if Peabody put all the records on a computer file, and if he's a lawyer who everybody thinks is honest and honorable, he could have done anything to the will, more importantly, anything to the real estate codicil, and no one is going to know the difference. I'm afraid we can have all the suspicions we want, but there is no way to prove it. What's on a server, or in a file is all we've got. The disc's gone and so are her good intentions. This guy wins. Unless they catch him dealing."

Katie stepped from the doorway, surprising them both. "Hey,

Dad. Mom and Barb say you are supposed to come out on the porch and stop talking about this."

"Okay, hon. I didn't even hear you come in." Calvin and Hockett turned to face her.

"I didn't want to interrupt what you were saying."

Calvin felt a twinge of anxiety. She had a flat tone to her voice and a somewhat distant expression. He feared she had overheard enough of the conversation to erase the therapeutic effect of the fun and carefree joy of the vacation day. It had happened before in the trouble with the metal-plate incident. His meddling put her in harm's away. She was such a delicate child—he didn't want her to slip into that frightening withdrawn condition again.

The red numbers of the digital clock glowed at 2:37. Calvin stepped toward the door that opened to the porch. The surf continued its comforting night sound and the breeze off the beach brought in refreshing coolness. He caught a glimpse of some movement out of the corner of his eye. It was a reflection in the sliding glass door, which opened into the living and dining room of the condo. He turned with a start to see Katie sitting at the counter bar with his laptop plugged into the wall and a modem cable to the telephone.

She turned quickly when he opened the slider.

"Dad, I know you're going to be mad, but listen, I've got something very important here!" She turned back to the laptop and spoke with more seriousness than he had ever heard. It got his attention.

"Dad, look at this. This is a download I got from Cyberfools. It's an old Y2K utilities kit. They found it and put it on their site."

He was, as usual, astonished at the cyber wisdom of his daughter's generation. They were computer techies, but not nerds. This was sophisticated stuff. Perhaps, if she was active, proactive, in dealing with the threat of bio-weapons, she'd feel more in control and less likely to withdraw again.

"I'm not sure what you've got here," Calvin said.

"What you can do is really neat. You can go into programs that were updated. Programs that were written before the new operating systems. Look at this. You can go into sites, and if they have any architecture that is built on the old operating systems or their updates, you can go into a file and get the date that file was written."

"Isn't that hacking? I mean, how can you do that?"

"It's not hacking and it's easy to do. Colleen's mom showed Colleen and me how to do it. Anyway, Mindy's dad works at the law firm you were talking about. I remember they have a funny name that Mindy makes fun of sometimes, like it's a real important thing. Anyway, I went to their site and searched it for King. I found an old file, used Sanibel as a search word and found a lot of pages. This is cool."

"More than cool. This is ice!"

"Yeah, whatever Dad. But look at these pages. They were all scanned and entered in February. You can see the date they were first entered and when the file was written and amended. They all have the same entry date and it says they were scanned in from hard copy on February 15. But look at this. See, these are the entry dates, and here are amendment dates. This one was amended April 3. It's the will and testament of Clara Grace King. Do you see what they did? Someone did something to this document after it was first entered by scanner."

"Katie, I can't believe it. I can't believe you're such a hacker."

"Dad, I told you it's not hacking. It's detective work."

"But I also can't believe how good you are. You've got proof that Peabody, or somebody—and I say Peabody—messed around with the document."

"But that's probably all. All we can show is that the will was changed. If it's been changed, then the real will has probably been overwritten."

"So the real will, the one before April 3, is gone?"

"Probably. Now it got scanned in on February 15 from a hard

copy. Maybe the hard copy is still around. That would be the real will."

"Well at least you've figured a way to show that someone changed the will. That's got to help some."

"Sorry, Dad. There may be a program that can go into the Word file on the change date and find what changes were made, but that is real hacker stuff."

"What is amazing and aggravating to me is that with the right skills you can simply change records and change history so quickly. These people just took over the King estate when she died. It's just a matter of having information."

"Dad, it is the Information Age. And the computer is the application."

"I know honey, but it's kind of scary when one or two people can have so much impact.

"See, no one thinks about the old pre-Y2K programs that have those ancient updates. They are so primitive, really bad geek stuff; the new software can just eat them up." She smiled sweetly and patted the computer.

◆ ◆ ◆

The mockingbird must have been at it for an hour before Calvin finally gave in. He had lain there thinking how the bird was like a morning sentry. First you hear the bird and then your consciousness is drawn to the sound of the surf. What a great way to wake up. He was sure Katie and Elizabeth must still be asleep. He figured Laney had been up for a sunrise walk on the beach. He was elated with what his tech-savvy daughter had been able to accomplish. Despite Hockett's doubts that anything could really be done about these evil persons, Katie had possibly found a way to crack Peabody's manipulation of the King records.

He'd tell Garret and Earl. He also gave himself the task of calling Southland to tell him. Maybe he could find out what happened April

3 or, better yet, find the original will. It was still unclear whether the original document could be recovered electronically, or if Katie had simply learned how to read that it had been altered. It was a long shot at best, and there was still a nagging doubt as to how admissible such evidence would be.

Nonetheless, he thought it amazing that a child was leading them on this technology. It gratified him that she was fighting back instead of retreating in fear, that she had found a way to do something tangible about a horrible mess created by adults. The situation was poetic and almost Biblical, he reasoned as he lay there, beginning to stretch. He also told himself to call Annie Riley at the station and try to get a copy of the tape they made of C. G. King. That could be the coup de grace to Bokanyev and Peabody's scam. Down here, that could be enough to get the legal changes made, to get the property out of Bokanyev's control.

This could be a great vacation after all, he thought. Then he realized he still had no hard evidence, no hard copy, and he wasn't sure Riley would be able to give him the tape. Regret tarnished the pleasant morning atmosphere. If only Judge Browne could have held onto the disc, hidden it, and kept it from being destroyed . . .

Mission Russia

DAVE HOCKETT WATCHED the flat land, small villages, and little *dachas* pass by as he rolled west on the trans-Siberia line. A hundred miles out of Khbarousk, they would switch from the electrical line to diesel for the seventeen-hour journey to Chegdomyn. Each time he made the trip, he slipped into a kind of task-driven or operational mind-set. The flight from San Francisco to Anchorage and then to Khbarousk was the prelude to a changing reality. Now, he was firmly set in the new reality.

On this train ride, he was in first class, with two bunks in the compartment. When he traveled with youth groups and choirs, they usually traveled second class, which meant four bunks to the compartment. He was grateful for the extra space and privacy. He had some things to work out in his head. He was troubled by the impact his frequent trips to Russia were having on his ability to work as a potter and to devote attention to his shop, but he sensed he was doing what was right by following his desire to do church mission work. He came, regularly, as his church had "adopted the town." They had goals: to deliver needed supplies, to establish a youth center and to help incubate a new business in the town. Still, it meant a personal conflict.

Over the last month, since the Calvins had gone back north,

Hockett had tried to put Bokanyev out of his mind to let the "official" route function. He had done a good job of doing so until Calvin called with the disappointing news that the television station had not kept the full interview done with C. G. King. All that was left was a little portion, that part which was used in the Annie Riley Faith Journey story. Riley told Calvin that she and her photographer, Stearns, had made a full copy of the interview so it could be converted to the video disc or CD, which C. G. had intended to become part of her international institute archives. With Judge Browne no longer in control of the house and possessions and with no corroborating evidence, to prove that Bokanyev and Peabody had been up to deceit, the case would be difficult. His anger had again surfaced, though his work to secure medical supplies for delivery in Chegdomyn was keeping him in check. Now that he was en route, he had time to filter all of the conflicting emotions and thoughts that had been troubling him.

He had a special "secret mission" that was also important. He opened his leather folder and turned to the place he had put the picture of Yuri Bokanyev. Earl had given it to Calvin, saying it came from an intelligence source. It was pixelated in the manner of computer files, but it was good enough to allow him to show it around to some of his Russian friends. In the past four years, Hockett had gotten to know many Russians during his frequent trips to Chegdomyn.

It was hard to explain Chegdomyn to the people back on Sanibel. The town was seventy years old, having been started as an exile community during the heyday of Joseph Stalin. There was a nearby coal mine, and political enemies were shuffled off to the wilderness to spend their lives in hard labor in the mine. With the collapse of the Soviet Union, people of Chegdomyn, children of exiles and political prisoners, people who had grown up in the town, began to look to the future with hope. Contact with people like himself and others on missionary trips fueled their hopes and brought assistance. Now Hockett was working with local people to start a brick and pottery factory. It was draining him of his ability to build his own business, but he had somehow been drawn to the plight of the hardworking, long-suffering, kind and giving peasants and workers in Chegdomyn.

After a few hours, the rumble of the rails and the throaty noise of the diesel engine acted as a sedative. The ride created in Hockett a different mood than he ever felt on Sanibel. Outside, heavy birch forests passed by, broken by open patches where acres of day lilies and other spring flowers bloomed. The train rolled over rivers and streams, tumbling fast over boulders and rocks. There were dozens of small waterfalls, and the daylight portion of the trip always reminded him of areas in Canada. He was at a similar latitude as that in Toronto, so although spring had come, it was still brisk and could be cold. The hours rattled away as Hockett thought about the business he had spent twenty years building. He realized that a healthy dose of providential help from good luck and friends made it happen. It had grown from a small, run-down wooden shack-like building to a lovely and well designed studio and shop on a corner lot of Sanibel, a destination for happy tourists and loyal islanders alike.

The business had flourished, allowing him and Barb to transition from sleeping on the floor in a side room of the shop behind a bamboo screen to owning a large and comfortable island home. He had gone from a northern outsider artist/potter to one of the island's leading businessmen. He was a busy churchman who was involved in capital campaigns, youth groups and church mission work. In that context, here he was.

At one time he had been counseled by a friend not to overcommit. Over-commitment could lead to burnout and disillusionment. Now, as he rattled toward Chegdomyn, thousands of miles from sunny Sanibel and his beloved Barb and Celia, he was full of questions. Was he still being nourished by the imaginative, idealistic tap root of his creative and business enterprise? Was he discontented with the life and business that had offered him opportunity? Was his life in some strange transition? Had he taken enough time to tell his staff and his customers how important they were to his life and his success? And, on a more sinister note, was Bokanyev about to bring some horrendous evil to his lovely island and its people? What was he to do about the tremendous conflict he felt and the anger he directed toward Bokanyev? What could he as a father do to alleviate Celia's nervous torment that was still appearing to grow more serious? The answer to that was, not much. The anguish of his own child and his goddaughter, Katie, were symbolic of the troubles children everywhere were experiencing in the complicated, violent world of smart bombs and bio-weapons. Still, there was one possibility.

◆ ◆ ◆

"Dave, you look very troubled. Are you not feeling well?" Randy inquired as the two walked to the dining car.

"No. Just sorting through a lot of stuff in my mind," Hockett responded to his fellow mission traveler.

"Well, this trip certainly gives you time to do that."

They took their seats and watched as the evening sky began to turn deep purple, then darken behind the wide birch forests. Hockett was hungry. He had not eaten since he had bread and coffee at Khbarousk.

"Looks like the standard: pork, rice, potatoes, and cucumber and potato salad," Randy observed.

"Well let's get it on this side of the trip," Hockett responded. He had learned several trips ago that what was served on the dining car to their destination was the same meal served on the way back. The fresh supplies were at Khbarousk, the starting end of the seventeen-hour trip. Any return trip from Chegdomyn meant the food had been put on at the other end of the line. Refrigeration was something that was largely unreliable, so cooking up and serving later was a standard procedure.

"I think I'm going to have a *Peva* tonight, Randy. How about you?" Hockett thought the Russian beer might help him to relax.

◆ ◆ ◆

Later, Hockett pulled the wool blanket up over his shoulder, listened to the clack of the rails, and felt the vibrations pulsating into the thin-mattressed bunk on which he was stretched. He had been tossing and turning most of the night and now waited to hear the matron at the end of the train car begin her routine of heating water for coffee and tea. They would arrive in Chegdomyn mid-morning. After traditional greetings of bread and coffee, they would be taken to the hospital, where the boxes and suitcases full of pharmaceuticals would be joyously delivered and received. Antibiotics, aspirin, ointments and countless other items taken for granted by Americans were in short supply here. Thinking of the gigantic smiles of Dr. Nikolai and his staff, and the haunting eyes of the orphaned baby who had captured his heart on his first trip four years ago, Hockett drifted into a twilight slumber.

The morning sun shone off the weathered wood train depot. Dust, stirred by the dozens of pairs of feet, swirled in shafts of sunlight and gave the welcoming scene a richly mottled light. It always deeply touched Hockett how these desperately poor people who barely eked out a subsistence with virtually none of the items he often took for granted, could be so hospitable. Somewhere, they had found old wallpaper and cut it into a crude, "Welcome Dave & Randy and Mission Russia" sign. The air was brisk and some of the older men still wore their *chapkas*. Hockett had purchased one of those fur hats, but it was packed in his bag. He was warm enough in his flannel shirt and heavy jacket.

"David, David. God bless you. It is good to see you on the mother soil." The big walrus-mustached and ruddy Sergei wrapped Hockett in a powerful bear hug and then slapped his upper arms. "Some of the women baked the traditional salt bread to welcome you back, to your second home, no?"

"I always get a wonderful feeling when I arrive, Sergei."

"It is the spirit which fills you. Dr. Nikolai waits at the hospital, so desperate they are for the medicines you bring. With the international situations so tense, it makes it even more impossible for people here to get these items. You had no trouble with the customs people?"

"We've come through enough times. We are recognizing them and they know us. Plus, we always have, you know, gifts for them."

"Ah, and this is why they know you. David, David, you are becoming a son of Mother Russia, or at least Mother Siberia. Tonight we go to Aleksander's dacha for banya and vodka toasts. This is also custom you like, no?"

"Yes. And I need some advice about a search I'm undertaking."

"Dave said it's been a great week mission-wise," Barb said into the phone. "An amazing thing. Last night he was told about a man who has lived in lower Chegdomyn for thirty years. His name is Bokanyevovich. He says Aleksander and Sergei don't really know him, but think it's worth trying to talk with him. Sometimes people shorten their names and, even though it's a long shot, he might tell Dave something. So far nobody knows anything. I think when he mentions that Bokanyev was KGB, everybody chills."

"Yeah, I'm sure it would scare them," Calvin replied, walking through his living room with the cell phone. "They have long and vivid memories of how brutal the KGB were."

"Tim, tell Barb what Garret told you," Laney instructed from another phone.

"He says the senior partner he's been working with at Peabody's law firm has just about all he needs to nail Peabody. They aren't going to do anything yet, but they've been checking on some of his efforts. He's apparently set up a dummy foundation for himself, taking over the properties C. G. put together for the real foundation. Basically he's put himself electronically in all the documents, taking out the local names. He's got seven locations, seven countries where C. G.'s money was supposed to put local people in charge, answerable to the international board, which was to be run by the study institute staff down there on Sanibel. Apparently he hasn't touched the bank accounts, so the money is still flowing internationally; people are still on the payroll, but, remember, this only started a few months ago and no one has really had time to figure out what's going on. By the time they do, he could be gone."

"It's amazing how clever he is. His timing is very good," Laney added.

"The situation is, if he changes the group leadership and puts himself, or someone he cuts a deal with, in control, then he doesn't have to play with the banking end of it. The money will still go to each operating group, but he'll get it."

"Boy! He is really a snake, isn't he?" Barb said.

"Apparently he hasn't done anything with the Sanibel bank, so that portion of her estate is untouched. Garret says that's good news. If the money had been touched or moved, it might have been tough to get it back into the real foundation. Part of what Judge Browne was doing was helping C. G. hire a staff when she died. He knows who she wanted to put in charge of the study center, institute headquarters staff."

"Is his memory improving that much?" Barb quizzed.

"Not really. He found a few notes at his home which Bokanyev's man didn't destroy. Anyway, until the property issue is settled legally, there really isn't anything to do with getting the U.S. staff in place. Apparently Bokanyev hasn't thought about the money, just the real estate. There are two places on Sanibel: King's on West Gulf and another place on San Carlos Bay. I guess Bokanyev is still in control of those. But Garret says that Don Southland says it looks like Peabody has either screwed up or has intentionally created some real tax issues for Bokanyev. That could be a federal violation, which means the good guys have a chance at getting the real estate back and, incidentally, charges filed against Peabody. Getting Bokanyev is going to be tougher."

"I just can't believe we are all in the middle of something like this again," Barb said spiritedly. "It's like that thing with the old plate you found on the beach. Kidnapping, monkeys running around—trouble."

"Oh, no!" Laney moaned.

The road was pocked and pot-holed, and it took the group past blocks and rows of gray, drab Soviet-style poured-concrete buildings. A few buildings still under construction spread behind the corner lot, with rusting cranes and equipment still standing in place. It looked as though work had stopped on them years ago. Over time, many usable parts had been pirated. The old man Bokanyevovich lived in a small flat which he had occupied since being exiled there in the late 1960s. One of Dr. Nikolai's nurses had an aunt who also lived in the building, and she told the party he was a fine old man, but a man with a heavy heart.

Peabody was amused by Bokanyev's Dominican citizenship, but then, of course, Bokanyev had also acquired an American passport. His old connections had given him the immunity to travel without hassle and without a past, or at least without a real past. The lawyer was mailing a packet of legal documents which would give Bokanyev clear title to the King estate and the land on Woodrings Point, a part of Sanibel even longtime residents knew little of. C. G.'s husband had purchased the land from the county after the cable and pipelines were laid in across the bay years ago. It was thick with mangrove trees and swampy footage, but it also had some bay frontage. Peabody could tell, from reading the real estate and title description, why Bokanyev was glad to get the property. There were a few small fishing shacks and old "leave us alone—we want our privacy" cottages on the point. Only in recent years had others looked at the stepchild waterfront property as being of value. According to the description, the Kings' Woodrings property was at the end of a dirt road and was virtually undeveloped.

There was no power, and the only building was an old, and apparently untended, boathouse that had been used by the cable-layers. It could be another storage or exchange point, again out of public view.

Bokanyev could have the two places, Peabody reasoned, but he'd better enjoy it quickly, because it wouldn't be long before tax problems were sure to loom. Mr. Bokanyev's little empire would come crumbling down while Peabody would have established himself as the proud owner of some of the world's finest beach-front real estate. By the time Bokanyev figured out what he had done, Peabody figured he would have left McAtee Cheskin Ford and Hendricks and proud old Don Southland as well as the manipulative Yuri Bokanyev behind to deal with their own problems.

Peabody wished he knew how to send some of the information to Bokanyev's old employer, the KGB, or whatever they call it now, just to make his life even more painful. It would serve him right after all of the control and manipulation he had exercised for so many years. Yes, soon Peabody would be free of the Russian's control; the packet of real estate papers and documents going into the overnight delivery box would cut the strings.

Bokanyev read the e-mail with a sense of accomplishment. Soon this Sanibel home would be his with legal documentation, which would allow Monica to get started with her redecorating schemes. He could then get the planning and zoning people off his back so he could finish work on his delivery point. In the meantime he would use the old boathouse on Woodrings Point for storage of his commodities, the Petrov-class gas he had purchased from an old comrade who was in league with a retired general from Kiev. He expected to receive the canisters, which had been stored in the Dominican cave, within a month. Already he knew it would be easier to do business from open-water places on Sanibel and Grand Cayman than making the overland journeys in the Dominican Republic. Some of the product was too unstable for the rough travel. Easier in and easier out on the two islands, he thought.

But again unwelcome and unasked for, the personal kept bursting into his mind and interfering with his schemes. Monica's insistence on getting more of the pottery had put him back, face to face, with things he couldn't forget. Troubling to him was the face of that lady at the pottery shop. He couldn't get it out of his mind. Barbara, she had been called. Her image had haunted him from the first time he was in the place. Her face, it reminded him of someone he had buried deep in his past, someone who he had kept sealed off in that dark part of his heart, someone who lived behind the scars. It was the face of his mother, or was it his sister? Touching the thought, sinking to that place where he had forbidden himself, he suddenly felt ill.

Dave Hockett had been immediately touched by the kindness of the old man, so typical of the people he had come to know and love during his mission visits to Russia. The apartment was tiny and the quarters were tight. They sat at the small kitchen table. There was barely enough room for the old man to stand between a chair and the small sink. Next to the table was a tiny hot-top stove on which he had boiled water. Two open shelves which lined a kitchen wall contained maybe only a dozen pieces of china; some of the pieces were chipped and cracked. Bokanyevovich explained they had belonged to his wife. They were old pieces that had been handed down through her family. That and the pictures were all he had of their life together; they were his prized earthly possessions.

Hockett blinked back tears several times as he watched the arthritic old man with gnarled fingers and long gray hair answer his questions. He'd look at the translator, then directly into Hockett's eyes as he awaited the translation. He had been a chemical engineer and lived in Moscow, where he taught and worked for the government on research projects. He had come from a family of merchants, as had his wife. They were both educated and, as they were expected to, joined the Communist Party. Their education, upbringing and party membership assured them a good life.

"So, then, how does it come that I live for the last thirty years alone here in this town of exiles?" he said through the translator. "So tragic is the story that my heart has been of lead. Only the children whom I teach give me life. I put in their hearts a seed of knowledge that life is more than our hard times, and it makes my old heart pump yet another day."

The group sat at the table and watched as the old man held, almost cradled, the wedding picture of him and his wife, taken, he said, more than fifty years ago. They smiled brightly as a somber Orthodox priest stood behind them. It was, he had said, "the happiest day of my life."

Hockett was reluctant to ask what had happened to his wife, when and how she had died. But he was seized by a thought as he looked onto the old picture. Bokanyevovich as a young man was a dead ringer for Yuri Bokanyev.

♦ ♦ ♦

Monica called through the door of the bathroom as she heard Bokanyev retch. "Do you want ice water? Pepto Bismol? Can I bring you something?"

"It is nothing. Only a flu or bad food," he responded, feeling more vulnerable than he had at any point in his life: weak, dizzy, exposed. Why had he opened that sealed chapter, allowed himself to delve so deeply into his past to come again to feel as though his heart had been cut from his chest. He trembled as he looked again at the faded yellow photograph, bent and torn, lying on the floor. There he was as a young boy, holding a wooden boat. An arm reached toward his shoulder. The body it belonged to had been ripped away, and what remained was only a jagged, faded edge of the picture. Standing on his other side had been the woman whose very image now caused him to tremble. He took a bite into a towel to muffle his sob. It was the face of the woman he had loved. When the picture was taken, he knew that tender woman to be his sister. Only a few years later, he would learn she was also his mother, an incest so rank and foul it had shattered his life and now clawed at his insides.

◆ ◆ ◆

The old man, Bokanyevovich, took the picture from Hockett's hands, held it at arm's length while his blue eyes stared laser-like at the pixelated image. Hockett felt the blood pressure in his own body begin to surge. There was a thick silence as he and the translator watched the old man scan the picture of Bokanyev. His hands passed over the face. After what seemed like several minutes, the man held the picture to his chest, sat back in his wooden chair, closed his eyes and titled his head back. It seemed to Hockett that he was trying to take the picture into his heart.

"Is it someone you know? Is it your son?" Hockett broke the poignant silence.

The old man blinked his eyes open. With both hands he carefully put the picture on the table in front of him as though it were a fragile piece of glass. He glanced up at the translator to say what he wished Hockett to know.

"This is the man who used to be my son," he said through the translator, carefully running his hand over the picture again as though stroking a child's face.

"I know this man. I have seen him." Hockett's throat felt tight and his tongue was suddenly dry and parched. "He is not involved in good things."

"I will tell you the secret of his heart. It is also the reason my heart is so like lead. I have not seen even a picture of him for thirty years. May I keep this? It will be a joy to me in the days I have left."

"Yes, of course." Hockett's head was whirling. The image of the man he had grown to despise, a man who aroused in him a desire to hate, the man who confused him spiritually—Hockett's feelings seemed somehow altered by the knowledge that he was loved by a father. His enemy was someone's beloved son. The translator's voice was soft, sympathetic.

"You have done the Lord's work. You bring to an old man a knowledge that his son is still alive. You must not hate this boy, even for bad things he does. His heart was made poison and he is a victim. I am old and I can say these things now." He crossed his knees and his eyes grew distant. "Thirty years ago, my son Yuri was a university student. He was not a great student, but his scores were in the upper third of his ranking. He was a good debater and even more accomplished in soccer and swimming. He was strong and handsome."

"I can see he was a good-looking boy." Hockett smiled and nodded to encourage the man to continue what was obviously a difficult story to tell. He disliked the pauses for translation, but they were necessary.

"Like young men his age, he was going from university to the military. Yuri had desired to fly and so hoped for the air corps, but instead he was recruited by KGB. Recruit is a term which makes it seem to be a choice. Yuri had no choice; he was told it was his obligation, and I think he welcomed the idea of serving his motherland by traveling in the world. One night he tells me his future. On the next day, my future is forever changed and I never again see Yuri." The translator finished the long translation. The old man paused and picked up a tea cup to sip at the by-now cool brew.

"This must be very difficult for you. I'm sorry."

The old man waved his hand even before the translation was complete.

"No, please. I must burden you more with my pain. On the next day, after Yuri and I celebrate his future, even though it filled me with a dread, men from the government came to my flat to tell me I was to be relocated for my protection. At that very moment, I was made to pack what I could in a case and leave. No farewell. No explanation to relatives, colleagues or the friends who lived nearby. Just in that moment, I was put out of my home with what I could pack and boarded on a long trip to Chegdomyn. Relocated, they said, because my son was to do—what do you call it—classified work in the government and I was to be 'protected.' Only later did I learn that meant protected even from contact with Yuri. So very sad never to say good-bye. Here I have been for thirty years." He was silent a moment, evidently considering those long years, then looked up again to speak to the translator, a frizzy-haired, middle-aged woman with sympathetic eyes.

"At first I was visited by agents of the government. I should say I was spied upon. I was told never to mention my son or his work. I was told never to explain my old life, only to say it was now my duty to teach science to the children of this region. After a few years they ceased to come, they ceased to care because they had broken forever the link between my flesh and blood and me." His eyes clouded with a mist of tears, which he blinked away.

Hockett was at a complete loss of what to say, or even to think. How odd that thousands of miles away on his sunny island, where his life was full of friends and customers, was the man who had grown to be his nemesis and who was, conversely, the object of such love and longing for this sad old man.

"Here now is the story which break his heart. Please to hand to me that little wooden chest," he said to Hockett. He pointed to a small, dust-covered little box with a lock sitting between some old books on a small shelf near the only upholstered chair in the small flat.

With the slow and deliberate movement of arthritic fingers, he unlocked and opened the box and removed a folded photograph.

"I know this is safe in your knowledge. For these years I have kept it, though it surely could have put me into the Gulag."

Hockett and the motherly translator looked upon the scene that the camera had captured. A young Yuri held a boat as the old man, years younger, extended his arm around his shoulder. Next to them was the smiling face of a younger woman. How odd! The woman actually looked a little like Barb.

"Is that your wife, Yuri's mother?" Hockett asked.

"No. This is the point of the great sadness. She is a woman named Yelana who was the young cousin of my wife. Yuri's mother, the love in my heart, Angelica, died from tuberculosis when Yuri was a small boy. Yelana, who had been trained in nursing, was there in the days of her sickness. My work would not permit me to care for Yuri alone and the only choice was send him to a government school to be trained. This I did not wish to do."

Hockett nodded again. "I can understand."

"Yelana was from a small village. To live in Moscow would permit her to know the city and to learn. She stayed with us, to be a mother to Yuri. Yuri knew her as his sister. He thought of her as his sister. I never tell him different, because in Russia to pretend a thing can be reason for prosecution. It seemed a little crime and to a young boy it was a comfort."

He leaned forward confidentially. "But when KGB get him and begin to train him, they tell him that Yelana was not only his sister, but also his mother. So disgusting a lie. I learn this many years later and know why Yuri never would write or visit. He has hate in his heart for me. He was made to think that I am a sick beast, that I had twisted lives by my own desires. He believes the poison the KGB use to steal away his life to make him belong to them. You see, if he hates me and wants to have no contact, then he can belong to them with all his mind and heart. This is how they did it. This is how they steal him from me. This is why his heart has grown so full of hate." The old man looked at Hockett. "Please tell me that he is in health and he is not destitute. Nothing more do I think I want to hear."

◆ ◆ ◆

Hockett let the intense heat of the banya sauna sear into his aching shoulders and neck. It had been three days since his conversation with a tearful Bokanyevovich, and he still had not reconciled his contradictory thoughts about the old man's son. He had been busy with the work of the mission trip and found that he could bury his emotions in the work. This evening, getting close to the time of his return to Sanibel, he was focused on the quandary.

Later, out of the sauna and in the garden of Sergei's dacha, he welcomed the rounds of vodka. Each shot, downed in a toast, was an antidote to the frustration and simmering anger. As the toasts continued and the good cheer of the fellow celebrants became louder, Hockett found that he wished to act on what he knew. Oddly, he wanted Yuri Bokanyev to have the knowledge the old man had given him, to know the truth about his life. It seemed only right. The desire in him was strong, but if and when that could ever happen only the Lord could know. It did not seem likely, given the circumstances.

The Sanibel Stopover

"I CAN'T BELIEVE WE got you off the island and over here in Fort Myers," Jayne said, handing glasses of champagne from the silver tray Brian held.

"This is one of the great unknown destinations in south Florida," Calvin responded, hoisting his glass of bubbles in a toast. His eyes swept the Bakers' Victorian garden, with sitting "rooms" and bejeweled walking stones. The place was rich and fragrant with herbs and blooming flowers; twinkling lights strung on palm trees and shrubs created a fairyland-like atmosphere.

"Well, we keep working on it and it keeps growing," Jayne laughed.

"We've got the time now," Brian added.

"We've hosted a couple of private parties here. People seem to enjoy it. It is different," Jayne said, taking a seat beneath the umbrella.

"This is amazing. You'd never know from the street this is behind your house. This is so neat," Elizabeth remarked, returning from the newest "room" in the garden, along a recently constructed fence wall.

Calvin sat back and relaxed in the mood of the mellow evening. Tomorrow the Calvins, Hocketts, and Bakers were flying to Grand Cayman for an early summer vacation. Laney, Elizabeth, and Katie were excited about snorkeling and beach time. Hockett had gotten over the nasty cold that had attacked him near the end of his mission trip to Russia, and he seemed more relaxed. He'd told Calvin he was "making peace with himself" over the Bokanyev problems.

Bokanyev had been stopped from occupying the King estate by a lawsuit filed by neighbors. Their protest centered on the unapproved construction project Bokanyev had tried to begin. The zoning board ruled on a temporary injunction. Only approved and environmentally certified building or construction projects were permitted on Sanibel, especially when it involved access to the gulf front. The former Russian spy had apparently spent most of the last month at a home someplace else. The FBI had continued to monitor him. Even though the King estate was his, there was still the concern about canisters of Petrov-class bio-weapons. For the time Hockett was content to let the system work.

The Bakers were also more relaxed. Their "retirement" after the sale of the Mad Hatter had given them a chance to catch their breath. Calvin, too, was looking forward to a week of downtime. It would be a great break, he thought. His stomach growled. Now he was also looking forward to Brian's new "discovery"—the Cameo restaurant on McGregor Boulevard, just about five blocks from Brian and Jayne's home and their magical garden.

"Gee, Sylvia, I wonder if the Sanibel crew knows that Bokanyev spends most of his time on Cayman. I mean it's a big enough island; there shouldn't be any trouble, but you never know." Doug Garret worked on his grill, moving hot charcoals about to balance the heat. Sylvia set the table on the upper deck, which offered a sweeping view of the lake and their long, rolling hillside lawn.

"Maybe you can call them, Doug. Tell them to keep their eyes open. I imagine they're just going to spend most of the time at the beach."

"Yeah, but Dave's a big guy and he and Bokanyev have already picked up some hostile vibes from each other. You know Dave probably wants to smash the guy. And our guys say Yuri's probably about to take possession of a shipment of stuff he's had stashed in the Dominican Republic. They're not sure if it's headed for Cayman or Sanibel."

"On the way where?"

"On the way to being sold, maybe to the guy behind the embassy bombings, maybe to a foreign power. Somebody who wants a weapon for mass destruction or suffering. Any terrorist group."

"Why are we so calm?"

"There's nothing we can do, and that steams me. It's working through the bureaucracy. There are jurisdictional issues. The feds have their hands tied. Our guys in Florida would love to shut him down, but what's he done? All we know is that we suspect canisters of bio-agents are on the way, but we don't know when or where. We've got nothing we can take to court. This guy didn't make it as a spy for thirty years because he's stupid. But remember this, Sylvia, we are smarter. Somehow, between the Dominican Republic and Sanibel, we're going to get to him."

"Honey, here come Amy and Andy. Let's drop it. I don't want the kids to hear any of this," Sylvia said, walking back into the sparkling kitchen.

◆ ◆ ◆

"What a find," Calvin said, hoisting the glass of Brunello. Brian smiled and nodded his agreement.

"Are you making notes?" Jayne asked, finishing the remains of her chervil-crusted salmon filet, accompanied by braised endive-vegetable soufflé, citrus couscous and chive butter sauce.

"Indeed." Calvin smiled as he continued to write on the back of the menu. He had started with the champagne lobster and pasta with caviar appetizer and had opted for the ostrich entree with a pistachio and dried cherry sauce. Others began with the wild mushroom, leek, and goat cheese brulée and the roast bob white quail with smoked sweetbread mousse served on truffled mashed potatoes and roasted shallot merlot reduction. Entrees had been passed around the table and included the roast rack of lamb Persille, roasted free range chicken with wild mushroom and foie gras duxelle, pilaf and lemon thyme, and the Chilean sea bass en papillote.

"You'd never know from the outside, just a little place in a strip mall, what's inside, would you?" Brian surveyed the beige-walled room, which was highlighted by a wall-sized mirror in the back. Each side was lined with four thick-padded and high-walled booths in green and orange. Two long tables had been pushed together for the Calvin-Hockett-Baker party. They stood in the middle of the carpeted, dimly lit room.

Tiramisu, cannolis, ice cream, and chocolate mousse accompanied by espresso, cappuccino, and a serenade by Alfredo, the manager-maître d', rounded out the notes Calvin made before the parties said good-night in the parking lot.

◆ ◆ ◆

"Doug was nervous about you being here tonight," Sylvia said to Larry and Mary Lou Conroy as they relaxed in the deck chairs, watching the Hoosier moon on an early June night. Amy Garret was clearing the table and Doug had gone to get the port.

"The sunset down here in Morgan County reminds me of my boyhood home, just a couple counties away," Conroy said, putting his feet up on a planter box. "The tenderloin was perfect. What did he have to be nervous about?"

"Actually, I was really concerned it was going to rain and we wanted to be out here by the lake," Garret said, striding back onto the porch with port and glasses on a tray. "It's not quite like your place on Captiva, but we love it."

"Oh, it's wonderful here," Conroy said, taking a port off the tray and examining it in the light of the moon. "Beautiful. You worried about rain? Well I talked with Lee Hamblin today. He said they had a lot of rain in May down on Sanibel and Captiva. He said it kept him off the golf course and at his computer. He says the report is just about done."

Garret clipped a cigar and offered it to Conroy. "Has he heard anything new on the King property?"

"He said Bokanyev has been pretty much stopped from doing anything with the estate until the restraining order issue is settled. Don't you love how sometimes the red tape works for you?" Conroy lit his cigar and took a couple of puffs, exhaling the smoke on a slight breeze. "In the meantime, his lawyer up here, Peabody, has quit McAtee Cheskin Ford and Hendricks, and Don Southland says there's an internal investigation that may end up going to the prosecutor. Internal issues and apparently what could be a prosecutable crime. Is that right?"

"Correct." Garret swatted at a mosquito. "I understand the IRS has something on him. I think the feds will get him on a few charges because of his takeover of some of King's foreign properties. Judge Browne's found his own batch of documents. He's going to send copies of them to some UN bodies. They had details of C. G.'s arrangements with several governments to set up the environmental centers. Peabody thought he had the complete file, so he pulled some chicanery, not realizing there were other records. They will at least show he hasn't played it by the book.

"Doug, you didn't tell me that," Sylvia said, leaning forward. "Let me have a puff on your cigar. I feel a little better about this now."

Garret handed her the cigar but gave her a long look. "But C. G.'s dream may die. The will is the governing document. We still don't have anything that proves the electronic version of the will is fraudulent. Katie Calvin's little discovery about amendment dates only raises a question; it doesn't prove anything."

"I guess her original wishes would have to be known, huh?" Conroy asked.

"Yep. That now seems impossible. I'm afraid the original will and all her intentions are like the lady herself, gone. It's a damned shame. Her idea of environmental control was pretty well thought out. But I do believe the IRS is going to get our little creep." Garret held his port glass up to the light to examine its rich luster.

"Well it's nice that one of our federal agencies is doing something in this mess. Man, this is a great port, Doug. Nice color too," Conroy said with relish.

"Thanks. You know what troubles me, Larry? Bokanyev is still in business, still expecting to operate on Sanibel, definitely on Woodrings Point, and so far there's nothing that can be done except stop the remodeling of the King estate. I think Ed Earl's got the neighbors riled up and organized enough they can keep Bokanyev tied up with legal hassles. But he's still got some hooks in."

"And God only knows where those canisters are," Sylvia said with disgust.

Seven Mile Sun

"WHAT DOES 'HE HATH founded it upon the seas' mean, Dad?" Katie asked as they moved through the customs line. She pointed to the large coat of arms that hung over the main doors of the Owen Roberts Airport terminal.

"That's the symbol of the island. 'He hath founded it upon the seas' is from the Old Testament. Do you see the turtle on top of the pineapple?"

"Yeah, and the lion and the stars."

"Very British, isn't it? It's a coat of arms. This is an English island. In fact, all those military planes on the runway are here for the air show which is part of the birthday celebration for the Queen. There'll be a big parade as well."

Celia joined them. "Cool. Will there be bands?" she asked. "I want to go back to the turtle farm too."

Calvin listened to the excited buzz of conversation of others waiting in line, eager to begin their time on the gleaming stretch of Seven Mile Beach and in the clear waters so inviting for divers and snorkelers. Katie and Celia were bounding with energy. Laney, Dave, Barb, and Brian were talking about restaurants and groceries, while Jayne and Elizabeth discussed the best dive spots.

Calvin was looking for their Cayman friend, Craig Merryman, whom they had met on their first visit years ago. Craig was a member of the Cayman Olympic bicycling team and was still a bit of an island celebrity, appearing on radio and television as an environmentalist and a planned-growth advocate. Calvin smiled as he thought of Craig's almost constant flow of chatter and the fact that he always called him "Jim." He had enjoyed recent conversations and e-mails with him over their friend Bokanyev. Then too, having a young friend on the island had always been a plus, he reasoned, and it gave the girls a cross-cultural, cross-racial experience.

A bright morning sun beamed on the pavement outside the terminal. All that was left to claim from the baggage track was the dive bag. Calvin watched as new pieces appeared from the back of the carousel.

"There's Craig," Laney chimed.

The large smile on the man's face reflected the island's mellow charm. "Hey, Jim, how you doin', mon? Oh, look at these ladies. They be looking like they ready for the island sun." He beamed at Celia and Katie who were suddenly bashful.

There were quick hugs and reintroductions all around.

"This is a cousin's van I've borrowed, mon, so we can save you a cab ride. But I've got to stop by the office real quick. You can see where I work if you'd like, yeah?" Craig said, pulling away from the taxi lane where he had commandeered a spot. Having so many relatives on the island gave him an advantage.

Craig Merryman explained that Merryman Security was responsible for the delivery and security details of all air cargo and freight that arrived on the island, after it was cleared and approved by Cayman Customs. The office was adjacent to the runway. Small and tidy, it was a busy working center. Phones, faxes, and two-way radios were alive and buzzing. Three women and two men were busy with the details of air commerce. Craig's office was along the back and featured a large window which overlooked the runway operations.

"Tools of the trade?" Calvin asked, pointing to a pair of binoculars and a long-lens camera on his desk.

"Oh, mon," Craig sighed. "They help but I be using them mostly for that strange cat who come to the island I told you about. He comes in the middle of the night, and his men who be surroundin' him all carry weapons. I've been payin' attention to this dude, mon. He's very rich. He buy up a lot of property. He even take an old resort and turn it into his own private place, mon."

"I know that heavy player," Calvin said. "We're on his trail."

"Very heavy, mon. Russian Mafia. I've checked him out—Yuri Bokanyev—and he is a very bad dude. And he is here now."

Calvin and Hockett exchange surprised glances. Could the timing have been worse? Could they never avoid the man?

"It's a very sad thing, mon. This evil man can wreck the tranquillity of your island and mine, just by himself and his greed." Craig sipped a beer while sitting in the shade of the cabana on Seven Mile Beach.

"I don't want Barb or Celia to know a thing about this," Hockett said resolutely.

"Same goes for Laney and the girls. It'd wreck the mood, ruin the week," Calvin added as he watched them on the beach and in the clear water, all full of smiles.

"I think Brian knows you have troubles on your heart, David. You've got to get some island mellow or he'll be buggin' you to know what is the problem. I myself do not like it at all. But I know the good Lord will work it out. He don't want a thing like that on this island."

"I've got something that may help get you into the island mind-set. I'm going to do salt fish and acee for dinner," Calvin said, smiling at Hockett.

"That's what you stunk up our condo with the last time we were here, right?" Hockett said emphatically. "You're not even thinking about using our kitchen, are you? 'Cause it's closed to salt fish and acee, mon."

"Oh, mon, you talking about one of the real dishes now. I may be workin' on me appetite." Craig's smile lightened the mood.

Right Side, Wrong Way

THE WEATHER WAS PERFECT, with warm blue skies and irresistible crystal clear water that broke into a cobalt blue or turquoise out below the horizon. The group had spent hours snorkeling, observing the fascinating reef world below. Elizabeth went diving with Brian and Jayne. Calvin served casual lunches each day and the late afternoon included discussions about the evening's dinner plans. "In the condo or out, what or where" rang out as the group gathered for wine or rum drinks and the turn of the earth signaled the onset of a Cayman evening. Relaxation was well seated in them all by Wednesday.

The group, minus Barb, Dave, and Jayne, loaded into the beach rover and were bound for Eden Rock for another round of astonishing snorkel views on the reef southwest of Seven Mile Beach off Georgetown. Nearby was Devil's Grotto, Parrot's Reef, and Seaview. Calvin thought he had done a good job of acclimating to the right hand drive, though he would occasionally flip on the wipers when he intended to get the turn signal.

He was driving east on West Bay Road when another tourist car pulled from the drive of the Grand Pavilion and lapsed into driving on the U.S. side of the road. It came straight toward the rover. Calvin honked and made a quick right onto a long drive to avoid collision.

Cars that had been coming from other directions and driveways darted at Calvin, as the offending driver tried to correct and spun out of control, threatening the tight knot of traffic. Calvin saw the other cars dash toward him, and he accelerated up the long grand driveway.

All they heard was the squealing of tires and the rip of gravel and road grit. No bang of metal, thank heavens.

"Everyone okay?" Calvin had stopped the rover and was turning to look at the group, some of whom had been sitting sideways on the benches behind the middle seats.

"We're okay. We're fine. Good maneuver!" Brian intoned.

"Dad, isn't this the place Craig was telling you about? The weird guy who bought the resort and turned it into his own home?" Elizabeth asked.

"You're right," Laney said. "Last time we were here, this was a resort. But they've done something with the lookout tower. Remember how it used to be open?"

Calvin's attention was drawn to the glass turret. Yes, he thought, they're right, this is Bokanyev's Cayman control center. One day when Craig was helping him fix a lunch, he had told Calvin about Bokanyev's estate. They were eventually joined by Elizabeth, who had been in another room of the condo. As a result, she knew more than he'd intended for her to.

"This place is awesome!" Celia observed, taking in the tennis courts, manicured gardens, and the size of the building.

"Quite a place for one guy," Brian said. "What kind of business is he in, or dare we ask?"

"It's dare we ask," Calvin said. He was faced with only one route out of Bokanyev's lair. He had to proceed up the drive to a circuit of the circle to return to West Bay.

"It's too far to back up. I'm going to swing around the circle," he explained.

"Oh, Tim. We shouldn't be doing this," Laney lamented.

As they headed toward the sprawling pink edifice, a man appeared on the circular drive. He wore dark glasses and, from what Calvin could see, he had a strong upper torso and arms with a narrow waist.

"Buddy the Bouncer," Brian sneered.

The man stood on the drive, blocking Calvin's progress on the circle.

"Sorry. We made a wrong turn. We were trying to avoid an accident. Didn't mean to bother you," Calvin said, leaning out of the window, feeling dumpy and out of shape as he looked at the specimen who stood with his hands on his waist and glowered at the car.

Calvin looked at the grand entrance on the porch. Two more men of similar build stood in the doorway; an attractive and elegantly dressed woman brushed past them. She briskly walked toward the man on the drive and said something to him, then headed back toward the house.

The man approached the car and looked in. Though his eyes were hidden behind the dark glasses, the motion of his head gave the indication he was examining everyone very thoroughly.

"This is private. Didn't you see the sign? Now leave!" His voice was harsh, intending to threaten.

The group in the rover was silent and their eyes were large as Calvin completed the circle of the driveway, drove past the grand entrance, and headed back up the long drive to West Bay.

Celia was the first to break the silence. "We know that lady." She turned on the bench seat to stare out the window as the group on the circle drive grew more distant.

"I saw her at the shop. They had a cool yellow car. They bought one of Dad's big vases. Her husband, or whoever he was, did something really weird. I saw him do it when I was riding up to the door. He got out of the car, got something out of the trunk, like a folder, and got a CD or something out of it. He put the CD thing down inside Dad's vase."

Calvin turned to look at Celia, not believing what he had heard. As his eyes darted toward her, he caught a glimpse of the turret tower, his attention captured by something glinting from behind the rounded glass wall.

Bokanyev stood with binoculars to his eyes, watching the rover loaded with tourists leave his driveway. He looked at his Rolex, which sparkled in sunlight coming through the open skylight. Nine-thirty. It was an old habit, checking the time as he observed. Another old habit asserted itself.

"Follow that group," he said into a speakerphone, knowing that in just moments one of his men would be on a motorbike and on the tail of the intruders.

Even the magnificence of the sights he was seeing as he snorkeled could not capture Calvin's attention. He was stuck on the revelation from Celia. Could it be the missing disc, the full interview, pictures and transcript and the complete file of C. G. King's plans for the international environmental study and monitoring centers? The thought of the existence of the disc warmed and elated him. But it also dismayed him. What if the disc had been destroyed? He wondered about the chances that it was now forgotten about, tucked away in a Hockett vase. He remembered Hockett telling him later about that first encounter with the odd Russian, whom he later learned was Bokanyev. They had purchased the large piece, only later to ask for a companion. Hockett had told him the woman said she wanted the ceramic creation for her Sanibel home which she was about to redecorate, an old estate they had only recently moved into and were still 'cleaning up.' Well, something had to be done about this. The old reporter's intuition was back. It was that same kind of hunch feeling that he had felt countless times since he was a kid. It was the same thing that drove him when he was working for his Ph.D. in history. It was the same force that kept him on the trail of the old metal plate in the "Sanibel Arcanum" business a few years ago. He was "onto something."

Now that he had located Bokanyev's Cayman estate, he just "felt" that in fact the Hockett vase was there someplace and probably contained the disc that could end all the mystery and definitively put

Bokanyev out of business and off the island. There was no hard reason to believe any of this, only a chance revelation and the instinct. Now all he had to do was get that disc.

Lately, Richie Peabody's North Meridian Street home seemed too small, as if it were collapsing in on him. Actually, it was his life that was imploding.

It had started in a small way. His step-kids seemed to hate him for moving them from Zionsville into what they called his "trophy house." Even their mother, his wife, had been riding him about it. Nasty nagging, but nothing serious—just unpleasant. He thought he could restore their favor when he told them he had suddenly acquired choice oceanfront property, but now that was never going to happen.

First he'd been put on notice by the IRS that he was the target of an investigation into falsified record keeping. He thought he could evade that by blaming it on phony records he had been given by a client. He had set Bokanyev up, so he could throw the blame elsewhere. But then he was drilled by the compensation committee at McAtee Cheskin Ford and Hendricks for violations of time accounting. It was that damn Don Southland who was behind the invasion of his professional life. The only way they could know what he'd done is if they read his private notes and his communications to and from Bokanyev. Just two hours ago, he learned that is exactly what had been done. Called before the senior partners group in a formal inquiry in the board room, they put his shredded documents on the table in front of him. They had been painstakingly pieced together by Southland's niece. Furthermore, they were considering seeking criminal charges.

But the coup de grace was the confrontation that occurred as he arrived home on what had been the worst day of his life. Oddly, his wife's Mercedes SUV was on the drive.

He entered the house to see her bags by the side door. Entering his study, he came face to face with his mother-in-law. She was sitting in his chair, behind his prized desk. His wife stood with her left hand on her hip, always a sign of anger, and her right hand holding a remote control. She shot him a lethal look, then clicked the remote control at his TV set.

There he was, on the tape, in Mexico city—naked, obese, and with two women. Before the tape had played even twenty seconds, his mother-in-law ejected it from the player, dropped it into a manila envelope, tucked it under her arm, took her daughter by the hand, and stood inches from his face.

"You'll be hearing from our attorney."

Peabody no longer felt clever.

Sweet Light Ride

"THIS IS SERIOUS," Calvin said quietly into the phone. "After we ended up at his estate, he put someone to following us. I saw one of the muscle guys at Eden Rock and again that night at dinner."

"Not a very good tail if you spotted him twice," Garret commented on the other end of the line from Indiana.

"Well I haven't seem him since."

"Probably just professional paranoia. He wanted you checked out, to make sure you weren't a cover. Stay away from him and you don't have anything to worry about."

"Doug, I'm almost sure the disc is here. I mean, I just know it is."

"Sorry, bucko, your hunch is nothing the authorities can go on."

"I know. Craig set us up with his cousin; he's one of the Queen's Council staff. They all know about Bokanyev, but they say there's very little they can do either."

"These spooks are like shadows. They can slip out of anyone's hooks. Bokanyev is a master spy."

"He's made significant contributions and has endeared himself to some of the Majority Party. Even those who are supportive think he's trouble, but he's given them absolutely no reason to challenge him. There's no hope of getting something like a search warrant."

"Listen, Tim, the guy's really smooth. He wouldn't have succeeded in his business if he wasn't good. You've got to let some people up here figure it out. Just stay away from it. You guys aren't pros."

"I'd like to take a look inside that place."

"Not on your life, ace. You could get in way over your head."

◆ ◆ ◆

The intense sun drove Calvin into long periods of baked slumber on the beach. As active as his mind was, the Caribbean heat and light and the splash of the waves caressed him into temporary relaxation. Hockett wasn't so easily distracted from his worry. He had spent most of the last day and half wearing a frown. Clearly he was trying to figure a strategy.

"Hey, mon, am I in time for lunch?" Craig's voice broke into Calvin's sun-induced cat nap. Hockett joined them from his recliner, which had been set under the cabana.

"Craig, how are you? I was off in space somewhere there. What do you know?" Calvin said.

"This is very good. The hanger says that Bokanyev plans to fly twice today. Sometime around three. He will be back about eight. Then he'll go back out tonight sometime. It will probably be around one or two A.M. The word is, he is going to Casa de Campo, outside Santo Domingo on the Dominican Republic. That's a short hop for his fast jet. He do a lot business there and make these jumps often. Then I believe he is to going to your island. So this is good news."

"How do you mean good news?" Calvin asked as he stood.

"We have been watching him, Jim. His comings and his goings. When he go like this for a short visit he leave only one security. And we know this security man has a girlfriend, who is also a cousin. It always work out that she call him when the boss be out of town."

"Pretty slick. Have you been in the place, then?"

"No, but we used the times to get pictures of the security systems and to see what we can. He got cameras around the place so we have to be careful. We know where the cameras are, because they were installed by some friends. This is a small island and we are almost one big family."

"So what are you saying?"

"I say we take a bike ride at five-thirty when the security man be with his woman. The sun be starting to set and the light will be golden. Easier to slip around by. The light off the water sparkles and reflects, so some of the back cameras close the iris down to like a squinty eye. We can evade 'em. So we know which door to go to and how to get around his alarm there."

"Oh, man, we're going to have to be cool. We can't let the gals know what we're doing."

"They be your ladies, mon. I leave that to you."

"The ride might be good for you, but you be careful, sweetie." Barb kissed Hockett as he headed toward where Calvin and Elizabeth were unlocking the bikes which went with the condo. Craig was astride his own road bike.

"I can't believe you're actually going for a ride," Laney said to her husband. "In all the years we've been coming here, you've never taken the bikes out."

"I don't think we'll be gone too long," Calvin said, masking the fear and frustration he felt. Elizabeth was on to what he, Craig, and Hockett were up to and now insisted that she be included. He was fearful that not only was he going to be in jeopardy, but that his eldest child was as well.

"I am an adult and have every right to decide for myself. I'm glad you still care what happens to me, but the truth is I'm in better shape than you are. You've got to let go," Elizabeth asserted. Craig assured him it would be no problem, and that she could stay as a lookout.

He was frustrated because he couldn't simply exert his parental influence. She was right. She was, after all, an adult. She was over twenty-one and was capable of taking care of herself. She probably was in better shape than he was. That hurt, and he was unhappy that he was unable to prevail and say no.

Brian was in their condo preparing an appetizer, and Jayne was at work on dessert. Barb and Laney had made a blender of piña coladas and were working on a fruit salad on the adjoining balcony patio. In the Hockett kitchen a pork loin was marinating. Hockett planned to grill it with fresh fish. Celia and Katie were on the beach and in the water. The good mood and relaxed state of mind was an easy ally for Calvin's getting the bike ride approved.

◆ ◆ ◆

Craig led the group along West Bay and into the parking lot of a hotel. From there they followed a service road around the nursery and equipment shed. To Calvin's surprise, there was an alley-like passage between several of the resorts and hotels. It was used for lawn and beach care vehicles and for the jitneys, which delivered the work staff to the large buildings out of the sight of the guests and tourists. Because Bokanyev's place had formerly been a resort, the alley led to its back side along the property line and beach access. It had been fenced and blocked with an out-shed which was easily breached at the beach approach.

Craig seemed confident enough.

"This is one of the camera angles that will be blinded by that sweet light. But stay close to the fence until we get back to the edge of the greenhouse. Then follow me and duck when I wave. Stay close, mon. Elizabeth, as soon as we go around that corner of the building, you stay on the corner of the patio porch and watch this way. If someone come, blow the whistle I gave you. Cool?"

"Cool," Elizabeth said calmly, and with a half smile held up an old-fashioned silver police whistle on a lanyard. "Don't worry, Pop. I'll keep you covered."

Calvin swallowed hard. He was proud, but also remorseful that he was exposing his daughter to this situation.

◆ ◆ ◆

"I see the vase! It's on the upper floor next to those French doors, right past the L-turn in the building," Hockett called out.

Everyone stopped and looked in the direction he pointed.

"That is not a problem. We can go in down here and get there in no time. Pray that it be the hiding place of the disc, mon," Craig said as he waved for everyone to squat or crawl along a shrub line toward a door and window.

Calvin reasoned that the door Craig approached was probably once the entrance for workmen who labored in the plumbing and electrical rooms on the back side, lower level of the building. Now it looked like it was rarely used.

"David, you stay here. Jim, I need for you to crawl when I do." Craig produced a chain of keys from his pocket, fishing for one that slid into the blue door. "So many cousins on this island," he said with a big grin as he opened the door and looked in.

After one false start, which led to a service area for pipes, Craig led them up a stairway and into the kitchen, then through a conservatory and up a staircase. They emerged into a grand room, which was bordered by the French doors opening onto the patio.

Suddenly Calvin remembered a similar escapade on the Dominican Republic—Rota's house and near disaster. How did he get into these situations? He was drawn to these things as a cobra is to a snake charmer. Then he saw the vase. It stood on a marble-topped table between the doors. Craig was in front of him and he stopped, turned his head and cocked his ear toward the vase before he picked it up. He looked into Calvin's eyes, smiled and said, "Here we go, mon."

Craig picked it straight up from the table and shook it back and forth, left and right, in a circular motion. Nothing. Not a sound.

Calvin sighed with a small a moan. Then he heard a plastic scratching sound as Craig shook the vase up and down.

"All right, mon. It must have been flat and got stuck." Craig held the vase out so Calvin could lend him a hand.

Like a shriek, a whistle ripped the air. Craig jumped and the vase slipped out of their hands. It cracked into two pieces as it struck the marble table. The pieces crashed to the wooden floor and shattered.

"Dave is running!" Craig said, looking out the window. "I don't see Elizabeth. We got to go fast, mon."

Calvin's heart pumped quickly. He was ready to run, but he first surveyed the shattered vase. He didn't see a disc. There were a couple of large chunks of the once-colorful vase still somewhat intact. He bent down to turn them.

"Jim, come! We got to run!"

Calvin saw Craig sprint for the stairs. He turned over a piece. Nothing. The whistle blasted the air again and it sounded as though it was coming from another location. He turned another large chunk of the broken ceramic shards. He spotted a piece of something and reached for it. He uncovered a Zip disc and a CD, rubber-banded together. He grabbed the bundle, stuffed it into his shorts pocket, and tardily dashed to catch up with Craig.

As the two emerged from the door, they heard the screech of the whistle again. It drew their attention to Hockett and Elizabeth, who had ducked down behind the cabana bar which stood at the end of the pool. Hockett was pointing furiously toward the fence line of the property which adjoined the neighboring resort, toward the beach.

They looked to where Hockett was directing their attention and saw the security man walking up the property line as though he too was trying to avoid surveillance cameras. It was obvious they had been sighted. The man stopped, took a stance, reached his hands behind his back, then noticed Craig waving to Hockett and Elizabeth to run. The security man stopped his action long enough to notice the other two.

They had discussed splitting up, should they be spotted and need to escape. Hockett and Elizabeth scrambled away from the edge of the cabana and dashed for the courtyard garden which led to the circular entrance.

"No, no!" Calvin called at them, as if directing their thoughts long distance. They were running away from their bikes. Craig and Calvin slid around the corner of the building to work the property line. "We're in trouble," he said to Craig. The bikes were on the other side of the fence line. To get to them they needed to work toward the beach, directly at the security man.

Calvin knew it was a long way down West Bay, and it wasn't likely they could hitch a ride before their chaser caught them. Their only hope was to retreat through the service alley and get lost in the crowds of a neighboring hotel before getting back out onto West Bay to make their way to the condo.

He tried not to panic. He wasn't worried about his own safety, but he was terrified for Elizabeth. He knew that Hockett would keep her as safe as he could, but it looked as though the security man had been reaching for a weapon. They were helpless and he wished he could stop the whole thing and embrace his child, like he did when she was younger and frightened.

"Hey! Over here!" Hockett's voice commanded their attention. He and Elizabeth had made a straight-line cut from the courtyard, past the circular drive and back toward the shed, which had been built at the edge of the property, separating it from the service alley they had ridden in on.

"Oh, good Lord, we be so lucky, mon," Craig said, as they quickly assembled, looking frantically for the pursuing security.

"Look. He went back to the end of the fence. All the way toward the beach to get around the barriers," Elizabeth told them with certainty.

She was really cool-headed, Calvin thought. They were in peril and they needed to get back to the condo, leaving this madness behind.

Hockett was giving orders. "We've got to clear out. See if you can hitch a ride."

"I got it!" Craig yelled. He had been fiddling with the keychain and he located the key that opened the service shed.

"Quick, get in here!" he barked.

As soon as they entered, Craig ran to the end of the building and kicked out a double-paned window.

"Out here. Hurry. The bikes are just down the line."

They all quickly scrambled out, Elizabeth first, then Craig and Calvin. Hockett worked his long frame through last. Hockett was just emerging from the shed as Craig and Elizabeth, on their bikes, started to pedal away. A motorcycle roared, and a Harley raced toward their spot on the other side of the fence. The rider twisted to look at the shed. Seeing what had happened, he zoomed toward the beach and made a dash for the end of the property, where he could get around the fence and then begin to close in.

"Split up!" Calvin yelled.

Calvin and Hockett worked toward the neighboring hotel. Craig and Elizabeth headed over rough ground toward West Bay onto a wooded expanse of no man's land between Bokanyev's old Royal Caymanian and the other pocket of civilization. Just past the old palm grove was a wall that led through the hotel's ornamental meditation garden. Beyond that was an entrance to the hotel courtyard and a path to West Bay Road.

Calvin heard the motorcycle approach and then roar beyond their path of flight. The biker was headed away from the bulk of people. Tracking differently than Elizabeth and Craig, he was headed toward the more isolated open patch of land that led away from the meditation garden. Seconds later there was a gunshot, then a second, loud explosion which echoed with a high whine. Calvin turned around and re-routed. He had to see what was happening.

It took him about two minutes to pedal back and across the rough ground toward the arched entrance to the meditation garden. As he rode near he could hear commotion, but no more gunfire nor motorcycle roar.

What he saw caused him to almost swallow his heart. Craig was just inside the entrance, kneeling next to Elizabeth, who lay facedown on the ground. The next moments were illuminated with strobe-like intensity as Calvin brought his bike to a stop and ran toward the scene. His worst fears were realized in the scene before him. Elizabeth was on the ground, and the back of her T-shirt was soaked in crimson.

"It's going to be okay. We'll get help." Calvin heard Hockett's voice alongside him. He didn't know Hockett had been so close. He felt like grabbing him for support, and then he saw Elizabeth sit up.

"Honey, lie still. You're bleeding," Calvin yelled.

"Hi, Pop," Elizabeth said, her voice groggy, as she continued to sit up and turn, shaking her head.

"I'm okay," she insisted.

"She is all right, mon," Craig said turning to Calvin and Hockett, "Most of the blood on the shirt is my own." He turned to reveal a cut lip and bloody nose.

"It is all so wild. It all happened so quickly," Craig explained.

Calvin was on the ground, hugging his daughter and making sure she was not injured.

"The crazy man, he shoot his gun and the bullets hit the stone wall. The stones fly away like sparks, mon, and one of them hits Elizabeth on the shoulder. She be yellin' and go down quickly. I be lookin' at her fall on the ground when the man come flyin' by me. Like a rocket, mon! Zoom. He be movin' so fast. He hit the sidewalk and go flyin' right into the traffic. That poor rasta dude in the red car not have a chance, mon. Voom, the bike is in front of him. I see his eyes go so wide like they going to explode or pop out of his head. He try to stop but he can't. He hit the crazy man. I think the poor brother was high and jammin' when all at once he hittin' a crazy man on a motorcycle." Craig's voice grew higher and his speech more rapid. "The poor dude go crazy himself and start yelling and crying. Elizabeth, she hear the sound when she pick herself up and she see the crazy man all mangled and bloody and everything so squished and she passes out. I be looking at all this craziness, mon, and I ride into the bench and smash my face. Then I be leaning over Elizabeth, telling her it all cool, and I bleed on her."

"All in the space of five minutes. That was wild, mon," Calvin said with a rueful smile, hugging Elizabeth.

Grilling With a Grudge

"I CAN'T BELIEVE WHAT you tried to do. Don't you dare say a word of this to Celia," Barb said to Hockett.

"Katie better not hear about it either," Laney added; she gave her husband a hard, judgmental look.

"Mom, it's okay. I'm all right. It probably won't even bruise. Craig is going to be fine. It's not Dad's fault. I made him take me along. I told him he had to or I'd tell you. I was a bit pushy, I guess." Elizabeth looked down at Katie and Celia sitting under the cabana snacking on cheese and crackers.

"I wonder if adventure lust is inherited?" Laney asked thoughtfully.

Calvin held up an item that glistened in the kitchen. "The great thing is, I've got the disc. Do you realize that if this is what we think it is, it'll completely shut Bokanyev down. It'll put him out of business."

"Put it someplace very safe," Hockett said, placing his beer on the condo counter. "Didn't you bring some other discs with your laptop?

"Don't you think Bokanyev's going to know you've got it?" Laney asked.

"If he does, he's going to have to get Caymanian authority to get it back. Craig is going to give it to a cousin for safekeeping. Probably the Queen's Council. It's going to be all right. Bokanyev is leaving the island tonight anyway." Calvin took the disc into the bedroom to put it with his computer bag.

"Well, I say we try to forget the whole thing and try to enjoy the last two days of our vacation. Right now I think we'd better think about dinner, or Celia and Katie will have a fit." Barb began getting items out of the refrigerator.

"After all of this? Is she really that cool?" Calvin asked Hockett.

"No. I can tell when she's pretending everything is fine. This means I'm in trouble deep."

"Oh," Calvin murmured. He caught Barb giving Hockett a side-ward look. He was happy that look was not intended for him.

"The coals probably have another ten minutes before they're ready for the pork. The fish is going on last." Hockett sneaked a look at Calvin. He gave him a grin and shook his head, but the hand that held the turning fork was shaking.

"I wouldn't feel so bad if it was just us. But we must be crazy to try this with the families here." Hockett was toying with the glowing coals in the grill, using the long tongs.

"The more I think about what happened back there, the more unnerving it is. I couldn't reach Garret. I left a message on the answering machine. The disc should help his buddies."

They were on the grill pad at the side of the condo units. A trade-wind breeze ruffled the top of the palms and blew the grill smoke toward the beach. The Caymanian evening had begun to mellow the tension and temperature, but it was still hot.

"Well, things are looking up. Thank heavens Craig's got so many relatives. We won't need to mess with the investigation."

"But I'm going to be mighty happy to get Barb and Cee back to quiet Sanibel." Hockett paused to survey the fire. "I've got a lot of chicken to go on with the pork. I'm going up for the first batch. You okay on beer?"

"I'm fine, but you might grab one for Craig."

They turned to greet him coming up the walk.

"Hey Jim. Hey Dave. I brought you some breadfruit and coconuts, mon. We need to mellow down with island food. Everybody be okay?"

"We're fine. The ladies have cooled down and your lip doesn't look too bad." Calvin extended his hand for an island grip.

"Naw. It all right man. It was just bleedin'. Only a little thing." He handed Hockett a sack full of raw breadfruit.

"Will Barb know what to do with this?" Hockett asked looking doubtfully at the round green fruit about the size of a giant grapefruit.

"Yeah. I tell her yesterday the recipe my dear mother be usin' all these years. She write it down. It like a bread. Be some good starch to soak up grease from your chicken and pork. It be good, mon."

Hockett headed upstairs while Calvin and Craig took a seat on the bench near the grill pad.

"Everything be cool. I tell my brother Perry, who you remember is an assistant chief inspector, what happen. He say 'no problem.' The man not gonna die. He be in hospital a while but then he is going to be sent to the Dominican Republic where he be wanted for a number of charges. He is a Russian and a bad fella. He not legal here, mon. This just be one more mark against Bokanyev. If we can get enough on him, then maybe we can throw his sorry butt off our island. You know what I mean, Jim?"

"Wish we could do the same thing on Sanibel Island."

"Now look at that, brother," Craig said, sipping his beer and using the bottle to point toward the horizon. The sky was a vivid pink and purple. The waves rolled in from a carpet of sea that shared a color with the sky. "Now I be thinkin' you got to have such natural beauty on your beach too, heh Jim? But do your people in America slow down enough to enjoy the thing? You don't got to answer, mon. I know. People be busy buildin' big things, buyin' new houses, drivin' fast cars. But they missin' the beauty in front of they eyes."

"Before you go this evening, I want to give you the disc for safekeeping."

"Have you looked at it yet, mon?"

"I brought both batteries for my laptop. But I left my Zip and CD drives at home, so we'll just have to wait until we get back."

"They be plenty of places here where we can look at it."

"Maybe sometime tomorrow. But we'll have to be cool about it. Laney and Barb want us to drop this whole thing."

"I not even going up there for a while. Don't want to walk into the fire of an angry woman's mouth, mon. I just chill out down here." Craig laughed and stretched out in the chair.

The first batch of grilled chicken had been put into the condo oven, while the pork roasted on the grill, getting ready for turning. The sky had darkened, leaving only a slight glow of orange just above the distant horizon. In the east, stars had begun to twinkle as Caribbean rhythms wafted down the beach, mellow sounds, launched from a poolside bar.

"I don't know how many dozens of times we've grilled together Dave, but it's one of the constants of life."

"We've gotten pretty efficient at it, haven't we? We've even brought Laney to the point where she doesn't mind if we leave the skin on the chicken."

Craig sat up like a shot. "What? She not like the skin, mon? That the best part when you do the jerk flavor. Course you got to keep it in a paper sack for a couple of days before you eat it. Then it be the best."

"I've heard they actually leave it in the bag unrefrigerated," Brian added.

"Naw. Not here, mon. They may do that in Jamaica. In Cayman, we use the fridge."

Tired of waiting for the dinner to be served, Katie and Celia decided to walk the beach. Brian volunteered to accompany them.

Craig, Elizabeth, and Laney strolled to the front of the condo units to look at some of the night-blooming orchid cactus. Calvin sat listening to the drifts of music and the mix of surf and voices. He was watching the smoke curl into the Caribbean sky, thinking about the evening's near miss and the similar escapade in the Dominican Republic.

Craig's voice interrupted the calm, "You makin' a big mistake, mon."

"Quiet. You know what we want," an accented voice said.

Calvin stood up and started to move when he saw Laney, Elizabeth, Bokanyev, and a second man appear with Craig. Bokanyev held Craig in control, jerking his arm behind him. Elizabeth was being held by her long hair by one of the men they had seen on the drive at the estate. Dazed and terrorized, Laney stood next to Elizabeth.

As the group approached, Calvin caught a glimpse of Hockett rounding the corner from the stairs, on the other side of the condo. Calvin threw his hands into the air above his head.

"Leave them alone. Don't hurt them," he yelled toward the oncoming group, hoping Hockett could see what was taking place on the other side of the building. He then had the satisfaction of seeing Hockett dash into Brian and Jayne's lower condo unit, click off the light, and quickly pull the drapes.

"Quiet, or the young lady gets her neck snapped." Bokanyev stepped from the shadows holding Craig in what was obviously a painful grip. Bokanyev waved a gun at Calvin.

"Which unit and who's in it?" he demanded.

"Upstairs. Two women." Calvin's mouth was going dry.

"I saw another man and a couple of kids in the car," the man who held Elizabeth said, stretching her back until she winced in pain.

"They're gone. They went into Georgetown to get some ice cream," Calvin said. Rage and fire were building in him, but he attempted to maintain control. He could not give the man any reason to injure his daughter.

"Get upstairs and don't say a damn word," Bokanyev ordered.

Calvin experienced the scene through a misty sense of unreality. His muscles moved him up the steps, but it was as though he was watching someone else ascend. He opened the door to the condo. Large smiles on the faces of Barb and Jayne suddenly turned to looks of panic when they saw who and what moved in behind him.

"Give me my property now," Bokanyev ordered.

Calvin watched Elizabeth with real distress. Should he lie about the disc? Hope to delay them?

"They not got it, mon," Craig blurted. "It be in the hands of island civilian authority. You are through here—"

Before he could finish his statement, Bokanyev floored Craig with an elbow to the jaw. The Russian stood, pointing his weapon at Craig.

"I've had enough of your jive," Bokanyev snarled.

"Let's do 'em now," the security man said with a cold voice.

"It's got to be clean," Bokanyev said.

Bokanyev's eyes darted around the condo and scanned the beach. His gaze landed on the stove.

"Gas," he said, looking to the front door and wall air-conditioning unit, which was about shoulder high next to the door.

He pointed to the air conditioner. "Turn it off," he ordered.

He walked to the sliding glass doors that led to the patio and locked them. He pulled the drapes shut.

"What a terrible accident. Such lovely tourists who do not understand how to work the island appliances."

"Oh my God!" Jayne gulped.

"We'll be all right," Barb said calmly, hugging Jayne. She stared defiantly into Bokanyev's eyes.

Calvin noticed the Russian almost flinch under Barb's scrutiny, and then anger came to his face. He looked toward the floor where Craig lay, holding his jaw.

"Put them in the chairs and on the couch," he barked to his man.

"Are they going to have an explosion or are they taking a long nap?" the man asked with a smile.

"We'll see," Bokanyev responded, dragging Craig to a lounger chair on the other side of the counter bar.

"Put the pilot light out," Bokanyev said as he moved to close the doors to the bedrooms and bath.

A buzzer ripped the tension of the room. It made a loud and annoying intrusion.

"What the hell is that?" the security man demanded.

"It's the baked beans. In the oven," Barb and Jayne offered, almost in stereo.

"You!" He pointed to Barb. "Turn it off!"

Barb stood up and started to the kitchen area across the open space when everyone's attention was directed to some whistling at the bottom of the stairs. It sounded as though the unknowing Brian had organized Celia and Katie into a mini chorus.

"It's the girls," Laney said. "Leave them alone."

"We could do that, couldn't we? Leave them alone, all alone? Little orphan tourists. No, I don't think so. We'll send them with you. Don't say a word. Let them come in or they'll hurt first and I mean real bad," Bokanyev said, moving back so the door would open.

"Turn that damn thing off!" the other man ordered Barb who had hesitated slightly when hearing the girls' whistle.

He moved in to stand next to Barb as she tapped the timer control and then reached down to open the oven.

"Check out that oven," Bokanyev called to his thug.

"Excuse me," she said, looking at the man who stood blocking the oven door.

He backed up a step toward the refrigerator and she pulled the oven door open. She grabbed the oven mitt from the counter and reached into to retrieve the beans. She started to pull it out and stopped.

"Uh oh," she muttered into the oven.

The man leaned forward to look. As he came forward, Barb pulled the beans out quickly and upturned the pan over his head. Two quarts of hot beans covered his head and ran onto his shoulders and neck.

His anguished cry was piercing. Bokanyev, startled, looked at the man doubled in pain. He was holding his face, running into the counter and table. In the moment Bokanyev was distracted, Elizabeth was out of the chair with a large conch shell in her hand. In a split second, she had driven the spike of the shell into the side of Bokanyev's face. He recoiled in pain. In the next moment, Laney kicked him in the groin. Calvin was going for the gun that the former agent had not relinquished.

Bokanyev's accomplice was down on his knees, holding his burned face and crying as though he was about to go into shock. Jayne managed to find a skillet and hammered him on the head, thus applying a crude anesthetic.

Bokanyev assessed the scene critically. It was out of control.

He grabbed the door, ready to take flight. At the bottom of the stairs, he surprised Brian and the girls. He leveled a shot at Brian who went down with a yell. Bokanyev grabbed Katie and held the gun to Celia's ear.

"You are coming with me," he snarled in almost a whisper.

"Hey, that hurts. Stop it!" Celia barked back, pulling away from his control.

He reached over Katie and grabbed Celia by her hair and slammed her head into the side of Katie's. Both girls cried out in pain. They were being held in a hammer lock by their hair.

He started to move toward the parking lot when he began to scream and curse in Russian about the fire of hell. Hockett had moved behind him and was squeezing the red-hot grill tongs on the back of the Russian's neck. Bokanyev was so shocked he let the girls go and dropped to his knees, releasing his weapon.

"Celia, kick that gun out of the way! Hey, give me a hand down here!" Hockett yelled.

Instead of kicking the gun, Celia bent down to grab it; Bokanyev made a halfhearted attempt to do likewise. Anticipating the movement, Hockett tightened the grip of the hot tongs; the former KGB agent gave up.

"For Pete's sake, Celia, don't play with that gun," Hockett grunted. "Give it to me."

Celia had backed up a step and was pointing the pistol at Bokanyev. Her hand shook and her eyes were wide. Katie, who had dashed to the side, looked at her friend with incredulity.

"Celia!" Hockett yelled.

Brian was suddenly at Celia's side, carefully taking the gun from her hand.

"What, like, you think you are someone bad? How tough are you now, Mr. Vodka-head?" Celia sneered at Bokanyev who by now lay on his stomach. His hands clutched his neck burns as Hockett stood with his right foot on the man's spine and the menacing tongs over his head.

Hockett kept a foot on Bokanyev. "Brian, are you all right? I thought you were hit."

"It was close. I just went down and faked it. Didn't want to give him another shot."

"The guy up here is scalded. He's in tough shape," Calvin said, bounding down the steps.

"Everyone else all right?" Brian yelled up the stairs.

"Yes. Craig is calling the police now." Calvin stood holding the weapon that had been pointed at him, thinking how absolutely bizarre it all was.

Fatherly Redemption

THE CAYMANIAN AUTHORITIES came and handled the aftermath of the potentially lethal situation in a laid-back and casual manner. There was a very proper securing of the scene and collection of evidence; three officers were involved in gathering statements. Everybody was totally mellow. There was none of the paramilitary attitude and bravado he had seen elsewhere or on cop shows. It was almost as though they were presiding over a family dispute instead of what could have been a murder scene.

It was in this setting that Calvin and Hockett were left with the senior officer and Bokanyev, who was sitting in a beach chair. Bokanyev was cuffed and his feet were in restraints. A medical technician had applied an ointment and dressing to the burns on his neck. Senior Officer Dawson, in his white-belted blue uniform, had been interviewing all three men, though Bokanyev had refused to answer most direct questions put to him. He had taken the line that he was simply after an item the men had stolen from him.

"That is no reason to be wantin' to hurt these fine people." Dawson was maintaining a casual attitude during his interview with Bokanyev.

A uniformed officer stood a few feet away from where Bokanyev, Calvin, and Hockett sat. Bokanyev simply glowered at Hockett. Calvin and Hockett tried to read in his expression what he might be thinking, what he might be prepared to say or even do. Surely he would take no action while cuffed and restrained, and police so nearby.

"You are an evil and arrogant horse's ass, Bokanyev. If it was left to me, you'd rot in hell," Hockett said, standing and taking a step toward the Russian.

Calvin tensed and dashed a look at the officer who had turned slightly to keep an eye on the trio.

"You think I should submit to you, because I am bound? Do you think you have the advantage of me? Do you think this island can hold me? This is nothing. Believe me when I say, you are nothing, this authority is nothing to me," Bokanyev sneered.

"You are giving me a real challenge, Bokanyev, but I'm not the one who will judge you. Someday we all meet our Maker, even you, and there is nothing you can do about it. You have no power to avoid it."

Bokanyev started to growl a response when he saw that Barb had come to stand next to Hockett; she handed him an envelope. Bokanyev's face was wet with perspiration. He rubbed his chest. He stared at Barb with a quizzical look.

"That face . . ."

"I know what you're doing, Bokanyev. You're thinking about your past and what you left behind," Hockett said, looking down on the Russian.

"What do you know of my past?" he sneered.

"I've been to Russia, to Chegdomyn."

Bokanyev frowned. "Yeah, so?"

"I've been on several church mission trips. We've gotten to know some people. The KGB isn't the only group in Russia with ways of learning things."

Bokanyev shifted in his chair. "So what do you think you know?"

"Just listen to me. It's time you got educated. I don't know why I'm doing this, but you're going to listen. I'm going to show you a picture. I'm going to tell you about your father and the big lie that poisoned your life."

"You know nothing. You are a little man. You spin clay pot toys and ornaments." Bokanyev spat at Hockett's feet.

Calvin watched his friend closely. Is he going to punch him? Hockett furrowed his brow and moved closer. The Caymanian officers tensed. As he stood almost directly over Bokanyev, Hockett's face lightened. He said:

"Listen to this, Yuri. The KGB lied to you. They drove you away from your father with a lie. They put hatred in your heart and used it to control you. Your mother died when you were young, you barely knew her." Bokanyev's face blanched. Hockett continued, his tone more subdued. "Your father could never tell you because of fear that you would be taken from him and sent to a state school. Look at the woman in this picture with your father," Hockett held the photograph close to Bokanyev's face. "She is your mother and this is their wedding day. I took this picture of him holding the wedding picture when I was with him in Chegdomyn about two months ago."

Bokanyev recoiled, refusing to look, sitting back in the chair as though he was trying to escape the reality that Hockett thrust at him.

"Yuri, look at this picture." Barb's voice was kinder than Calvin thought the man deserved.

"Do you remember the day it was taken?" she asked. "You're the little boy with the boat. See, your father has his arm around you. The woman next to you is not your mother. She is not even your sister. She was a relative of your mother. She cared for you as though you were her son. She loved you like you were her brother. She did not leave you. Your father told my husband she was one of the millions who simply disappeared. By then you were older, but still not old enough to know why or to understand. That's what your own father said." Barb had come forward and was standing next to Bokanyev, showing him the picture.

Bokanyev turned from Barb and stared at the picture and then back to her. His chest heaved and his body shuddered. He tried to control himself.

"Can't you believe what we are saying?" Hockett spoke with a controlled voice. "After your years in the KGB, can't you believe what they did to you? They sold you the terrible lie. There was no incest. See the difference in the women? The picture Barb is holding is not your mother." Hockett held out the picture he had taken of the old man holding the wedding picture. Bokanyev looked at it sadly.

"This was your mother. They are different women." He paused, watching Bokanyev stare at the photo. "Your father is well. He is an old man, but he has never given up loving you. He knows of your hatred for him, but he knows you were tricked. He still loves you." Hockett choked on the last sentence he delivered, obviously aware that Yuri Bokanyev's path in life had not been entirely of his own doing, that he too was a victim.

Barb put her hand on Bokanyev's shoulder. "None of what they told you about your father is true." She turned to Hockett and they walked away, leaving Bokanyev sitting alone.

◆ ◆ ◆

Here in the midst of his pursuit of these meddling people, in the middle of the humiliation of being apprehended by a small island police department, Bokanyev knew instinctively they were right. The way he felt, the reality of his situation, was in direct contradiction to how he had been trained to behave and respond. He sat with his head in his hands, looking at the sand around his feet. He tried to make sense of his thoughts. Cold and calculating dispatch had been his way of life. But the convincing way Hockett told him details of his father's life, and the kind concern of the woman Barb, negated that. That inner, secret longing for his father, that private desire for the joy he had known as a child, the wish to love again, all of that he had denied and buried, but it was now liberated.

In his own stoic way, he had always hoped there had been a greater truth, though he had never permitted that thought even a glimmer of life. Now it hit him. The last thirty years of his life, the deception and pain, had been perpetrated by a fraud. His anger grew, but it was now directed at his faceless handlers in the KGB.

Calvin and Hockett watched as the Caymanian authorities led Bokanyev to the car. Laney and Barb had gathered the girls upstairs.

"This be the reason for the governor to deny him access here. Perry think they may even be able to seize his property because they find so many weapons there. Not even the politicians who get his money gonna be able to be backin' him now, Jim," Craig said, as he joined Calvin and Hockett at the driveway.

"As I was watching him, when you and Barb were working on him with the pictures, I got this sense that he was turned inside out, that you really struck a nerve," Calvin said turning to Hockett.

"Well, we did what we could. We told him the truth. Barb was wonderful. I tried, but I just couldn't be that loving," Hockett responded.

"The Lord moves in mysterious ways, don't he?" Craig added with big grin. "Dave, you was a bad dude tonight, mon. I say you was grilling with a grudge."

Rush to Sanibel

THE TWILIGHT SKY GLOWED pink and orange out the window of the airplane. Calvin considered Katie—a fragile silhouette of a girl next to the bold swatch of horizon—in a concerned way. They were heading into their approach to Southwest International, and Calvin knew the next few days would be tense. The escalation began the evening after the confrontation. Bokanyev had admitted that a shipment of Petrov-class bio-weapons were bound for Sanibel, or perhaps had already been received. They had been moved from the caves in the Dominican Republic, loaded onto a private yacht, and motored toward north Florida. The name and registration of the personal pleasure craft was unknown to the Russian. The arrangements had been made by his ally Abelardo Rota; the contraband was to be received by his assistant Josef.

Hockett and Calvin tried to keep the fact that bio-weapons were heading toward Sanibel from the rest of the party, but after the late evening visit by Craig and his brother and Calvin's call to Garret, Laney and Barb confronted them for the truth. The girls were to be kept sheltered from the news, as were Brian, Jayne, and Elizabeth. This was the kind of news to keep under wraps.

◆ ◆ ◆

Ed Earl and Doug Garret waited until the Bakers had collected their bags and bade farewell before they presented themselves to the Calvins and Hocketts. Calvin would ride back to the island with them, while Hockett would drive the rest of the party back home. None of this went unnoticed by Elizabeth.

"What's up, Pop?" Her face was troubled.

"There are some things I have to talk to Ed and Doug about." He tried to dismiss her casually.

"C'mon Pop. This is about something serious."

"I'll tell you later, kiddo. I don't want your sister to get upset."

"She's not dumb. She knows something's going on, or why would these guys be here and why wouldn't you be driving home with us?"

"Then help us out. We're trying to close in on a couple of bad operators. Don't make a big deal out of this. Try to get Katie and Celia occupied with something else. Would you please?"

She scrutinized his face and then shrugged. "Sure Pop. I guess so. But you be careful."

Calvin watched the frigate birds, with their pterodactyl-like wing-span and short V-shaped tails, soar high on the late evening thermals, crossing each other's trail. They looked faintly menacing in the quickly darkening sky. He considered what Garret and Earl had told him. Neither the CIA nor the FBI, according to their sources in the agencies, had any hard knowledge of the alleged shipment. On top of that, no one had been watching Josef, and there was virtually no way to know which of the thousands of private watercraft could be carrying this phantom shipment.

"Unless they are prepared to stop and board everyone, there's not a snowball's chance in hell to know who it is," Garret said.

Calvin was angry. "Weapons lethal enough to kill everybody on the East Coast are headed to this island."

"It's just complicated. How can we do anything? We can't sound a warning to all the harbor masters and docking points between here and the Dominican Republic. Think about that. First, that would tip our hand, and secondly, it would create a panic." Earl tapped his finger decisively against the steering wheel as he drove across the causeway.

Garret turned toward Calvin. "We've figured a couple of routes. This is only a guess, but I'm saying they probably loaded the stuff and left from El Macao on the east end of the Dominican Republic. That seems to be the closest port near the jungle, where you did your tripping with the Tainos. That's where the storage caves are. I doubt if they took the stuff anywhere else. Then it's one of two routes. The first option is a northern route along the old Bahamas Channel, which means he could put in on Great Exuma or Andros Island, then back to the Santaren Channel and up to the Keys."

"I'm trying to picture that route," Calvin said as he watched Sumerlin pass by outside.

"Don't sweat it. Ed'll show you maps when we get to Hockett's. Now if that's the route, then he'd cut the Keys between Grassy and Long or below Marathon and then up to Sanibel."

"What's the second route?"

"Well, this geek could go south toward Cuba. He could stay south of the channel and fuel up at Matanzas or up at Havana. From there he's wide of Key West and he shoots back toward Sanibel. Either way, this guy's probably carrying enough stuff to kill the entire population of the areas he traveling through. Situation is critical," Garret said.

"I remember Lee Hamblin said that grade of weapon could be very unstable. Who knows what kind of crew he's got handling the stuff, or if they even know how lethal it could be," Calvin enjoined. "At least we've got the disc, including the whole C. G. King interview that she gave to Annie Riley."

"That'll be enough for the judge to get the property back for the conservancy and study center." Earl guided the car to a stop at the drawbridge.

"That means nothing though, if the bio agent gets into the wind," Garret said watching the bridge come up.

◆ ◆ ◆

"Mom, I might be able to help. I know how serious this is," Elizabeth said as she, Laney, Barb, and Dave sat on the Hockett porch awaiting the arrival of Calvin, Garret and Earl. Celia and Katie were in Cee's room upstairs.

"Oh, I just wish this would go away. It scares me so much," Laney said, her voice quavering.

"We've got to face up to it," Barb said, looking at Laney.

"Mom, you can't be so emotional. You've got to be in control. It's not fair to leave me in the dark."

"I suppose you're right. Dave can tell you what he knows, but this just makes me sick."

Hockett explained that a shipment of bio-weapons was bound for Woodrings Point, the old cable-crossing boathouse now owned by Bokanyev, but that even Bokanyev wasn't sure when it would arrive. Laney sighed audibly several times. Elizabeth sat and listened and occasionally reached over to console her mother.

"Your mom is so, like, freaking out, Katie," Celia whispered behind the door of her room which opened onto the balcony, within earshot of the adults.

"Yeah, I know. She's real nervous sometimes. Dad says she's so dramatic."

"My mom and dad don't know that their voices always come up here. They have these private talks and stuff about the business and things. I can hear them, but they like think that I can't. Plus they forget that I'm precocious."

"Oh. What do you mean, precocious?"

"Too smart for my age. But I can't help it." She watched Katie's eyes widen. "But you're really cool on the computer, so let's see what we can find about Petrov bio-weapons. Go online."

"Okay, but do you know where Woodrings Point is?"

"Yeah. I even rode my bike there once."

"Cool."

Being Held at Bay

THE SUN HAD NOT YET broken the eastern horizon, but the sky had begun to lighten. Calvin, Elizabeth, Hockett, Garret, Conroy, Earl, and boat owner George Roppe were on the bay.

"Coffee always tastes better on the water," Earl spoke through the steam rising out of his cup.

"If there is no sign of a boat at the dock, what do we do?" Calvin asked.

"I think we'd have to consider ground surveillance," Garret said, looking up from a nautical map of the San Carlos Bay.

"Actually, that's what Donna and Claudia are up to," Conroy said through his beard, his grin widely apparent.

"What do you mean, Larry?" Garret asked, as Earl also trained his stare on the affable businessman.

"Claudia Prouse, my executive assistant and Donna Iemer, a state government worker, are on leave to help Lee Hamblin with his report. Used to work for him. They're helping us with this." Roppe looked puzzled. Conroy directed his attention back to Garret and Earl. "There's some property for sale up on Woodrings Point. They're starting to build some of these fancy homes up there among the loners. Claudia and Donna are going to look around, as if they are shopping for property."

Earl looked deep into Conroy's eyes, searching for an assurance the two political operatives would not overreach their skills. "Just as long as they don't try anything. Josef is a tough hombre. He's been with Yuri for years, does a lot of his muscle work as well. And now he's on his own. With Yuri in the can, Josef stands to collect whatever the sales arrangements are."

"No, they'll be all right. They've been around the block a few times and Donna handled the kidnappers in Caracas."

Calvin put his hand on his daughter's shoulder. "If she's very careful, and I mean she promises me that, then Elizabeth can do a dive off the back side of the boat and take a close-up look around the boathouse."

"It's your call. I think she can get in and get out without being noticed. If she's noticed, she could just play dumb," Earl said. "Josef doesn't know her."

Elizabeth's blue eyes were serious. "I'll be very careful, Pop, don't worry."

"Well, I don't want to move into the point area for a while," Garret said. "I want to stay wide in the bay, get some long-distance looks. We've got to pretend to be fishing, looking for spots. That way we can get some wide looks at the boathouse and see if there's any traffic." Garret spoke with the authority of a man who had been on surveillance missions before.

◆ ◆ ◆

"Since your dad has some extra business down here, we are staying a couple of extra days. Your computer camp doesn't begin until the middle of next week, so we'll have plenty of time to get you packed," Laney said to Katie as they sat on the Hockett porch overlooking the lake, eating hot breakfast muffins.

"That's cool. Celia and I are going to take a bike ride today. Then maybe this afternoon we can get some ice cream at Pinocchio's."

"Whose bike are you going to use?"

"She can use mine," Barb said. "Just remember to stay on the bike paths, but still be extra careful. You know how some of these tourists drive."

"When do you think you'll hear from your friend in the Dominican Republic, Pedro?" Garret asked as he and Calvin sat on deck chairs behind the cabin.

"Not sure. He was going to try to find Enrique to see if he had any information about activity around the caves. I told him we'd like to know when they loaded at that end, and the name of the boat. I gave him my cell number and the one George has here on the boat."

Hockett, Roppe, and Elizabeth were setting fishing rods now that the boat had halted in the bay. Garret, Earl and Calvin sat just behind the wheel on the flying bridge. Garret was holding a list of boats he had obtained from harbor masters. He and Earl viewed the moving watercraft with field glasses. They'd call a name and check it off the list. Calvin had a certain sense of enjoyment in the surveillance mission, though he was anxious about permitting Elizabeth to dive and snoop.

"What are we going to do when we get there?" Katie asked Celia as they biked out of Gumbo Limbo and onto the bike path on the side of the Dixie Beach Road which ran toward the Woodrings Point end of the island.

"We'll see if there's anything that looks like the pictures you got off the Internet, like oxygen or propane tanks." Celia's face reddened with heat and exertion as she pedaled faster.

"Well, let's be careful. I don't want to do anything silly," Katie responded.

"We may have to be daring."

"Like when you pointed the gun at the man on Grand Cayman?"

"Yeah. What a jerk!"

"Oh, terrific!" Katie bleated plaintively.

◆ ◆ ◆

"All right, here's what Enrique learned," Calvin declared emphatically. "It's the *Gary Go Fast*, registered out of Grand Cayman. It's owned by a retired auto dealer and race car owner. He uses it in the winter. It's chartered and rented in the summer. Apparently, a business associate of the owner had been using it down at Casa de Campo where it's been parked. It left the Dominican Republic two days ago."

"Your hallucinogenic Taino buddy is a pretty good field man," Garret said.

"He is definitely motivated. He told Pedro that the owner of the cave, Bokanyev, is considering giving his land to the University in Santo Domingo to use in their archeology research."

"Sounds like Yuri's working on a deal," Earl said with the knowledge of a former prosecutor. "Nothing like a little generosity to help sweeten a plea bargain, especially with his connections."

◆ ◆ ◆

"Watch those two girls on bikes," Claudia said as Donna maneuvered the rental car on the gravel road back towards the paved Dixie Beach Road.

"They're a long way out here, aren't they?" Donna said, watching them as they approached.

"My God. That's Katie Calvin, Tim's daughter. What is she up to?" Claudia wondered, snuffing out her cigarette. "Pull over."

The girls stopped their bikes as they saw the car pull to the side of the road. They looked at each other, wide-eyed—with some fear.

"Katie. Katie Calvin. It's Claudia. Remember, I gave you the little male kitten you named Claude, after me?" She closed the car door and began to walk to the girls.

"Oh, yeah. Hi." Katie smiled as she remounted the bike and rode toward Claudia and the car.

As Katie reached the car at the side of the road, Donna emerged. Katie and Celia pulled up, dismounted, and kicked down the kickstands so they could chat. As Katie got off the bike, a sheaf of papers fell out of her back pocket.

"Here, you dropped these," Donna said, retrieving the stack of papers. "Hm. Interesting reading for summer vacation. 'United Nations Analysis of the Petrov-class of Chemical/Biological Agents.'" Donna gave Katie a steely smile as she handed her the papers.

Larry Conroy pulled up the antenna of his cell phone, listened, then said, "That's better. Yeah. Well, maybe you'll need to head back that way and keep an eye out for them. Sure, I'll tell him. We think the boat's been there and gone. We saw it moving west toward Redfish Pass in the Pine Island Sound. It was moving away from the Point end of Sanibel. Yeah, call again in about a half an hour." He clicked off the phone and directed his attention to Calvin.

"Tim and Dave, your daughters are up on Woodrings Point. Claudia and Donna left them about fifteen minutes ago. Claudia said Katie had an Internet report on Petrov-class weapons. The girls told them they were just taking a bike ride."

"Celia, you're going to be grounded for a year," Hockett muttered.

Calvin's stomach did flips. Elizabeth was in a wet suit, waiting for the boat to reach a strategic point so she could submerge and scuba dive around the suspect boathouse. His youngest was heading that way on bike. This adrenaline rush thing and the thrill of mystery was apparently in the bloodline. It was out of control. Was he to blame?

The girls had hidden their bikes inside the mangrove thicket on the north side of the road. They had secreted themselves behind a pile of Brazilian pepper cuttings on the property about seventy yards from the old boathouse. Their present concern was the dog who patrolled a patch about twenty-five yards in front of the side door to the boathouse. They saw no car on the property.

"If we can get around the dog, we'll be able to go in," Celia said with a smirk, reaching into the pocket of her cargo shorts.

"He looks mean," Katie said, worried.

"Remember, I'm precocious. This will take care of the doggie, doggie, doggie." Raising her voice to call the rottweiler, she stepped from behind the woodpile.

Katie watched with wide eyes and held her breath. Celia walked toward the dog with her right hand extended, offering a combination of a still partially frozen raw hamburger patty and some ham scraps which, until that morning, had been in the Hockett freezer to be used in a soup stock. In her left hand were the plastic bags. The snarling dog snapped at Celia. She held her ground and tossed a portion of the pattie in his direction. Before long, she had the dog under control.

"Cool," Katie said.

"I saw the dog-treat thing in a movie, but it was poisoned there. I wouldn't do that."

The two left the dog to the frozen ham scraps as they dashed to the door. Celia grabbed the handle and turned. The door opened with a creak and they walked inside.

"This is easy," Celia said as she and Katie stood inside the large old boathouse on a deck, looking at a small powerboat and jet ski tied up in the water below them. A motorcycle was parked just inside the door on the left.

No sooner had Celia finished her comment than Josef stood up from behind the boat, pointing a gun at the girls.

"You little bitches. What are you doing? This is private property. Are you thieves? Should I shoot you for trying to steal my boat?"

"We're just lost. We're on an adventure bike ride," Katie said quickly. Tears began to well up in her big blue eyes.

"You can't talk to us that way. And you have no business with that gun. I'll tell my dad. He knows the police chief and they'll arrest you."

"Celia!" Katie said, looking at her with surprise.

"You've got a real mouth on you, don't ya?" Josef said. He walked toward the girls, holding the gun on them and smiling darkly. He reached Celia and backhanded her with his left hand.

Celia dropped to her knees and cried out. Katie hugged her in a desperate act of protection. When she did, Josef saw the papers in the back pocket of her shorts.

His eyes went wide when he read the Internet reprint.

"Maybe I will have to kill you after all," he said as he poked the gun into Celia's neck. She and Katie both screamed as Josef reached behind them for nylon rope.

Elizabeth had surfaced, turned toward the boat and gave a thumbs up to Calvin and Earl who were watching with binoculars. She resubmerged and headed toward the boathouse, which was less than a quarter mile away. Even though the water was dark and somewhat turgid, the dive light cleared a swath which she followed. When she saw the pilings and pier posts, she trimmed the light and clipped it to her belt.

The sunlight cut the bay with enough wash that she could see when she had slipped under the edge of the boathouse. She took her mouthpiece out, slipped up to just under the surface and got a corner of her goggles out of the water to grab a quick view. She was on the back side of a boat. It was large, bigger than the powerboat she was behind. She wiggled her toes in a fashion to turn her fins into a propeller, sliding around the corner of the boat. She saw the jet ski to the left, tied to a piling post.

To her dismay, beyond a large open space she saw the girls and the man who held a gun on them. They were standing on an elevated deck. Celia and Katie were tied to a post, back-to-back. How in the world had they gotten here? Crazy kids. The goggles were steaming up and it was hard to see clearly, but it looked as though Katie was crying. A motorcycle stood near the door.

Elizabeth dropped below the surface to refit her mouthpiece. Seeking depth, she bumped something. She froze, and then turned to move away from the object. She moved back in the direction of the boat and the edge of the boathouse. When she had slipped a few feet away, she turned on her light to see what she had bumped. Before her was something that looked like a giant version of a drinking-glass storage rack used by restaurants in their large dishwashers. It was an oversized metal basket, holding, in this case, several canisters resembling oxygen tanks. She began to kick furiously toward the boat.

◆ ◆ ◆

"Damn!" Garret said, turning off the cell phone. "Now that we're in a go position, we've got to wait. It's a jurisdictional thing. The FBI has to work it through the process for a warrant and authorization. That'll be tomorrow. We don't want to tip the locals."

"Why not?" Calvin demanded indignantly.

"They'd come with lights on. It'd create a security issue and a real panic. If we get the hazardous materials guys out here, it'll be a circus. Trust me on this. I know." Garret shook his head. "The army will send a team if we can give them more info, but it'll take several hours. We haven't been able to contact our guys who can reach CIA, but heaven only knows what they'd want to do. We're stuck where we are for the time being."

Calvin turned away grumbling

"It's not your fault. Neither of you," Elizabeth said as she gave her dad's shoulder a squeeze.

Calvin and Hockett sat quietly, both full of a sense of desperation.

"I've got Claudia on the phone," Conroy yelled toward the group on the bridge.

"Tell them to stay at the road, back away from the boathouse," Earl said with a calm but forceful voice. "Tell them if he comes out on a motorbike to get to the inside quickly and check on the girls. Make sure they got that. The girls are their issue, not Josef."

"We'll get them out of there," Garret said to Calvin.

◆ ◆ ◆

"If these guys are dealing with Bin Laden, they'd think nothing of killing the girls," Claudia said as she and Donna considered the instructions Larry had relayed to them from the boat.

"Maybe we can take him. Only one guy. But how do we go in?" Donna asked, scratching her chin.

"Let's use the honey trap. We go as a couple of interested property buyers, just checking with the locals. Unbutton your blouse and give him the eye."

"What he's going to do, drop the gun and jump my bones right there?"

"Well, if we can get him outside, maybe something will come to us." Claudia lit a cigarette.

"Sounds pretty thin, but what the heck."

◆ ◆ ◆

"Okay, here's the situation," Earl said to the group on the bridge. "Doug says Immigration and Naturalization Service and Customs can stop him, just on suspicion. The boat may not be registered. Waiting for locals to check it out can tie him up. If he's on the jet ski, we let the locals take him or follow him. We move toward the boathouse, not enough to spook him, but close enough to get a look at what's going on and to go with him if he leaves."

"I've got to tell you, Claudia and Donna—these are two tough gals. I just don't think they're going to wait around," Conroy confessed.

"We need some backup on the road. Is there anyone you can trust?" Garret looked at Hockett.

"Yes. Like I said, I can call the chief, Chief Stiner. I know he's a good man and he's going to have to know about some of this sometime. I think we can trust him not to overreact."

"Go with it. But don't tell him about the chemicals. Ask him to stand by, out a bit."

"I told him about what happened on Cayman. I'll just tell him this could be related and he'll be cool." Hockett reached to punch up the cell phone.

"Helloooo. Anybody around?" Claudia crooned, standing outside the boathouse. Donna checked her cleavage exposure and looked for a stone she could slip into her fist.

The sound of an engine starting gave them both a sudden chill. Claudia gambled and went for the door.

"Helloooo," she yelled outside the door.

Donna stood next to her. She needed to remember to be flirtatious when her instinct was to smash the guy's face when he opened the door. She unbuttoned another button, shook her back her hair, and licked her lips.

"What are you doing here? This is private," Josef said, opening the door and standing inside the threshold.

"Oh, I'm soo sorry to bother you. But my friend and I here are thinking about buying the property next to yours," Claudia told him.

Josef stepped out of the door to see Donna, who stood with her hands on her hips. She made a slight twisting action in the waist, causing her blouse to flutter teasingly. She smiled at him with a coy deflection of her eyes, taking in his physique.

"My goodness! Are you taking a ride in a boat?" Claudia asked wonderingly. "Maybe we could ride with you? We'd love to see the view from the water."

"Maybe sometime when I'm not so much in hurry," Josef said, keeping his eyes on the wiry blonde who stood a few feet away from the door.

"Well, I might be your neighbor. Do you think we'd like it here?" Donna started to walk toward him, looking him up and down.

Josef stepped out of the boathouse door toward Donna. As he stepped out, Claudia dashed inside the dark old boat-storage shed. She caught a glimpse of the girls to her left, on the pier beside the jet ski.

She started to reach for the door's edge, to slam it shut, but was stopped abruptly by Josef.

He slammed a forearm into Claudia's shoulder and neck, forcing her to the ground. He bounded into the boat, where the engine was already purring. Donna came inside to see Claudia rolling in pain as Josef struggled with a tie-line on the front of the boat. He was trying to jerk it loose from the pier. It looked as though he might just force the boat away by powering the engine, snapping either the line or pulling the tie-rope holder away from the boat or the pier. He had given up on jerking at the rope and was ready to grab the wheel in a standing position. As Claudia lay on the pier, she noticed a boat hook, a long rod with a tipped hook end, used to draw the boat close to the pier or to shove it off. She rolled toward the twelve-foot pole, grabbed it and rose to her knees. Donna was playing the role of a surprised airhead, trying her best to look perplexed and confused, all the while giving Josef her best "come hither" stare and supposedly ignoring her friend on her knees and two girls tied to a post.

Josef hesitated only a moment in sliding the throttle arm, but it was long enough for Claudia to take aim. She guided the pole for a trajectory that would intersect directly with Josef's manhood. She stood up and, in a flash, Josef turned to see her, but not before she had used her arms to strike on target with a powerful lift and drive. She raised the pole with such force and precision that it pushed Josef backwards and out of the boat, but not before he grabbed the throttle. The engine roared and the boat behaved like a tied bronco. It ripped and strained and tugged in a chaotic whirl until it broke loose.

"Oh man! The boat is breaking loose. It's really kicking up a wake in the boathouse," Garret looked through binoculars.

"Dave, I see the girls," Calvin yelled, looking through his field glasses. "They're okay. Claudia's untying them."

"Donna is trying to get into the boat. Damn, she almost got thrown. Oh, look out, the boat's loose, it's coming out, it's turning around, it's shooting out into the bay," Garret announced in a surreal play-by-play.

"George, stay clear of that boat, but let's get inside that boathouse," Earl said to the owner.

"No! No!" Calvin yelled. "It looks like some of the tanks are bobbing to the surface."

◆ ◆ ◆

Donna had used Claudia's weapon to pull Josef from the water. He had been hit by the bucking boat and was bleeding from a head wound. She hooked his belt with the pole and pulled him to the deck, where he was lifted out by both of the women. He was breathing but barely conscious. The water in the boathouse was foam-filled and agitated, like the water in a high-power spa. The force of the propwash had worked on the containers of bio-agents, and three had flopped to the surface. They were still tethered to the basket container, but were being jerked by water currents and banging into each other.

"My God, we've got to get out of here!" Claudia yelled.

"But it can be carried on the wind. It can go anywhere," Katie said, rubbing her wrists, which bore the burn of the rope.

They were stopped by a sickening sound, the bang of metal as another tank porpoised to the surface, clanging its neighboring canister as if it were about to lift into the air. As it did so, its top valve unit made direct contact with the side of another tank. The valve top, constrained by the tether line, broke away from the rising tank. Driven by the water pressure, it lifted onto the surface of the deck, just feet from where Katie, Celia, Donna, and Claudia stood.

The tank began to hiss and emit a steamy vapor. Donna grabbed a plastic bag that lay on the deck. She ran to the tank, trying to cover its open portal.

"We're going to die!" Claudia exclaimed.

"I'm never going to get a driver's license," Celia mourned

Nauseated, Katie began to heave over the side of the deck.

George Roppe carefully put the boat into the berth on the outside of the boathouse. Even before he had slowed the engine and Hockett had tied it off, Garret, Earl, and Calvin were off the boat and onto the deck, running toward the crisis.

"This is wrong. Something is weird here," Garret said, surveying the open tank. He noticed Donna, who straddled the tank in the water, holding one arm around the ladder while the other hand grasped a baggie tightly on the open valve.

"I'm trying to keep it under water," Donna said looking up, noting that the men on the deck above her seemed to be staring at her mostly exposed chest. "But some of it got out. I even felt a coolness on my hand, but nothing yet. Is this a delayed reaction? You've got to get people out of here."

"Maybe we're not going to die," Claudia said. "Damn, I need a cigarette!" Everyone turned to stare at her. "I know, I know—not here!"

◆ ◆ ◆

By the time Lee Hamblin arrived, all but the open tank had been returned to the underwater basket device, which was only inches below the surface. The open tank had either sealed itself or had been drained. Chief Stiner and Garret had tied it up, and it now floated peacefully in the bay water inside the boathouse. The girls had been driven home by Claudia. Hockett went with them to explain the events. Donna stayed with the party, waiting for her boss, the former congressman, whom everyone hoped might have some explanation as to why they were still alive after the gas escape. The injured Josef had been taken away and put into custody, with a gash on his head and a sore groin.

"Perhaps the toxin had been weakened," Donna speculated. "Or maybe it needed a mixture, and only one valve opened."

"This is all blind conjecture, though the fact is we are still alive," Conroy said.

"The girls are fine. But Donna said she even felt it on her hand," Calvin added.

"Yes, yes," Hamblin said as he knelt to examine the tank with almost a bemused look, referring to a notecard he pulled from his pocket. He noted particularly the markings.

"You all must be terrified and, I suppose, perplexed by all of this. The good news is, the worst is over. The bad news is, there is no consumer product commission or better business bureau that potential victims of this stuff can turn to for relief of emotional suffering." He rose from his kneeling position to sit on an old crate.

"You've got to explain this, sir," Garret said intensely.

"Well, on the ironic side, there may be no charges that you can bring against Bokanyev either. You see, this is all a phony, a dud, maybe some kind of decoy. I'm sure Yuri Bokanyev didn't know it was phony. He probably thought he had purchased the real thing."

"What? This is a knock-off bio-weapon? Who the hell ever heard of that?" Claudia's voice was excited.

"I mean, what's the point?" Calvin asked.

"Hold on, folks. I think I know where this is going," Ed Earl added quietly.

Hamblin smiled slightly. "There's an awful lot of counterfeit trade in the arms black market these days, especially among the old KGB crowd. I guess they used to make a lot of dummies, phony cases of these tanks, and other weapon systems, so that the intelligence estimates would be inflated. I guess that happened in Moscow and Washington. I've been reading some declassified KGB files during the past months, and it's all laid out there."

"Disinformation. 'Pug wash' is what the spooks call it," Garret interrupted.

"That's exactly what they used to call it when they came up to testify before the oversight committee. Well, anyway, it seems a lot of people bought into it because a lot of this stuff is being sold."

"You mean there's no threat, Lee?" Conroy asked.

"No, the Petrov-class is real. If this had been, sadly, a real tank, none of you would be here now. For that matter, this end of the island would a huge casualty. No, I suspect what we have is ammonia gas, maybe just helium. We know the Russian government is trying to figure how much of this stuff is out there. I know for a fact the Russian tax people would like to know how much some of these black market merchants have made selling the phony agents."

"Isn't that ironic. Even the Ruskie tax man wants his bite," Claudia said.

"Kind of funny when you think about it. Even some of what we used to think were real supplies, back in the height of the Cold War, were just mock-ups and counterfeits. Now the free-market capitalism of the underground arms market is letting more people get taken for a ride. I guess it's good that some of this stuff is in play. It is ultimately better that this gets into a Bin Laden's hands than the real thing. What a strange little twist to this sad business. Well, this will certainly make an interesting anecdote for the report I will deliver to Congress and the UN."

Kir Royales at Jean Paul's

CALVIN COULD SEE Jean Paul embracing and kissing Jayne and then Sylvia. Brian and Doug were given warm handshakes. The Hockett van pulled off Tarpon Bay Road into the clearing known as the French Corner. He watched as the congenial proprietor graciously waved his special guests into the cozy charm of his romantic cafe. Hockett pulled his van alongside the Baker car. The gravel parking lot was almost empty.

"What a treat," Laney said, smiling widely.

"He's a real friend, isn't he?" Hockett said as he stopped the van, turned off the engine and opened the door.

"You mean he opened tonight just for us?" Elizabeth asked.

"Cool," Katie assessed.

"I hope he's got the onion soup tonight, Mom," Celia said to Barb as they walked up to the door.

"We'll see," Barb said, as she approached Jean Paul and turned her cheek for a kiss.

Hugs, kisses and embraces were all around for the ladies, as Calvin and Hockett smiled at the scene.

"Tim, it is so good to see you again. So good that you are fine. And now we see that you and David have become heroes again," Jean Paul said with his French accent and warm smile.

"Heroes we're not. Glad to be here, we are. It's so kind of you to come off a vacation to open for us tonight."

"It is my pleasure. Please come in. Bill is making Kir Royales. The Bakers and your friends the Garrets are here already. The Earls called to say they will be a little late. Judy was too exuberant in her shopping."

"Easy to do down here."

"Well, she wasn't at A Touch of Sanibel," Hockett said as they walked inside. "I'll have to get on that rascal."

It had been four days since the discovery of the fake canisters, and the story had been trumpeted all over the news. Lee Hamblin was in Washington with Claudia and Donna. The President and congressional leaders wanted to take advantage of the current media interest, so they had arranged for a special White House meeting, featuring Hamblin's preliminary report. Claudia had delayed a trip to England with a niece to help with arrangements. The Conroys were on business in New York but were stopping in Washington as guests of Hamblin. Calvin and Hockett had declined an invitation to attend.

"I'll read about it," Calvin said.

"I've got a pottery business to run," was Hockett's response.

The natural wood tones and mellow lighting had immediately put the gathering into a relaxed and reflective mood. Jean Paul had prepared a choice of either filet mignon au poivre vert de Madagascar (filet in green peppercorn sauce) or his saumon frais (Norwegian salmon with fresh dill sauce).

Garret tapped a spoon to his wine glass about halfway through the meal. "You know, in all this recounting of what has happened, we've forgotten something. Here's to the fat little weasel who will soon be in hock up to his eyeballs now that the IRS has busted him. To that chubby sissy Richie Peabody and—"

"Hold it." Ed Earl stood. "Doug, if you don't mind, let's remember Mr. Peabody, but let's not toast him. I amend your sentiment so that we may honor that most despised of federal agencies, the IRS. Just like the mounties, this time they got their man, the right man. Cheers."

◆ ◆ ◆

As they awaited dessert, Sylvia looked across the round table to Calvin. "You know, what I'd like to really know is, did you really do that Taino ritual with the smoke and stuff, or was that just a bad dream."

"The more I think back, the more it seems that the whole thing was a bad dream. To be honest though, my instinct tells me it was real. But I've got to say, the anti-malaria medicine I was taking has been known to cause wild dreams and hallucinations."

"That's the problem here, Calvin," Hockett said as the rest of group began to chat in several little conversations. "Your hallucinations become my nightmares."

"All's well that ends well," Calvin said.

"I wouldn't want to go through it again, but you're right. I've learned a lot," Hockett pulled his chair out and turned as he and Calvin continued their private chat.

"Like what, if I may ask?"

"What can we really ever know about another person's soul, about their life? You know, I was convinced Yuri Bokanyev was evil. I know he did a lot of horrible stuff in his life. He was trying to sell poison and death, just to get rich. The things he did were evil, but was it really his fault? There was his old man, still loving him. You know, if he could just have had his father's love, maybe he'd never have taken the path he did. But the wonderful thing is, he can change. 'Once you were in darkness, now you are in light. Be like children of the light.'" Hockett's eyes smiled distantly, thoughtfully.

"When you told us he was making a donation to the building of the youth center and wanted it named for his dad, I almost choked up." Calvin sipped at the wine.

"He's lucky he's such a rich man. By giving away so much of his fortune, he's really buying his freedom. The Sanibel properties go back to their intended use. He's been forced to sell on Grand Cayman. He has made a trip to Russia and reconciled. He and his father will be comfortable in the Dominican Republic. And Monica—he took Monica and his father likes her. Perhaps she wasn't just with Yuri for the money. So what about you?"

"When we came down here at Christmas, I was in a weird space. Middle-age slump, I guess. A little post-publication letdown, lots of uncertainty about business. And, you know, it's hard to accept getting older. Inside is still the kid who fell in love with *Treasure Island* and who wanted to go off on adventures like *Journey Without Maps*, but, you know, you don't have unlimited time. So, like a big baby, I guess, I got all hung up in trying to figure out my life. It was kind of self-obsessed."

"I want to listen to this," Laney said, turning away from the conversation knot she'd been a part of.

"Sure, you've had to live with it. I guess I was feeling trapped. And then this whole thing blows up. Worrying about the girls, fearing for their well-being, thinking about the idea of bio-weapons and the hell they could create right here on this little paradise. All of it just shoved my own, call them ruminations, out of mind. Didn't have time to think about myself, and that's the point. I think that's the lesson here."

"I'm not sure I follow you," Hockett said.

"I'm with Dave. What are you saying?" Laney asked.

"It's a question of focus. If all we ever do is think about ourselves, then of course we're going to find problems. We need to focus on others, if you will, emptying ourselves. Look it. I've got some talents and skills, God-given. The point is this: I want to use those, to offer those, to do something worthwhile. Specifically, I want to devote effort to being a peacemaker, to work to eliminate these kinds of weapons. I want to stand against them, in my own way. And I want to make stewardship of the planet a real priority. We've got to care about this earth. There are countless ways we can each play a role. I want to be very active about it."

"Tim, I know you well enough to pick up this new vibe. We've been friends too long for me not to realize what you're going through right now. You're committed to those ideas. It's the way I feel about the mission work."

"Okay guys, here's the tough question for my husband, whom I probably know as well as anyone. What about the need for adventure? Your 'unquenchable thirst' for a mystery? The Jim Hawkins in you?"

"My dad had it figured out, hon. I know I'm a lot like him."

"Your mom says you're more like him the older you get."

"He had it right. He used to say, 'Make the most of each day. Do the best you can, but take it just one day at a time.' That's the guidance I'm going to follow. That's my inner navigation. The adventure, Laney, is to see how rich you can make your life with experiences. It's not money; it's life lived fully, it's making memories, making a difference. The journey without maps is the plunge into the future. I'm still going to travel, one day at a time."

"Hey, Pop, I didn't hear what you said about your next adventure trip. You know what? I think I'm going to go to Alaska. You guys might want to think about it too. It's the last frontier," Elizabeth said from across the table.

"Oh, puh-lease!" Laney said, putting her napkin on the table.

Calvin's eyes twinkled. He glanced at Katie and saw her raise her eyebrows as a smile began to wrinkle her mouth.

About the artist . . .

JAMES WILLE FAUST is an important American artist with a growing national reputation. He first achieved national recognition when he was commissioned to depict Indiana for the award-winning Absolut Vodka "Absolut Statehood" campaign of 1992–1993. Faust's work has been exhibited in several Midwestern galleries, including the Indianapolis Art Museum, the Richmond (Indiana) Art Museum, and at the Chicago International New Art Forms Exposition. He resides in Indianapolis.

Thanks to Lana for her unending support, enthusiasm, and love; to Kristin and Katherine for being wonderful daughters who make their father proud and fill him with joy. Respect to Mary Helen for her faith and spirit.

My appreciation to friends who understand. Bravo to Wille for a sensational work of art. Gratitude to Nancy Baxter for the creative midwifery; Sheila Samson for the classy design; Jennifer and Andy for the promo push; Ben Strout for his producer's eye; Sharon for saving a crashed file; and the islands of Sanibel, Grand Cayman, and the Dominican Republic for their allure and magnificence.

Any similarities to persons alive or deceased is in the eye of the beholder and attributable to the power of mystery and the dance of the muse.

Laboratory Workbook & Program Documentation

CALCULUS CONNECTIONS
A *MuLTimedia* Adventure

Douglas Quinney • Robert Harding • IntelliPro, Inc.

JOHN WILEY & SONS, INC.

New York • Chichester • Brisbane • Toronto • Singapore

DOCUMENTATION

CALCULUS CONNECTIONS
A MULTIMEDIA ADVENTURE

Douglas Quinney
Robert Harding

ISBN 0-471-02111-3

Printed in the United States of America

10 9 8 7 6 5 4 3

About the Calculus Connections Authors

Dr. Douglas Quinney, University of Keele, UK and Dr. Robert Harding, Cambridge University, UK, have written, developed and published multimedia mathematics software since the mid 1980's. Their groundbreaking works in multimedia mathematics include The Renaissance Project, commissioned by Apple Computer UK published in 1992 to demonstrate effectiveness of interactive multimedia technology in higher education, and major contributions to The United Kingdom Mathematics Courseware Consortium that includes over 20 UK Mathematics departments concurrently creating interactive multimedia modules for various mathematics courses.

About the Calculus Connections Developer

IntelliPro, Inc. is a leading developer of interactive courseware in mathematics, engineering and the sciences. It brings to the project extensive expertise in multimedia, mathematical simulation, computer graphics and animation, and instructional system design to construct this interactive multimedia environment for teaching and learning calculus.

Table of Contents

Laboratory Workbook

Program Documentation

Workbook Overview

This Laboratory Workbook is a key component of the Calculus Connections multimedia teaching and learning experience. One workbook chapter accompanies each software module and is designed to:

- Provide background information
- Extend ideas introduced in the software
- Test understanding of concepts
- Apply this understanding to new situations

Connecting with the Software

We have designed each Workbook chapter to enhance your experience and maximize your potential for success with the corresponding software module. Chapters begin with necessary prerequisites, mathematical objectives, and a discussion of how the concepts you explore in each module relate to applications from engineering, physics, the sciences and daily life in general.

The Workbook uses your experience with the software as a springboard to explore other examples, exercises and new situations. It encourages multiple pathways for investigation, via approaches that call for pencil and paper, for computers, and for expressing your mathematical ideas and discoveries in sentence form. The pages in this book are perforated so that you can record your results on the Problem worksheets, tear them out, and hand them in to your instructor.

The Multimedia Experience

Our goal for Calculus Connections is to spark your imagination, deepen your mathematical intuition and give you opportunities to explore connections between mathematical theory and the world around you. We encourage you to question results, to construct "what if" scenarios and to experiment by changing parameters, inputting your own functions and generating your own graphics. Most of all, we encourage you to be curious, to be open-minded, and to have fun with this multimedia adventure!

D. Quinney
R. Harding

Chapter 1

Lines, Functions, and Equations

Prerequisites

Before you study this chapter make certain that you understand this fundamental material:

(1)   Basic algebra, including the simplification of expressions and the manipulation of brackets.

(2)   Coordinate geometry, including how to plot points.

(3)   The equations of a straight line and the solution of quadratic equations.

Objectives

The main purposes of this module are to explain what a mathematical function is, how it can be defined, and how functions can be classified and visualized. Initially, functions are classified as linear or nonlinear, with the distinction being demonstrated graphically. More complicated functions can be built up by combining simpler functions, (by adding, multiplying and dividing, for example).

Another purpose of this module is to help distinguish between the definition of a function $f(x)$ and solving equations of the form $f(x)=0$.

Connections

Accompanying this module are two applications that introduce mathematical functions and their construction.

The first application illustrates how many mathematical functions that appear to be very complicated can often be built up from more familiar functions. This process, which is called function composition, can often be unraveled so that we can understand complicated functions by looking at their individual components.

The second application uses tables of data, in this case the height of trees in a forest, and shows how to estimate values at nontabular points. This process is called interpolation. The application also shows how we can estimate values beyond the tabular points; this is called extrapolation. We begin by looking at the simplest possible method, known as linear interpolation, before considering more complicated techniques.

Why do we need mathematical functions?

Mathematics is a shorthand that enables us to write expressions succinctly. For example, if r is the radius of a circle then the area of the circle, A, is given by the product of π times r times r or

$$A = \pi r^2.$$

This is a relationship between two variables called A and r. We can also represent this relationship by a graph.

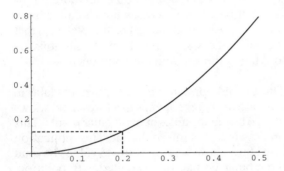

Figure 1.1. The mathematical function $A = \pi r^2$.

For each value of r we can determine the corresponding value of A and plot the point generated. For example, $r=0.2$ gives $A = \pi 0.2^2 = 0.125664$ and so we plot the point $(0.2, 0.125664)$. This generates the curve shown in Figure 1.1. Since for each value of x there is a unique value of y, we say that y is a function of x. We can also represent this function by a table of values, such as Table 1.1.

r (in)	A (in^2)
0.0	0.000000
0.1	0.031416
0.2	0.125664
0.3	0.282743

Table 1.1. Numerical values from the function $A(r) = \pi r^2$.

There are many ways of representing math-ematical functions: algebraic, geometrical and numerical, in addition to the original wordy form. Each has its own uses, but they all provide essentially the same information.

In general, if two variables x and y are related by a function f, we write $y = f(x)$. The variable x is called the independent variable, and y is called the dependent variable. For each value of x there is only one value for y.

Classifying Functions

There are many ways of classifying mathematical functions. We begin by distinguishing between linear functions and nonlinear functions.

A linear function is one that is represented by a straight line. But what characterises straight lines? In answering this question we will see that the expression $y = mx + b$ always represents a straight line. But why, and what is the meaning of the parameters m and b?

Example 1.1
Figures 1.2 and 1.3 show the linear function $f(x) = mx + b$ for
    (i) $b=0$ and $m=-4,-3,-2,-1,1,2,3,4$
    (ii) $m=2$ and $c=-4,-3,-2,-1,1,2,3,4$
We see that m determines the slope of the line and b determines its position.

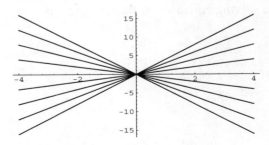

Figure 1.2. $y=mx$ for $m=-4,-3,...,3,4$.

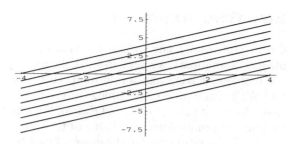

Figure 1.3. y=x-c, for c=-4,-3,...,3,4.

 Exercise 1.1

Plot the functions $y=mx+c$, for values of $m=-5$, $-4,-3,...,3,4,5$, $b=-5,-4,...,4,5$ for yourself. What the effect does changing m and b *have* on the graph?

Since two points, (x_1, y_1) and (x_2, y_2), determine a line, how can we find the equation that represents it? If the point (x_1, y_1) lies on the line $y=mx+c$ then we have

$$y_1 = mx_1 + b$$

and, similarly,

$$y_2 = mx_2 + b.$$

This gives two equations in the two unknowns m and b. Solving for m gives

$$m = \frac{y_2 - y_1}{x_2 - x_1}$$

and then $b=y_1 - m\,x_1$.

Example 1.2

Find the linear function passing through the points (2,2) and (4,6). The slope of the line is given by

$$m = \frac{6-2}{4-2} = 2.$$

Hence, $y=2x+b$. Since $y=2$ when $x=2$, this gives $2=4+b$, or $b=-2$, and so the required function is given by $y(x)=2x-2$. (Check: $y(2)=4-2=2$, $y(4)=8-2=6$.)

Given the equation $y=mx+c$, where m and b are now known, for each value of x we can find a corresponding value of y. We say that y is a function of x. In particular, since the graph of this function is a straight line, we say that y is a linear function.

We have been able to fit a straight line through two points. Now we can use the resulting equation to find other points on the line, either between the given points, which is called **linear interpolation**, or outside them, which is called **extrapolation**.

Example 1.3

The equation of the linear function passing through the points (2,2) and (4,6) was determined in Example 1.2 as $y(x)=2x-2$. Interpolation at $x=3$ gives $y=4$. Extrapolation at $x=5$ gives $y=8$.

 Exercise 1.2

Find the equation of the line through (1,2) and (4,7). Interpolate this line at $x=2$ and extrapolate it at $x=5$.

Nonlinear Functions

The difference between linear functions and nonlinear functions is made clear by looking at the graphical representations. For a linear function the graph is always a straight line but for nonlinear functions it is a curve. (See Figure 1.4 for an example).

Many mathematical problems result in nonlinear functions. In some cases it is possible to approximate nonlinear functions by linear ones. This idea is fundamental to many mathematical procedures.

Example 1.4

If we look at the function $y=e^{-x}\sin(x)$ over the range $0\le x\le 2\pi$, then it is clearly a curve. However, if it is plotted over the interval $2\le x\le 3$, it looks more like a straight line. See Figures 1.4 and 1.5.

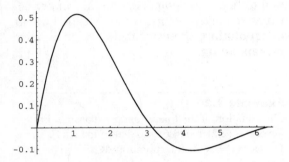

Figure 1.4. $y=e^{-x}\sin(x)$, $0\le x\le 2\pi..$

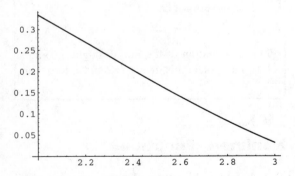

Figure 1.5. $y=e^{-x}\sin(x)$, $2\le x\le 3.$

The more closely we look at any curve, the straighter it appears to be.

Exercise 1.3

Plot the function $y=x^3$ for $0\le x\le 1$. Zoom in and see what happens over the ranges (0.4,0.6), (0.49,0.51), and (0.499,0.501).

Equations f(x)=0

Given a function, f, and a value x, we can evaluate $f(x)$. Sometimes, we need to solve the opposite problem, that is, when a value of $f(x)$ is given and we require x. For example, we could be asked to find a value x such that $f(x)=0$. We are looking for points where the value of the function vanishes, or in terms of the graph of $y=f(x)$, where the curve $y=f(x)$ cuts the axis. Such points are called *solutions*, or *roots* of the equation $f(x)=0$ or *zeros* of the function f. For example, the function shown in Figure 1.6 has zeros at the points $x=1$ and $x=2$.

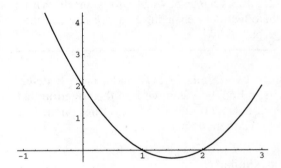

Figure 1.6. A function with zeros at $x=1$ and $x=2$.

For some functions, $f(x)$, it is possible to develop a formula for finding the solutions; for more general equations, $f(x)=0$, we must use alternative methods.

Quadratic Equations

The solutions of the quadratic equation $ax^2+bx+c=0$ are given by

$$x=\frac{-b\pm\sqrt{b^2-4ac}}{2a}.$$

For each value of *a*, *b*, and *c* we can evaluate this expression. Notice that there are always two solutions, they are either both real, equal, or involve the $\sqrt{(-1)}$; in which case we call them "complex" roots.

Example 1.5

Find the solutions of

  (i) $x^2 - 4x + 3 = 0$

  (ii) $x^2 + 2x + 1 = 0$

  (iii) $x^2 + 2x + 6 = 0$

(i) $x^2 - 4x + 3 = 0$:

$$x = \frac{4 \pm \sqrt{16-12}}{2} = \frac{4 \pm \sqrt{4}}{2} = 1 \text{ or } 3.$$

(ii) $x^2 + 2x + 1 = 0$:

$$x = \frac{-2 \pm \sqrt{4-4}}{2} = -1 \text{ twice.}$$

(iii) $x^2 + 2x + 6 = 0$:

$$x = \frac{-2 \pm \sqrt{4-6}}{2} = \frac{-2 \pm i\sqrt{2}}{2}.$$

These functions are shown in Figure 1.7. Notice that for (i) the curve $y = x^2 - 4x + 3$ cuts the y axis twice, at 1 and 3. For (ii) the curve $y = x^2 + 2x + 1$ just touches the y-axis at x=-1. But the curve given by (iii), $y = x^2 + 2x + 6$, does not cross this axis, that is, it is never zero.

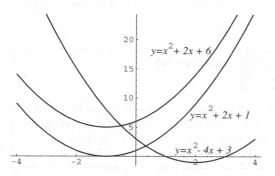

Figure 1.7. The zeros of the quadratics in Example 1.5.

 Exercise 1.4

Plot the functions $y = 3x^2 - 3x - 1$. Show that there are two solutions for the quadratic equation $3x^2 - 3x - 1 = 0$ and determine them.

Solving f(x)=0

Although we have a formula for the roots of a quadratic equation, there are many other types of equation for which no formula can be found. Example 1.6 shows how a technique known as the **bisection method** can be used to find roots to any desired accuracy.

Example 1.6

Figure 1.8 shows that the equation $\cos(x)=x$, $x>0$, has only one solution and that this solution lies between x=0 and x=1.

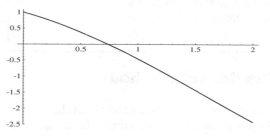

Figure 1.8. y=cos(x)-x.

Let $f(x)=\cos(x) - x$, and notice, in particular, that

$$f(0)=1>0, f(1)=\cos(1) - 1 = -0.459698 < 0.$$

Now consider the midpoint between x=0 and x=1, that is, x=0.5. Since $f(0.5)=0.377358>0$, the solution must lie between x=0.5 and x=1, so we consider the midpoint of this interval x=0.75. Again, since $f(0.75)$=-0.018311<0 and $f(0.5)$=0.377358>0, the solution now lies in the interval x=0.5 to x=0.75. Hence, we consider the midpoint x=0.625 where

$f(x)$=0.18593>0. The solution must therefore lie between x=0..625 and x=0.75, and so we bisect again to consider x=0.6875, and so on. This generates the following intervals:-

(0.6875,0.75)

(0.71875,0.75)

(0.73438,0.75)

(0.73438,0.74219)

(0.73828,0.74219)

(0.73828,0.74023)

(0.73828,0.73926)

and so on until both values agree to 0.73909. The required solution is, therefore, 0.73909 to 5 decimal places.

Exercise 1.5

Plot the function $f(x) = e^{-x} - x$ to show that it has a zero in the interval $0 \le x \le 1$, and then find the solution of $e^{-x} - x$=0.

The Secant Method

Although the bisection method is a reliable way of finding approximations for roots, faster methods are sometimes useful. One approach is to approximate the curve $y=f(x)$ near the solution by a straight line and to use linear interpolation close to the root we want to find. Figure 1.8 shows a function that has a zero in the interval $a \le x \le b$. We now join the points $(a,f(a))$ and $(b,f(b))$ by a secantt and consider where this line cuts the x-axis.

We see that the secant joining the points $(a,f(a))$ and $(b,f(b))$ cuts the x-axis close to the solution we need. We call this point c and then repeat this process with the points $x= a$ and $x=c$. This is called the **secant method**.

Notice that this method effectively replaces the curve by a linear approximation over the interval (a,b).

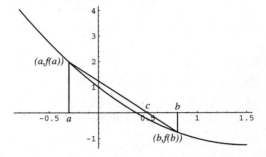

Figure 1.9. The secant method for solving $f(x)=0$.

Example 1.5
Find the solution of the equation $\cos(x)=x$, x>0 using the secant method.

First we let $f(x)$=$\cos(x)$ - x for which $f(0)$=1 and $f(1)$=-0.459698. Then following the construction in Figure 1.9, we join (0,1) and (1,-0.459698) by the line

$$y=-1.459698x+1.$$

We now determine where this line cuts the x-axis. This gives x=0.68507 at which f(0.68507)=0.0893. We then repeat this process with a=0.68507 and b=1 to generate the next approximation at x=0.736299. Repeating this process again gives the approximations 0.73912, 0.73909, and 0.73909. Therefore, the required solution is 0.73909 to 5 decimal places.

Exercise 1.6

Determine both solutions of the quadratic equation $3x^2$-3x-1=0 using the bisection method and the secant method. Which is the faster method? Which is the easiest to apply and why?

The basis of the secant method is shown in Figure 1.9. In this figure we can see that the function is effectively approximated by the secant, and the next approximation by linear interpolation between $x=a$ and $x=b$.

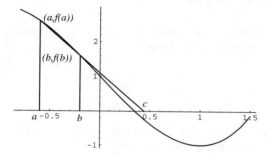

Figure 1.10. The secant method for solving f(x)=0.

In fact, we do not actually need $f(a)$ and $f(b)$ to have opposite sign as Figure 1.10 shows. We can still join the points $(a,f(a))$ and $(b,f(b))$ and then extend this line to where it cuts the x-axis, which gives a new approximation. Effectively, this is using extrapolation to estimate the required solution.

 Exercise 1.7

Determine the smallest positive solution of the cubic equation $x^3 - 3x + 1 = 0$ using the secant method and the initial intervals:

(i)   (0,1);

(ii)   (-0.5,1).

WORKED EXAMPLE 1.1: HIGHWAY SERVICE STATIONS

As an example of the way in which mathematical functions can be composed we will consider the costs involved in maintaining a highway. Let us assume that the major costs during the life of the station are the cost of running the service stations and then the traveling costs of moving equipment and engineers to carry out repairs. If we decide to build very few stations, then the traveling costs will be high. If we build a lot, then the traveling costs are lower but station running costs are larger. Can we represent this by a mathematical function?

First, we identify any variables and their units:

n	Number of service stations
A	Cost of running one station ($M)
T	Total cost ($M)
L	Length of the highway (km)
d	Distance between stations (km)
N	Number of incidents attended per year
k	Traveling costs per kilometer

Next we decide how these variables are related.

Station Running Costs

As each service station costs A and there are n stations the total running cost is nA.

Traveling Costs

As the stations are d km apart, the maximum distance traveled to an incident is $d/2$, and so the total traveling cost is at most $Nk\left(\dfrac{d}{2}\right)$.

However, since the complete length of the highway is L, $dn=L$ which gives the total maximum traveling costs to be $Nk\left(\dfrac{L}{2n}\right)$.

Total Costs

The total cost is given by adding the running and traveling costs to give

$$T = nA + \frac{NkL}{2n}$$

which is a combination of a linear function nA and a nonlinear function $NkL/(2n)$.

Notice that as n tends to zero the total cost rises, similarly, as n gets bigger so does the total cost. Is this what you would expect?

If we wish to build 4 stations then the total cost would be

$$T(4) = 4A + \frac{NkL}{8}.$$

Alternatively, if we were given a total budget of $100M for the stations then to find n we need to solve the equation $T(n)=100$ or

$$100 = nA + \frac{NkL}{2n}.$$

Simplifying this gives a quadratic equation

$$2n^2A - 200n + NkL = 0$$

which has two solutions.

Which root do we need and what is the significance of the other?

WORKED EXAMPLE 1.2: FORESTRY DATA PROBLEM

This problem concerns the growth of trees and how data can be plotted and used to assist commercial exploitation. Consider the data given in Table 1.2 below.

Age (yr)	Height (m)
10	7
20	10
30	14
40	16
50	18

Table 1.2. Heights of trees recorded as a function of time.

How can we estimate the height of the tree when it is 25 years old?

When is the tree approximately 13 m high?

First, we identify any variables and the units in which they are measured:-

H Height of the tree (m)

t Age of the tree (yr)

The data in Table 1.2 is plotted in Figure 1.11.

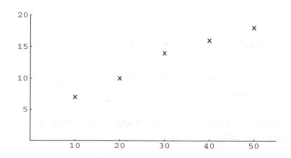

Figure 1.11. Tree data from Table 1.2.

Figure 1.11 shows that trees do not grow linearly, but over any short period we can make such an approximation. To estimate the height of the tree at any time between 10 and 20 years, we can fit a straight line between the points (20,10) and (30,14).

Let us suppose that the equation of the required line is

$$H(t)=mt+b.$$

The slope of the line joining the points (20,10) and (30,14) is

$$m = \frac{14-10}{30-20} = 0.4$$

and $b=2$ so that

$$H(t)=0.4t+2.$$

The height of the tree after 25 years will be $H(25)= (0.4)(25) + 2 = 12$ m.

To determine when a tree was 13 metres high we need to solve the equation $H(t)=13$. This gives

$$0.4t+2=13$$

or

$$t=27.5 \text{ years.}$$

The interpolating function, $H(t)=0.4t+2$, derived for the range $20 \leq t \leq 30$, predicts that the trees will be 18 metres high after 40 years and yet the original data give a height of only 16. What do you conclude? (We have assumed that we can extrapolate the data given to find the height of the tree outside the range $t=20$ to $t=30$.)

To illustrate the problems inherent in this procedure let's look at some extreme cases.

What happens when $t=0$ or $t=1000$ years?

When $t=0$, $H(t)=0.4t+2$, gives $H(0)=2$, that is, the trees are 2 metres high.

After 1000 years the tree will be given by $H(1000)=402$ metres. Is this sensible?

What do you conclude about extrapolation?

WORKED EXAMPLE 1.3: FORESTRY DATA PROBLEM

In Worked Example 1.2 we considered interpolating the data in Table 1.2 using linear functions. To do this we selected two points and *fitted* a straight line

$$H(t) = mt + b.$$

It is clear, from Figure 1.10, that a straight line is not a good approximation over the whole range. Hence, we might decide to fit a curve instead. For example, we could use the quadratic function

$$H(t) = a + bt + ct^2.$$

As there are now three coefficients to find, we need three equations to determine them. For example, if this function is to pass through the points (10,7), (20,10) and (30,14) we need to ensure that $H(10)=7$, $H(20)=10$ and $H(30)=14$. This produces the equations

$$a + 10b + 100c = 7$$
$$a + 20b + 400c = 10$$
$$a + 30b + 900c = 14$$

Solving these equations produces values for the coefficients a, b, and c; hence,

$$H(t) = 5 + \frac{3}{20}t + \frac{1}{200}t^2.$$

This predicts that the height of a tree after 25 years will be 11.875 m (compared with the predicted value of 13 m in Worked Example 1.2).

Similarly, in Worked Example 1.2 we estimated when the trees would be 13 metres high. Now we need to solve the quadratic equation

$$13 = 5 + \frac{3}{20}t + \frac{1}{200}t^2.$$

The solutions of this quadratic equation are $t=27.72$ years and $t=-57.72$ years.

What is the significance of the negative root?

What happens when $t=0$ or $t=1000$ years

When $t=0$ then $H=5$, that is, trees start 5 metres high?

After 1000 years the tree will be 5155 metres high. Is this sensible?

Figure 1.12 shows the function $H(t)$ and the remaining two points from Table 1.2.

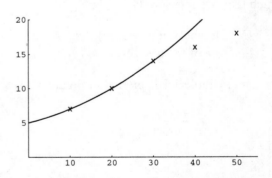

Figure 1.12. The interpolating quadratic through (10,7), (20,10), and (30,14).

What do you conclude about this example of the use of extrapolation?

PROBLEM 1.1: HIGHWAY SERVICE STATIONS

Name: _____

Date: _____

Section: _____

In Worked Example 1.1, a function was developed to determine the cost of *n* highway service stations. Use this function to answer the following questions for a highway which is 400 km in length, where each station costs $4M/year, the maximum number of incidents is 500 per year and the costs of traveling to an incident are 200$ per km.

(Write your answers in the spaces provided or use the reverse side of this page.)

How much will it cost if 5 depots are used?

$2n^2 A - 200n + NkL = 0$

$50 \times 4 - 1000 + \frac{500 \cdot 200 \cdot 400}{40000000}$

$T = nA + \frac{NkL}{2n}$

$200M - 1500 + $

$240M - 1000$

$= 16M + \frac{500 \cdot 200 \cdot 400}{10}$

$= 16M + 4M = 20M$

If a maximum of $50M is available each year, what is the maximum number of service stations that can be built?

$50M = nA + \frac{NkL}{2n}$

$\Rightarrow 200n M = 2n^2 A + NkL$

$\Rightarrow 2An^2 - 200m \cdot n + NkL = 0$

$8n^2 - 200n + 40 = 0$

$\Rightarrow n = \frac{200 \pm \sqrt{4000 - 1280}}{8}$

$= \frac{200 \pm 52}{8}$

$31 \text{ or } 18$

If inflation increases the running costs of each service station by 5%, what effect will this have on the number of stations that can be afforded?

If traveling costs increase by 5%, what effect will this have?

PROBLEM 1.2: POLYNOMIAL INTERPOLATION

Name: _____

Date: _____

Section: _____

In Worked Examples 1.2 and 1.3, linear and quadratic functions were fitted to the data in Table 1.2. What is the highest degree polynomial that can be fitted through all five points given? (Hint: Two points determine a linear function and three determine a quadratic. What will four points determine, and so on?)

(Write your answers in the spaces provided or use the reverse side of this page.)

Construct a cubic polynomial passing through the first four points in Table 1.2. Interpolate at t=25. Estimate when the trees were 13 m high.

Construct a polynomial that passes through all the points in Table 1.2. Interpolate at t=25. Estimate when the trees were 13 m high.

Compare the estimates computed above with those determined in Worked Examples 2 and 3. What do you conclude about the results as the number of points included increases?

NEW SITUATIONS

1. Metal Tray

A metal tray is to be formed from a sheet that is 2 ft by 1 ft by removing a small square at each corner and folding the sides. Find an expression that relates the volume of the tray so formed in terms of size of the square removed.

2. Coffee Cup Problem

Coffee is frequently served in polystyrene cups that are in the shape of a truncated cone. Find an expression for the surface area and volume of such a cone in terms of its dimensions. If the cup must contain exactly half a pint and the angle of the sides is fixed at a, find an expression for the surface area in terms of the height of the cup. Plot a curve of the surface area as a function of the height.

3. Solving equations

Find the smallest positive solution of the equation $ae^{-x} = \sin(x)$ when $a=2,4,6,8,10$. Plot the function given by

$F(a)=\{$Smallest solution of $ae^{-x} = \sin(x)\}$.

Is $F(a)$ a continuous function?

A point $x=a$ is called a zero of a function $f(x)$ if $f(a)=0$. This is equivalent to being able to write $f(x)=(x-a)g(x)$. If $g(a)\neq0$ then $x=a$ is called a simple zero. If $g(a)=0$ then in turn we can write $g(x)=(x-a)l(x)$, hence ;

$$f(x)=(x-a)^2l(x)$$

and the function f is said to have a double

root. At a double root show that $f(a)=0$ and $f'(a)=0$.

Show that the equation

$$ae^{-x} = \sin(x)$$

has a double root when a is approximately 8 and find this root correct to 5 decimal places.

4. The Secant Method

The secant method generates a sequence of approximate solutions for a root of the equations $f(x)=0$, which we will call x_0, x_1, x_2, x_3, and so on. To find this sequence let $x_0=a$ and $x_1=b$, where $f(a)$ and $f(b)$ have the opposite sign. Find the equation of the linear function passing through $(x_0,f(x_0))$ and $(x_1,f(x_1))$ and show that if this function vanishes at x_2, then

$$x_2 = x_1 - \frac{f(x_1)}{\left(f(x_1) - f(x_0)\right)}(x_1 - x_0).$$

Derive the general expression for the secant method in the form

$$x_{n+1} = x_n - \frac{f(x_n)}{\left(f(x_n) - f(x_{n-1})\right)}(x_n - x_{n-1})$$

where x_n is the n-th approximation for the required solution.

5. Accuracy

In many instances when data are recorded the accuracy is limited by the equipment that is used. Measuring the heights of trees is clearly subject to a certain degree of error. In Worked Examples 2 and 3 we used the data in Table 1.2 to estimate the height of trees when they were 25 years old. Now let us suppose that the heights given in Table 1.2 are only accurate to 5%. How accurate are the computed coefficients and the interpolated value? How accurate is the extrapolated value produced in Worked Examples 1 and 2? Would you expect to achieve an overall accuracy of 5%?

6. Extrapolation

The population of a colony of geese is observed over an 8 year period and produced the following results.

Year	Population
1980	2000
1982	4528
1984	5458
1986	5800
1988	5973

Table 1.3. The population of a colony of geese.

By fitting a "suitable" polynomial to this data predict the geese population in 1990 and 2000.

What do you conclude from your results?

7. Conditioning

The solutions of the quadratic equation $ax^2+bx+c=0$ are given by

$$x=\frac{-b\pm\sqrt{b^2-4ac}}{2a}.$$

As the values of a, b, and c change the solutions will change with them. However, do small changes in the coefficient produce small changes in the solutions of the quadratic?

Find the solutions of

$$x^2-39x+380=0$$

and

$$x^2-39x+380.5=0.$$

What do you conclude? Is this polynomial subject to similar problems when the other coefficients are changed by similar amounts?

Are the solutions of the quadratic equation

$$x^2-3x+2=0$$

subject to a similar problem. Investigate the circumstances under which the roots of quadratic equations suffer from this type of problem.

Chapter 2

Limits

Before you study this chapter, you should be familiar with:

(1) The idea of a function and how it is defined.

(2) How functions can be classified and visualized.

Objectives

The main purpose of this chapter is to introduce limits. A limit is a value that can be "approached as closely as you like", but perhaps never "attained". Limits are essential to the theory of the calculus. It is the idea of a limit that will enable us to define the slope of a curve, and later to introduce differentiation and integration.

What do we really mean by saying, for example, "as I passed the road sign I was doing 30 mph"? The idea of a limit is no harder than this simple everyday concept, although there is a precise mathematical way of describing this idea.

There are special techniques for finding limits in certain cases. More generally, the concept of a limit provides the essential link between some mathematical ideas and their useful interpretation in everyday applications.

In this chapter the "Achilles and Tortoise" paradox is introduced. If you are not familiar with the paradox, run the software that illustrates it fully. The paradox interested the ancient Greeks and led them and, later, mathematicians to accept that a process with infinitely many steps can for common sense reasons have a finite limit, and that the limit is "real" in the sense that it is obvious that Achilles catches the Tortoise. The software will enable you to replay the race as a simulation, which will bring home the nature of the paradox as well as being an example of a limiting process.

The software also includes a video of a typical road trip where a limiting situation arises. On a road with a 60 mph speed limit, if you observe the limit then your average speed can never reach 60 mph. This illustrates from everyday experience a limit that we do not expect to attain.

Achilles and the Tortoise: Zeno's Paradox

The Achilles and Tortoise paradox is presented in the software, and shows that there are some puzzling features in the concept of a limit. Common sense tells us that Achilles catches the Tortoise, and obviously Zeno knew that! The point of his perverse logic is that it is hard to explain it away, because the sequence of steps into which he divides the progress of the race is infinite. So what is wrong, if anything, with Zeno's way of looking at the race? The paradox will be resolved later in this module, and it will require us to accept the idea of a limit.

Exercise 2.1

Simulation of the race.

Simulate the paradox step by step. Alter the starting places of Achilles and the Tortoise and their running speeds, and see that the paradox has nothing to do with the particular values chosen.

Start with the default values shown. Then try giving the tortoise a bigger start, a smaller start, and then give it different speeds (but lower than Achilles!). What is the common sense effect on the place where Achilles catches up, and how long this takes? What is the effect on Zeno's analysis?

Now suppose that Achilles isn't feeling well and cannot run as fast as the Tortoise, and choose some speeds accordingly. How does Zeno's analysis deal with this situation?

Further problems and activities are suggested in the software.

Exercise 2.2

The common sense solution to Zeno's Paradox

Suppose that Achilles gives the tortoise a 100 m start, and that Achilles runs with speed u and the tortoise at speed v. Show that the time for A to catch $T = 100/(v\text{-}u)$.

Hint: what is the relative speed of Achilles with respect to the tortoise?

Average speed

In the video clip and simulation of the trip, it is important to note that the average speed for the whole trip can never *reach* the cruising speed, but if the drive on the highway can go on indefinitely then the average can get *as close as you like* to the cruising speed.

Example 2.1

Suppose the trip starts with a delay of p sec, but then resumes at a constant speed of s m/sec. Then the distance traveled after t sec (for $t>p$) is $d = s \times (t - p)$. Therefore, the average speed over this distance is $v(t) = \dfrac{s \times (t - p)}{t} = s - \dfrac{sp}{t}$.

Here the variables are all positive, so $\dfrac{sp}{t}$ always represents something positive, which is subtracted from s. Therefore, the average speed is always less than s. However, by making the time t long enough, you can make the reduction as small as you like, but it can never be zero.

Exercise 2.3

In the trip simulation, alter the starting delay and cruising speed. Convince yourself that the average speed is always less than the cruising speed.

Upper and lower bounds

A function $f(x)$ over a given interval of values x can have an upper bound, or a lower bound, both, or neither.

An upper bound is a value that the function never goes above.

A lower bound is a value that the function never goes below.

It is important to emphasize that the bounds usually depend on the interval of x over which the function is considered. However, some functions have "global" bounds; that is, they can be bounded on the interval $-\infty < x < +\infty$. Although the computer cannot plot over an infinite interval, you can usually investigate the behavior of the function sufficiently well over a finite interval to predict the global behavior with confidence.

Exercise 2.4

Run the software in the concept "Upper and Lower Bounds". There are a number of functions and a number of intervals that are pre-set, and you can plot any function over any of the intervals. Determine which have finite global bounds. Which functions have a global lower bound but no finite global upper bound?

Exercise 2.5

Do the problems suggested in the software: "Areas of Circles".

Further problems and activities are suggested in Problem 2.1 later in this chapter.

Limits: sequences and series

The idea of a limit applies also to sequences and series. Here, we will use these terms with the following meanings (which are not formal definitions).

A *sequence* is an ordered set of values a_n. For example,

$$1, 2, 3, 4, 5, 6, 7, \ldots$$

is a sequence with $a_n = n$, and

$$1, \frac{1}{4}, \frac{1}{9}, \frac{1}{16}, \frac{1}{25}, \ldots$$

is a sequence with $a_n = \frac{1}{n^2}$.

A *series* is formed by adding together the values of a sequence. Thus the following are series:

$$1 + 2 + 3 + 4 + 5 + 6 + 7 +$$

$$1 + \frac{1}{4} + \frac{1}{9} + \frac{1}{16} + \frac{1}{25} + \ldots$$

If a sequence is defined for all integer n (so there are infinitely many members of the sequence), then the corresponding series is called an *infinite series*.

The question arises: Does a sequence of values have a limit? In other words, is there a value a that a_n approaches as n gets larger and larger? If there is such a value, it is called the "limit as n tends to infinity", and this would be written as $a_n \to a$ as $n \to \infty$. It is obvious that the sequence $a_n = n$ does not have a limit: in fact, $a_n \to \infty$ as $n \to \infty$, whereas the sequence $a_n = \frac{1}{n^2}$ does have a limit: in fact, $a_n \to 0$ as $n \to \infty$. If a limit exists, the sequence is said to *converge*; otherwise, it is said to *diverge*.

When the terms of a sequence are added to form a series, then it is often of interest to know whether the sum of the series converges to a limit.

Example 2.2

Consider the geometric series $a + ar + ar^2 + ar^3 + ar^4 + \ldots$. In this case define $S_n = \sum_{k=1}^{n} ar^{k-1}$. It can be shown that $S_n = a\dfrac{1-r^n}{1-r}$. If $r < 1$, then $r^n \to 0$ as $n \to \infty$, and so $S_n \to a\dfrac{1}{1-r}$ and the series converges. If $r > 1$, then $r^n \to \infty$ as $n \to \infty$, and so $S_n \to \infty$, and the series does not converge. What happens if $r = 1$?

Example 2.3

The divergence of a sequence or series does not necessarily imply that values increase with unbounded magnitude. In Example 2.2, take $a = 1$ and $r = -1$. The values S_n form the sequence $+1$, -1, $+1$, -1, $\ldots$. This behavior is still called divergent, because there is no limit, but it may also be described as *oscillatory*.

Limits: functions

A limit of a function $f(x)$ is defined as a value that can be approached as closely as required. Sometimes a limit can be rather obvious and trivial.

Example 2.4

The function $f(x)=x$ has the limit 1 as x approaches 1. This is obvious because we can actually take $x=1$ and also get as close as required to 1 (for example, x=0.9, 0.99, 0.999, 0.9999, etc.). Mathematically this is written as $f(x) \to 1$ as $x \to 1$. It is also true that $f(x)$ attains the limit when $x=1$.

In the above example, the function $f(x)$ could be evaluated directly at the point where the limit was required. This cannot always be done, as the next example shows.

Example 2.5

Consider the function $f(x) = \frac{1}{x}$, which gets smaller and smaller as $x \to \infty$. Here $f(x)$ can be made as small as desired, but can never actually be made zero. The value 0 is a lower bound for $1/x$ in the region $x>0$. So $\frac{1}{x} \to 0$ as $x \to \infty$. This is the same as the statement "the limit of $\frac{1}{x}$ as x tends to infinity, is zero". In this case the function does not attain the limit.

The "limiting value" of a function is sometimes used to define the value of that function at points where it is otherwise undefined.

Example 2.6

Consider $f(x) = \dfrac{sin(x)}{x}$. It is not possible to evaluate this function at x=0, because that would require dividing by zero. However, it *is* possible to evaluate this function for nonzero values of x "as close as you like" to zero. It will be seen that $f(x)$ approaches the value of 1 in this case, and so it is reasonable to define $f(0)=1$. It will also be seen that there is a precise mathematical way of expressing the concept of being "as close as you like" to some value.

Types of Convergence

In situations where a function or sequence diverges (that is, does not converge) there are several possible types of behavior. The types that will arise in our examples are (a) unbounded divergence, or (b) oscillation without convergence. A function is said to diverge if it tends to $\pm\infty$ as x tends to the value in question. Note that in divergent cases the direction of divergence can depend on how the limit is approached.

Oscillation without convergence (as opposed to oscillatory convergence) implies that the value rises and falls without approaching a limit. Thus, for example, $1/x$ diverges to $+\infty$ if $x \to 0$ from above, but diverges to $-\infty$ if $x \to 0$ from below. The function $\cos(x)$ oscillates as $x \to \pm\infty$.

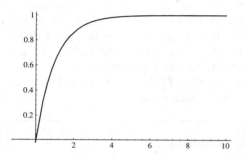

Figure 2.1. A function that increases monotonically to a limit as $x \to \infty$.

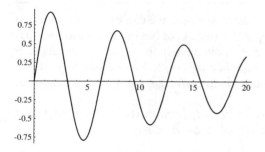

Figure 2.2. A function showing oscillatory behavior.

Exercise 2.6

Look at the software examples shown on the concept "Types of Convergence". Each example has an expression that approaches some limiting value as closely as you like. Each is illustrated with a graphical demonstration so that you can see what is happening. Note that most of the examples exhibit monotonic convergence to a limit, but at least one shows oscillatory convergence.

Average speed: the ε game

In the preceding sections of this chapter, you have learned how sequences and functions can approach limiting values. In the examples that approached limits, the statement "approach as close as you like" has not been proved rigorously, but was stated as obviously true from observation and mathematical intuition. Mathematicians like to be more precise than this, and this section demonstrates how a precise mathematical meaning can be given to the phrase "approach as close as you like".

Examine once again the example showing the average speed of a trip, as shown in the concept "Limits of Average Speed" and in Example 2.1 above. Using the same variables as in Example 2.1, we have seen that the average speed is

$$v(t) = \frac{s \times (t - p)}{t}.$$

For illustration, take $s=60$ mph, t as the time in minutes, and p as 9 minutes (convince yourself that you can express t in any units you like as long as you express p in the same units as t).

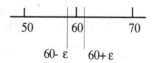

Figure 2.3. An interval containing values that are close to the value 60 mph.

First we must concentrate on what we mean by "close", and give this word a precise mathematical meaning. This can be done by thinking of a relatively small positive number, traditionally denoted by ε (Greek epsilon), and then saying that any value $v(t)$ within the interval 60-ε

$< v(t) < 60+\varepsilon$ will be called "close" to 60. For example, we might agree that any speed within the interval 59 to 61 mph is close to 60 mph (i.e. take $\varepsilon=1$ mph).

This definition goes part of the way towards what is needed, but being close some of the time is not enough! If 60 is to be a limit, then we will require that there is some critical time T beyond which $v(t)$ remains in this band for **all** times $t > T$. This is true in this example, because the function $\dfrac{60 \times (t-9)}{t}$ increases monotonically towards 60 as $t \to \infty$.

Exercise 2.7

Verifying a limit.

Show that for all $t > T$, where $T = \dfrac{540}{\varepsilon}$,

$60 - \varepsilon < \dfrac{60 \times (t-9)}{t} < 60 + \varepsilon$.   Verify   the

formula for $\varepsilon = 0.1, 0.01, 0.0001$.

Even this requirement is not sufficient to express fully our intuitive concept of a limit. Imagine an auto with a faulty cruise control unit that varies the speed cyclically by 1/2 mph so, for instance, $v(t) = \frac{1}{2}\sin(t) + \dfrac{60 \times (t-9)}{t}$. There is a time beyond which the speed stays within the 59 to 61 mph band, but we would not agree that the limit is 60 mph, since the speed ends up oscillating about this value. If we were to choose $\varepsilon=1/4$ mph, then our requirement for a time beyond which the average speed stayed with a band from 59.75 to 60.25 mph could not now be satisfied. We see therefore that a rigorous definition of a limit must not rely on just one value of ε, but must hold for **any** $\varepsilon > 0$, how-

ever small (positive but nonzero). Mathematically, the requirement that $v(t)$ tends to the 60 mph limit is stated as:

"Given any $\varepsilon>0$, there exists a value T such that for all $t>T$, $60-\varepsilon<v(t)<60+\varepsilon$."

You can think of this as a simple mathematical game between two players A and B. To win, A has to think of an ε for which B cannot find a value T. B wins if she can show that whatever ε is chosen by A, she can always find a value T such that for all $t>T$, $60-\varepsilon<v(t)<60+\varepsilon$. If B wins, we say that a limit exists.

Exercise 2.8

Take the part of Player A in the ε game against the computer for the average speed function. Convince yourself you can never win!

It is easy to see how we can extend this idea to a sequence. Instead of having a continuous variable t, we now have index numbers for terms in the sequence a_n (say). Mathematically, if the sequence is to converge to a limit a, we require:

"Given any $\varepsilon>0$, there exists a value N such that for all $n>N$, $a-\varepsilon < a_n < a+\varepsilon$."

Exercise 2.9

Do the problems suggested in the software: "Introduction to Limits".

Exercise 2.10

Prove that the sequence $a_n = (1/n)$ converges to 0 as $n \to \infty$ by finding a formula for N (which will depend on ε).

The ε game for x → x₀

You have seen in the preceding sections how a limit can be defined precisely in the two situations (a) of a continuous variable (e.g., time t) tending to infinity, or (b) of an integer variable (e.g., n) tending to infinity. But you have also seen instances where it is of interest to consider a limit as a continuous variable approaches a finite value. For example, $Lim_{x \to 0} f(x)$ where

$$f(x) = \frac{\sin(x)}{x} \text{ as in Example 2.6.}$$

This new situation is met with a simple adjustment to the definition of a limit. Suppose it is required to show that $Lim_{x \to x_0} f(x) = L$, or in alternative notation that $f(x) \to L$ as $x \to x_0$. In terms of the game between two players, A still sets a value for ε that defines a band (which we will call the f-band) within which $f(x)$ has to stay. The f-band will be the interval L-ε < $f(x)$ < L+ε. In this situation B must find a corresponding band for values of x, say, x_0-δ < x < x_0+δ (which we will call the x-band) for which $f(x)$ stays within the f-band set by A.

It may help to look at a situation where there isn't a limit. Consider the case shown in Figure 2.4 with $f(x)$ = -1 for all x < 0, and $f(x)$ = +1 for all x > 0. Leave $f(0)$ undefined for the moment. Consider the limit of $f(x)$ as $x \to 0$ (take $x_0 = 0$ in this example). Player A easily wins, because she only has to choose ε=$\frac{1}{2}$. It is obvious that however small player B chooses the x-band -δ < x < +δ, the function varies between -1 and +1 throughout the x-band, and cannot possibly lie in the f-band set by A. For example, if B chooses δ = 0.01, then for -0.01 < x < 0 we get $f(x)$ = -1, and for 0 < x < 0.01 we get $f(x)$ = +1. Hence, the width of the f-band in which values of $f(x)$ lies is 2, whereas player A has challenged B to make the width of the f-band less than 2ε=1.

Notice that whatever $f(0)$ is defined to be, the function still has no limit as $x \to 0$. Take $f(0)$ = 0, for example, and reconsider the statements in the preceding paragraph.

The formal definition becomes:

"If $f(x) \to$ a limit L as $x \to x_0$, then given any ε>0, there exists a value δ > 0 such that for all x for which x_0-δ < x < x_0+δ , L-ε < $f(x)$ < L+ε."

Exercise 2.11

Do the problems suggested in the software: "Finding Limits".

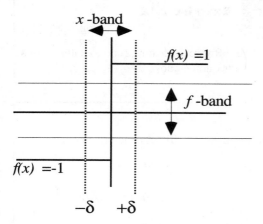

Figure 2.4. The e-game for a discontinuous function.

Instantaneous speed

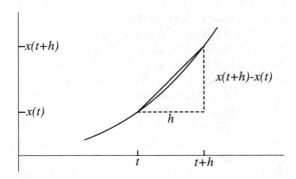

Figure 2.5. Speed as the slope of a distance vs. time graph.

Now that the meaning of a limit has been examined, the idea can be applied to the everyday concept of instantaneous speed. A manufacturer of speedometers can test them by timing a vehicle electronically over a measured distance. Suppose the vehicle's position along a track is given by $x(t)$. Suppose the timer starts at t and stops at $t+h$. Then the average speed over this interval is $\dfrac{x(t+h) - x(t)}{h}$. This is, of course, just the slope of a small segment (chord) on the distance-time graph. If this quantity tends to a limit as $h \to 0$, then this limit can be called the "instantaneous speed" at time t. This idea will be explored more fully in later modules.

Zeno's paradox resolved

Zeno knew, of course, that Achilles will catch up with Mr. T. What puzzled Zeno and his contemporaries was, where was the flaw in their logic?

The common sense solution is based on the idea that A's speed relative to T is $(v-u)$, and A has 100 m to run relative to T, so for a 100 m start, the time for A to catch T is $\dfrac{100}{v-u}$. For example, if A runs at 6.67 m/s (which is approximately "4 minute mile" speed) and T moves at 0.03 m/s (approximately 100 m/hr), then the catching-up time is $\dfrac{100}{6.67 - 0.03} = 15.06$ sec. The paradox is set out in Table 2.1.

Continuing this process gives a total time that is the sum of the infinite series $S = (100/u)(1 + v/u + (v/u)^2 + (v/u)^3 + (v/u)^4 + \dots)$. The paradox is resolved if we can recognize that an infinite series can have a sum with a finite limit, since then although the number of separate steps in Zeno's analysis is infinite, the sum of all the individual times is finite.

Exercise 2.12

Run the software to see how Zeno's analysis gives the results quoted above.

Table 2.1: Zeno's Paradox

	Time for stage	Total time so far
1. A runs to T's original position T advances a distance *(100/u)v*	*100/u*	*100/u*
2. A runs to T's new position T advances a distance *(100v/u²)v*	*100v/u²*	*(100/u)(1 + v/u)*
3. A runs to T's new position T advances a distance *(100v/u²)v* and so on …	*100v²/u³*	*(100/u)(1 + v/u+(v/u)²)*

PROBLEM 2.1
UPPER AND LOWER BOUNDS

Name: _____

Date: _____

Section: _____

Consider the average speed problem, based on Example 2.1.

Suppose that the trip starts at speed u m/sec and this speed is maintained for p sec. Then the speed rises to s m/sec for the remaining time, where $s > u$. Show that the average speed is always less than s.

(Write your answers in the spaces provided or use a separate sheet of paper.)

Find the distance traveled in time t for (i) $t \le p$, (ii) $t > p$.

Use the previous result to obtain an expression for the average speed over the trip from t=0 up to time t, where t>p.

Write the above result in the form s - z, and show that z is positive provided that s > u.

Now use pencil and paper to answer the following questions, and then check your results using the software.

Suppose u=0 and p=10 sec (which gives the same situation as Example 2.1) and the cruising speed s is 28 m/ sec (approx. 100 kph, approx. 60 mph). How long into the trip before the average speed is just above (a) 20 m/sec, (b) 27 m/sec, (c) 27.9 m/sec, (d) 27.99 m/sec?

Now suppose that the initial speed u is 14 m/sec and that this is maintained for 600 secs. How long into the trip before the average speed is just above (a) 20 m/sec, (b) 27 m/sec, (c) 27.9 m/sec, (d) 27.99 m/sec?

PROBLEM 2.1
UPPER AND LOWER BOUNDS
(continued)

Think of some functions that have global upper bounds but no global lower bounds.

Hint: if you know the bounds of a function f(x), what can you say about the bounds of -f(x)?

Find the global upper and lower bounds (if they exist) of some more functions:

cos(x)   *tan(x)*   *(1+x)/(1-x)*   *(1-x)/(1+x)*

1/(1+x²)   *(1-x)/(1+x²)*   *exp(x)*   *exp(-x)*

exp(-x²)   *exp(x) over -∞ < x ≤ 0*

log(x) over 0 < x ≤ 1   *log(x) over 1 ≤ x < ∞.*

PROBLEM 2.2
LIMITS OF FUNCTIONS

Name: _____

Date: _____

Section: _____

Consider each of the following functions as $x \to \infty$. Use the software to decide whether they are oscillatory or monotonic, and whether they converge or diverge.

(Write your answers in the spaces provided or use a separate sheet of paper.)

Hint: see the software section "Finding limits ".

(1) f(x) = x sin(x), (2) f(x) = cos(x)/x², (3) f(x) = sin(x)/(1+cos(x))

(4) f(x) = exp(x)/x5, (5) f(x) = log(x), (6) f(x) = log(x)/x

(7) f(x) = (1+x)/(1-x), (8) f(x) = (1-x2)/(1-x), (9) f(x) = (1+2x)/(1+x)

(10) f(x) = (1+2x)²/(1+x²).

If they converge, what are their limits?

Repeat for x → −∞. Are there any for which the question cannot be answered?

PROBLEM 2.2
LIMITS OF FUNCTIONS
(continued)

Which of the convergent cases have the same limit?

Use the software to find the limits shown, or discover how they behave if there is no limit.

Hint: it may help you to attempt to plot the function over a suitable interval, and then use the function calculator to evaluate the function closer and closer to the limit.

If the function diverges, say whether it diverges to +∞ or -∞.

(1) $\dfrac{\sin(x)}{x}$ *as* $x \to 0$　　(2) $\dfrac{\tan(x)}{x}$ *as* $x \to 0$　　(3) $\dfrac{\cos(x)}{1 - \frac{1}{2}x^2}$ *as* $x \to 0$

(4) $x \log(x)$ *as* $x \to 0$　　(5) $\sin(\frac{1}{x})$ *as* $x \to 0$　　(6) $\dfrac{(1 - x^2)}{(1 - x)}$ *as* $x \to 1$

(7) $\dfrac{(1 + x^2)}{(1 - x)}$ *as* $x \to 1$

(8) $\exp(\dfrac{1}{x-1})$ *as* $x \to 1$ *from below*　　(9) $\exp(\dfrac{1}{x-1})$ *as* $x \to 1$ *from below*

PROBLEM 2.3
SEQUENCES AND SERIES

Name: _____
Date: _____
Section: _____

(i) Use the software to decide whether the following sequences are oscillatory or monotonic. Which of them converge, and which diverge?

(Write your answers in the spaces provided or use a separate sheet of paper.)

$a_n = (-1)^n/n$ $b_n = 1/n$ $c_n = 1$ $d_n = (2)^n$

$e_n = (-2)^n$ $f_n = (2)^n/n!$ $g_n = (-2)^n/n!$ $h_n = (20)^n/n!$

$j_n = (-20)^n/n!$ $k_n = (1+n)/(1-n)$ $p_n = (1-n^2)/(1-n)$ $q_n = (1+2n)/(1+n)$

$r_n = (1+2n)^2/(1+n^2)$ $r_n = a^n$ for $a>1$ $s_n = a^n$ for $-1<a<+1$ $t_n = a^n$ for $a=\pm1$.

For those that converge, what is their limit?

(ii) Verify the formula quoted in Example 2.2 for the partial sum of a geometric series for the following cases, by using the software to find numerical values for several choices of n, and comparing the values with the value obtained from the formula. You should easily be able to predict which converge to a limit, and which do not.

$1 + \frac{1}{2} + \frac{1}{4} + \frac{1}{8} + \frac{1}{16}\cdots$ $2 + 6 + 18 + 54 + 162 + \ldots$

$1 - \frac{1}{2} + \frac{1}{4} - \frac{1}{8} + \frac{1}{16}\cdots$ $2 + 0.2 + 0.02 + 0.002 + \ldots$

PROBLEM 2.3
SEQUENCES AND SERIES
(Continued)

(iii) Investigate the limit of the sequence $a_{n+1} = \frac{1}{2}\left(a_n + \frac{2}{a_n}\right)$. You will need to choose a suitable starting value for a_0. Are there any restrictions on your choice of a_0 if the sequence is to converge? If a suitable starting value can be found, what will be the limit of the sequence $a_{n+1} = \frac{1}{2}\left(a_n + \frac{x}{a_n}\right)$ for x>0?

(iv) Investigate the sequence $a_n = \left(1 + \frac{k}{n}\right)^n$. Suppose that $a_n \to E$ for $k = 1$. Investigate the limit for $k = 2, 3, 4$ and give a prediction for a general result.

The software also contains a derivation to show that

$$S = a(1 + r + r^2 + r^3 + r^4 + r^5 + \ldots) = \frac{a}{1-r}.$$

What expressions for a and r must be chosen to make the series correspond to Zeno's analysis?

Substitute back for a and r and show that this result is the same as the commonsense solution.

Let $S_n = \sum_{k=1}^{n} ar^{k-1}$. *Show that* $S_n = a\frac{1-r^n}{1-r}$.

Hint: you can use a method similar to the method used in the software to derive the limiting sum of the series.

NEW SITUATIONS

1. Finding limits

When functions can be evaluated easily, then limits are also easy to work out and you may not think the concept of a limit is particularly useful, or needed. For example,

$$x^2 \to 1 \text{ as } x \to 1$$

$$\frac{1}{x} \to \frac{1}{2} \text{ as } x \to 2 \quad .$$

$$x^3 + 3 \to 30 \text{ as } x \to 3$$

In these cases the limits are attained, because when $x = 1, 2,$ or 3, respectively, the functions equal their limits.

The concept of a limit is more useful when a function is either

(i) undefined at some value $x=a$, or

(ii) when we want to know what happens when x "gets very large" (i.e. "tends to" $\pm\infty$).

Investigate the examples below, using the software if you want.

(i) Undefined values can result from division by zero and logarithms of zero:

$$\frac{\sin(x)}{x} \to ? \text{ as } x \to 0$$

$$x \log(x) \to ? \text{ as } x \to 0$$

$$\sin(x) \log(x) \to ? \text{ as } x \to 0$$

(ii) Typical examples of limits as x "tends to" $\pm\infty$:

$$\frac{1}{x} \to ? \text{ as } x \to +\infty$$

$$\frac{1}{x} \to ? \text{ as } x \to -\infty$$

$$\frac{1+x}{2+x} \to ? \text{ as } x \to \pm\infty$$

$$e^{-x} \to ? \text{ as } x \to +\infty$$

$$\frac{\log(x)}{x} \to ? \text{ as } x \to +\infty$$

There is no general rule for finding limits, but graphical and numerical investigation will often help to indicate the value of a limit.

2. Limits of quotients

Mathematical expressions in the form of quotients $\dfrac{f(x)}{g(x)}$ are quite common, and it is often possible to see what their limiting values are by examining the numerator $f(x)$ and denominator $g(x)$ separately.

For example, consider $\dfrac{4x^2 - 5x}{2x^2 + 10x}$ as $x \to \infty$.

The value of the numerator $4x^2 - 5x$ will eventually be dominated by the term $4x^2$. When $x=100$, say, the two terms evaluate to (40000-500). In other words, as $x \to \infty$ the numerator is approximated well by the term $4x^2$ alone. Similarly, the denominator is approximated well by the term $2x^2$ alone as $x \to \infty$. Since

$$\frac{4x^2}{2x^2} = 2,$$

we deduce that as $x \to \infty$,

$$\frac{4x^2 - 5x}{2x^2 + 10x} \to 2.$$

A similar line of reasoning helps us to see the limit as $x \to 0$. Now it is the other terms that dominate: for example, when $x=0.01$, the numerator evaluates to (0.0004-0.05) and the denominator to (0.0002+0.1). Therefore, we can deduce that as $x \to 0$, $\dfrac{4x^2 - 5x}{2x^2 + 10x} \to \dfrac{-5x}{10x} = -\dfrac{1}{2}$.

Even when there is no limit, this technique can predict the approximate behavior of a function as x approaches some region of values of interest. For example,

$$\frac{x^3 \sin(x) - 2x \cos(x) + 3}{x^2 + x + 1} \rightarrow x \sin(x)$$

as $x \rightarrow \infty$.

The top line is dominated by the x^3 term, and the bottom line by the x^2 term.

By examining the following expressions, predict their limiting values (if there is a limit) or their behavior as $x \rightarrow -\infty$, $x \rightarrow 0$ and $x \rightarrow \infty$. Verify your results by using the software.

(i) $\dfrac{4x^2 - 5x}{2x^2 + 10x}$

(ii) $\dfrac{x^3 \sin(x) - 2x \cos(x) + 3}{x^2 + x + 1}$

(iii) $\dfrac{x^3 + e^x}{xe^x}$

(iv) $\dfrac{3x^4 - 2x^2 \sin(x) + 100}{100 - x}$

(v) $\dfrac{1 + e^x \cos(x)}{1 - e^x \sin(x)}$

(vi) $\dfrac{1 + \ln(x)}{1 - \ln(x)}$ as $x \rightarrow 0$ and as $x \rightarrow \infty$

3. One-sided limits

It is worth noting that it is now possible to define "one-sided limits", in which the value of x approaches a limit point from one direction. For a decreasing sequence of x-values for which , $x \rightarrow x_0$ we say " $x \rightarrow x_0$ from above". To consider the limit of $f(x)$ as $x \rightarrow x_0$ from above, instead of using the x-band *centered* on x_0, use $x_0 < x < x_0 + \delta$. To consider the limit of f(x) as $x \rightarrow x_0$ from below, use $x_0 - \delta < x < x_0$.

As an example, consider the function $f(x) = -1$ for all $x < 0$, and $f(x) = +1$ for all $x > 0$. Show that $f(x) \rightarrow 1$ as $x \rightarrow 0$, from above. Choose an $\varepsilon > 0$. For any d, > 0 we have that $f(x) = +1$ for all x in the x-band $0 < x < d$. Therefore, $f(x)$ lies in the f-band $1 - \varepsilon < f(x) < 1 + \varepsilon$ for all ε, and we conclude that $f(x) \rightarrow 1$ from above.

Find the following one sided limits:

(i)   As $x \rightarrow 0$ from below, $\dfrac{|x|}{x} \rightarrow$?

(ii)   As $x \rightarrow 0$ from above, $\dfrac{|x|}{x} \rightarrow$?

(iii)   As $x \rightarrow 1$ from above, $\sqrt{x-1} \rightarrow$?

Chapter 3

Rates of Change and Differentiation

Prerequisites

To take full advantage of this module make sure you understand. the following material.

(1) How to plot functions.

(2) How to find the slope of a straight line (Module 1).

(3) The concept of limits (Module 2).

Objectives

The phrase **rate of change** is frequently used in many different contexts. The objective of this module is to explain what it means mathematically. Once the idea is understood we will then ask:

"If we are given two variables, related by a given function, is it possible to determine the rate of change of one variable with respect to the other?"

This simple idea led to one of the most important mathematical tools: **The Calculus.**

Connections

The two video presentations for this module illustrate the fundamental importance of rates of change. Many physical laws use this idea. For example, one of Newton's laws of motion states:

"The **rate of change** of linear momentum is equal to nett forces acting."

Other examples are provided by Newton's Law of cooling:

"The **rate** at which a body looses heat is proportional to its excess over the ambient temperature"

and the law of radioactive decay is given by:

"The **rate** at which a radioactive substance decays is proportional to the mass of the radioactive material present."

What is meant by **rate** in these examples?

The first application concerns the motion of a car as it moves along a road. The speedometer measures its speed. What do we mean by speed? If the car is traveling at 30 miles per hour does it mean that we have to wait for 1 hour before traveling 30 miles? In fact, in 1 minute the car will cover half a mile. In 1 second the car will travel 44 feet. So to say that the car is traveling at 30 miles per hour means that the average rate of change of distance is equivalent to 30 miles per hour. If we refine the interval further so that it tends to zero, we get the instantaneous rate of change distance with time; the speed of the car. This limiting process forms the basis of the differential calculus.

The second application concerns the rate at which a hot air balloon rises or falls as the gas burner is used to control the flight. As the air inside is heated, the balloon will rise; as it cools the balloon will descend. You will be able to investigate such a situation with the animation provided with this module.

Rate of change and slope

The linear function $y=mx+c$ represents a straight line for which the slope is the same at each point. Given any two points on the line, the rate of change of y with respect to x is the slope of the line.

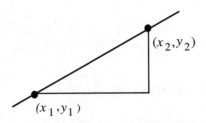

Figure 3.1. The straight line between (x_1,y_1) and (x_2,y_2).

For example, the slope of the line joining (x_1,y_1) to (x_2,y_2) is given by

$$\frac{\text{difference in } y \text{ values}}{\text{difference in } x \text{ values}} = \frac{\Delta y}{\Delta x} = \frac{y_2 - y_1}{x_2 - x_1} = m$$

therefore, the rate of change of y with respect to x is m.

Example 3.1

The slope of the line joining the points $(1,1)$ and $(3,2)$ is $1/_2$ as shown in Figure 3.2.

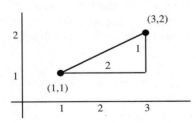

Figure 3.2. The line joining the points (1,1) and (3,2).

In the preceding example it was possible to find the slope of a straight line because the slope was the same at every point, but how can we find the slope of a curve at any point?

A line that just touches a curve is called a tangent. It is distinguished from a secant, or chord, which cuts the curve twice as shown in Figure 3.3. However, as the points of intersection of the chord with the curve get closer together, the chord approaches the tangent.

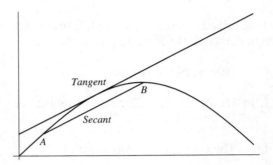

Figure 3.3. Secants and tangents.

 Exercise 3.1

Plot the function $y=0.1x^2+3$. Sketch the tangent to this curve at the point $x=2$. Draw the secant between the points on the curve when $x=0$ and $x=4$. Investigate what happens to the slope of the secant as the points $x=0$ and $x=4$ approach $x=2$.

Differentiation as a limit

In the Figure 3.3 there were two points, A and B, that were being adjusted simultaneously. We can now simplify this approach by keeping one point, A, fixed where the tangent touches the curve and moving the other, B, as shown in Figure 3.4.

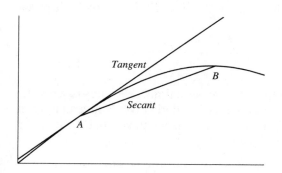

Figure 3.4. Secants and tangents.

As the point B approaches A, along the curve, the angle between the secant and the tangent approaches zero. In the limit, as AB tends to zero, the slope of the secant approaches the slope of the tangent which is the same as the slope of the function.

Exercise 3.2

Investigate the secant approximation to the function $y=^1\!/_2\,e^x$ at $x=1$.

The approach outlined above is graphical; a more analytical approach is needed. Let us begin by looking at the simplest non-linear function, $y=x^2$. At the point $x=1$ we consider the secant joining the points on the curve from $x=1$ to $x=2$.

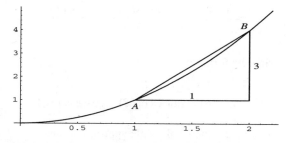

Figure 3.5. Finding the slope of the line AB.

From Figure 3.5 the slope of the secant AB is given by the rise divided by the run. For the function $y=x^2$ this is given by

$$\frac{2^2-1^2}{1}=\frac{4-1}{1}=\frac{3}{1}=3$$

As B gets closer to A we should get better and better approximations for the slope of the curve.

Exercise 3.3

Investigate the slope of the secant joining the point $A=(1,1)$ on the curve $y=x^2$, to the points given below.

B	slope
$(1.1,1.1^2)$	2.1
$(1.01,1.01^2)$	2.01
$(1.001,1.001^2)$	2.001

What happens to the slope of the chord as the points get closer?

Differentiation of functions

To carry out the procedure in Exercise 3.3 for every function is just too complicated, so let us look for a simplification. Consider the general point x and a point close to it, $x+h$. Taking $x=1$ and $h=1$ would give Figure 3.5. The slope of the chord is now

$$\frac{(x+h)^2-x^2}{h}=2x+h.$$

Taking $x=1$ and $h=1$ this becomes 3, as before, but we can also consider all other values as well. For $x=1$ and $h=0.001$ this gives the slope equal to 2.001. Now taking the limit as h tends to zero, we get

$$\underset{h \to 0}{\text{Limit}} \frac{(x+h)^2 - x^2}{h} = 2x.$$

This is equivalent to saying that the slope of the curve $y=x^2$ at the point x is $2x$. We have been able to associate with the function x^2 another function $F(x)=2x$ according to the rule

$$F(x) = \{\text{the slope of } y=x^2 \text{ at } x\}.$$

Rather than introducing another function, we write $F(x)=y'$ so that if $y=x^2$ then $y'=2x$. This new function is called the derivative and may also be written as

$$\frac{dy}{dx} \text{ or } \dot{y}$$

The number of different notations reflects the diverse origins in the development of the Calculus. The process of obtaining the function y' from y is called differentiation; the function y' is called the *derived function* or *derivative*.

We can apply this rule to any function $f(x)$ by using the same approach.

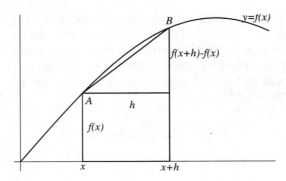

Figure 3.6. Estimating the slope of $y=f(x)$ from the slope of the line AB.

The slope of the line AB in Figure 3.6 is given by

$$\frac{f(x+h) - f(x)}{h}.$$

If this approaches a limit, as h tends to zero, the result is called the derivative. Notice that h can be made as small as we please but it can never reach zero.

Example 3.2

Find the derivative of the function $f(x)=x^3$ and hence its slope at $x=2$. From the definition of the derived function we consider

$$\frac{f(x+h) - f(x)}{h} = \frac{(x+h)^3 - x^3}{h}$$

$$= 3x^2 + 3xh + h^2,$$

and so

$$\underset{h \to 0}{\text{Limit}} \frac{(x+h)^3 - x^3}{h} = 3x^2$$

therefore, the function $f(x)=x^3$ has derivative $f'=3x^2$. At $x=2$ the slope is 12.

Example 3.3

To find the derivative of the function $f(x)=\sin(x)$ we consider

$$\frac{f(x+h) - f(x)}{h} = \frac{\sin(x+h) - \sin(x)}{h}$$

$$= \frac{\sin(x)\cos(h) + \cos(x)\sin(h) - \sin(x)}{h}$$

using the formula

$$\sin(A+B) = \sin(A)\cos(B) + \cos(A)\sin(B).$$

Next we use the small angle approximations,

$$\sin(h) \approx h \text{ and } \cos(h) \approx 1 \text{ for small values of } h,$$

so that

$$\frac{\sin(x) + \cos(x)h - \sin(x)}{h} \rightarrow \cos(x).$$

Therefore, if $f(x)=\sin(x)$ then $f'=\cos(x)$.

Exercise 3.4

Use the procedure outlined above to show that:

$y(x)$	$y'(x)$
mx+c	m
x^4	$4x^3$
x^n	nx^{n-1}
$\cos(x)$	$-\sin(x)$

Linearity

The more closely we look at any curve, the straighter it appears to be. This suggests that, in the limit, we can find the slope of the curve by approximating it by a straight line. This is not surprising since the slope of the curve at any point is given by the slope of the tangent at the point.

Example 3.4

If we look at the function $y=x^2$ over the range $0\le x\le 1$ it is clearly a curve. However, if it is plotted over the interval $0.49\le x\le 0.51$, it looks more like a straight line. See Figures 3.7 and 3.8 for these graphs.

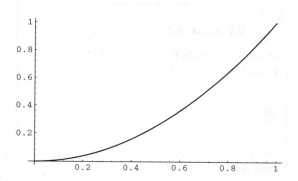

Figure 3.7. $y=x^2$, $0 \le x \le 1$.

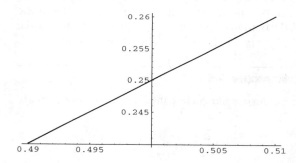

Figure 3.8. $y=x^2$, $0.49 \le x \le 0.51$.

Exercise 3.5

Plot the function $y=x^3$ for $0\le x\le 1$. Zoom in and see what happens over the ranges (0.4,0.6), (0.49,0.51), and (0.499,0.501).

Rules of differentiation

We now know how to find the derived function for x^2 and x^3, but what about the sum x^2+x^3? It would be nice if the derivative of the sum of two functions were the sum of the derivatives. It is!

Exercise 3.6

Show that the slope of the chord joining the points x and $x+h$ on the curve $f(x)=x^2+x^3$ is given by

$$\frac{f(x+h)-f(x)}{h}=3x^2+3xh+h^2+2x+h.$$

Show that as h tends to zero, this approaches a limit and that $f'(x)=3x^2+2x$.

What about the product of functions? If we know that the derivative of $f(x)$ is $f'(x)$ and the derivative of $g(x)$ is $g'(x)$, what is the derivative of $f(x)g(x)$? Is it $f'g'$? The answer is no.

Example 3.5

Let $f(x)=x$ and $g(x)=x$, then $f(x)g(x)=xx=x^2$ so that

$$\frac{d}{dx}(fg)=\frac{d}{dx}(x^2)=2x.$$

However, $f'=1$ and $g'=1$ so that $f'g'=1$; therefore,

$$(fg)'\neq f'g'$$

How, then, do we differentiate functions built up from simple combinations of other functions?

Let $f(x)$ and $g(x)$ be differentiable functions and a any constant, then:

Multiple rule: $(af)'=af'$ (1)

Addition rule: $(f+g)'=f'+g'$ (2)

Difference rule: $(f-g)'=f'-g'$ (3)

Product rule: $(fg)'=gf'+fg'$ (4)

Quotient rule: $\left(\dfrac{f}{g}\right)'=\dfrac{gf'-fg'}{g^2}$ (5)

We will not attempt to justify these rules here they can be found in any Calculus textbook. We will, however, give an example.

Example 3.6

Differentiate the function $f(x)=(x+2)\sin(x)$. The function f is made up from the product of two simpler functions each of which it is easy to differentiate. Putting $u(x)=x+2$ and $v(x)=\sin(x)$ gives $f(x)=u(x)v(x)$. To differentiate f we use the product rule,

$$f'=uv'+vu'.$$

Here $u(x)=x+2$ and thus $u'=1,v(x)=\sin(x)$ so that $v'=\cos(x)$. Combining these results (4) gives

$$\begin{aligned}f'=uv'+vu'&=(x+2)\times\cos(x)+(1)\times\sin(x)\\&=(x+2)\cos(x)+\sin(x)\end{aligned}$$

The Chain Rule

Mathematical functions are often built up by composing functions. For example, given the function $3x+2$ we can compose this with the sin function to get $f(x)=\sin(3x+2)$. The chain rule gives us a method for differentiating such functions.

Chain Rule: $(f(g))'=f'g'$ (6)

The chain rule looks very complicated, but it is often easier to think of it as differentiation by substitution. To consider the function $f(g(x))$ we set $f=f(g)$ and $g=g(x)$, then

$$\frac{df}{dx} = \frac{df}{dg}\frac{dg}{dx}.$$

Example 3.7

To differentiate the function $f(x)=\sin(3x+2)$, we put $g=3x+2$ so that $f(x)=f(g)=\sin(g)$. Now we differentiate f with respect to g to get

$$\frac{df}{dg} = \cos(g).$$

However, we want df/dx, which the chain rule gives as

$$\frac{df}{dx} = \frac{df}{dg}\frac{dg}{dx} = 3\cos(g) = \cos(3x+2).$$

Example 3.8

To differentiate the function $f(x)=(x+1)^3$, we could expand f to get $f(x)=x^3+3x^2+3x+1$. Differentiating this function gives $f'=3x^2+6x+3$. Alternatively, applying the chain rule to f, we put $g=x+1$ so that

$$f(x)=g^3 \quad \text{and} \quad \frac{df}{dg}=3g^2$$

giving

$$\frac{df}{dx} = \frac{df}{dg}\frac{dg}{dx} = 3g^2 = 3(x+1)^2$$

because $\dfrac{df}{dx}=1$. Which then is easier? Here there is no doubt, but what if the function were a little more complicated? For instance:

(i) $f(x)=(x+1)^{10}$, where the expansion would be difficult but if now we put $u=x+1$ then

$$\frac{df}{dx} = \frac{df}{du}\frac{du}{dx} = (10u^9)(1) = 10(x+1)^9$$

(ii) $f(x)=(x+1)^{-5}$, where the chain rule gives

$$\frac{df}{dx} = \frac{df}{du}\frac{du}{dx} = (-5u^{-6})(1) = -5(x+1)^{-6}$$

(iii) $f(x)=\sqrt{(x+1)}=(x+1)^{1/2}$, where the chain rule gives

$$\frac{df}{dx} = \frac{df}{du}\frac{du}{dx} = \left(\frac{1}{2\sqrt{u}}\right) = \frac{1}{2\sqrt{(x+1)}}$$

The preceding examples are a little complicated but demonstrates that the rules for differentiation can be applied one by one as needed to the differentiation of most functions.

Higher Order Derivatives.

The derivative of a function is itself a function and we may be able to differentiate it as well. The derivative of a function $f(x)$ determines the rate of change of a function or the slope of the curve $y=f(x)$. The derivative of f' determines the rate of change of the slope and is related to the curvature of a function.

The derived function is called the first derivative. The derivative of the first derivative is called the second derivative and so on.

Example 3.9

Find the second and third derivatives of $y=x^3$. The first derivative is given by $y'=3x^2$ which can also be written as $\dfrac{dy}{dx} = 3x^2$. The derivative of this function is $6x$, and therefore we write

$$y''=6x$$

or

$$\frac{d^2y}{dx^2} = \frac{d}{dx}(\frac{dy}{dx}) = \frac{d}{dx}\left(3x^2\right) = 6x.$$

In the same way $y'''=6$.

 Exercise 3.7

Find the derivative of $f(x)=\cos(2x)$.

(i) Where is the derivative largest?

(ii) Where is it smallest?

(iii) To which points on the function $f(x)$ do these points correspond?

(iv) What do you notice about the way the graph is "curving" at these points?

(v) What is f'' at these points?

WORKED EXAMPLE 3.1:
WHAT IS SPEED?

The distance of a car from a fixed point is measured and recorded in Table 3.1.

Time (sec)	Distance (ft)
0	0
1	48.01
2	92.08
3	132.27
4	168.64

Table 3.1. Recorded Distances of a Car for $0 \leq t \leq 4$.

How do we estimate the speed after 2 seconds? Over the complete interval the car covers 168.64 feet in 4 seconds, an average of 42.16 ft/sec. Over the interval $t=1$ to $t=3$ the car travels 132.27-48.01=84.26 ft. The average speed over this interval is therefore 84.26/2=42.13 ft /sec. If we want to find the speed at $t=2$ we need more information. For example, if the distance traveled after t seconds is given by

$$s(t)=50t-2t^2+0.01t^3$$

then the rate of change of s with respect to time gives the car's speed. During the interval $t=1.9$ to $t=2.1$ the car will cover s(2.1)-s(1.9)=8.42402 feet at an average speed of 42.1201 ft/sec. Over the interval $t=1.99$ to $t=2.01$ it will cover

$$s(2.01)- s(1.99)=0.84240002 \text{ ft}$$

at an average speed of 41.120001 ft/sec.

Similarly, over the interval (2,2.01) it will cover s(2.01)-s(2)=42.1006 feet at an average speed of 42.1006 ft/sec.

In the same way over an interval t to $t+k$ the car will have moved from $s(t)$ to $s(t+k)$, that is, it will have traveled a distance

$$
\begin{aligned}
s(t+k) &- s(t) \\
&= 50(t+k) - 2(t+k)^2 + 0.01(t+k)^3 \\
&\quad -(50t - 2t^2 + 0.01t^3) \\
&= 50k - 4tk - 2k^2 + 0.03t^2k + 0.03tk^2
\end{aligned}
$$

The average rate of change of s over this interval is then

$$\frac{s(t+k) - s(t)}{k} = 50 - 4t - 2k + 0.03t^2 + 0.03tk.$$

Then as k gets smaller this expression approaches $50-4t+0.03t^2$, and therefore, we write

$$s'(t)=50-4t+0.03t^2.$$

Equivalently, we differentiate $s(t)$ to get the same result. From this we find that the speed after 2 seconds is $s'(2)=42.212$ ft/sec.

WORKED EXAMPLE 3.2: BALLOON FLIGHT

A hot air balloon that encloses 180,000 ft^3 is heated by a burner which generates 8,000,000 Btu. (A normal house furnace generates between 60,000 and 100,000 Btu). The mass of the balloon, the gas cylinders and the passengers is 2810 lb. The balloon rises in still air which is at 5° C. If the burner is on for 10 seconds, then switched off for 5 seconds before burning for another 10 seconds find the rate of climb after 25 seconds.

Air Temperature (°C)	Lift/1000 ft^3 (lb)
0	20
5	19.5
10	18
15	17
20	16

Table 3.2 Lift Generated per Thousand Cubic Feet of a Balloon that has Internal Temperature 100° C.

The volume of the balloon is 180,000 ft^3, therefore if the ambient temperature is 5° C the lift generated is 180×19.5 lb = 3510 lb. The total mass being lifted is 2810 lb and therefore, the difference is 710 lb.

We now assign variables that in this case are

$v(t)$ velocity at time t (ft/sec)

L lift when the burner is on (lb)

m mass of balloon (lb)

When the burner is off, we assume that the balloon will fall under gravity so that

$$m\frac{dv}{dt} = -mg$$

where m=2810 and g=32 ft/s^2.

When the burner is on, the equation of motion is

$$m\frac{dv}{dt} = (L-m)g,$$

where L=3510.

These equations determine the rate of change of velocity of the balloon. They reduce to

$$v' = \frac{700 \times 32}{2810} = 7.97 \text{ft/sec when the burner is on,}$$

and v'=-32ft/sec when the burner is off.

Initially, v'=7.97, so that the graph of v against t is a straight line with slope 7.97, that is, v=7.97t+c, for some c. However, when t=0, v=0 and so c=0, giving v=7.97t. After 10 seconds the vertical velocity is $v(10)$=79.7 ft/sec.

The burner is now turned off so that v'=-32, which means that the graph of v is a straight line with slope -32, giving v=-32t+c. When t=10 the balloon is ascending at 79.7 ft/sec so that now 79.7 = -32×10 + c which gives c = 399.7 and v=-32t + 399.7. After 5 seconds with the burner off, t=15, the rate of climb is $v(15)$=-80.3 ft/sec and the balloon is falling rapidly. (How do we know it is falling?)

If the burner is now switched on then v'=7.97, so that the graph of v is a straight line with slope 7.97, that is v=7.97t+c, for some c. When t=15, v = -80.3; therefore c=-199.85 giving v=-199.85+7.97t. After 10 seconds, when t=25, the vertical velocity is $v(25)$=-0.6 ft/sec. (Which direction is the balloon moving at this point?)

Now try plotting the function that is given by $v(t)$, 0 ≤t≤25.

PROBLEM 3.1:
CAR ACCELERATION

Name: _____

Date: _____

Section: _____

In Worked Example 3.1 we were able to approximate the speed of a car by looking first at the average rate of change of distance over smaller and smaller intervals and then, the instantaneous rate of change of the function $s(t) = 50t - 2t^2 + 0.01t^3$. In the same way we can determine the acceleration of the car at any time. Acceleration is the rate of change of velocity with time.

(Write your answers in the spaces provided or use the reverse side of this page.)

Tabulate the speed of the car at one second intervals during the period t=0 to t=4 seconds.

Find the average acceleration over the interval t=2 to t=3 seconds.

Find the average acceleration over the intervals (1.9,2.1), (1.99,2.01), (2,2.1), (2,2.01).

Find the derivative of s´ at t=2 seconds.

PROBLEM 3.2:
BALLOON EXTENSION

Name: _____

Date: _____

Section: _____

For the balloon in Worked Example 3.2, the altitude is a function of t, which we can write as $s(t)$. Since velocity is the *rate of change* of distance with respect to time, if the balloon rises with velocity $v(t)=at+b$, then the distance traveled after time t is $s(t) = \frac{1}{2} at^2 + bt + c$. This can be easily confirmed by differentiation. For the worked problem, when the burner is initially on, the velocity during the first 10 seconds is $v=7.97t$ so that $s(t) = \frac{1}{2} 7.97t^2 + c$. As the balloon is initially at rest on the ground $s(0)=0$ giving $s(t) = \frac{1}{2} 7.97t^2$ and $s(10)=398.5$ ft.

(Write your answers in the spaces provided or use the reverse side of this page.)

Find the height of the balloon after 15 seconds if the burner is off for 5 seconds.

Find the height of the balloon after 25 seconds if the burner is turned on for 15 $\leq t \leq 25$.

Plot the altitude of the balloon over the interval $0 \leq t \leq 25$.

What would happen if the flight had taken place on a warmer day?

NEW SITUATIONS

1. Mathematical Functions

Determine rate of change of each of the following functions at the points shown,

(i) $y = x3 - 3x + 3$, $-2 \le x \le 2$, $x = -1, 0, 1$,

(ii) $y = e^{-x^2}$, $-2 \le x \le 2$, $x = -2, 0, 2$,

(iii) $y = x^2 e^{-x^2}$, $x > 3$, $x = 10, 20, 100$.

2. Folding a Tray

A metal sheet which is 2 ft by 1ft is shaped into a tray by removing a small square at each corner and folding the sides. Find an expression that relates the volume of the tray in terms of size of the square removed. Find the rate at which the volume changes as a function of the surface area .

3. Coffee Cup Problem

Coffee is frequently served in polystyrene cups that are in the shape of a truncated cone. Find an expression for the volume of such a cone in terms of its dimensions. What is the rate of change of the volume for a fixed height with respect to the angle of the sides?

4. Radioactive Decay

"The half-life of plutonium is 24,000 years"

What does this mean? If 1 kg of plutonium was placed in a room it would decay. But, in doing so it would give off lethal radiation, so that after 24000 years there would be 500 g of plutonium remaining. This determines the half-life of plutonium. After another 24,000 years there would be 250 g and so on. How long will it be before there is only 1 g left? The rate at which the plutonium decays is proportional to the amount of plutonium present. If there is a large amount it decays rapidly; if there is a small amount then it does so slowly. This can be written as

$$\frac{dM}{dt} = -kM,$$

where M is the mass of Plutonium and k is a positive constant. (This equation is called a differential equation and it will be discussed in a later module.). Show that the function $M(t) = M_o e^{-kt}$ satisfies this equation for any value of M_o. When $t=0$, $M(0)=1000$, and when $t=24000$, $M(24000)=500$; show that $k = {}^{-\log(2)}/_{2400}$. How long will it be before the original mass is reduced to 1 g?

5. Drinking Coffee Problem

Coffee is usually made up of 90 percent coffee taken from a hot urn and 10 percent cold milk taken from a refrigerator. The rate at which either cools or warms up is proportional to the difference between the temperature of the particular liquid and the surrounding air. If the coffee is made by putting the milk in first and waiting 1 minute before adding the coffee, does it cool quicker than if the coffee is put in first?

6. Newton's Method

The secant method for solving the equation $f(x)=0$ was described in Chapter 1. The basis of the secant method is shown in Figure 3.9.

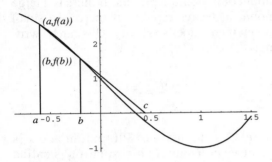

Figure 3.9. The secant method for solving $f(x)=0$.

For the secant method we join the points $(a,f(a))$ and $(b,f(b))$ and then extend this line to where it cuts the x-axis at c, which gives a new approximation for the solution of $f(x)=0$. However, as a and b get closer together the slope of the secant will approach the slope of the tangent, which is given by the value of the derived function at the point of contact.

Show that if x_0 is an approximate solution then

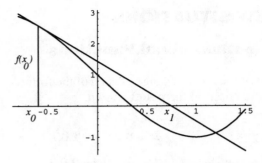

Figure 3.10. Newton's method for solving $f(x)=0$.

$$x_1 = x_0 - \frac{f(x_0)}{f'(x_0)}$$

gives a better approximation. In general if x_n is an approximate solution then

$$x_{n+1} = x_n - \frac{f(x_n)}{f'(x_n)}$$

generates a sequence of approximations that will nearly always converge to a solution if $f(x)=0$.

Use Newton's method to find all the solutions of

$$\cos(x)=x.$$

Compare the results with those given by the secant method for this problem.

Chapter 4

Inverse and Transcendental Functions

Prerequisites

Before you study the material in this module you should know about:

(1) Functions and how they can be classified and visualized (Module 1).

(2) Elementary trigonometric and exponential functions.

(3) The derivative and differentiation of simple functions, (Module 3).

Objectives

The concept of a mathematical function was introduced in Chapter 1. Recall that a function is a process for associating a value, y, with an argument x. For example, in Figure 4.1, for the value $x=0.8$ there is only one value for y, namely, 0.64. We write $y(x)$ to denote that y is a function of x, but is x also a function of y?

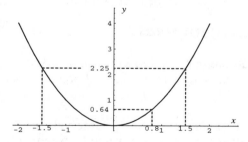

Figure 4.1. The mathematical function $y=x^2$.

Inverse functions arise when we interchange the roles of the dependent and independent variables: given a value of y, what value of x will make $y=f(x)$? In terms of the x-y graph, we are now choosing a value on the y-axis and reading off the corresponding x value. If this can be done, then

we can write $x=g(y)$ where g is the *inverse function* of f. The notation $g=f^{-1}$ is also used. For example, for the graph in Figure 4.1, the value $y=2.25$ gives two values of x, one at $x=1.5$ and a second at $x=-1.5$. Therefore, x is **not** a function of y. However, if we allow x to take only positive values, then for the function $f(x)=x^2$, $x>0$, each value of y determines only one value for x. In this case the function f is said to have an inverse, or to be *invertible*.

This Chapter will consider which functions have inverses, how they can be found, and their derivatives.

Connections

We need to find a simple condition to determine if a function is invertible. It turns out that whenever a function has a maximum or minimum the function is not invertible. To illustrate the idea of maximum or minimum, (which are collectively called extrema[1]), the first application considers a roller-coaster ride. Rides contain all the features about extrema to be studied: high points, low points, horizontal parts, and so on. Here, you will be able to simulate and replay sections of the ride, including features of interest like a high point, or maximum.

The second situation illustrates how transcendental functions can arise. The simulation associated with this application looks at the construction of part of a flight simulator.

---

[1] Extreme vaues, maximum or minimum are called collectively - "extrema" - if you use Latin plurals, or "extremums", if you prefer English plurals.

Intervals and Extrema

Figure 4.1 shows that the function $y=x^2$ is not invertible if all values of x are permitted. However, if we restrict the definition of this function to positive values of x then for each y there is a unique value of x and the resulting function is invertible. How, then, do the functions

$$\text{(i) } y=x^2,$$

and

$$\text{(ii) } y=x^2, \ x \geq 0,$$

differ? In terms of the Calculus the difference is that the derivative of the first function takes both positive and negative values; the derivative of the second is always the same sign. This is the key to determining whether or not a function is invertible. Alternatively, if a function has either a minimum or maximum, or both, then the slope of the curve $y=f(x)$ has at least one zero, therefore, the derivative changes sign.

The concepts of maxima and minima are well illustrated by a roller-coaster track. In the graph of a typical function, think of a maximum as a typical high point and a minimum as a typical low point. In some sense the start and end of the ride must be a high or a low too, but these points obviously cannot be like the typical hump or trough found in mid-ride (because it is not possible to pass through the start or end-points). A start-point or end-point is usually described as an extremum, but may not necessarily be a maximum or minimum.

It is important to note that there can be several highs and lows in a rides. Hence, places like these are sometimes called local maxima or minima, to make a distinction between them and the global extrema, which are the places that are at the greatest or least heights over the whole ride.

 Exercise 4.1

Simulation of the roller-coaster ride.

Use the software to simulate the roller-coaster ride.

Locate: a maximum, a minimum, an extreme value that is neither a maximum nor a minimum.

Observe the behavior of the slope as you go from a maximum to a minimum, and from a minimum to a maximum.

Alter the shape of the track and observe how the positions of any minima and maxima change.

Exercise 4.1 should confirm the following results.

"At a minimum or maximum on a curve $y=f(x)$, which is not an end point of the interval where the function is defined, the derivative either vanishes or is undefined."

Defining intervals

Intervals are important to a precise description of extrema, and there is a special notation for them.

The statement "x lies in the interval $[a,b]$" means that x can take any value between and including a and b. The value of a should be the lowest of the pair a,b. The statement can also be written:

$$a \leq x \leq b .$$

Note that when the end-points of the interval are included (as here), the interval is known as a *closed interval*.

The statement "*x* lies in the interval (*a,b*)", means that *x* can take any value between but *not* including *a* and *b*. The statement can also be written:

$$a < x < b.$$

Note that when the end-points of the interval are not included (as here), the interval is known as an *open interval*.

The notation may be adapted in the obvious way to describe intervals that are open at one end and closed at the other. For example, the statement "*x* lies in the interval [*a,b*)" can be written:

$$a \le x < b,$$

and the statement "*x* lies in the interval (*a,b*]" can be written:

$$a < x \le b.$$

Exercise 4.2

View the "Intervals & Extrema" concept from the software. Select functions and ranges from the lists available. Drag the interval markers on the graph to see examples of different intervals. Enter some other functions of your choice.

Exercise 4.3

View the "Intervals & Extrema" concept in the software. This illustrates how intervals describe different sections of a curve.

Find some intervals where:

    the highest point is at one end of the interval;

    the highest point lies inside the interval;

    the lowest point is at one end of the interval;

    the lowest point lies inside the interval.

Turning Points and Extrema

An *extremum* is a place where a function takes its highest or lowest values in some local interval. For example, in Figure 4.2 there are two obvious extrema, a "high" at *x* =-1 and a "low" at x= ⅓, but if the interval [-2, 1] is being considered, then the values of *y* = -1 at *x* = -2 and *y* = 2 at *x* = 1 are also extrema.

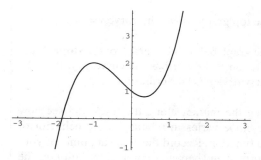

Figure 4.2. $y = x^3 + x^2 - x + 1$.

In the graph representing the roller-coaster track, a maximum is a place where the ride reaches a "high". At a maximum that is not at the start or end of the track, the ride switches over from going up to going down. The car will be instantaneously traveling horizontally.

A minimum is a place where the ride reaches a low. At a minimum that is not at the start or end of the track, the ride switches over from going down to going up. The car will be instantaneously traveling horizontally.

In general, at a turnimg point the slope changes sign. All minima and maxima are turning points. However, notice that all turning points are extrema but not all extrema are turning points.

Exercise 4.4

Look at the "Turning Points & Extrema" concept in the software.

Verify that the slope of the curve changes as just described.

Notice the screens where both the function and its derivative are shown.

The top graph shows the curve $y=f(x)$.

The graph below it is a graph of the **slope**. If the function $f(x)$ describes the curve $y=f$, then the **derivative** $f'(x)$ describes the slope.

Drag the marker along the track and see how the slope varies in relation to the behavior of the function. Record the slope at points of your choice at and between extrema, to show how the slope varies.

Mathematical Functions

Any function which can be constructed by using only multiplication and addition of an independent variable is called a *polynomial function*.

Example 4.1

The following functions are polynomial functions:

(i) $2x^2+3$, $5 \leq x \leq 5$

(ii) $x^4 + 3x - 2$, $-2 \leq x \leq 2$

(iii) $x^7 + x^2 - 2x$, $0 \leq x \leq 4$

A *rational function* is the ratio of one polynomial function to another.

Example 4.2

The following functions are rational functions:

(i) $\dfrac{1}{x}$, $2 \leq x \leq 5$

(ii) $\dfrac{x+1}{x-3}$, $-2 \leq x \leq 2$

(iii) $\dfrac{x^2+1}{x^2-4}$, $0 \leq x \leq 1$

Transcendental Functions

Polynomial and rational functions are built up by a finite number of additions, multiplications and divisions. Polynomial and rational functions are examples of *algebraic functions*, as is any function that is constructed by using integer or fractional powers, such as $\sqrt{}$, of the independent variable or any constants. All non-algebraic functions are called *transcendental functions*.

Example 4.3

The following functions are transcendental functions:

(i) $y=\log(x)$, $x > 0$

(ii) $y=\sin(x)$

(iii) $y=\tan(\cos(x))$

(iv) $y=e^{-\sin(x)}$

Inverse Functions

From Figure 4.1 we see that a function f which is either always increasing or always decreasing is invertible. However, if the slope is zero at any point, that is, $f'=0$, then the function may not be invertible. If the function has either a minimum or a maximim then it will not have an inverse.

Example 4.4

Show that the function $f(x)=x^2-3x+2$ has a maximum at $x=1.5$ and that if this function is defined on any interval containing this point, it will not be invertible.

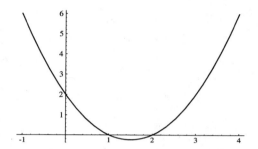

Figure 4.3. The function $f(x)=x^2-3x+2$.

The derivative of this function, which is given by $f'=2x-3$, vanishes when $x=1.5$. Notice from the graph in Figure 4.3 that in any interval that contains $x=1.5$ there are two values of y for each x, therefore, this function is not invertible.

To be able to invert this function we need to consider intervals of the form (2,10), (-20,1) or even (0,1.49995) just so long as the function does not include the turning point.

Example 4.5

From Example 4.4, the function of $f(x)=x^2-3x+2$, $x>1.5$, is invertible. The inverse function is given by solving the quadratic equation

$$x^2-3x+2-y=0$$

to give

$$x = \frac{3 \pm \sqrt{9-4(1-y)}}{2} = \frac{3 \pm \sqrt{1+4y}}{2}.$$

However, since $x>1.5$ we need to take the positive root so that

$$x = f^{-1}(y) = \frac{3 + \sqrt{1+4y}}{2}.$$

Exercise 4.5

Sketch the function $f(x)=x^3-3x+1$ and determine the largest interval containing $x=0$ where this function is invertible

Warning!

Provided $f'\neq0$, on an interval (a,b), the function f is invertible. However, this does not mean that we will be able to write down an expression for the inverse!

Example 4.6

The function $f(x) = x^5 + 5x^3 + 2$ has derivative $f'(x) = 5x^4 + 15x^2 > 0$ and so this function is *invertible*. However, to find the inverse function, we need to solve the quintic equation

$$x^5 + 5x^3 + 2 - y = 0.$$

Therefore, is not possible to give y as an explicit function of x.

Plotting inverse functions

Even if we are unable to find an explicit expression for the inverse function, we can still plot it given a graph of the function itself!

Recall that to plot the function $y=f(x)$ we draw the x-axis horizontal and the y-axis vertical. For the inverse function $x=f^{-1}(y)$ we need to interchange the x and y-axes, that is, we draw the y-axis horizontal and the x-axis vertical. This is equivalent to rotating the original graph through 90 degrees about the origin before flipping the resulting graph about the new horizontal axis.

Example 4.7

In Example 4.5 it was shown that the $f(x)=x^2-3x+2$, $x \geq 1.5$, is invertible. The graph of the inverse functions as constructed in Figure 4.4a, b and c.

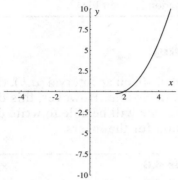

Figure 4.4a. The function $f(x)=x^2-3x+2$.

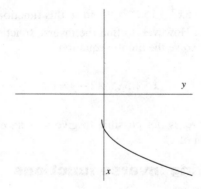

Figure 4.4b. Rotating Figure 4.4a through 90 degrees.

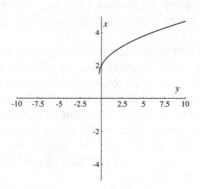

Figure 4.4c . Flipping the curve in Figure 4.4b about the y-axis determines the graph of the inverse function.

Example 4.8

The function $y=\sin(x)$ is invertible on the interval $(-\pi/2, \pi/2)$ and its inverse function, arcsin(y) is shown in Figure 4.5c.

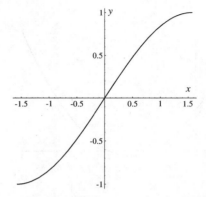

Figure 4.5a. The graph of y=sin(x).

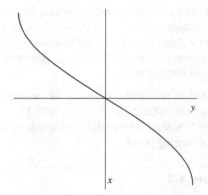

Figure 4.5b. Rotating Figure 4.5a through 90 degrees.

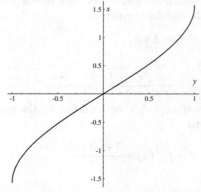

Figure 4.5c. Flipping the curve in Figure 4.5b about the y axis.

Exercise 4.6

Sketch the function given by $f(x) = x^3 - 3x + 1$. Determine an interval where this function is invertible and sketch its derivative.

Exercise 4.7

For each of the following functions determine an interval where the function is invertible and sketch the inverse function.

(i) $\cos(x)$

(ii) $\tan(x)$

(iii) e^x

(iv) $\log(x)$

Differentiating Inverse Functions

As it may not always be possible to find an explicit expression for an inverse function how then can we differentiate it?

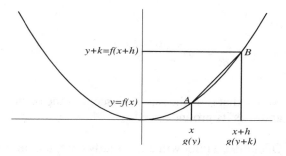

Figure 4.6. The relationship between the derivative of a function and its inverse.

Let us assume that a function f is both differentiable and invertible. If it is differentiable then

$$\frac{df}{dx} = \underset{h \to 0}{\text{Limit}} \left(\frac{f(x+h) - f(x)}{h} \right).$$

Graphically, this is equivalent to the slope of the line AB in Figure 4.6 approaching the slope of the curve as h tends to zero. Now write $f^{-1} = g$, then since f is an invertible function we have that $y=f(x)$, $y+k=f(x+h)$, $x=g(y)$ and $x+h=g(y+k)$. Substituting these expressions into $\frac{df}{dx}$ gives

$$\frac{df}{dx} = \underset{h \to 0}{\text{Limit}} \left(\frac{f(x+h) - f(x)}{h} \right)$$

$$= \underset{k \to 0}{\text{Limit}} \left(\frac{y+k-y}{g(x+h) - g(x)} \right) = \frac{1}{\left(\dfrac{dg}{dy} \right)}$$

Therefore, $[f^{-1}]' = 1/_{f'}$ or equivalently

$$\frac{dy}{dx} = \frac{1}{\left(\dfrac{dx}{dy} \right)}.$$

Example 4.9

Example 4.8 shows that the function $y=\sin(x)$ is invertible on the interval $(-\pi/2, \pi/2)$ and now the derivative of the inverse function, arcsin, is found as follows. If we set

$$x = \arcsin(y)$$

then

$$\frac{dx}{dy} = \frac{1}{\left(\dfrac{dy}{dx} \right)} = \frac{1}{\cos(x)} = \frac{1}{\sqrt{1 - \sin^2(x)}} = \frac{1}{\sqrt{1 - y^2}}$$

Exercise 4.8

For each of the following functions, determine an interval where the function is invertible and determine the derivative of the inverse function.

(i) $\cos(x)$

(ii) $\tan(x)$

(iii) e^x

(iv) $\log(x)$

WORKED EXAMPLE 4.1
FLIGHT SIMULATOR

As a plane approaches the end of a runway the pilot is able to control the rate of descent and ground speed of the plane. Find the angle the glide path makes to the runway and the rate of change of this angle if the pilot is to make a smooth landing.

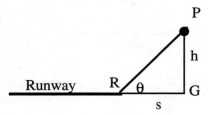

Figure 4.7. The plane at P approaching the runway R.

Firstly, we identify any variables and their units:

θ the angle of the glide path (radians)
h vertical height of the plane (m)
s distance to the end of the runway (m)
t time (s)

From simple trigonometry we have that

$$\tan(\theta) = \frac{PG}{RG} = \frac{h}{s}$$

or

$$\theta = \arctan(^h/_s),$$

since the tan function is increasing between 0 and $\frac{\pi}{2}$.

If the plane follows this glide path it will land rather heavily. Instead the pilot will aim to reduce q so that at touchdown q tends to zero. In order to investigate this we need to find $\frac{d\theta}{dt}$.

We could differentiate $\arctan(^h/_s)$ with respect to t to give $\frac{d\theta}{dt}$, but instead let us consider

$$\tan(q) = ^h/_s$$

which we differentiate as follows:

$$\frac{d}{dt}(\tan \theta) = \sec^2 \theta \frac{d\theta}{dt} \quad \text{(chain rule)}$$

$$\frac{d}{dt}\left(\frac{h}{s}\right) = \frac{sh' - hs'}{s^2} \quad \text{(quotient rule)}$$

Combining these results gives us

$$\sec^2 \theta \frac{d\theta}{dt} = \frac{sh' - hs'}{s^2}$$

or

$$\frac{d\theta}{dt} = \cos^2 \theta \frac{sh' - hs'}{s^2}$$

Notice that h' is the rate of descent of the plane and s' is its ground speed.

Of course, a pilot will not actually compute this value but if we want to model the landing of a plane, it will be necessary to do so.

PROBLEM 4.1
EXTREMA OF FUNCTIONS

Name: _____

Date: _____

Section: _____

The function $f(x) = x^3 + x^2 - x + 1$ is shown in Figure 4.2. On the interval $-2 \le x \le 1$ this function has extrema at $x = -2, -1, \frac{1}{3}$, and 1.

Use the function plotter to plot some other functions of your choice. Chose intervals and record their extrema. Say whether each is an end-point value, a maximum, a minimum; give the coordinates of each.

(Write your answers in the spaces provided or use the reverse of this page.)

The "Intervals" screen has a list of functions that you could try. Think of some others.

Function...   Interval...

Extrema:

Function...   Interval...

Extrema:

Function...   Interval...

Extrema:

Function…   Interval…

Extrema:

PROBLEM 4.2
INVERSE FUNCTIONS

Name: _____

Date: _____

Section: _____

For each of the following functions sketch $y=f(x)$, and determine an interval, containing the given point, where the function is invertible. For the selected interval, sketch the inverse function and find its derivative.

(Write your answers in the spaces provided or use the reverse of this page.)

(*i*) $\sin(x^2)$, $\quad x=0$, (*ii*) e^{-x^2}, $\quad x=1$, $\qquad$ (*iii*) $\dfrac{1+x}{1-x}$, $\quad x=0$,

(*iv*) x^3+3x+2, $x=1$, $\quad$ (*v*) $\cos(x)$, $x=\pi$, $\quad$ (*vi*) $\log(1-x)$, $x=\dfrac{1}{2}$.

Function (i)

Sketch:

Function (ii)

Sketch:

Function (iii)

Sketch:

Function (iv)

Sketch:

Function (v)

Sketch:

Function (vi)

Sketch:

PROBLEM 4.3
FLIGHT SIMULATOR

Name: _____

Date: _____

Section: _____

In Worked Example 4.1 we constructed a simple model to consider the glide path of a flight simulator in terms of the ground speed and rate of descent. Now suppose that an instrument on the plane detects a radio beacon at the end of the runway and is able to find the distance to the beacon and the rate at which this distance is changing. Find the rate of change of the angle of the glide path in terms of the rate of change of the distance between the plane and the end of the runway.

(Write your answers in the spaces provided or use the reverse of this page.)

Express the angle of the glide path in terms of the plane's height and direct distance to the end of the runway.

Differentiate the result obtained to find the rate of change of the glide path angle.

NEW SITUATIONS

1. Population Growth

Many populations can be modeled by a logistic curve as shown in Figure 4.8.

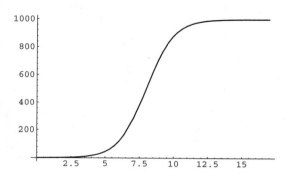

Figure 4.8. A logistic curve.

The population starts small but grows rapidly since there is little competition from the same species. As the population grows, there is more competition for food, therefore, the growth of the population decreases. Finally, the population approaches a limit as it saturates the environment where it lives. The mathematical equation for a logistic curve is given by the function

$$p(t) = \frac{M}{1 + Ae^{-at}}.$$

Show that for all values of M, A, and a this represents the curve shown in Figure 4.8. What is the significance of the parameters M, A, and a?

Show that this function is always increasing and, hence, find t as a function of p. If $M=1000$, $a=-1$ and $A=20e^5$ determine t as a function of P and determine when the population will be 750.

2. Balloons

The volume of a spherical balloon is given by

$$V(r) = \frac{4}{3}\pi r^3$$

Find the rate of change of the volume with respect to the radius. If the balloon is leaking air at a rate 10 cc/sec how fast is the radius changing?

3. Intrepid Tourists

A tourist stands beside the Statue of Liberty and looks toward it. If he stands very close to the base, the angle between the top of the plinth and the top of the statue is very small. As he moves away it will increase until he is some way off when the angle will be small again. Find an expression that determines this angle as a function of tourist's distance from the base of the statue.

If the tourist walks away from the statue at 5 feet per second find the rate of change of the angle sight between the plinth and the top of the statue.

At what distance from the statue is the angle of sight largest?

Chapter 5

Applied Maximums and Minimums

Prerequisites

The discussion in this chapter involves the Calculus. Before you begin to study it make sure that you understand the following material:

(1) Differentiation (Module 3);

(2) Intervals and Extrema (Module 4).

Objectives

The objective of this module is to learn how the Calculus, by looking at the slope of a function, can be used to find any minimums and maximums. In some cases it may be possible to do this by simply plotting the function and reading any maximum or minimum from a graph. For example, consider the function

$$f(x)=x^3+x^2-x+1$$

shown in Figure 5.1. There is a maximum near $x=-1$ and a minimum near $x=0.4$.

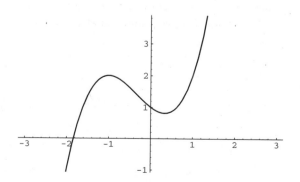

Figure 5.1. $y= x^3+ x^2- x +1.$

Now suppose that a function f involves a parameter, such as b in

$$f(x)=x^3+x^2+bx+1.$$

It is not possible to plot this function, so how can we find out if there any minimums or maximums? More importantly, how does the position of any minimum or maximum depends on the parameters?

Connections

The need for determining minimums and maximums arises all around us. How will you maximize the score you obtain on this course? How will you find a job that will maximize the return for your efforts? How is it possible to get a maximum return on any financial investments made? Sometimes, we may not be able to construct a mathematical function to minimize or maximize but in many cases we can. Once constructed how do we optimize such functions?

This module looks at two applications. The first concerns minimizng the loss of productive land in the event of a fire breaking out in a forest; the second involves determining the optimum size of a cylindrical canister of a given volume.

Finding Turning Points

We need a simple recipe for determining whether a given function has any maximum or minimum and how to find them. From Figure 5.2, notice that, on either side of a maximum, the slope of the curve changes from positive to negative. Similarly, on either side of a minimum the slope changes from negative to positive. In either case at the peak or trough the slope is zero. This is the clue to finding minimums and maximums.

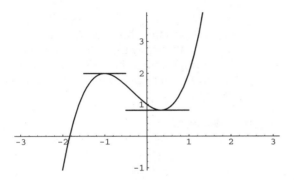

Figure 5.2. $y=x^3+x^2-x+1$.

Turning Points of Functions

At a "turning point" of a function $f(x)$ the slope of the curve $y=f(x)$ is zero. Therefore, to find the minimums and maximums we need to identify such points.

Example 5.1

The function $f(x)=x^3+x^2-x+1$ is shown in Figure 5.2. For all values less than -1 the slope is positive, for values between -1 and 0 it is negative. Somewhere in between the slope is zero, this is when the tangent is horizontal. Likewise, for values between 0 and 0.3 the slope is negative, whereas beyond 0.4 it is positive. Therefore, there is a point between 0.3 and 0.4 where the slope is horizontal. This gives a second turning point.

Exercise 5.1

Investigate the turning points of the function $f(x)=x^3-2x^2-x+1$ graphically.

Turning Points and Derivatives

The differential calculus gives an analytical method for determining turning points. Since the slope of a curve $y=f(x)$ is given by its derivative, wherever the derivative vanishes determines a turning point.

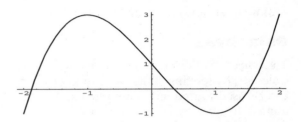

Figure 5.3. $y=x^3-3x+1$.

Example 5.2

Consider the function $f(x)=x^3-3x+1$ shown in Figure 5.2. The derivative of this function is given by $\dfrac{df}{dx}=3x^2-3$ and is shown in Figure 5.4. Notice that, the derivative vanishes at two points $x=\pm1$. At $x=-1$ the function has a maximum and at $x=1$ a minimum.

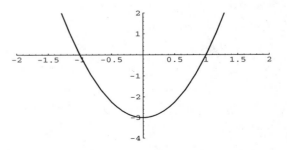

Figure 5.4. $y=3x^2-3$.

Example 5.3

The derivative of $f(x)=x^2-3x+1$ is $\dfrac{df}{dx}=2x-3$. This vanishes when $x=\frac{3}{2}$ which is the only turning point of this function.

Example 5.4

The slope of the function $f(x)=x^3+3x+1$ is given by $\dfrac{df}{dx}=3x^2+3>0$, and so there are no turning points.

Even when it is difficult to determine the derivative analytically we can always sketch the derived function given the graph of the function.

Example 5.5

Sketch the graph of the derivative of the function $f(x)$ shown in Figure 5.5.

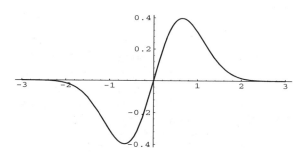

Figure 5.5. $y=f(x)$.

Notice that at $x=-2$ the slope is small and negative and so we can mark this on the sketch of the derivative. At $x=-1$ the slope is more negative. However, for $x=0$ the slope is positive. For $x=1$ it is again negative and at $x=2$ it is still negative but much smaller. These points are plotted in Figure 5.6. We can then join the plotted points to help us to visualize the graph of the derived function.

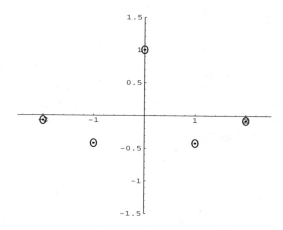

Figure 5.6. *Values of the derivative at selected points for the function in Example 5.5.*

Exercise 5.2

Plot the sketch of the function

$$f(x)=\frac{x^2-4}{x^2-16}, \quad -3 \le x \le 3,$$

and sketch its derivative. Locate the turning points of this function.

Extrema and Turning Points

It is important to distinguish between minimums and maximums, both of which are turning points, and extrema as described in Module 4. All turning points are local extrema but not every extremum is a turning point.

Example 5.6

The function $f(x)=x^3+3x+1$, $0<x<3$, has no turning points but has a global minimum of 1 when $x=1$ and a global maximum of 37 when $x=3$. Neither of these extrema is a turning point.

Classifying Turning Points

From Figures 5.3 and 5.4 it is obvious which points are minimums and maximums, but can we tell from the mathematics? We will now show how it is possible to determine which turning points correspond to maximums and which to minimums by looking at the second derivative.

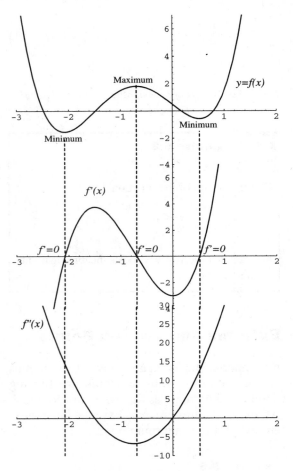

Figure 5.7. Using the second derivative, f'', to distinguish between minimums and maximums.

Figure 5.7 shows a function $f(x)$, its derivative $f'(x)$ and also its second derivative $f''(x)$. At the minimum near $x=-2$, the derivative is zero

but the second derivative is **positive**. Likewise, at the other minimum near $x=0.5$. However, at a maximum near $x=-0.7$ the derivative is zero but the second derivative is **negative**.

In general:
(i) A function $f(x)$ has a **minimum** at $x=a$ if $f'(a)=0$ and $f''(a)>0$.
(ii) A function $f(x)$ has a **maximum** at $x=a$ if $f'(a)=0$ and $f''(a)<0$.

  Exercise 5.3

It is also possible for both $f'(a)$ and $f''a)$ to be zero. What does this mean in terms of the graphs of $y=f$, f' and f''? Try to think of a function that has this type of behavior.

If $f'(a)=f''(a)=0$ then the curve is said to have a **point of inflexion** at $x=a$.

Example 5.7

The derivative of the function $f(x)=x^3-3x+1$ is $f'=3x^2-3$. This expression vanishes at two turning points, $x=\pm1$. The second derivative of f is $f''=6x$. At the turning point, $x=1$, $f''(1)=0$ and $f''(1)=6>0$ and so this point is a minimum. At the other turning point, $x=-1$, $f'(-1)=0$ and $f''(1)=-6<0$, which is a maximum.

Example 5.8

The minimums and maximums of the function $f(x)=xe^{-ax}$ can be investigated by considering its derivative

$$\frac{df}{dx}=e^{-ax}-axe^{-ax}.$$

This vanishes when $x=1/a$. At $x=1/a$ the second derivative is $-ae^{-1}$. If $a>0$ then $-ae^{-1}<0$ and so the point $x=1/a$ is a maximum. If $a<0$ then $-ae^{-1}>0$ and the point $x=1/a$ is a minimum.

WORKED EXAMPLE 5.1: FORESTRY

Fire is one of the major threats to the natural resources provided by large areas of forestry. If a fire breaks out then large areas of forest can be lost. To avoid this, tracts of forest are often divided by firebreaks. A typical firebreak is a strip of land from which the trees and undergrowth are removed. Clearly the number and position of firebreaks is crucial; for example, they are frequently placed at right angles to the prevailing wind as shown in Figure 5.8. (Why are they placed in this way?).

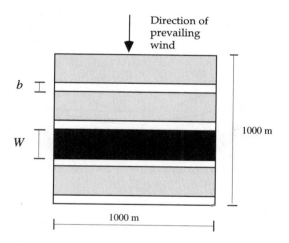

Figure 5.8. A typical square km of forest with firebreaks.

The major question is how many firebreaks should be placed in a one kilometer square of forest. If too few firebreaks are used then each block of forest will be large, and if a fire breaks out the losses will be large. If too many firebreaks are used then the area of a block of forest lost will be smaller but large areas of productive land will be used for firebreaks. Is there an optimum number?

First, we identify any variables we might use and their units:

W Width of forested section (m)

b Width of the firebreak (m)

n Number of firebreaks

A Area of productive land lost (m²)

Next we determine how the variables are related. If there are *n* firebreaks then the total productive land lost is one stand of trees plus the area of all the firebreaks, that is,

$$A = 1000(nb + W) \text{ m}^2.$$

However, from Figure 5.8,

$$n(W+b) = 1000 \text{ m (1 km)},$$

and eliminating *W*, gives

$$A = 1000\left(nb + \frac{1000}{n} - b\right).$$

Now we try to minimize *A*, the area of land lost, with respect to the number of firebreaks, *n*. Differentiating with respect to *n* gives the rate of change of *A* with respect to *n*, that is,

$$\frac{dA}{dn} = 1000\left(b - \frac{1000}{n^2}\right)$$

Therefore, $\frac{dA}{dn} = 0$ when $n^2 = \frac{1000}{b}$ which gives one positive turning point. Differentiating again shows that $\frac{d^2A}{dn^2} > 0$ for $n>0$, from which we conclude that this turning point is a minimum. For example, if $b=10$ then $n^2=100$; implying that there should be 10 firebreaks.

This result suggests that if we quadruple the width of the firebreaks then we need only halve the number of firebreaks. Is this sensible?

WORKED EXAMPLE 5.2: TIN CANS

This application concerns the millions of tin cans produced and discarded every day. How can we find the dimensions of a cylindrical canister that has a given volume and a minimum surface area. To consider this problem, first recall how a tin can is made. It is built from three parts and for each of these parts we can find an expression for the area. Notice that the volume depends on two variables, the height of the can and the radius of the ends. These two variables are not independent but are linked by the fact that the volume is fixed; if we change the height the radius will also change.

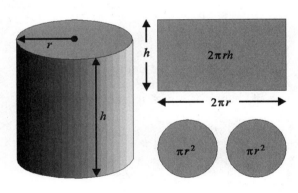

Firstly, we assign names to all variables that will be used and determine their units:

r Radius of the top (in)
h Height of the can (in)
V Volume of the can (in³)
S Surface area of the can (in²)

Next we decide how the variables are related. The can has volume $V=\pi r^2 h$ and surface area $S=2\pi rh+2\pi r^2$; therefore, the surface area is given by

$$S = \frac{2V}{r} + 2\pi r^2.$$

If V were given then we could find the best value of r by simply plotting S as a function of r. (See Figure 5.9.)

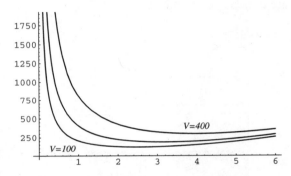

Figure 5.9. Surface area, S, for V=100,200, 300 in³.

In general,

$$\frac{dS}{dr} = -\frac{2V}{r^2} + 4\pi r \; r.$$

This vanishes when $2V/r^2=4\pi r$, that is. when $r^3=V/2\pi$. The second derivative is always positive and so this turning point is a minimum.

Notice that since $V=\pi r^2 h$, the height of the can is $h=V/\pi r^2 =(V/\pi r^3)r = 2r$. What basic shape does the can have? Does this agree with the shape of the cans you see most often?

PROBLEM 5.1
FORESTRY EXTENSION

Name:

Date:

Section:

In Worked Example 5.1 we assumed that the firebreaks ran in one direction. What would happen if they were arranged in two sets of parallel lines? Would we loose less productive land if a fire breaks out?

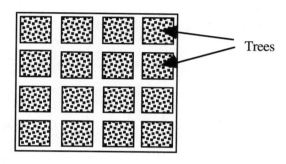

Trees

Figure 5.10 . Revised layout for 4 firebreaks in each direction.

(Write your answers in the spaces provided or use the reverse side of this page.)

Identify any variables and assign units.

How are the variables related? In particular describe how the area lost in the event of a single fire depends on the number of firebreaks?

Find the rate of change of the area lost with respect to the number of firebreaks and hence identify a value of n that gives the optimum result.

PROBLEM 5.2
TIN CANS EXTENSION

Name: _____

Date: _____

Section: _____

In the Tin Can problem, Worked Example 5.2, we ignored the cost of welding the top and bottom on to the can. If the cost of this welding a unit length is twice the cost per unit area of the can, determine the optimum shape of the can.

(Write your answers in the spaces provided or use the reverse side of this page.)

Identify the variables and assign units.

How are the variables related? In particular, how does the cost of the can depends on the radius and height?

Find the rate of change of the cost with respect to the radius and hence find the optimum dimensions.

NEW SITUATIONS

1. Mathematical Functions

Determine whether each function has any turning points in the range shown and then classify them.

(i) $y=x^3-3x+3$, $-2 \leq x \leq 2$

(ii) $y=e^{-x^2}$, $-3 \leq x \leq 3$

(iii) $y=x^2e^{-x^2}$, $x \geq 2$

2. Enclosure

A farmer wishes to enclose a rectangular area of a field by using 200 yards of wooden fencing. If he needs to fence off the maximum area what dimensions should the enclosure have?

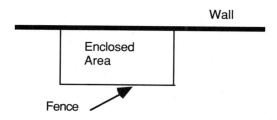

If the farmer discovers an additional 50 yards of fencing but decides to enclosed an area without the use of the wall, can he enclose a larger area?

3. Folding a tray

A metal tray is to be formed from a 2 ft by 1 ft sheet by removing a small square at each corner and folding the sides. How much should be removed to get the maximum volume?

4. Cylindrical Canister

A cylindrical canister has surface area 250 square inches. Find the dimensions that will give it maximum volume. How does this affect the solution compared with the tin can problem in the module?

5. Car Replacement

As a car gets older its value decreases but its annual running costs increase. How is it possible to decide the best time to sell a car and replace it? The value, $v(t)$, of a car is shown below together with an estimate of the annual running costs, $c(t)$.

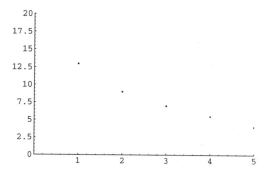

Figure 5.11. Value of the car, v(t).

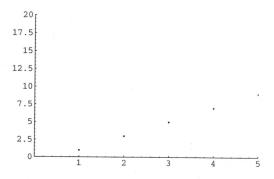

Figure 5.12. Annual running costs. c(t).

How would you estimate the annual costs of running this car? When is best to exchange it and get another car?

Chapter 6

Areas as Limits

Prerequisites

To take full advantage of this module make sure that you:

(1) Know how to plot functions (Module 1).

(2) Know about bounds and limits (Module 2).

(3) Understand rates of change (Module 3).

Objectives

You may think that area is a very simple idea which you understand well. But when you think about it, measuring areas when the shape is not rectangular is not straightforward at all! It is even necessary to ask: What is *meant* by the area of a nonrectangular region? This question can be tackled with the help of the concept of limits, a concept introduced in Chapter 2.

The concept of area for a nonrectangular shape in turn allows the idea of "area under a curve" to be considered. The process of finding an area under a curve plays a vitally important part in mathematics and the calculus. Many physical, chemical, and biological laws are linked to rates of change, and it is often the purpose of mathematical formulations to predict the actual value of the quantity that is changing. To do this, a process called *integration* has to be carried out, and this turns out to be closely related to the problem of finding an area under a curve.

In later modules, you'll also learn how integration and differentiation are closely linked. Integration and differentiation are inverse processes, meaning that one process undoes the effect of the other. Understanding the idea of area as a limit is vital to mastering these twin ideas, on which the whole of calculus is built.

Connections

In the software there are two situations with video clips which illustrate how areas can be found.

The first situation is land surveying, and it shows how areas of irregularly shaped pieces of land can be estimated. The idea of limits and bounds from earlier modules is essential here. There is an associated simulation activity in which you can estimate areas for yourself.

The second situation is about rainfall. You will already have an intuition that when it is raining hard, a rainwater collector will be filling up more rapidly. There's an everyday meaning to describing how hard it is raining (for example, saying "it's raining cats and dogs", or "it's drizzling"); hence, there is a generally shared intuitive idea about the rate at which it is raining, even if it is not precisely expressed. However, a meteorological station rain gauge does not measure the *rate* of rainfall, only the *accumulated rainfall* since the collector was last emptied.

Areas and rates of change

The Land Area Survey simulation in the software is designed to show that area can be defined for shapes other than simple cases, such as rectangles, and that in order to do this, mathematical processes involving limits are required. The rainfall simulation is designed to show that there is a link between areas and rates of change.

Exercise 6.1

Land area survey

Use the software to simulate the land area survey, as illustrated on the video clip. Change the shape of the river boundary and alter the size of the squares used to estimate the area.

Observe for yourself that:

1. The true area lies between the upper and lower estimates.

2. As the size of the squares gets smaller, the two estimates converge.

The area of the site is the limit of the estimates as the size of the squares tends to zero.

Example 6.1

If it rains at the rate of 2 mm/hr for one-half hr, then the rain falling in this time is

$2 \times \frac{1}{2} = 1$ mm. If it rains at the rate of r mm/hr for t hours, then the rain falling in this time is rt mm.

Exercise 6.2

Simulation of rainfall

Run the rainfall simulation. Alter the weather profile, and observe the connection between the rate at which it rains and the level of water in the collector.

Problem 6.1 suggests further activities that illustrate these ideas.

Areas of shapes

The area of a square is a familiar idea. Areas for many other shapes may be estimated by dividing the shapes into small rectangles.

First divide the shape up into rectangles, all of which lie inside the shape; the total area of these rectangles will be an underestimate for the shape's area (Figure 6.1). Now add more rectangles until every part of the shape is covered by a rectangle (Figure 6.2); the total area of these rectangles will now be an overestimate. By taking small enough rectangles, the two estimates will approach each other and thus the area can be found as accurately as you like. (This will be true for all the normal well-behaved situations met in practice. Strictly speaking, the assertion that the two estimates will converge should be qualified by a proviso that the shapes have sufficiently smooth boundaries.)

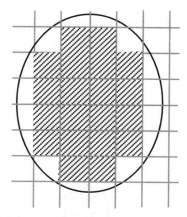

Figure 6.1. An area containing rectangles.

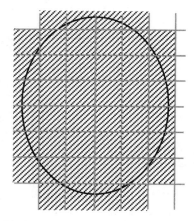

Figure 6.2. An area covered with rectangles.

Problem 6.2 suggests using the software to verify that areas can indeed be estimated in this way.

Integrals as areas

Consider a curve of $y = f(x)$. Since areas can be enclosed by curves, it should be possible to obtain a mathematical expression for the "area under the curve".

Define a function

$A(a, b)=\{$The area under a curve $y=f(x)$ between $x=a$ and $x=b$ $\}$.

Clearly this is very long winded, and in true mathematical style we use the shorthand notation $\int_a^b f(x)dx$, where $\int$ is called an "integral sign" and the notation "dx" indicates that the area between the curve and the x-axis is being measured. A definite area (such as the shaded area in Figure 6.3) starts and ends at values of x, which are called limits (the values a and b as illustrated in this case), and these can be included with the integral sign.

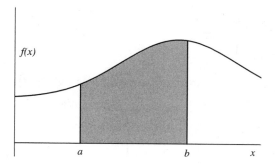

Figure 6.3. Area under a curve.

Thus $\int_a^b f(x)\, dx$ means:

"the area under the curve $f(x)$ between $x=a$ and $x=b$". This expression is called the *definite integral* of the function between the limits a and b.

The area can be estimated in the same way as areas of any other shapes. To define an area under a curve for a given interval of x, make a shape by using the part of the x-axis corresponding to the interval, the corresponding section of the curve, and two lines parallel to the y-axis, as shown in Figure 6.3.

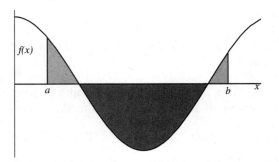

Figure 6.4. Graph of f(x)=cos(x), showing positive and negative regions of area under a curve.

If part of a curve lies below the x-axis [so $f(x)$ is negative, as in Figure 6.4], then the area in that section counts as negative.

Example 6.2

To show that $\int_0^\pi \cos(x)\,dx = 0$, first divide the interval of integration into two parts $\left(0, \frac{\pi}{2}\right)$ and $\left(\frac{\pi}{2}, \pi\right)$. Since the total area is just the sum of subareas, we have

$$\int_0^\pi \cos(x)dx = \int_0^{\frac{\pi}{2}} \cos(x)dx + \int_{\frac{\pi}{2}}^\pi \cos(x)dx.$$

But $\cos(x) = -\cos(180 - x)$, so the area between the curve and the x-axis in the interval $\left(\frac{\pi}{2}, \pi\right)$ is exactly $(-1)\times$ the areas for $\left(0, \frac{\pi}{2}\right)$. Therefore, $\int_0^{\frac{\pi}{2}} \cos(x)dx = -\int_{\frac{\pi}{2}}^\pi \cos(x)dx$, and we have the result.

Limit of upper and lower sums

To recapitulate, $\int_a^b f(x)\,dx$ means:

"the area under the curve $f(x)$ between $x=a$ and $x=b$".

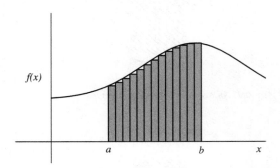

Figure 6.5. Using strips to give a lower sum estimate for area.

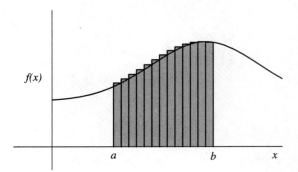

Figure 6.6. Using strips to give an upper sum estimate for area.

Estimating areas can be done by square counting just as with shapes, but for integrals (which are just areas under curves) it is easier to use rectangular strips. As with shapes, the strips can be chosen to give upper and lower estimates.

The height of the strips can be chosen so that they lie inside the curve. Then their area is less than the true area, and is it called the "lower sum".

Or, the height of the strips can be chosen so that the area under the curve lies within the strips. Then their area is greater than the true area, and it is called the "upper sum".

By reducing the width of the strips, the area can be found to any required accuracy. Worked Examples 6.1 and 6.2 show applications of this technique to some simple functions.

A similar interpretation works for rainfall. Suppose the graph in Figures 6.5 and 6.6 represents the rate at which it is raining, and that the width of the strips corresponds to 1 hour. A meteorologist checks the gauge every hour, but before checking the gauge she likes to guess how much she'll find. Suppose the rain is getting heavier, so that at the beginning of a 1-hour period it rains at (say) 5 mm/hr, and at the end the rate is 10 mm/hr. This could be represented by the portion of the graph to the left of the maximum. If the meteorologist guesses at the start of the hour, she'll come up with the underestimate of 5 mm in the collector; if she guesses at the end of the hour, just before reading the gauge, then she will guess 10 mm, an overestimate. Notice that the underestimate will be exactly the area of a strip in the graph under the curve (as in Figure 6.5), and likewise the overestimate will correspond to a strip that goes above the curve (as in Figure 6.6). If the time between checking the gauge is shorter, her estimates will be improved. For example, it is quite plausible in this example that the rainfall rate could have increased to 6 mm/hr after 15 minutes, so the two estimates for the amount of rain falling in the first 15 minutes would be 1.25 mm and 1.5 mm. Not only is the discrepancy smaller

(not unexpected because only a quarter of the time has passed), but it is smaller relative to the amounts involved. This argument leads to the conclusion that the area under the rate of rainfall curve in any interval of time gives the amount of rain that falls in that time.

WORKED EXAMPLE 6.1
AREA UNDER A LINE

It is often necessary to find the area under a general curve $y = f(x)$. We make a start on this general problem by considering the function $y = mx$, and its area under the section from the origin to a given value of x. This is given by the

definite integral $\int_0^x f(x)dx = \int_0^x mx\, dx$.

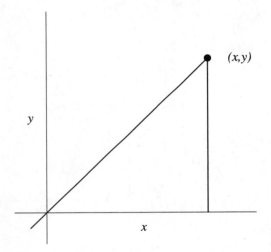

Figure 6.7. The function y=mx.

This area can easily be found because it is the area of a right-angled triangle $= \frac{1}{2}xy = \frac{1}{2}mx^2$. Although this is the most direct way to get this result, we shall now go on to obtain it by using the method of Upper and Lower Sums, and will show that the same answer is obtained.

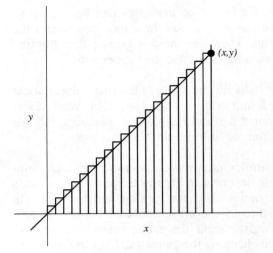

Figure 6.8. The function y=mx and strips giving an Upper Sum.

Divide the interval $(0, x)$ into n equal intervals each of width $\frac{x}{n}$. Draw n strips all lying above the line $y = mx$ as shown in Figure 6.8. The kth strip has height $mk\frac{x}{n}$. The total area of the strips is the "Upper Sum" U, given by

$$U = \sum_{k=1}^{n}\left(\frac{x}{n}\right)\left(\frac{mkx}{n}\right) = \frac{mx^2}{n^2}\sum_{k=1}^{n}k.$$

Now a formula is needed for $\sum_{k=1}^{n}k$. This will be given by any good computer algebra package, or it can be obtained by pairing up the terms from the front and back of the sequence: the sum of the kth and $n-(k-1)^{th}$ terms is always $(n+1)$, so the average value of the terms is $\frac{1}{2}(n+1)$. Therefore, $\sum_{k=1}^{n}k = \frac{1}{2}n(n+1)$, and using this result gives $U = \frac{1}{2}mx^2\frac{n(n+1)}{n^2}$.

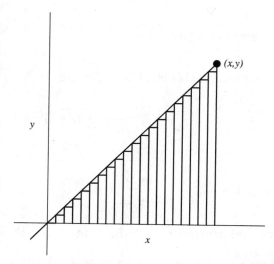

Figure 6.9. The function y=mx and strips giving a Lower Sum.

Let us now consider strips that lie under the line as in Figure 6.9. Note that the height of each strip is now defined by the left-hand edge rather than the right-hand edge, and hence the first strip has zero height.

The kth strip now has height $m(k-1)\dfrac{x}{n}$. The total area of the strips is the "Lower Sum" L, given by

$$L = \sum_{k=1}^{n}\left(\frac{x}{n}\right)\left(\frac{m(k-1)x}{n}\right) = \frac{mx^2}{n^2}\sum_{k=1}^{n}(k-1),$$

and, therefore, $L = \frac{1}{2}mx^2\dfrac{(n-1)n}{n^2}$.

By inspection, $U > L, U \to \frac{1}{2}mx^2$ from above, and $L \to \frac{1}{2}mx^2$ from below. This allows us to conclude that the area $= \frac{1}{2}mx^2$, agreeing with the result obtained geometrically.

Therefore, $\displaystyle\int_0^x mx\,dx = \frac{1}{2}mx^2$.

WORKED EXAMPLE 6.2
AREA UNDER Y=AX²

The Upper and Lower Sums method can be applied in situations where the area cannot be found from a simple geometrical argument. Consider the case $y = ax^2$.

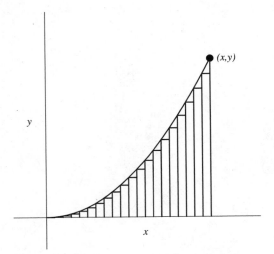

Figure 6.10. The function $y = ax^2$ and strips giving an Upper Sum.

Divide the interval $(0, x)$ into n equal intervals each of width $\dfrac{x}{n}$. Draw n strips all lying above the curve $y = ax^2$ as shown in Figure 6.10. The kth strip has height $a\left(k\dfrac{x}{n}\right)^2$. The total area of the strips is the "Upper Sum" U, given by

$$U = \sum_{k=1}^{n}\left(\frac{x}{n}\right)a\left(\frac{kx}{n}\right)^2 = \frac{ax^3}{n^3}\sum_{k=1}^{n}k^2 .$$

To proceed, we need to know that $\sum_{k=1}^{n}k^2 = \frac{1}{6}n(n+1)(2n+1)$. This can be looked up in a computer algebra package, or proved by induction.

This gives $U = \frac{1}{3}ax^3\,\dfrac{n(n+1)(2n+1)}{2n^3}$.

The Lower Sum is obtained similarly as

$$L = \sum_{k=1}^{n}\left(\frac{x}{n}\right)a\left(\frac{(k-1)x}{n}\right)^2 = \frac{ax^3}{n^3}\sum_{k=1}^{n}(k-1)^2$$

giving $L = \frac{1}{3}ax^3\,\dfrac{(n-1)n(2n-1)}{2(n-1)^3}$.

By inspection, $U > L$, and since $\dfrac{n(n+1)(2n+1)}{2n^3} \to 1$, as $x \to \infty$, $U \to \frac{1}{3}ax^3$ from above, and $L \to \frac{1}{3}ax^3$ from below. Therefore, $\displaystyle\int_0^x ax^2\,dx = \frac{1}{3}ax^3$.

P R O B L E M   6 . 1
R A I N F A L L

This problem relates to the rainfall simulation in the software. All the results can be obtained working with pencil and paper, but you might like to use the software to illustrate and check your results.

How much rain falls in a 4-hour period if:

(i) Rain falls at a constant rate of r mm/hr?

(ii) Rain falls at rate r for 1 hour, then $2r$ for the next hour, then $3r$ for the next, then r for the last hour?

(iii) The rainfall increases linearly from 0 at the start of the period to r at the end of the fourth hour?

(Hints: use the software for various values of r of your choice; what is the average rate of rainfall?)

(iv) The rainfall increases linearly from zero at the start of the period to r at the end of the second hour, then linearly back down to zero at the end of the fourth hour?

(Hint: what is the average rate of rainfall in the first 2 hours?)

PROBLEM 6.2
AREAS OF SHAPES

Name: _____

Date: _____

Section: _____

1. Use the software to obtain upper and lower bounds for the areas of shapes provided by the software, and hence estimate their areas to within 2 percent accuracy. Record your results here.

Triangle

Circle

Ellipse

Parabola

2. Area of an ellipse.

Go to the problem section of the software and look at the problem "Area of an ellipse". An ellipse is defined by

- its semimajor axis a, and
- its semiminor axis b.

When $a=b$, the ellipse is exactly the same as a circle of radius a.

Record your results here.

For a circle of radius a =..., what square size gives a result accurate to within 2 percent? ......

Now change b to ka, and use the same square size to estimate the area of the ellipse. Try for example, k=1.5, 2. What factors does the area change by?

a =..., k=1.5a, area =...

a =..., k=2.0a, area =...

Can you guess what is the formula for the area of an ellipse?

PROBLEM 6.3
AREAS USING UPPER
AND LOWER SUMS

Name: _____
Date: _____
Section: _____

1. Use the software to estimate the areas under curves as shown to 2 significant figures. You should do this by adjusting the strip sizes so that the upper and lower sums agree to this accuracy. Then you know that the true answer lies within these bounds.

(i) $\int_0^{10} x^2 dx = \dots$

(ii) $\int_{-10}^{10} x^2 dx = \dots$

(iii) $\int_{-10}^0 (1+x) dx = \dots$

(iv) $\int_0^{\pi/2} sin(x) dx = \dots$

(v) $\int_{-\pi/2}^{\pi/2} sin(x) dx = \dots$

(vi) $\int_0^1 e^x dx = \dots$

(vii) $\int_{-4}^4 (x^3 - \frac{1}{2}x^2 - x + 1) dx = \dots$

Do several of the problems suggested in the software problems "Areas under curves for various *f(x)*".

Record your results here:

...   .

...   .

NEW SITUATIONS

1. Integrals as functions

In the integral $\int_a^b f(x)\,dx$, for any particular values of a and b, preceding sections of this chapter have shown how the area can be found. If one limit (usually the upper limit) is thought of as a variable (conveniently done by calling it x, say), then the integral can be thought of as a function. For example, define

$$F(x) = \int_a^x f(x)\,dx.$$ $F(x)$ gives information about the way the area changes as x varies.

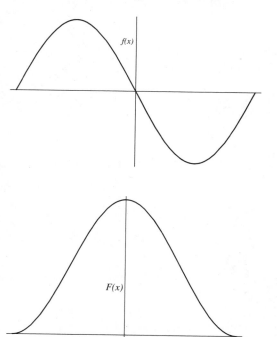

Figure 6.11. Area as a function of one limit .

Note that with these limits $F(a) = 0$, and that when the upper limit (x in this case) is less than the lower limit (0 in this case), the integral is counted as having the opposite sign to the area.

Exercise 6.3

Addition of integrals

Convince yourself by experimenting with the software that

$$\int_a^b f(x)dx + \int_b^c f(x)dx = \int_a^c f(x)dx.$$

Start with values $a \le b \le c$. Then look at the situation $a \le c \le b$, and deduce that this means

$$\int_b^c f(x)dx = -\int_c^b f(x)dx.$$

2. Integrals as functions

Define $F(x) = \int_0^x f(x)\,dx$. Use the software to explore the properties of $F(x)$ for a variety of functions. Why is $F(x) = 0$ in every case?

First verify the results of Worked Examples 6.1 and 6.2. Use the technique of Problem 6.3 to evaluate

$$\int_0^1 x\,dx = \ldots \qquad \int_0^2 x\,dx = \ldots \qquad \int_0^3 x\,dx = \ldots$$

$$\int_0^4 x\,dx = \ldots \qquad \int_0^5 x\,dx = \ldots$$

and verify that $\int_0^x x\,dx = \frac{1}{2}x^2$.

Verify that $\int_0^x x^2 dx = \frac{1}{3}x^3$.

Now evaluate $\int_0^x x^3\,dx$ for several values of x and suggest a general result. Repeat for $\int_0^x x^4\,dx$. Hence suggest a general formula for $\int_0^x x^n\,dx$.

Now use the result of Exercise 6.3 to suggest a general formula for $\int_a^b x^n\,dx$.

Chapter 7

The Fundamental Theorem of Calculus

Prerequisites

Before you study the material in this chapter you should know about:

(1) Elementary trigonometric and exponential functions.

(2) Differentiation of simple functions (Module 3).

(3) Integration and areas (Module 6).

Objectives

In Module 6 we wrote

$$\int_a^b f(x)dx$$

to represent the area enclosed between a continuous function and the x-axis, from $x=a$ and $x=b$. It was investigated by "counting squares" or as limits of sums. However, no systematic approach was given as to how this integral can be found analytically. In this module we will show that there is function F such that

$$\int_a^b f(x)dx = F(b) - F(a).$$

This is the first half of the Fundamental Theorem of Calculus. The second part of this theorem shows that F is differentiable and

$$\frac{dF}{dx} = f(x).$$

From this result we can conclude that differentiation and integration are inverses of each other.

Connections

Many physical, chemical, and biological laws are phrased in terms of the rate of change of physical quantities, and it is often necessary to determine the actual quantity that is changing. The Fundamental Theorem of Calculus provides a tool to do this. To find the indefinite integral of a function all we need to do is find another function which when differentiated reduces to the integrand given.

To illustrate this the first application considers a car that is traveling with velocity $v(t)$ and shows how the distance traveled, $s(t)$, can be found. This can be achieved since velocity is the rate of change of distance, that is,

$$\frac{ds}{dt} = v,$$

therefore, by the Fundamental Theorem

$$s(t) = \int v(t)dt.$$

To find s we need to integrate v. Alternatively, if $s(t)$ is thought to be *the* integral we can check whether it *is* the integral by differentiating it.

The second application looks at the acceleration of a sky diver falling from a plane under uniform gravity, g. As acceleration is the rate of change of velocity we need to find a function $v(t)$ which when differentiated is always equal to g.

What is the Fundamental Theorem of Calculus?

FUNDAMENTAL THEOREM OF CALCULUS

If f is a continuous function on an interval $[a,b]$ then there exists a function F such that

$$\int_a^b f(t)dt = F(b) - F(a).$$

Furthermore, the function F is differentiable and

$$F(x) = \frac{df}{dx}.$$

The function F is called an antiderivative or indefinite integral of f.

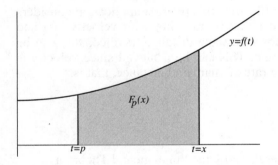

Figure 7.1.   The area under the curve y=f(t) between t=p and t=x.

Let $F_p(x)$ denote the area enclosed by the shaded area in Figure 7.1. This region is bounded by the curve $y=f(t)$, the fixed vertical line through $t=p$, the horizontal axis and the vertical line through the variable point $t=x$. We shall refer to an area between a curve and the axis, as here, as the "area under the curve". $F_p(x)$ determines a function of x.

Using the notation of Chapter 6 we can write $F_p(x)$ as the definite integral

$$F_p(x) = \int_p^x f(t)dt.$$

If we take any other point, $t=q$, then

$$F_q(x) = \int_q^x f(t)dt.$$

However,

$$F_p(x) - F_q(x) = \int_p^x f(t)dt - \int_q^x f(t)dt$$

$$= \int_q^p f(t)dt,$$

which represents the area enclosed by the curve between $t=q$ and $t=p$.

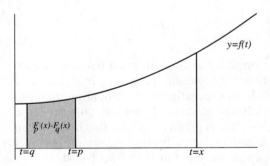

Figure 7.2.   The area represented by $F_p(x)$-$F_q(x)$.

Notice that $F_p(x)$-$F_q(x)$, which is shown in Figure 7.2, is independent of the choice of x, hence, $F_p(x)$ and $F_q(x)$ differ by an additive constant, and we can write

$$F_p(x) = F_q(x) + C,$$

whatever, the choice of p or q.

Now let us return to the definite integral and use the definition of $F_p(x)$ to write

$$\int_a^b f(x)dx = F_p(b) - F_p(a)$$

$$= [F_q(b) + C] - [F_q(a) + C]$$

$$= F_q(b) - F_q(a).$$

Therefore, it does not matter whether we start at p or q. We always get the same result and so we can drop the suffix to write

$$\int_a^b f(t)dt = F(b) - F(a).$$

This is the first part of the Fundamental Theorem of Calculus. The function F is called an antiderivative or indefinite integral of f. We write

$$F(x) = \int f(x)dx + C$$

where C is called a constant of integration. The only problem now is how do we find the function F. The FTC does not tell us how to find it, but it does tell if a given function is or is not an antiderivative.

Example 7.1
Which of the following functions represents an antiderivative for $\log(x)$?

(i) $\dfrac{1}{x}$

(ii) $\log(x^2)$

(iii) $x\log(x) - x$

(i) The derivative of $y = \dfrac{1}{x}$ is $-\dfrac{1}{x^2} \neq \log(x)$ so we

can conclude that this is not an antiderivative for $\log(x)$.

(ii) The derivative of $y = \log(x^2)$ is $\dfrac{2}{x} \neq \log(x)$ and

so we conclude that this is not an antiderivative for $\log(x)$ neither.

(iii) The derivative of $y = x\log(x) - x$ is

$$\frac{d}{dx}\left(x\log(x) - x\right) = \frac{d}{dx}\left(x\log(x)\right) - 1$$

$$= x\frac{d}{dx}(\log(x)) + \log(x)\frac{d}{dx}(x) - 1$$

$$= \frac{x}{x} + \log(x) - 1 = \log(x)$$

so we conclude that $x\log(x) - x$ is an indefinite integral of $\log(x)$, hence, we can write

$$\int \log(x)dx = x\log(x) - x + C$$

 Exercise 7.1

Which of the following functions is an indefinite integral of $\tan(x)$?

(i) $\tan(x^2)$

(ii) $-\log(\cos(x))$

(iii) $x\tan(x)$

Justifying the FTC

To justify the Fundamental Theorem we return to the area function $F_p(x)$ given in Figure 7.1. We need to show that the rate of change of F_p is always f irrespective of the choice of p. To do this we need to find an expression for the derivative of F_p. From Chapter 3 we have that

$$F_p'(x) = \underset{h \to 0}{Limit}\left(\frac{F_p(x+h) - F_p(x)}{h}\right).$$

However, $F_p(x+h)$ is the area under the curve $y = f(t)$ between $t = p$ and $t = x + h$, and $F_p(x)$ is the area between $t = p$ and $t = x$ and therefore,

$$F_p(x+h) - F_p(x)$$

is the area under $y=f(t)$ between $t=x$ and $t=x+h$. This is the shaded area shown in Figure 7.3.

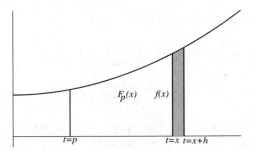

Figure 73. The area given by $F_p(x+h) - F_p(x)$.

As h gets smaller and smaller the area given by $F_p(x+h) - F_p(x)$ approaches a rectangle with area $hf(x)$ and so

$$F_p'(x) = \underset{h \to 0}{Limit}\left(\frac{F_p(x+h) - F_p(x)}{h}\right)$$

$$= \underset{h \to 0}{Limit}\left(\frac{hf(x)}{h}\right) = f(x)$$

Exercise 7.2

View the concept "Justifying the FTC" in the software to see how the above limit is achieved.

Standard Integrals

To evaluate the definite integral

$$\int_a^b f(x)dx$$

we need to find a function $F(x)$ such that

$$\frac{dF}{dx} = f.$$

Alternatively, to check if a function $F(x)$ is an indefinite integral of $f(x)$ we differenti-

ate F, and if $F'=f$ then F is the required indefinite integral.

Power functions

The derivative of $y=x^n$ is $\frac{dy}{dx} = nx^{n-1}$ and, therefore,

$$\int nx^{n-1}dx = x^n + C .$$

Similarly,

$$\int x^n dx = \frac{x^{n+1}}{n+1} + C, \qquad n \neq -1.$$

Check:

$$\frac{d}{dx}\left(\frac{x^{n+1}}{n+1} + C\right) = \frac{1}{n+1}\frac{d}{dx}\left(x^{n+1}\right) = x^n$$

as required.

Exercise 7.3

Why does the formula

$$\int x^n dx = \frac{x^{n+1}}{n+1} + C, \quad n \neq -1,$$

exclude the case when $n = -1$? Show that

$$\int x^{-1}dx = \log(x) + C .$$

Example 7.2

The indefinite integral of x^3 is $\frac{x^4}{4} + C$.

Check:

$$\frac{d}{dx}\left(\frac{x^4}{4} + C\right) = \frac{d}{dx}\left(\frac{x^4}{4}\right) = x^3$$

as required.

Polynomial functions

A polynomial is the sum of power functions. If we know how to integrate x^3 and x^2, how do we integrate x^3+x^2?

Recall from Chapter 3, that the derivative of the sum of two functions is the sum of the derivatives. Similarly, by the FTC the integral of a sum is the sum of the integrals, that is,

$$\int (f(x)+g(x))dx = \int f(x)dx + \int g(x)dx$$

To see this, let

$$F(x) = \int f(x)dx$$

and

$$G(x) = \int g(x)dx$$

that is $F'=f$ and $G'=g$. Then, from the differential calculus

$$\frac{d}{dx}(F+G) = \frac{dF}{dx} + \frac{dG}{dx} = f + g$$

and, hence,

$$\int (f+g)\,dx = \int \left(\frac{d}{dx}(F+G) \right) dx$$

$$= F + G = \int fdx + \int gdx.$$

Notice, also, that since

$$\frac{d}{dx}(aF) = a\frac{dF}{dx} = af,$$

for any constant,

$$\int af dx = \int \frac{d}{dx}(aF)\, dx = aF = a\int fdx$$

again by using the FTC.

Example 7.3

The indefinite integrals of $x^4 + 3x - 2$ is given by integrating x^4 to get $\frac{1}{5}x^5$, $3x$ to get $\frac{3}{2}x^2$ and 2 to get $2x$ so that

$$\int x^4 + 3x - 2dx = \int x^4 dx + \int 3xdx - \int 2dx$$

$$= \frac{x^5}{5} + 3\frac{x^2}{2} - 2x + C$$

Check:

$$\frac{d}{dx}\left(\frac{x^5}{5} + 3\frac{x^2}{2} - 2x + C \right)$$

$$= \frac{d}{dx}\left(\frac{x^5}{5} \right) + \frac{d}{dx}\left(3\frac{x^2}{2} \right) - \frac{d}{dx}(-2x)$$

$$= x^4 + 3x - 2$$

as required.

Trig Functions

Example 7.4

The derivative of $F(x)=\sin(x)$ is given by
$$F'(x)=\cos(x),$$
therefore,

$$\int \cos(x)dx = \sin(x) + C.$$

Example 7.5
The derivative of $G(x)=\cos(mx)$ is $-m\sin(mx)$, therefore,
$$\int \sin(mx)dx = -\frac{1}{m}\cos(mx) + C$$
Check:

$$\frac{d}{dx}\left(\frac{1}{m}\cos(mx) + C \right) = -\frac{m}{m}\sin(mx) = -\sin(mx)$$
as required.

Example 7.6

The derivative of $G(x) = \log(\sec(x))$ is $\tan(x)$, therefore,

$$\int \tan(x)dx = \log(\sec(x)) + C.$$

Check:

$$\frac{d}{dx}\big(\log(\sec(x))+C\big)=\frac{\sin(x)}{\cos(x)}=\tan(x)$$

as required.

Exponential Functions

The derivative of $F(x)=e^x$ is $F'(x)=e^x$ therefore, $\int e^x dx = e^x + C$

Example 7.7

The derivative of $G(x)=e^{mx}$ is me^{mx}, and so

$$\int e^{mx} dx = \frac{1}{m} e^{mx} + C.$$

Example 7.8

The derivative of $G(x)=e^{mx}$ is me^{mx}, and so

$$\int e^{mx} dx = \frac{1}{m} e^{mx} + C$$

STANDARD INTEGRALS

$$\int x^n dx = \frac{x^{n+1}}{n+1} + C,\ n \neq -1 \quad \text{since} \quad \frac{d}{dx}\left(\frac{x^{n+1}}{n+1}\right) = x^n$$

$$\int \frac{1}{x} dx = \log(x) + C \quad \text{since} \quad \frac{d}{dx}\big(\log(x)\big) = \frac{1}{x}$$

$$\int \cos(mx) dx = \frac{1}{m}\sin(mx) + C,\ \text{since} \quad \frac{d}{dx}\left(\frac{1}{m}\sin(mx)\right) = \cos(mx)$$

$$\int \sin(mx) dx = -\frac{1}{m}\cos(mx) + C,\ \text{since} \quad \frac{d}{dx}\left(-\frac{1}{m}\cos(mx)\right) = \sin(mx)$$

$$\int e^x dx = e^x + C \ \text{since} \quad \frac{d}{dx}\big(e^x\big) = e^x$$

$$\int \log(x) dx = x\log(x) - x + C \ \text{since} \quad \frac{d}{dx}\big(x\log(x) - x\big) = \log(x)$$

Finding Areas Using the FTC

From the Fundamental Theorem of Calculus

$$\int_a^b f(x)dx = F(b) - F(a),$$

where F is an indefinite integral of f, that is,

$$\frac{dF}{dx} = f.$$

We write

$$\int_a^b f(x)dx = F(b) - F(a)$$

with

$$\int_a^b f(x)dx = \left[F(x)\right]_a^b$$

$$= F(x)\big]_a^b$$

$$= |F(x)|_a^b$$

as possible alternative notations.

Example 7.9

Evaluate the integral $\int_1^3 x^3 dx$. An indefinite integrand for x^3 is given by $F(x) = \frac{1}{4}x^4$, since $F'(x) = x^3$; therefore,

$$\int_1^3 x^3 dx = F(3) - F(1)$$

$$= \frac{1}{4}3^4 - \frac{1}{4}1^4 = \frac{1}{4}80 = 20.$$

Non-positive functions.

If a function is positive, then the value of the integral,

$$\int_a^b f(x)dx = F(b) - F(a)$$

gives the area enclosed by the curve $y=f(x)$ and the x-axis between $x=a$ and $x=b$. However, if the function changes sign this is not the case, unless the areas below the x-axis are counted as negative.

Example 7.10

Evaluate the integral $\int_0^{2\pi} \sin(x)dx$.

An indefinite integrand for $\sin(x)$ is $F(x)=-\cos(x)$ since $F'=\sin(x)$. Therefore,

$$\int_0^{2\pi}\sin(x)dx = -\cos(2\pi) - (-\cos(0)) = -1 + 1 = 0$$

and yet from Figure 7.4 the area of paper enclosed by this function and the x-axis is clearly nonzero.

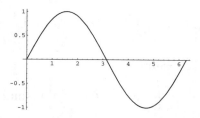

Figure 7.4. The function $f(x)=sin(x)$, $0 \le x \le 2\pi$.

The reason for this is obvious. Only when the function is positive is a positive contribution made to the area enclosed. To find the total area enclosed, we need to split the function into domains in each of which the function has the same sign.

Example 7.11

Find the area enclosed by the curve $y=\cos(x)$ between $x=0$ and $x=2\pi$. If we evaluate the integral $\int_0^{2\pi}\cos(x)dx$, using the indefinite integral $\sin(x)$, then

$$\int_0^{2\pi} \cos(x)dx = \sin(2\pi)-(\sin(0))=0-0=0$$

and yet from Figure 7.5 the geometrical area enclosed by this function and the x-axis is clearly nonzero.

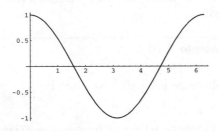

Figure 7.5. The function f(x)=cos(x), 0≤x≤2π.

This function is positive between 0 and $^\pi/_2$, negative between $^\pi/_2$ and $^{3\pi}/_2$ and positive between $^{3\pi}/_2$ and 2π. The geometrical area enclosed is therefore given by

$$\int_0^{\frac{\pi}{2}} \cos(x)dx + \int_{\frac{\pi}{2}}^{\frac{3\pi}{2}} (-\cos(x))dx + \int_{\frac{3\pi}{2}}^{2\pi} \cos(x)dx$$

$$=\left[\sin(\tfrac{\pi}{2})-\sin(0)\right]+$$

$$\left[-\sin(\tfrac{3\pi}{2})+\sin(\tfrac{\pi}{2})\right]+\left[\sin(2\pi)-\sin(\tfrac{3\pi}{2})\right]$$

$$=[1-0]+[1+1]+[0+1]=4.$$

Exercise 7.5

Evaluate the following integrals and determine whether they represent geometrical areas under the curve.

(i) $x^2+2x+1,$ $0 \le x \le 1$

(ii) $x^2-3x+2,$ $0 \le x \le 2$

(iii) $\sin(x),\ -1 \le x \le 1$

(iv) $e^x,$ $-1 \le x \le 1$

(v) $x\sin(x^2),$ $0 \le x \le 2$

WORKED EXAMPLE 7.1

Distance Traveled

The speed of a car is noted at 1 second intervals and is recorded in Table 7.1.

Time (seconds)	Speed (m/s)
0	40
1	45
2	48

Table 7.1. Recorded speeds at 1 second intervals.

How can we estimate the distance traveled over this period?

First, we identify any variables and their units

- s Distance traveled (m)
- v Velocity of the car(m/sec)
- t Elapsed time (seconds)

Plotting the data given in Table 7.1 produces

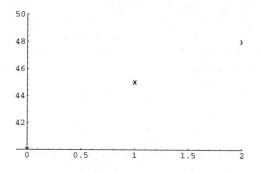

Figure 7.6. Velocity vs. time for Table 7.1.

If we assume that the car traveled smoothly we can approximate its velocity at any point between those given in Table 7.1 by a curve of some form. As the points are not quite linear, let us try fitting a quadratic function to them.

If we assume that

$$v(t) = at^2 + bt + c$$

then $v(0)=40$, $v(1)=45$ and $v(2)=48$ giving

$$v(t) = -t^2 + 6t + 40$$

To find the distance traveled we need to integrate $v(t)$ over the interval [0,2], that is,

$$s(t) = \int_0^2 (-t^2 + 6t + 40)dt.$$

To do this we need the indefinite integrand of $v(t) = -t^2 + 6t + 40$. Integrating term by term gives

$$\int (-t^2 + 6t + 40)dt = -\frac{1}{2}t^3 + 3t^2 + 40t + C.$$

We can check this is the case since

$$\frac{d}{dt}\left(-\frac{1}{2}t^3 + 3t^2 + 40t + C\right) = -t^2 + 6t + 40.$$

If we write $F(t) = -\frac{1}{2}t^3 + 3t^2 + 40t$, then

$$\int (-t^2 + 6t + 40)dt = F(t) + C$$

and so the distance traveled is approximately

$$\int_0^2 (-t^2 + 6t + 40)dt$$
$$= F(2) - F(0) = 89.33 \text{ m.}$$

What would happen if the speeds given were inaccurate? How much effect would this have?

WORKED EXAMPLE 7.2

Terminal Velocity

When sky divers leave a plane they fall under the influence of gravity and accelerate towards the ground. However, they do not accelerate forever but approach a terminal velocity of about 130 mph vertically downwards. This is because as they move faster they encounter more drag due to air resistance which opposes the force of gravity. To a good approximation, the amount of air resistance is proportional to the velocity. Estimate how long it will take for a man of mass 180 lb to reach 90% of terminal velocity.

Let

v	Velocity measured vertically **downwards** (ft/sec)
t	Elapse time (seconds)
m	Mass of the sky diver (pounds)
g	Acceleration due to gravity (ft/sec^2)
k	Constant of proportionality between air resistance and velocity

Using Newton's second law of motion

$$mv' = mg - kv.$$

When the terminal velocity, v_T, is reached, the forces due to gravity and drag will balance out so that $mg = kv_T$; that is, $v_T = \dfrac{mg}{k}$. If the terminal velocity is $v_T = 130\,\text{mph}^1$, then

$$k = (180 \times 32)/\left(130 \times \frac{88}{60}\right).$$

Now write

$$mv' = mg - kv$$

as

$$mv' + kv = mg$$

---

^{1} v_T is +130 since we are measuring distance vertically downwards.

and set $v(t) = u(t)e^{-\frac{k}{m}t}$ then

$$mv' + kv = m(-\frac{k}{m}ue^{-\frac{k}{m}t} + u'e^{-\frac{k}{m}t})$$
$$+ kue^{-\frac{k}{m}t}$$
$$= mu'e^{-\frac{k}{m}t}$$

Therefore,

$$u' = ge^{\frac{k}{m}t}$$

and, hence

$$u(t) = \frac{mg}{k}e^{\frac{k}{m}t} + C = v_T e^{\frac{g}{v_T}t} + C,$$

by the Fundamental Theorem of Calculus. Consequently,

$$v(t) = v_T + Ce^{-\frac{g}{v_T}t}$$

where C is a constant of integration. This gives a large number of possible expressions for $v(t)$, but as the sky diver starts from rest we have that $v(0)=0$ and so $C=-v_T$ giving that the velocity at time t is

$$v(t) = v_T\left(1 - e^{-\frac{g}{v_T}t}\right)$$

$v(t)$ reaches 90% of terminal velocity when

$$1 - e^{-\frac{g}{v_T}t} = 0.9$$

which is when

$$t = \frac{v_T}{g}\log(10) \approx 13 \text{ seconds}.$$

When the sky divers leave the plane they will have a horizontal velocity equal to that of the plane. How will this affect the time for them to reach the terminal velocity?

P R O B L E M   7 . 1
S K Y   D I V E R

Name: _____

Date: _____

Section: _____

In Worked Example 2 we determined the time it would take for a sky diver to reach 90% of terminal velocity. This problem is about determining the distance fallen in this time.

(Write your answers in the spaces provided or use the reverse of this page.)

The velocity of the sky diver is given by the function $v(t) = v_T(1 - e^{-\frac{g}{v_T}t})$. Find an integral representing the distance traveled as a function of time.

Evaluate the integral and determine the distance traveled before the velocity reaches 90% of the terminal velocity.

PROBLEM 7.2
FIND THE GIVEN
INTEGRALS

Name: _____

Date: _____

Section: _____

Evaluate the following integrals . In each case determine whether the given integral is equal to the geometrical area enclosed by the curve and the *x*-axis.

(Write your answers in the spaces provided or use the reverse of this page.)

(i) $\int_{0}^{1} x^3 + 3x + 2\, dx$,

(ii) $\int_{-1}^{1} x^3 - 3x + 2\, dx$,

(iii) $\int_{0}^{2\pi} \sin(2x)\, dx$,

(iv) $\int_{-1}^{1} \tan(x)\, dx$

(v) $\int_{0}^{1} xe^{-x^2}\, dx$,

(vi) $\int_{0}^{1} \frac{1}{1+x^2}\, dx$.

Integral (i)

Sketch:

Integral (ii)

Sketch:

Integral (iii)

Sketch:

Integral (iv)

Sketch:

Integral (v)

Sketch:

Integral(vi)

Sketch:

NEW SITUATIONS

1. Finding the area of a circle

To determine the area of a quarter circle of radius r as shown in Figure 7.6, we divide the area into small slices as shown in Chapter 6. As the width of each slice approaches zero the sum can be replaced by an integral:

$$\int_{x=0}^{x=r} y\,dx = \int_{x=0}^{x=r} \sqrt{r^2 - x^2}\,dx$$

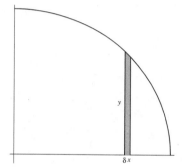

Figure 7.6 Finding the area of a circle

Show that the function

$$F(x) = \frac{x\sqrt{r^2 - x^2}}{2} + \frac{r^2 \sin^{-1}\left(\frac{x}{r}\right)}{2}$$

is an indefinite integral of $\sqrt{r^2 - x^2}$ and show that the area shown is $\frac{\pi r^2}{4}$. Extend this to find the area of an ellipse given by

$$\frac{x^2}{a^2} + \frac{y^2}{b^2} = 1.$$

2. Carbon Dating

How do archaeologists date ancient arttifacts?

All living organisms absorb oxygen in some way and in doing so they absorb small traces of a radioactive element, carbon 14. When the organism dies the carbon 14 decays. In 5730 years the amount of carbon 14 will decay to half its original amount, this is the half-life of carbon 14. If the sample has 75% of the amount of carbon 14 found in a living specimen, can we determine the age of the sample?

If $M(t)$ is the mass of carbon 14 then it decays at a rate proportional to the mass, that is,

$$\frac{dM}{dt} = -kM.$$

Make a change of variable to set $M(t) = e^{-kt} f(t)$ and show that $f'=0$. Show that f is necessarily a constant and find an expression for it in terms of the original mass.

Show that if the half-life is 5730 years, then

$$k = \frac{1}{5730} \log_e 2$$

and determine age of the specimen.

3. Serving Aces

The aim of all top tennis players is to serve as many aces as possible. An ace is achieved when the ball that is served at a speed V m/sec at an angle a below the horizontal, just clears the net and lands on the edge of the service area. To a first approximation the ball can be considered as a projectile that moves under gravity and we will ignore spin, air resistance ,and other complications. If we take the service base line as the origin and let the horizontal distance traveled be $x(t)$ and the height of the ball above the court be $y(t)$, then by Newton's laws of motion

$$y''=-g \ , \ x''=0.$$

Integrate these equations and show that if the ball is struck at a height h, then

$$y = h - x \tan \alpha - \frac{5x^2}{V^2 \cos^2 \alpha}.$$

If the height of the net is 1 m, the distance from the baseline to the net is 12 m, and the distance from the net to the edge of the service court is another 6 m, estimate the speed at which the ball must be struck to serve an ace if it leaves the racket at a height of 2.5 m.

Chapter 8

Mean-Value Theorem for Integrals

Prerequisites

Before you study this material, you should be familiar with:

(1) The elements of differential and integral calculus (Modules 3, 5, 6 and 7).

(2) The concept that an integral can be thought of as "area under the curve" (Module 6).

(3) The integration of simple functions (Module 7).

Objectives

The objectives here are to explain two related concepts. The first arises from the observation that the "area under a curve" can be deformed without changing the total area; in particular, this means that for any function curve it is possible to visualize a "melting icebergs" effect in which peaks melt away and troughs fill in until there is a level "pond" of melt water having the same volume as the original irregular iceberg. On a graph of y against x, this is the equivalent of flattening out a curve into a horizontal line that represents the average value of the function (see Figure 8.1).

The first concept then comes down to saying that for any integral that exists over a finite interval, it is possible to replace the function with a constant value, and that this value may be chosen to leave the value of the integral unchanged. This value is the "mean value" of the function.

The second concept arises from the question, does the original function itself ever take this mean value? The "Mean Value Theorem" says that if the function is continuous (in the interval of integration being considered) then the answer is, yes.

Connections

Averages, or "Mean Values" as they are more precisely known in mathematical terminology, play an important part in our lives. Among the most familiar examples are grade points, average scores of your favorite team, and references to people as being of above or below average height. These averages are found from discrete data: for example, add up all the points scored by a team and divide by the number of games. But there are also averages that we use from continuous data (examples are weather statistics and travel speeds), and to find these averages requires integration, which it helps to think of as an area under a curve.

The software has two video clips which illustrate the mean values of quantities that vary with time. The first clip is about two weather measurements, rainfall and temperature. Rainfall can come in bursts. You can have showers that start abruptly, rain constantly for a few minutes, and then abruptly stop. Several such showers over a day will still allow the meteorologist to calculate an average rate of rainfall over the entire day, such that were it to drizzle at a constant rate for this time, the total rainfall over the day would be the same as the total from all the showers. Yet at no time did it ever rain at this drizzle rate.

Temperature, on the other hand is a different story. Temperature can't change abruptly. We can find an average temperature for the day by the same mathematical technique, just deforming the temperature graph to be a straight line while preserving the area. This time, there will be at least one time in the day when the temperature is *exactly* at the mean. Because temperature must vary smoothly, the Mean Value Theorem says there must be a time when this happens.

The second video clip shows a train trip. Train speeds must vary continuously - they need time to speed up and slow down. The "iceberg melt" effect can be used to illustrate the averaging process. Because speed is a continuous function, there will be at least one time in the trip when the train is moving at exactly the mean speed for the whole trip.

The practical uses of knowing mean values are fairly clear. If you visit Alaska, knowing the mean temperature will help you decide what clothes to take. Knowing typical mean travel speeds will help you to plan trips. These examples are very simple, but the mathematical importance of the mean value theorem is more subtle than this, and it will turn out to be useful in deriving some more advanced, more powerful results. For example, Taylor's Theorem will tell us how to construct a series to find the value of a continuous function to any required accuracy, and the proof will require the Mean Value Theorem.

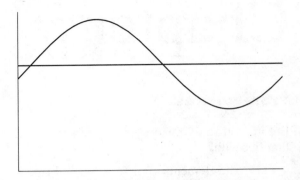

Figure 8.1a. Mean Value and the melting iceberg effect.

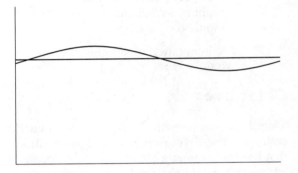

Figure 8.1b. Mean Value and the melting iceberg effect.

Mean values: rainfall

It is known from previous chapters (see Chapter 6, in particular) that the area under the curve for the rate of rainfall gives the total rainfall. To work out the mean rainfall over a day, work out the total rainfall for that day (in millimeters say) and divide by the number of hours: this gives the mean rainfall in millimeters per hour.

Example 8.1

Measure time in hours from midnight, when the rain gauge collector is emptied. If the rate of rainfall is *r(t)* mm/hr, then the total amount of rain collected will be a function of time,

$$R(t) = \int_0^t r(t)dt .$$

Note that $R(0)=0$, because the collector is empty at $t=0$.

The total rainfall over a 24-hr period will be

$$R(24) = \int_0^{24} r(t)dt$$

Imagine a day in which it rains constantly at a steady rate $\bar{r}$ and the same total amount of rain falls as before. Now $r(t) = \bar{r}$, a constant, and

$$R = \int_0^{24} r(t)dt = \int_0^{24} \bar{r}dt = \bar{r}\int_0^{24} dt = 24\bar{r} .$$

$$\therefore \bar{r} = \tfrac{1}{24}\int_0^{24} r(t)dt .$$

Rain can start and stop suddenly, so now imagine a day when its either raining cats and dogs or not raining at all. There is as before a value for the mean rainfall, but it is quite possible that there is never a time in the day when it rains at the mean rate.

 Exercise 8.1

Rainfall
Use the software to simulate rainfall, as illustrated on the video clip. Change the rainfall profile and observe the relation between mean rainfall and the rate of rainfall curve.

Mean values: temperature

The mean temperature for a day is calculated in a very similar way to finding mean rainfall, except that unlike rainfall "temperature-fall" cannot be physically collected. The area under the graph can be found, however, and divided by the total time to give the mean.

Example 8.2

Take $t=0$ to be midnight as in Example 8.1. If $T(t)$ is the temperature at any time, then the mean over 24 hr is given by

$$\bar{T} = \tfrac{1}{24}\int_0^{24} T(t)dt .$$

Temperature varies continuously, and there will be a time in the day when whatever the variation, the temperature will be exactly at the mean value for the day. This is essentially what the Mean Value Theorem says.

 Exercise 8.2

Temperature
Use the software to simulate a temperature profile over a day. Observe that there is always a time when the temperature equals the mean.

Mean speed of a train trip

Every trip has an average speed that can be calculated by dividing the total distance traveled by the total time taken. We learned in previous chapters (Chapter 7, for example) that the area under the graph of speed against time gives the total distance traveled.

Example 8.3

If a trip starts at $t=0$, and the speed at any time is $v(t)$, find the mean speed for the trip. The distance traveled since $t=0$ as a function of time t is given by

$$x(t) = \int_0^t v(t)dt.$$

Now imagine a trip made at a constant speed, equal to the mean, $\bar{v}$, say. We have for $t > 0$

$$\bar{v} = \frac{x(t)}{t} = \frac{1}{t}\int_0^t v(t)dt.$$

The Mean Value Theorem says that at some point in the trip, the train will have a speed exactly equal to the mean speed. In fact, there can be several such times.

 Exercise 8.3

Mean speed in a trip
Use the software to simulate a train trip. Find a speed profile where the train travels at the mean speed on four occasions.

The Mean Value Theorem for Integrals

If a given function $f(x)$ is continuous over a finite interval from $x=a$ to $x=b$ and the integral of $f(x)$ from a to b equals I, then there is a value ξ, such that I also equals the integral of the constant value $f(\xi)$ on the same interval. This is stated mathematically as follows:

The Mean Value Theorem for Integrals:

If $f(x)$ is a continuous function in the interval $[a, b]$, then there exists a constant $\xi \in [a, b]$ such that

$$\int_a^b f(x)\, dx = \int_a^b f(\xi)\, dx = (b-a)f(\xi).$$

The final term in the statement arises because the definite integral of a constant is given by the area of a rectangle, length $(b-a)$ and height $f(\xi)$ in this case.

Example 8.4

Consider the function $f(x) = x^2$ over the interval $[0, 2]$. By using standard integration techniques we have $\int_0^2 f(x)\, dx = \left[\frac{1}{3}x^3\right]_0^2 = \frac{8}{3}$. The mean value of $f(x)$ over this interval is therefore $\frac{4}{3}$, and $f(\xi) = \xi^2 = \frac{4}{3}$, giving $\xi = \sqrt{\frac{4}{3}}$.

Further exercises of this type are suggested in Problems 8.1.

The Mean Value Theorem and Integrals of Discontinuous Functions

The Mean Value Theorem does not apply when the integrand is not continuous, as in the example involving rainfall. However, a mean value for a function over an interval can often still be found, just as there is still a mean rainfall even though rainfall may not vary smoothly.

Example 8.5

Consider the Heaviside Function $H(x)$, defined as:

$$H(x) = \left\{ \begin{array}{l} 0 \text{ if } x \le 0 \\ 1 \text{ if } x > 0 \end{array} \right..$$

On the interval $[-1,2]$ (for example),

$\int_{-1}^2 H(x)dx = 2$, so the mean value of $H(x)$ over $[-1, 2]$ is $\frac{2}{3}$.

There is no value ξ such that $H(\xi) = \frac{2}{3}$.

See also Problems 8.2.

WORKED EXAMPLE 8.1
MEAN VALUE EXAMPLES

(i) Find a value in the interval [0, 2] such that

$$\int_0^2 (1+x^2)\,dx = 2f(\xi).$$

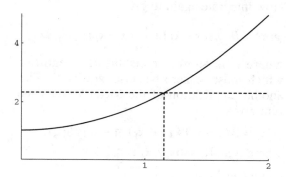

Figure 8.2. $f(x) = (1+x^2)$.

Applying standard integration methods to the integral gives

$$\int_0^2 (1+x^2)\,dx = \left|x + \tfrac{1}{3}x^3\right|_0^2 = 2 + \tfrac{8}{3} = \tfrac{14}{3}.$$

Therefore, ξ must satisfy $2f(\xi) = \tfrac{14}{3}$, which requires $1+\xi^2 = \tfrac{7}{3}$.

Solving this gives $\xi = \sqrt{\tfrac{4}{3}}$.

(ii) Find values of ξ in $\left[0, \dfrac{5\pi}{2}\right]$ such that .

$$\int_0^{\frac{5\pi}{2}} \cos(x)\,dx = \frac{5\pi}{2} f(\xi)$$

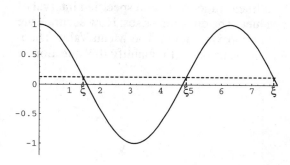

Figure 8.3. $f(x) = \cos(x)$.

Applying standard integration methods to the integral gives

$$\int_0^{\frac{5\pi}{2}} \cos(x)\,dx = \left|\sin(x)\right|_0^{\frac{5\pi}{2}} = 1.$$

Therefore, ξ must satisfy $\dfrac{5\pi}{2} f(\xi) = 1$, which

requires $\xi = \cos^{-1}(\dfrac{2}{5\pi})$.

Solving this gives $\xi = \alpha,\ 2\pi - \alpha,\ 2\pi + \alpha$, where α is the principle value of $\cos^{-1}(\dfrac{2}{5\pi})$.

WORKED EXAMPLE 8.2 APPROXIMATION

In the application "Tree Growth" of Chapter 1, tree sizes were predicted by using linear interpolation between two data points on a graph. In effect, the tree growth function is approximated by a linear function over a specified interval of x-values. The question arises: How accurate are such approximations? The Mean Value Theorem helps us begin to quantify this question.

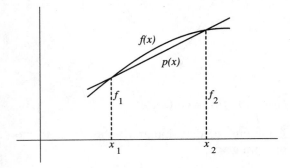

Figure 8.4. Linear approximation.

Consider a function $f(x)$ for $x_1 \le x \le x_2$. Let $f_1 = f(x_1)$ and $f_2 = f(x_2)$. Now let

$$p(x) = f_1 + m(x - x_1), \text{ where } m = \frac{f_2 - f_1}{x_2 - x_1}.$$

The function $p(x)$ is a linear function, and its graph is a straight line that intersects the curve $y = f(x)$ at the points (x_1, f_1) and (x_2, f_2). The problem can now be stated:

To obtain an expression for an upper bound to $|f(x) - p(x)|$ for x in $x_1 \le x \le x_2$.

Begin by defining $g(x) = f(x) - p(x)$, so that $g(x_1) = g(x_2) = 0$. Now note that because $p(x)$ is a linear function, its second derivative must vanish, and therefore $g''(x) = f''(x)$. Integrat-

ing gives $g'(x) = A + \int_{x_1}^{x} f''(x)dx$ where A is a constant of integration. Using the Mean Value Theorem, we find that for each x there must be a ξ such that $g'(x) = A + (x - x_1)f''(\xi)$ and $x_1 \le \xi \le x$.

Now integrate again to give

$$g(x) = B + A(x - x_1) + \int_{x_1}^{x} (x - x_1)f''(\xi)dx,$$

where B is another constant of integration, which must be zero because $g(x_1) = 0$. Then another application of the Mean Value Theorem gives

$$g(x) = A(x - x_1) + (x - x_1)(\eta - x_1)f''(\zeta),$$

where η and ζ satisfy $x_1 \le \eta, \zeta \le x$,

and we can now write

$$g(x) = A(x - x_1) + k(x - x_1)^2 f''(\zeta)$$

where $0 \le k \le 1$ (because $\eta - x_1 \le x_2 - x_1$). We also know that $g(x_2) = 0$ giving $A = -k(x_2 - x_1)f''(\zeta)$ for some value of k and ζ.

Therefore,

$$g(x) \le |A(x - x_1)| + k(x - x_1)^2 |f''(\zeta)|$$

and, hence,

$$|g(x)| \le 2(x_2 - x_1)^2 \operatorname*{Sup}_{x_1 \le x \le x_2} |f''(x)|.$$

The result gives an upper bound for the error in the linear approximation to f(x) over the interval . Better bounds can be obtained by more advanced techniques, but this result contains useful information. In particular, it can be seen that the bound depends on the square of the interval size, and the result tells us that to set a bound it is not necessary to know about the behavior of derivatives higher than the second derivative.

PROBLEM 8.1
MEAN VALUE EXERCISES

Name: _____

Date: _____

Section: _____

Problem 8.1a

Use the screen "Mean-Value Theorem for Integrals". Find values x and $f(x)$ satisfying the Mean Value Theorem for the following integrals:

(i) $f(x)=x,$ $[a, b] = [0, 2]$: $\xi =\ldots, f(\xi) = \ldots$

(ii) $f(x)=x,$ $[a, b] = [-4, 4]$: $\xi =\ldots, f(\xi) = \ldots$

(iii) $f(x) = \frac{1}{3}x^2,$ $[a, b] = [-4, 4]$: $\xi =\ldots, f(\xi) = \ldots$

(iv) $f(x) = e^x,$ $[a, b] = [-1, 1]$: $\xi =\ldots, f(\xi) = \ldots$

(v) $f(x) = \frac{1}{x},$ $[a, b] = [1, 2]$: $\xi =\ldots, f(\xi) = \ldots$

(vi) $f(x) = \log(x),$ $[a, b] = [1, 2]$: $\xi =\ldots, f(\xi) = \ldots$

PROBLEM 8.1
MEAN VALUE EXERCISES
(Continued)
Problem 8.1b

Use pencil and paper to find mathematical formulae for the mean values of integrals of the following functions using the intervals shown, and verify that the formulae correctly give the results obtained in the previous activities.

(i)   f(x)=x: $[a, b] = [0, 1]$: $\xi = \ldots$, $f(\xi) = \ldots$

(ii)   *f(x)=x*:   for general $[a, b]$ $\xi = \ldots$, $f(\xi) = \ldots$

(iii) $f(x) = \frac{1}{3}x^2$, $[a, b] = [-4, 4]$: $\xi = \ldots$, $f(\xi) = \ldots$

(iv) $f(x) = e^x$, $[a, b] = [-1, 1]$: $\xi = \ldots$, $f(\xi) = \ldots$

(v) $f(x) = \frac{1}{x}$, $[a, b] = [1, 2]$: $\xi = \ldots$, $f(\xi) = \ldots$

(vi) $f(x) = \log(x)$, $[a, b] = [1, 2]$ $\xi = \ldots$, $f(\xi) = \ldots$

(vii) $f(x) = \cos(x)$, $[a, b] = [0, n\pi]$: $\xi_1 = \ldots$, $f(\xi_1) = \ldots$, $\xi_2 = \ldots$, $f(\xi_2) = \ldots$, $\ldots$

Distinguish between your results for *n* odd and *n* even.

(viii) $f(x) = e^x$, $[a, b] = [0, t]$: $\xi = \ldots$, $f(\xi) = \ldots$

(ix) $f(x) = \log(x)$, $[a, b] = [0, t]$: $\xi = \ldots$, $f(\xi) = \ldots$

(x) $f(x) = \cos(x)$, $[a, b] = [0, t]$: $\xi = \ldots$, $f(\xi) = \ldots$

(xi) $f(x) = \sin(x)$, $[a, b] = [0, t]$: $\xi = \ldots$, $f(\xi) = \ldots$

PROBLEM 8.2
DISCONTINUOUS CASES

Name: _____

Date: _____

Section: _____

Problem 8.2a

Use the screen "Mean-Value Theorem and Integrals of Discontinuous Functions". Construct examples where it is not possible to find values ξ and $f(\xi)$ satisfying the Mean Value Theorem. Sketch typical cases here.

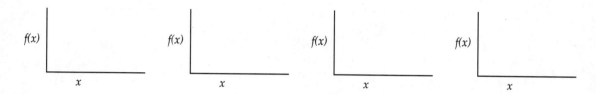

Problem 8.2b

Why does the Mean Value Theorem not work for the following? Use the software to investigate, or sketch the functions for yourself. Answer each case with a sketch and brief explanation.

i) $f(x) = \frac{1}{x}$, [a, b] = [0, 2]

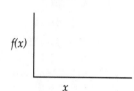

((ii) $f(x) = \frac{1}{x}$, [a, b] = [-2, 2]

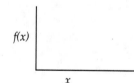

(iii) $f(x) = \sin(\frac{1}{x})$, [a, b] = [0, 2]

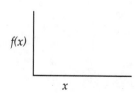

(iv) $f(x) = \log(x)$, [a, b] = [0, 1]

(v) $f(x) = \tan(x)$, $[a, b] = [-\pi/2, \pi/2]$

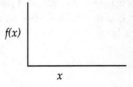

(vi) $f(x) = \dfrac{1}{1-x^2}$ in ranges $(-\infty, -1)$, $(-1, +1)$ and $(+1, \infty)$

NEW SITUATIONS

1. Multiple Solutions

Why should you expect the Mean Value Theorem to apply to the integral

$\int e^{-x} \sin(x)\,dx$ over any finite interval? Justify you answer. How does the number of possible values for ξ [such that $f(\xi)$ = mean value of the integrand] vary with the interval chosen?

Construct examples where the Mean Value Theorem applies over any interval of integration, and indicate how the number of possible values for ξ varies with the interval chosen.

2. Effect of interval

For $f(t) = \dfrac{(1+kt)}{(1-kt)}$, what intervals of integration are possible in which the Mean Value Theorem can apply? Find analytic (i.e., closed form) solutions where possible.

3. Trapezium Rule

The Trapezium Rule is a simple method for estimating the value of definite integrals numerically. It works by dividing the integration interval into a number of equal intervals and approximating the integrand by a line for each interval. The area under the curve in each section is then approximated by a trapezium, giving the rule its name.

For example, consider $\int_a^b f(x)\,dx$ with intervals. Let h be the width of each interval, so that $h = \dfrac{b-a}{N}$. The intervals are defined by a set of

points $\{x_k,\ k = 0 \ldots N\}$ with $x_k = a + kh$. Note that $x_0 = a$ and $x_N = b$, so there are $N+1$ points defining N intervals. Now define the value of the integrand $f(x)$ at the kth point to be $f_k = f(x_k) = f(a + kh)$.

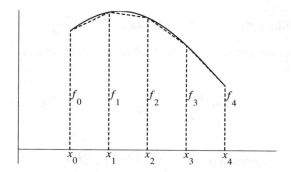

Figure 8.5. The Trapezium Rule.

The area enclosed by the trapezium on the interval $[x_{k-1},\ x_k]$ is $\dfrac{h}{2}\big(f_{k-1} + f_k\big)$.

Summing these gives an estimate $T_N(a,b)$ for the integral $\int_a^b f(x)\,dx$ where

$$T_N(a,b) = \frac{h}{2}\big(f_0 + 2f_1 + 2f_2 + \ldots 2f_{N-1} + f_N\big).$$

To be useful, any estimate must be accompanied by an indication of accuracy. The Mean Value Theorem can now help to give this information.

Generalizing the result obtained in Worked Example 8.2 so that it is applied to the interval $[x_{k-1},\ x_k]$, the difference $g_k(x)$ between the integrand f(x) and the straight line approximating it in this interval satisfies

$$\big|g_k(x)\big| \le 2(x_k - x_{k-1})^2 \underset{x_{k-1} \le x \le x_k}{Sup} \big|f''(x)\big|.$$

The error in the estimate for the integral therefore satisfies

$$\int_{x_{k-1}}^{x_k} |g_k(x)|\, dx \le 2h^3 \underset{x_{k-1} \le x \le x_k}{Sup} |f''(x)|.$$

Since there are N intervals and $h = \dfrac{b-a}{N}$, an upper bound for the error of the estimate is given by:

$$2\frac{(b-a)^3}{N^2} \underset{a \le x \le b}{Sup} |f''(x)|.$$

As we noted previously in Worked Example 8.2, this estimate is on the generous side and a tighter error bound can be found. But this result is still very useful, telling us in particular that if, for example, the number of intervals were to be doubled, then the error should decrease by a factor of 4.

Program Documentation

Navigation

When the program has installed, you'll see 3 icons: *Main Menu, Intro, Readme*. Refer to the Readme file for any installation or performance problems. Click on Intro for a 2-minute Introduction to the philosophy of the program. Click on Main Menu to get to the content of the program.

System Requirements

Windows 3.1 or higher (including Windows 95), 486DX microprocessor, 8MB RAM, 10MB free hard disk, Multispin CD-ROM drive, SVGA graphics card and monitor (256 colors), 100% compatible Soundblaster™ sound card.

Main Menu

The main menu lists the titles of the 8 modules in this volume. Click on the topic you want to access.

Module Menu

Our goal is to make the software as user-friendly as possible, so each module is set up exactly the same way. There are Applications (move the cursor over the Applications icon to see list, and then click on the topic you want to explore), Concepts (move the cursor over the concepts icon to see list, and then click on the topic you want to explore), and Exercises (ditto). From this module menu you can access anything in the module, in any order you choose.

Installation Instructions

1 Insert CD-ROM into CD drive

2 In the Windows Program Manager, click *Run* under the *File* menu

3 Click *Browse*

4 Choose the CD-ROM drive by clicking in the lower right corner

5 Click *install.exe*

6 Click *OK* twice

7 Follow the instructions on screen

Start Connections

There's also a prescribed pathway through the Applications, Concepts and Exercises in each module. Bring the cursor up from the bottom middle of the screen, upwards toward the middle until "Start Connections" pops up. Click on "Start Connections" to enter this prescribed mode. This pathway takes about 45 minutes to 1 hour to complete so it's perfect for one lab session. This suggested route makes it effortless for instructors to make assignments, or for students to always know where in the program they are, and where to go next.

Navigational Icons and Tools

Navigational icons are located on the bottom right of each screen. Use them to:

- *Go to next screen*
- *Return to previous screen*
- *Rewind to beginning of section*
- *Fast forward to next section*
- *Return to module menu*

Other navigational icons are presented when appropriate. Use them to:

- *Repeat voiceover or animation*
- *Give additional information, problem statements or instructions to run a simulation*

Other Icons and Tools

Hotwords

Words highlighted in a contrasting color are "hot." Click on them for definitions and other information.

Calculus Connections provides convenient on-line Help, Options, Tools and References. Bring up this menu by passing the cursor over the bottom of the screen, and click to select.

Help

On-line interactive Help is always available. Click Help for information on:

- *Entering equations*
- *Syntax errors*
- *Interacting with plots*
- *Main module menu*
- *Menu bar navigation*
- *Menu bar icons*
- *Menu bar pull downs*

Options

Click to change setup, colors, sounds and Preferences.

Mathematical Tools

Click on Maple, Mathematica, Derive or Mathcad for access if they are resident on your computer.

Calculus Connections provides custom 2-D and 3-D Graphing Tools. You can plot, manipulate and save graphs of functions without complicated syntax or other software.

References

Click on References for definitions and biographical information.

Exit

Exit lets you quickly access the Main Menu, Module Menu, or Introduction to Calculus Connections. You can also quit the Program from the Exit menu.

Technical Assistance

Call **212-850-6753**, or send email to **math@jwiley.com** for assistance.

Calculus Connections Volumes 2 & 3

Volume 2 *(available summer 1996)*

Definite Integrals

Rectilinear Motion

Simpson's Rule

Sequences and Series

Differential Equations

Spherical and Polar Coordinates

Parametric Equations

Mathematical Modeling

Volume 3 *(available spring 1997)*

Scalar Functions of More than One Variable

Vector Valued Functions

Directional Derivatives and the Gradients of Functions of One Variable

Double and Triple Integrals

Triple Integrals in Cylindrical and Spherical Coordinates

Centroids, Center of Gravity and Moments of Inertia

Line Integrals

Surface Integrals

To Order Volumes 2 & 3

To purchase a copy of Calculus Connections Volume 2 & 3, visit your favorite bookstore or call Wiley directly at **1-800-225-5945**.

Wiley will pay shipping and handling costs for all pre-paid orders.

Index